# ANGEL IN BLACK

By Max Allan Collins:

*The Memoirs of Nathan Heller:*

*Angel in Black*

*Majic Man*

*Flying Blind*

*Damned in Paradise*

*Blood and Thunder*

*Carnal Hours*

*Dying in the Postwar World*

*Stolen Away*

*Neon Mirage*

*The Million-Dollar Wound*

*True Crime*

*True Detective*

MAX ALLAN COLLINS

# ANGEL IN BLACK

A NATHAN HELLER NOVEL

NEW AMERICAN LIBRARY

New American Library
Published by New American Library, a division of
Penguin Putnam Inc., 375 Hudson Street,
New York, New York 10014, U.S.A.
Penguin Books Ltd, 27 Wrights Lane,
London W8 5TZ, England
Penguin Books Australia Ltd,
Ringwood, Victoria, Australia
Penguin Books Canada Ltd, 10 Alcorn Avenue,
Toronto, Ontario, Canada M4V 3B2
Penguin Books (N.Z.) Ltd, 182–190 Wairau Road,
Auckland 10, New Zealand

Penguin Books Ltd, Registered Offices:
Harmondsworth, Middlesex, England

Published by New American Library, a division of Penguin Putnam Inc.

First Printing, March 2001
10 9 8 7 6 5 4 3 2 1



LIBRARY OF CONGRESS CATALOGING-IN-PUBLICATION DATA:

Collins, Max Allan.
Angel in black : a Nathan Heller novel / Max Allan Collins.
p. cm.
ISBN 0-451-20263-5 (alk. paper)
1. Heller, Nathan (Fictitious character)—Fiction. 2. Private investigators—California—Los Angeles—Fiction. 3. Short, Elizabeth, 1924-1947—Fiction. 4. Los Angeles (Calif.)—Fiction. I. Title.
PS3553.04753 A82 2001
813'.54—dc21 00-066844

Printed in the United States of America
Set in Sabon
Designed by Leonard Telesca

Printed in the United States of America

*In memory*
*of Nate Heller's Second City friend*
*Del Close*
*dark angel of comedy*

Although the historical incidents in this novel are portrayed more or less accurately (as much as the passage of time, and contradictory source material, will allow), fact, speculation, and fiction are freely mixed here; historical personages exist side by side with composite characters and wholly fictional ones—all of whom act and speak at the author's whim.

"She was a lazy girl and irresponsible; and, when she chose to work, she drifted obscurely. . . ."

—JACK WEBB, on Elizabeth Short

"I've had that recurring dream since I was about twelve—that I murdered somebody."

—ORSON WELLES

"She gets around town, she's the queen of downtown, my angel dressed in black."

—WARREN ZEVON

# 1

The two pieces of her lay porcelain-white in the ankle-high grass and weeds of a vacant lot on South Norton Avenue, like the upper and lower sections of a discarded marionette. No strings could ever reanimate this disassembled figure, however—a sadistic puppeteer had made certain of that.

"Jesus frig," Fowley said, as ashen as the bisected corpse that lay, bizarrely posed, alongside the sidewalk. "Where's a fuckin' photographer when you need one?"

We were in a neighborhood of Los Angeles called Leimert Park, an area where development had been stalled by the war, and the weedy lots retained sidewalks, driveways and fire hydrants, as if the houses had been whisked away by a particularly tidy tornado.

"Yeah," I said, "Richardson wouldn't want to leave entertainment value like that just layin' around."

James H. Richardson was Fowley's boss, the city editor of Hearst's morning *Examiner*, and Bill Fowley—son of a legendary New York *American* editor—was one of about twelve guys who fancied themselves Richardson's star reporter.

A rumpled gray porkpie hat sitting tight on his round skull, Fowley had the same reddish brown hair as me, only his was cropped close to the scalp, like a guy going to the electric chair. He was small, a good five inches shorter than my six feet, and forty pounds lighter than my one-ninety; he was almost swimming in a baggy light brown suit, wind whipping it—I wasn't swimming in my tan double-breasted gabardine, but the wind was making waving flags out of my pantlegs, too.

"What am I thinkin'?" Fowley said, pacing at the feet of the spread-eagled, on-its-back bisected corpse. "Felix keeps a spare Speed Graphic in the trunk. Here . . ."

He lobbed me the keys and I caught 'em.

". . . grab it outa there, Heller. You know how to use a friggin' Speed Graphic, don't you?"

I was not a reporter, star or otherwise. I was, and for that matter am, Nathan Heller, at that time president of the A-1 Detective Agency of Chicago, which is to say a private detective. And since a good deal of my business, over the years, had been divorce work, yes, I knew how to use a friggin' Speed Graphic.

But I didn't feel like shooting grim pinup photos of a nude, dead, once-beautiful woman, and declined, graciously.

"Fuck you, Fowley," I said. "Take your own ghoulish goddamn pictures."

Whirling, Fowley—who looked like a pleasant bulldog, only right now his expression wasn't all that pleasant—said, "You want to keep me happy, don't you, gumshoe? Or don't you and your partner still want that free publicity?"

"No need to get shitty about it."

"Maybe you cheap bastards would rather hire a p.r. agent than get the *Examiner*'s goodwill, for fucking free."

I unlocked the trunk and fetched the camera. Fowley was normally an amiable joe, but he had just caught front-page fever: the bisected body in this vacant lot had all the earmarks of a headline story . . . a beautiful woman, butchered by some maniac. Sex and murder—ideal breakfast reading.

The morning was almost cold under a gun-metal sky, the breeze bristling the weeds into tickling the two halves of the girl, who—unlike the rest of the scattered refuse, rusty cans, disintegrating cardboard, broken bottles—had been carefully arranged, as if by an artist; buzzing flies circled this lurid masterpiece, critics having a closer look.

Her arms were above her head, as if someone had poked a gun at her and demanded money; her legs were spread wide, as if in carnal invitation. But there was nothing inviting about this young woman, not anymore. Her raven hair a tangle of damp curls, she had been cleaved at the waist, the two sections crudely aligned, the top half of her angling somewhat into the lot while her left foot pointed to the nearby sidewalk. Her lily-white flesh had a waxy look, and appeared strangely clean, despite slashes to her face and to either well-formed breast, and to one shapely thigh; a nasty vertical gash extended from her navel to her wispy pubic thatch.

"Not much of a bush on her," Fowley pointed out.

"Jesus, Fowley."

"All I mean is, she's just a kid," he said, shaking his head as he scribbled in his notepad. The buzz of flies sounded like fluorescent lighting shorting out. "She could be fifteen."

"Or twenty," I said, and the bisected corpse strobed even whiter under the Speed Graphic's flashbulb.

In the ten or eleven inches separating the two sections of her, green grass waved in the wind, except where her distended liver matted it down.

A sick feeling boiled in the pit of my stomach. I was not a novice to crime scenes; I had seen my share of grisly homicides. I was thirty-eight years old and an ex-cop and a combat veteran and it took a hell of a lot to make me sick.

But this was the worst, most brutal, as well as saddest homicide victim I'd ever seen—a once-lovely young woman, carved in two, then arranged with thumb-to-the-nose glee by the sick fuck responsible. Yet there was more to my reaction than the tragic loss of young life and the grotesque sadism that had caused it.

Memories were stirring in me. I had been part of an investigation in Cleveland, not quite ten years before, and had been at a similar crime scene, a rubble- and rubbish-infested dump in the middle of town, where the torso of a young woman had been found. In some respects that one had been even worse: the head, the arms, legs, and feet had been severed and scattered about the dump like so much garbage, making a puzzle out of a human being to be reassembled by the police. The murder had been one of thirteen torso slayings attributed to the same maniac.

And we had found that psychotic son of a bitch, my friend Eliot Ness and I, and we had given him a lifetime enrollment in an Ohio laughing academy—the Mad Butcher of Kingsbury Run, the newshounds had called him. He was safely tucked away in a padded suite; nonetheless, the resemblance of this bisected torso slaying to the Butcher's modus operandi stirred memories in me, and nausea.

When that memory had passed, as I kept playing photographer for Fowley ("Here, I'll stand blocking her dirty parts, Heller, and you shoot from behind me, and we'll get something Richardson can goddamn publish"), another memory, jogged by the windblown grass, kicked in. . . .

*After the Japs had come at us in the morning, up a slope of golden* kunai *grass, screaming* "Banzai," *machine guns chattering, we cut them down with our M-1s and they dropped into the grass, scattered about like ragdolls, bodies in the weeds, flung there by our bullets, bodies barely visible, and that afternoon as we waited for the next wave of them, their dead lay puffing and ripening in the sun, sending a sweet foul wind riffling through the grass. . . .*

I lowered the camera, turned away.

"Heller! Nate . . . are you okay?"

I nodded.

"Shit, man, you look whiter than she does."

When I turned back around, Fowley—porkpie hat shoved back on his head now—was hovering over the fly-attended corpse, way too close.

Anger blotted out the nausea, and I charged over and yanked him back. "What the hell are you doing? You're tainting a crime scene! Stay away from her!"

Close up like this, I noticed for the first time the purple bruises and rope burns around her wrists and ankles. She'd been tied up, probably tortured.

"I was just gonna close her eyes," Fowley said. He looked shaken.

That was when I got my first real look at the girl's face; I'd been avoiding it, I guess, because the sadistic artist had reserved perhaps his most grotesque touch for her high-cheekboned, movie-star-pretty countenance: she had been slashed ear to ear, widening her mouth into a garish clown leer of death.

And her eyes—which were of a lovely clear mountain-lake blue—were indeed half-lidded open.

"Go ahead," I said numbly.

Fowley knelt, closed the woman's eyes gingerly, gently, and moved away. I already had.

In fact, I was standing in the street, legs unsteady, weaving. Because the worst memory of all the memories invoked by this gruesome crime scene had come to me, on that closer look at her.

*I knew this girl.*

Jesus Christ, I knew this girl!

Detectives do not believe in coincidence. Some of us believe in fate, a few even believe in God; but none of us believe in coincidence—when we see it, we know it's not true, we know something smells, we know somebody's trying to fuck us.

Nevertheless, my knowing this girl, whose dead body we'd stumbled onto, was a coincidence, pure and simple—and I would just have to live with it (and you will just have to take my word for it). Trouble was, this pure and simple coincidence would look impure and complex to the cops.

And as for reporters and coincidence—newspapermen like Fowley, here, and his boss Richardson—they would hang me out to dry, by the short and curlies.

So how did I come to be standing in this vacant lot in the University section of Los Angeles, over the bisected corpse of a girl I had known? Let's start with what a Chicago boy was doing in California in the first place—the usual reasons: business and pleasure. The business aspect had to do with the branch of the A-1 Detective Agency I was opening, going partners with Fred Rubinski.

Fred was an ex-cop from Chicago who'd been running his own one-man agency out of the Bradbury Building in downtown L.A.

since before the war; he also had a piece of a Sunset Strip restaurant and good connections with the movie industry, both studios and stars. He was at the point where he needed to expand, much as I had done a few years earlier. Throwing in together would benefit both of us. So Fred was now Vice President of the A-1, with offices in Chicago and Los Angeles; and we were looking toward New York.

I'd arranged to stay for at least a month, getting the new partnership up and running, during which time—here's the pleasure part—I would be on an extended honeymoon. Today—January 15, 1947—was in fact our one month anniversary, the former Peggy Hogan and me.

My wife and I were staying in a bungalow at the Beverly Hills Hotel—expensive digs, but the A-1 had landed a security-consultant contract with the hotel management, and this was a perk, a hell of a nice one. Less than half an hour before I found myself shooting photos of a bisected nude corpse in a Leimert Park vacant lot, Fowley had picked me up at my hotel, after breakfast, in a blue '47 Ford.

I had the use of one of the agency's cars, but my wife would be taking it to go shopping (I prayed it wasn't Rodeo Drive again), so Fowley was escorting me to his paper, where he and I and Jim Richardson were supposed to work out the exclusive arrangement whereby the A-1 fed information to the *Examiner* in exchange for ongoing, positive publicity, starting with a big spread that would announce the merger of the Rubinski and Heller agencies.

"You understand, Bill," I'd told him, as he made his leisurely way east along Venice Boulevard, "the A-1's clients' interests come first."

"Do I look like a T-bone steak?"

"Not particularly."

"Then spare me the friggin' A-1 sauce." Fowley said this with a friendly sneer, cigarette dangling. "Sure, a couple Chicago boys like you would never think of sellin' out a client."

"Well, we wouldn't. It's not good for business."

He shrugged. "My biggest worry about this arrangement is your pal Bugsy Siegel."

I shifted in my seat, spoke up over the police radio calls Fowley was monitoring. "He's not my pal, and I wouldn't call him 'Bugsy' to his face, if I were you."

"Didn't you work with him in Vegas?"

"I worked for Ben Siegel in Vegas, yes. Did a security job at the Flamingo. Taught his little private police force how to nab pickpockets, and stopped the pilfering that was nickel-and-diming him."

"Yeah? So who was doing the pilfering?"

"His little private police force."

Fowley sailed his spent cigarette out the window, spraying sparks of color into the gray morning. "I'm just warning you that the boss has a hard-on against Siegel—they're blood enemies."

"I thought Richardson relished the idea of my clients including the likes of Capone and Frank Nitti."

"Oh, he loves that. Chicago gangsters are colorful. It's the West Coast variety Jim hates—they're criminals, y'know . . . except for Jim's pal Mickey Cohen, of course."

Fowley's Ford was approaching Crenshaw Boulevard when a crackling voice on the shortwave said, "A 390 W down, 415, empty lot one block east of Crenshaw between 39th and Coliseum. Please investigate—Code Two."

Code Two meant proceed quickly but without red light or siren; a 390 W was a drunk woman, and 415 was a public disturbance. This all added up to a drunk woman passed out in a vacant lot.

Fowley reacted like an old firehorse hearing a familiar bell. "Huh! We got a naked drunk dame, just a block or so over! Let's have a look. . . ."

"Stop the presses. What the hell makes you think she's naked?"

"She's disturbing the peace and she's unconscious; 'bout the only way a broad can pull that off is to pass out in the buff. Where's your sense of adventure, Heller? Maybe she's a looker!"

"Christ, Fowley, I don't wanna follow you on some wild goose—"

But he was already turning south on Crenshaw; next it was east on 39th, where he started to crawl through the barren warzone landscape of vacant lots, some of which were staked off every thirty feet or so. Traffic was nil.

"Pretty wide-open spaces," Fowley said. "See that lot over there? That's where Ringling Brothers and Barnum and Bailey used to put the circus on, before the war."

"There she is," I said, pointing to a bare white foot in the weeds.

Fowley slowed, craned his neck. "Hell, that's not a woman—that's a store mannequin or something. . . ."

"I don't think so," I said.

There'd been no sign of whoever called it in to the cops; not surprising a citizen would take a pass on getting involved in the likes of this.

Now—some minutes later—Fowley was scribbling frantically as I took a few more flash pictures, the Speed Graphic spitting blackened flashbulbs onto the crime scene; any moment a patrol car, having heard the same police call, would roll up and take over. Me, I wished they'd hurry.

But, as I may have mentioned, I was a detective, and, for better or worse, that's how I looked at things. And I heard myself saying to Fowley, "You notice anything weird about this?"

Flies were blowing me the raspberry.

Fowley looked up from his notepad, raising his eyebrows, smirking as he said, "Oh hell no. This is about as routine as they come, Heller."

"Where's the blood?"

"The blood . . ." His eyes slitted, then widened. "Where the hell *is* the blood?" Suddenly Fowley was looking around like somebody who misplaced his car keys.

From the sidewalk, I pointed to the two-part corpse. "Look at the wounds—no signs of coagulation."

Nodding slowly, Fowley said, "The grass isn't bloody around the body, either—not even . . . you know, between the halves."

"No sign of any other internal fluids, either. See that grayish white knob? That's her spine. It looks like some organs have been removed."

"What is this guy? A friggin' vampire?"

"Maybe a werewolf."

"Hey, that's good!" Eyes popping, he scribbled that down. "That'll make a swell headline . . . 'Werewolf Murderer Butchers Beauty'!"

"Mention me at the Pulitzer dinner." Tentatively, I stepped closer; thinking like a detective gave me distance, and kept the nausea in check. "Can you see that vertebrae? Lower part of her."

"What about it?"

"No bone granules. It's a clean cut—not sawed . . . severed."

"Heller, look at this. . . ."

"Get back, Fowley! You're too close."

He was waving away the flies. "Aren't those . . . bristles? God, they're embedded right in her skin. Like off a wire brush!"

"You may be right, and that would make sense. There's no way she was killed here. This isn't a murder scene—it's a dump site. She was bisected, drained of blood, scrubbed clean, and carted and dumped here, off the main drag, probably before dawn."

I looked at the gray sky, wondering if it would keep its threat of rain and wash this lot clean of evidence. There was no rumble of thunder and this was, after all, California; it had been three weeks since it last rained. Still, maybe I needed to keep playing photographer. . . .

Slowly I scanned the vacant lot and its scant scattering of refuse; then my eyes fixed on a discarded cement sack, its limp gray cloth draped in the grass a few feet from the girl's head. Going over to it, but trying to keep my distance and not further pollute the scene, I saw on the cheap gray material a few droplets of what might have been dried, watery blood.

"This may have been used to haul one half of her," I said, and pointed out the possible blood drops to Fowley. "Not inside the sack, more like using it as a sling."

"Brother," Fowley said, snugging his porkpie back down, "she musta been drained damn near dry."

I took a flash picture, retrieved the spent bulb.

Returning to the sidewalk, I said, "There's a few drops here, too. . . ." I recorded that with the Speed Graphic, then kept looking. "Hey! This might be a piece of luck. . . ."

On the driveway to a house that had never been built was the dried-blood imprint of a shoe's heel, half of one, anyway, partly obscured by an automobile tire track. Probably a man's shoe, possibly a woman's oxford.

"So our killer pulled in here," I said, kneeling over the partial heel print in the driveway, taking a flash picture, "made two trips hauling 'garbage' out of his trunk, making this heel print . . ." I glanced toward the street. ". . . then he took the hell off, backing over and partially smearing it. . . ."

I got up and went to the street. Skid marks were burned into the gutter. Whether these were marks made by the car screeching to a stop, or peeling out, it was impossible to say. I took another picture.

"He was headed south," Fowley said.

I nodded, rising.

As if the skid marks had come to life, squealing tires behind us announced a patrol car pulling in. Two uniformed cops climbed quickly out.

One of the cops was lanky, about thirty, the other was much younger, a rookie with a linebacker build; hard-eyed and pasty-faced under their uniform caps, both were undoing the safety straps of their holstered revolvers.

"Take it easy, fellas!" Fowley called out, holding up his hands; mine were already up. "I'm a reporter on the *Examiner*."

Then Fowley reached inside his suitcoat pocket and the revolvers jack-in-the-boxed into the cops' hands.

"Jesus Christ, boys," Fowley sputtered, "I said I'm a reporter! Fowley's the name! Let me show you my i.d."

"Get 'em up," the older one said, then to his partner added, "Check his i.d."

The young one made his way over to reach inside Fowley's coat and have a look.

"He's okay," the young cop said.

Nobody bothered to check my i.d.—the camera in my hand was apparently sufficient: I was an *Examiner* photographer.

Then the younger cop angled over toward the weeds, to get a gander at the drunk woman disturbing the peace. "Oh my God—Mike . . . Mike!"

"What?"

"This girl—poor girl, Jesus Mary, somebody's cut her in half!"

The older cop, holstering his revolver, had a look at the body in the weeds, joining his partner, who was weaving like he was the drunk.

"Get on the radio, Jerry," Mike told the boy, steadying him with a hand to a shoulder. "Get put straight through to the watch commander. Have 'em get a team over here pronto."

Jerry nodded, but paused, thinking about whether or not to puke, didn't, and—on unsteady legs—somehow got over to the patrol car, reaching in for the dash mike, calling in a dead body "at the 390 location—probable homicide."

That seemed a fair assessment.

"Monitoring police calls, Mr. Fowley?" the older cop asked.

Fowley shrugged. "Yeah. I mean, hell, it's legal, Officer."

"Compromising a crime scene isn't."

Fowley was reaching in his pants pocket; but this time no revolver jumped into the hand of the man in blue. "Listen, Officer . . . I'd like to phone this in to my city editor."

"You just stay put." But somehow the cop didn't sound like he meant it; a ritual was in progress.

Fowley handed the guy a folded-up tenspot. "Maybe you got change for this buck."

The patrolman took the tenspot, put it in his pocket, and came back with a nickel, which he flipped to Fowley.

"Go make your call," the cop said.

This would have never happened in Chicago—a buck would have covered it. Maybe two.

"Your photographer stays," the cop said.

"Fine," Fowley said, "swell, not a problem." Then he turned to me, took the Speed Graphic out of my hands, and said, "I'll be right back."

"Thanks," I said, just thrilled to be left here on deposit.

Then I was alone with the two cops, and the dead girl, under a gray sky, waiting for all the other cops in L.A. to show up.

"Poor kid," the older cop said to the younger one, shaking his head. "That was a nice body 'fore it got butchered. What a waste."

Jerry swallowed; he was as pale as she was. "Geez . . . I wonder who she is?"

"You mean you wonder who she was," the older cop said.

I wonder.

# 2

I suppose I would have been happier hearing my bride say she was pregnant if my girl friend hadn't phoned that same day with similar news.

Former girl friend, that is—what kind of heel do you take me for?

"This is Elizabeth," the voice on the phone had said. The voice was soft, low, husky, vaguely refined.

It was early on a Thursday evening, six days prior to that vacant lot in Leimert Park.

I was in the living room of our bungalow at the Beverly Hills Hotel and my wife was sitting on the sofa next to me. The bungalow, a modest affair with a marble fireplace and French doors looking out on a private patio, was outfitted in plush furnishings that matched the peachy-pink walls and pink-and-green floral carpeting. My wife's dainty yet curvaceous frame was outfitted in a dark green bolero slacks suit with a white top; her open-toe-sandaled feet were on the Queen Anne coffee table, ankles crossed.

"Who?" I asked the phone. The voice had been familiar but I didn't immediately place it.

"You know—Beth. Beth Short."

"Oh!" I glanced at my wife, who glanced back at me, pausing

as she leafed through the latest *Silver Screen* magazine, in that chilling "Who is that, dear?" manner known by all men who've received a phone call from a woman while their wife is in the room.

"I take it you remember me," said the sultry voice on the phone.

"Yes. Of course."

And here is why looking at my wife reminded me of who the girl on the phone was: they looked alike.

The girl on the phone had lustrous brown hair so dark it almost appeared black; so did Peggy. The girl on the phone was not quite as petite as Peggy, but they had similarly creamy pale skin, slender shapely figures, and big beautiful eyes (Beth's were blue-green, Peggy's were Elizabeth Taylor violet). Both of them had fabulous smiles, slightly chubby chipmunk cheeks, with movie-star features reminiscent of screen songbird Deanna Durbin. And both liked to wear white flowers in their dark hair.

I had known the former Peggy Hogan—my bride of almost a month—since 1938; but we had gotten serious in the summer of '45, and soon were more or less engaged; then by the end of the next summer, we had broken it off. Rather, Peggy had broken it off, and gone gallivanting to Las Vegas to work for a friend of mine. Soon she and that "friend" were romantically inclined, which is to say reclined, so for about three and a half months—roughly the fall of '46—I had been a spurned, rather bitter lover.

And like so many a man enraged with the woman who cast him aside, I had promptly gotten myself involved with another woman whose striking physical resemblance to my lost love would allow me to bask in equal parts joy and misery.

But my affair with Beth—and you will get the details of that, in time . . . patience—had been brief, and I had not given the little waitress with the movie-star looks a single thought since our final night together, back in Chicago, last November.

Because in December, when Peggy's affair came to an abrupt and rather unpleasant end, she ran back into my arms and I gratefully accepted the gesture. We were married a day later, in one of those shabby little Las Vegas wedding chapels, and spent several days thereafter frantically fucking, desperately reassuring each other that we were desperately in love with each other (as opposed to just plain desperate), never discussing, never mentioning the fact that she was mine on the colossal rebound.

"You're surprised to hear from me," the girl on the phone said.

"Yes," I said, master of understatement that I am. "I didn't think it was widely known I was in L.A., and the last time I saw you—"

"Was in Chicago. But, Nathan—you knew I was a California girl. Remember, we talked about you opening an office here? You were going out in December. Remember?"

I remembered. I only wished she hadn't.

"Listen," the girl on the phone said, "I'm . . . I'm in trouble."

"What kind?" I asked, sitting up. "Kind you need a private detective for?"

"No . . . you know. I'm in *trouble*."

"Trouble?" I asked numbly, knowing.

"Nathan, I'm two months late."

Not private detective trouble, then; private dick trouble.

"I see . . . and it's, uh, it's . . ." I glanced at my wife, who was still paging through the movie magazine, pausing intermittently to frown curiously at me.

"It's yours, Nathan," the girl on the phone said. Beth said. Her low-pitched voice managed to seem worldly and youthful at the same time.

I swallowed, smiling and shrugging at my wife, saying into the phone, "Forgive me, but . . . there's no doubt of that?"

"I haven't been with anybody but you." Dreadful certainty in the voice. "Not for over a month before we were together, and not at all since."

Fighting dizziness, I said, "Frankly, I don't, uh, remember even . . . being with you."

Other than those incredible blow jobs. Yes, I am a classy guy.

"Oh, Nathan, please, please don't tell me . . ." The husky voice caught, a sob trapped in her throat. ". . . don't tell me you were too drunk . . . too drunk to remember. . . ."

What I did remember was that I had indeed been drunk that last night with her. Yes, sir, class act all the way.

"This is a bad time," I said.

Now Peggy was looking at me, really frowning.

"We have to talk," Beth's voice said.

"Can't this wait till business hours? I can be in my office at the Bradbury Building tomorrow morning."

"I know about your office," Beth said. "How do you think I found you? Your friend Mr. Rubinski gave me your number."

My friend Mr. Rubinski and I would have to have a little talk.

"I just need your help," she said, "you know, to . . . get rid of it."

So she wanted money. What a shock.

"It must be something, staying at the Beverly Hills Hotel," Beth's voice was saying, the sob gone now, replaced with a sort of purr. "I always dreamed of staying there."

"Yeah, it's a swell place," I said. Swell place to be staying when somebody was sizing you up for a shakedown.

Peggy said, "Who is that?"

I covered the mouthpiece, whispered, "A client."

Peggy smirked irritably and returned to her movie magazine.

Into the phone, I said, "Where can I reach you?"

The response had an edge in it: "I want to talk now."

"How about in an hour?

". . . All right. I'm at the Biltmore—Fifth and—"

"I know where the Biltmore is."

"Why don't you come down here, Nathan, and meet me in the lobby?"

"That's impossible. I'll call you back."

"I'm in a pay phone."

"Well give me the number."

She did; I scribbled it down on a pad by the phone on the end table.

"I'll be waiting, Nathan," Beth said. "Let it ring a long time—I'll be sitting in the lobby, listening for your call. Don't disappoint me."

The click in my ear was a relief—a momentary one. I felt sick to my stomach, head whirling. Pretty much the symptoms of morning sickness, but then this was evening, and I was a man. Sort of.

"Do these people have to bother you at home?" Peggy asked.

She looked lovely tonight—as she had on every day of our marriage, thus far—her dark hair up, a fetching pile of raven curls, her cute nose trailed with freckles, her wide full lips lushly lipsticked. No flower in her hair tonight; we'd have to settle for the cut flowers in crystal vases spotted about our cozy honeymoon shack.

"I mean," Peggy continued, movie magazine in her lap now, "you're not even really working any cases in this town, are you? Isn't that Fred's job?"

"I thought you liked it out here."

"I do. You know how I feel about that."

I knew well. We'd been here over three weeks, and Peggy had made it clear she liked Los Angeles, specifically Hollywood. I had made it clear I did not: to me Hollywood was one big movie set, a world of cheap fancy facades, especially the people.

I should have known I was in trouble the moment Peggy got a load of the Beverly Hills Hotel, with its pink-and-green stucco Mission-style-meets-Art-Moderne buildings strewn about grounds swarming with flowering shrubbery and colorful gardens. Staying at that hotel—a pastel, palm-flung make-believe land whose airy lobby was garnished with stunning floral arrangements and luxurious plants and overstuffed furniture for patrons with overstuffed wallets—was like living inside a movie, a sensation reinforced by having the likes of Cary Grant, Hedy Lamarr, Jimmy Stewart and Rosalind Russell sitting at the table next to you, in the hotel's main dining room or its Polo Lounge.

Back in the late '30s, when I met Peggy Hogan, she'd been studying at Sawyer Secretarial College, earning money on the side as an artist's model, posing for Brown and Bigelow's Chicago-based calendar artists. The business schooling was at her family's insistence, as her ambition had been to become an actress. She had lived in Tower Town—at that time, the Chicago equivalent of Greenwich Village—and had some minor success in the Little Theater scene.

By the time she and I got together, though, Peggy had abandoned her show business aspirations and used her considerable business skills—she was particularly adept at accounting—to help support her family, after her father's second and fatal stroke. She was one of seven kids, and her only brother, Johnny, had been killed in the war.

That burden was off her back now, however, because her uncle James Ragen—a client of mine—had died last August and left Peggy's mother a tidy sum. Jim Ragen had been the head of Continental Press, a racing wire service used by bookies nationwide, and he had died—despite my best efforts to prevent it—at the hands of "rival business interests."

Close to her uncle and looking up to him, Peggy had been around that kind of people all her life—underworld figures, I mean (she even at one time dated a Capone bodyguard)—and had an unfortunate propensity toward fancying the "glamorous" world of bigtime gangsters.

I guess my reputation for having mob ties myself—really exaggerated—maybe lent me a little of that same shady allure, from Peggy's point of view. So maybe I shouldn't have complained about her yen for the likes of her late uncle, and Capone bodyguards, and did I mention the friend of mine she'd run off to Las Vegas with was Benjamin "Bugsy" Siegel?

All of which is to say, Peggy had been around, yet at the same time was naive about certain things. She could be impressed by the phony glitz of Ben Siegel's Flamingo Hotel, the aura of excitement, danger and affluence that emanated from bigtime gamblers and gangsters, surrounded as they were by fawning sycophants and beautiful women in jewels and fur.

And of course, by his own crafty design, Ben Siegel's Las Vegas was the bastard brother to Tinsel Town; so I suppose it should have been no surprise to me that honeymooning in Hollywood would stir certain dormant leanings and longings within my bride.

Not right away, though. The first week of our honeymoon in the Southland (as Southern California liked to call itself) had been blissfully uneventful—really your typical honeymoon, three parts sightseeing, one part fucking. Maybe two parts fucking.

On a delightfully sunny day, we prowled the foot trails of

Elysian Park, up and down arroyo-gouged hills, through a snarl of creepers, wild roses, blue gum eucalyptus, slouching pepper trees and twisted oaks; from Point Grand View, the city and mountains lay stretched before us, as if the world was ours for the taking. The view at night at Griffith Park planetarium (within and without) widened those possibilities to the universe, though the next morning we settled for a rowboat ride on the shady, landscaped waters of Westlake Park, ogled the oozing bubbling bog of the La Brea Tar Pits in the afternoon and, that night, took in the colored lanterns and the festive music from cafes of brick-paved, shop-strewn Olvera Street.

But the sights that most thrilled Peggy were the movie palaces of Hollywood Boulevard, the ridiculous pagoda of Grauman's Chinese—where we compared footprints with the stars (my feet were bigger than Gable's, hers smaller than Lombard's) and took in *Till the Clouds Roll By*—and the Egyptian, where we caught *The Shocking Miss Pilgrim* and coerced a passerby to snap our picture in front of the ancient god standing guard in the forecourt.

To me the perfect symbol of this phony burg was that shabby HOLLYWOODLAND sign on Mount Lee, a deteriorating remnant of a failed real estate deal, letters thirty feet wide and fifty feet tall studded with burned-out lightbulbs, a decaying relic whose chief function over the years had been to provide a platform for the suicide dives of failed starlets. Still, the looming letters from a distance, if you squinted, looked impressive. They certainly impressed Peggy, who was cross with me when I suggested that maybe someday somebody would have the good sense to tear the goddamn thing down.

"You have no romance," Peggy said.

We had just made love on the bungalow's Axminster broadloom carpet in the glow of the marble fireplace.

Nuzzling her neck, I said, "If that's what you think, you haven't been paying attention."

"That's not what I mean . . . Can we talk?"

I had not been married long enough to recognize the three deadliest words in the English language, known by husbands everywhere.

"Aren't we?" I asked innocently. "Talking?"

Now she nuzzled my neck. "I just wanted to ask you something."

"Ask me something?" I ran a hand along the smooth side of her, following the sensuous sweep down to her waist and up the swell of her swell hip. "Sure. Ask me anything."

"Could we stay longer?"

"Where? California? Why?"

The violet eyes were wide and seemingly guileless. "Never mind why. Could we?"

I leaned on an elbow, watching the flames of the fireplace lick her, burnishing her supple curves. "Well, not at the Beverly Hills Hotel. I think we can squeeze a month, maybe a month and a half out of 'em. You got any idea what these bungalows go for, a night?"

"I know that. I just thought maybe we could rent a little place."

". . . You don't mean you'd like me to work out of the L.A. office? Peggy, you can't be serious. . . ."

She was studying me, affectionately, a hand fiddling with my hair. "Why don't we throw something on and go to the lounge?"

Polo Lounge, she meant.

Soon we were sharing one of the private booths overlooking the garden patio, the trees of which were festooned with twinkling lights. This was a week night, around eleven, and the place wasn't all that busy. The only celebrity couple was Lucille Ball and Desi Arnaz, who—like us—were married and seemed deeply, hopelessly in love.

Peggy—in a pink pantsuit with shoulder pads that would have done Joan Crawford proud—sipped her stinger, cherry-lipsticked lips kissing the red plastic straw, and I worked on my rum cooler, wondering what was on her mind.

Finally, she said, "Being out here has got me thinking."

"About?"

"Giving it another try."

"Giving what another try?"

"Acting!"

The word was like a blow to the pit of my stomach, and I probably sounded winded, echoing, "Acting?"

"You knew that was always my dream."

"I thought we'd kinda thrown in together on a mutual dream, Peg—the white-cottage-white-picket-fence variety?"

"Nate, you don't expect me to be just another drab little housewife, do you?"

Now I felt a black cloud settling over my head, like that shrimpy guy in *L'il Abner*, the one trouble followed.

Trying to be gentle, I said, "Baby, don't be fooled by this mink-lined hellhole."

The violet eyes glittered, looking as lovely—and as hard—as precious gems. "I know it's a tough town. I know sooner or later I have to check out of the Beverly Hills Hotel and back into reality. But I have talent, Nate—you remember how good I was, in *Winterset*, at the Playhouse? Don't you see? This could be my last chance to make something of myself."

And here I thought she'd made something of herself becoming Mrs. Nathan Heller.

"Baby," I said, "thousands of pretty young things flock out here to knock Lana Turner off the screen, and the only roles they get, on or off the screen, are as waitresses, salesgirls, and car hops."

Her eyes tightened. "Are you saying I'm too old?"

"No! Hell, no, baby—"

Her whole face seemed to harden. "That I can't compete, just because I'm almost thirty?"

I felt like a kid who'd peeked in the oven at cookies baking and got his face scorched.

"You're the most beautiful woman in this town," I told her, grasping her hand. And it wasn't a lie. First of all, she was my bride and we were on our honeymoon and I loved her; and second of all, the former Peggy Hogan was a knockout. But knockouts approaching thirty were, in fact, long in the tooth for this sleazy trash heap of a town.

"I think it's an advantage, not being some naive little beauty contest winner," she said, trying to convince herself as much as me. "Let those little tramps try to sleep their way to the top. I have something they'll never have."

"Talent," I said, nodding, going along with her.

"Well of course talent, but I was talking about connections. Your connections. My late uncle's connections. Ben's connections."

It was the first time Ben Siegel had been referred to since we'd tied the knot.

"Ben's connections," I echoed numbly.

She shrugged a single shoulder, as if the bombshell she'd just dropped was the tiniest firecracker. "Ben owes us. He owes you and he owes me. He has more Hollywood friends than Hedda Hopper."

"I'd rather not bring Ben back into our lives, in any fashion. Okay?"

She raised her hands in gentle surrender. "All right, bad suggestion—but your partner Fred has a black book filled with movie colony bigwigs. Isn't that why you threw in with him—the movie studios and stars he works for, and with? It would be easy for him to line up some interviews, some auditions for me."

"You've really been thinking about this, haven't you?"

"Yes. Yes, I have."

"And I'd just move out here, and what? Let Lou Sapperstein run the Chicago office?"

"Sure, and you can fly back and forth some. We could maintain two residences. We can afford it."

I knew when Peg got up a full head of steam like this, there was no stopping her—and, frankly, I didn't see the harm. She did have a little talent—a little—and, yes, she had the looks. She was pretty with a nice shape, and with all the Technicolor pictures they were making these days, those violet eyes would show up nice.

But the reality was, she didn't stand a chance, even with a little string-pulling. At twenty-nine, she really was too old for this town, to be starting out, anyway. So I didn't see the harm. Let her try, let her get her hopes dashed, and let her come running back into my arms in tears.

The second agent she tried out for signed her. I chewed Fred out, asking what the hell he thought he was doing, had he twisted this guy's arm or what?

Fred—a small, compactly muscular, nattily dressed man in his forties with sharp dark eyes, a rumpled face, and a shiny bald head—sat behind his desk in the Bradbury Building and shrugged elaborately. "Who'd a thunk it? I didn't ask for any favors, except to let Peg read for him. I said she was my partner's wife and would he please humor her. He said sure, and now this!"

I was pacing. "Humor her is right. She goes out on audition at Fox tomorrow!"

"Having an agent is nothing."

"Nothing! There's ten thousand beautiful babes out there that would screw you silly for an in with an agent!"

"Maybe in the future I should keep that in mind." Fred sat forward, patted the air reassuringly. "Listen, Nate, don't worry. Roles are not that easy to come by. You think she's gonna get the first part she reads for? No way in hell!"

Fred was right. She got the second part she read for, a bit as a waitress in a Bob Hope picture at Paramount.

She was thrilled, giddy with it, and I did my best not to be a rat, and seem happy for her.

Anyway, Peggy taking this flier at the movies didn't bother me as much as the notion of relocating to Los Angeles; and Fred Rubinski wasn't crazy about it, either, because he was used to running his own office. Taking me on as a partner had been predicated on my ass staying in Chicago.

"I don't know what to do about it," I said to him, in a booth at Sherry's, the swanky restaurant he owned a piece of on Sunset. "I could divide my time between Chicago and here, maybe three weeks back there and one in L.A."

"That might work," Fred said, lighting up a cigar, pushing a plate of cheesecake crumbs aside. I was still working on my dessert, a rum and Coke.

"Trouble is," I said, "knowing how susceptible Peggy is to this show biz baloney, I'm afraid Errol Flynn or Robert Taylor or somebody would be in her pants before I got off the plane in Chicago."

"Nice, you got such faith in your bride."

"Listen, I love Peggy and I think she loves me, but I got no illusions about this marriage. I got her on the boomerang and I have my work cut out, holding on to her without her flying into somebody's else's arms."

"Siegel?"

"No. But somebody rich and slick and handsome."

Fred's rumpled face formed a lopsided smile. "Well, Nate, you may not be rich, but you're workin' on it, and lots of people think you're slick, maybe too slick—and more than your share of ladies have found you handsome enough, over the years."

"Yeah, but I'm not a movie star. Listen, Fred, if I stay out here, it's still your office—just make me your chief investigator."

"Jesus, Nate, you're the president of the company!"

"That's all right. Even back home I spend my time working cases . . . I just use my clout to pick and choose."

Fred contemplated awhile, then shrugged and said, "Might work out at that. We can play this publicity angle better with the *Examiner*, if that comes to pass, with you doing a 'private eye to the stars' number. We could get nice ink out of that."

"Maybe."

So I had told Peggy that night, in our bungalow, that I had decided to stay in L.A. We'd rent a house and I'd work out of Fred's office, and she could take a real stab at a career in movies.

She melted into my arms. "Oh, Nate, you're wonderful . . . I love you so much. . . ."

"Why don't you try to think of a way to properly thank me, then?"

I cupped her small perfect behind and drew her close.

"Oh, yes, darling . . ." Her fingers were fiddling in my hair. ". . . but one thing . . ."

"Yeah?"

"I think we should start . . . you know, using something."

"Huh?"

"I'm going to get pregnant if we don't start using some precautions."

Over the first weeks of our marriage, we had certainly thrown caution to the wind, with no thought of anything but good old-fashioned honeymooners' lust. Possibly in the back of my mind had been the thought of making some little Hellers—I was older than Peg, after all, pushing forty, a returning vet seeking that idyllic postwar world, and settling down had been part of the process.

But that night I used a Sheik, like old times, and soon she was using a diaphragm. We still made love like honeymooners—well, maybe dropping back to twice or even once a day—and Peggy was constantly affectionate, grateful for the sacrifice I was making for her, and her career.

On the evening I received the phone call from Beth Short, I had noticed a certain moodiness on Peggy's part—almost a sullenness, though she hadn't been unpleasant or anything.

After I cradled the phone—already starting to work on the story that would allow me to slip away to a pay phone where I could call Beth back and start dealing with this mess—Peggy tossed her movie magazine on the coffee table beside red-painted toes peeking through her sandals, and said those three words again.

Not "I love you"—the three deadly ones.

"Can we talk?"

"Well, sure, honey."

"We haven't had dinner, you know."

Somehow it was an accusation.

"I thought we'd just go over to the Polo Lounge," I said. "Or maybe order room service."

"Let's go out." Abruptly, she stood, smoothing her bolero slacks outfit. "I need to go out."

So I took her to La Rue, a chic joint on the Strip owned by Billy Wilkerson, publisher of *The Hollywood Reporter*. Unlike the nearby Ciro's and the Trocadero, La Rue was chiefly a restaurant, not a nightclub, and the mood was relaxed—no blaring big band, just a piano playing Cole Porter. The only celebrities I spotted were Rita Hayworth and Orson Welles, sharing one of the striped booths; weren't they divorced? Hayworth looked angry and Welles, heavy-lidded, seemed half in the bag. I knew Welles, having met him in Chicago years before, but he didn't recognize me, or anyway acknowledge me. I got over it. We moved along to our own cozy striped booth, where we ate, conversing little. Peg had lobster newberg, which she barely touched, and I had a lamb chop, just picking at the thing.

We were both preoccupied—I was thinking about that phone call to the Biltmore I was supposed to make, Beth's hour deadline having nearly elapsed; and Peggy had as yet to elaborate on those three little words: "Can we talk?"

Finally, after our plates had been cleared and the crumbs brushed from the linen tablecloth and we'd both declined dessert and ordered coffee, I asked, "How did the audition go this morning?"

"It wasn't an audition," she said.

"I thought it was an audition."

"It wasn't. It was a doctor's appointment."

"Doctor's . . . are you all right?"

"Yes. No. I don't know."

I scooched around beside her in the booth, slipped an arm around her. "Peg, what's wrong?"

"I was late."

"Late?"

"You know . . . *late*?"

I couldn't be hearing this.

"And I'm *never* late," she went on, her tone as light as a Noel Coward play, and as ominous as an obituary, "so I made a doctor's appointment . . . just to be safe, you know? I'm pregnant, all right."

"Well," I said thickly, "that's . . . that's wonderful."

"Wonderful?" The violet eyes glared at me: *are you insane?* "You can't be serious. This couldn't come at a worse time."

She didn't know how right she was, but I said, "It's a great time—we're newlyweds and we're going to be parents. That's great. It's the American dream."

"It's a nightmare. It doesn't fit in with our plans at all!"

"Our plans?"

"Nate, I'm going to be in a movie next week. I have an agent. My dreams are all coming true."

"Don't you have any dreams that involve me, and starting a family?"

She sighed impatiently, glancing away. "Of course I do . . . just not right now."

"What are you suggesting?"

"I think we should . . . consider . . . you know."

"Consider what?"

"Must I say it?"

". . . Getting rid of it?"

Now her manner turned businesslike. "Surely, with your connections, you know people that could . . . take care of this."

My connections again.

"Peggy," I said, scooching away a little, pawing the air, "no more discussion. You're having this baby. *We're* having this baby."

She huffed, she puffed, she blew my house down: "I should have known you'd take that selfish attitude."

Whatever happened to the good old days, when you knocked up a woman, she tried to talk you into getting married, and you tried to talk her into having an abortion instead?

"You're my wife," I said, "and I love you, and you're going to be the mother of my . . . of our . . . child."

"You're impossible," she said, and she began to cry, and when I tried to comfort her, she slapped at me and rushed off to the powder room. Other patrons glared at me, wondering what terrible thing I'd done to this poor girl.

I took the opportunity to use the pay phone to try the number at the Biltmore. I let it ring and ring and ring.

Finally a male voice answered. "This is a pay phone."

"I know. Is there a pretty girl sitting there, waiting in the lobby? Dark hair, almost black? Real dish?"

"Yeah, I seen her, she was hangin' around awhile. She blew, though."

"Thanks."

Shrugging, I hung up; what the hell—what had been her damn rush, anyway? Beth Short knew where to find me.

So I leaned against the wall outside the ladies' powder room, nodding to Bogart and Bacall as they strolled by, heading to the bar; Bogart nodded back and Bacall bestowed a smile. Nice couple. Glad somebody was happily married.

Well, at least I could be sure of something: I might be one fertile son of a bitch, but none of the women in my life wanted to have my kid.

# 3

Flies were not alone in swarming around the milky-white cleaved cadaver in the weedy vacant lot on South Norton Avenue—within minutes of Bill Fowley abandoning me by driving off to make his phone call, cops and reporters and assorted rubberneckers were getting grisly glimpses.

It began slowly, with another radio patrol car pulling up, a uniformed sergeant who'd been cruising Slauson having heard the 390 call. Though he was older, and obviously experienced, the sarge whitened and shook his head and backed away from the body, mumbling, "Man oh man oh man." Shortly thereafter a blue '41 Ford with a press sticker on the windshield drew up, parked in the street, and a fortyish fireplug of a woman in a raincoat, her short red hair uncovered, hopped out and headed over, trailed by a photographer—a real one—loading a bulb into his Speed Graphic.

Round faced with pleasant features given an edge by her hard bright eyes and firm set jaw, Aggie Underwood might have been a schoolteacher; instead she was the first rival reporter to arrive at the scene. Sort of a rival, anyway: like Fowley, she worked for Hearst, just a different paper, the afternoon *Herald Express*.

Trouble was, Aggie knew me—we were friendly acquaintances, having met when I came to L.A. in late '44 on the notorious Peete case; Louise Peete—currently sitting on death row—was scheduled to be the second woman in California history to be executed. Aggie was regarded by many as the best police beat reporter in L.A., with a tough-as-nails, aggressive reputation that I knew from personal experience was well deserved.

She didn't notice me at first—I was standing off to one side—and when the younger uniformed officer, Jerry, stepped forward, holding out a traffic-cop palm, saying, "Just a minute, lady!" she brushed past him, speaking to the older cop, Mike, notepad and pencil at the ready.

"Remember me, Officer?" she said chirpily. "Underwood of the *Express?*" Still charging forward, she jerked a thumb back at her photographer, who was ambling up behind her. "Jack here took that swell picture of you that made page three last month—that school fire?"

"Miss Underwood, please stay back—"

"What have we got here?"

"It's a bad one, ma'am, please prepare yourself . . ."

Aggie laughed at that—the thought of any crime scene bothering a tough cookie like her being simply absurd—and then the laugh caught, and Aggie froze, one foot on the sidewalk, the other on the grass, almost stepping on the corpse's left leg. The blood drained out of Aggie's face, leaving her complexion fish-belly white under the shock of red hair.

"Christ almighty," she breathed. Swallowing, she said, "This poor kid's been cut in two!"

Nice to have a reporter on hand, to spell that out for the rest of us.

And now Aggie was doing something she probably had never done before: she was moving away from a big story, walking backward till she dropped off the curb and stumbled against the nose of that first squad car. She covered her mouth, clearly queasy.

Finally she said, "What kind of sick son of a bitch would do something like this?"

Nobody bothered answering—not that anybody had an answer.

I didn't have one, either, but I figured I better break the ice, just the same. Better I make myself known than wait to be noticed.

Joining her where she was propping herself against the patrol car, I said, "Been a while, Aggie."

She turned to me blankly; then recognition narrowed her eyes and she smiled, faintly, shaking her head, saying, "Nate Heller. Heard you were in town. . . .What brings a handsome devil like you to these picnic grounds?"

Without mentioning I'd played photographer, I told her I'd been tagging along with Fowley for a meeting at the *Examiner*, to get some ink for my new partnership with Fred Rubinski.

"And you didn't come to me first?" she said, fumbling in her purse for cigarettes. She was shaking, a little. "After all we've meant to each other? . . . Jack! Get off your dead keister and take some goddamn pictures!"

Jack—thin, thirty, a burning cigarette bobbing—looked at her with wide eyes that supposedly had seen everything, and said, "What the hell picture can I take of that?"

"You take every picture, every angle you come up with, and leave the worries to the airbrush boys."

He sighed smoke. "Gotcha."

Aggie offered me a cigarette, a Camel, and I took her up on it. Like a lot of servicemen, I'd started smoking overseas; I'd managed to shake the habit, during my postcombat trauma stay in the mental ward at St. Elizabeth's. But now and then I got the craving—stressful situations, mostly.

"So the *Examiner* beat me here," she said, plucking a tobacco flake off her tongue. "Well, too bad for them they only got a morning edition. . . . Did he have a photographer with him?"

"No."

"It doesn't matter, anyway. Jack's right. This is gonna be a hard one to print pictures of."

I was lighting up off a book of matches she'd tossed me. "You okay, Aggie?"

"Yeah. But, Nate, I swear to God that's the worst one I ever saw. I mean, I caught some bad traffic accidents, and plenty of nasty homicides, from ice picks to axes . . . but, hell, this . . . the sick bastard put that poor little dame on display. It's like a French postcard sent by the Marquis de Sade."

The younger cop was saying to the sergeant, "I make her for about thirty-five. What do you think, Sarge?"

But it was Aggie who answered the question, trundling over, saying, "I got girdles older than that kid—she's barely out of her teens." Fully recovered, Aggie knelt over the corpse and pointed. "She's got smooth skin. Get a load of those firm thighs, boys—she's young and I think she might've been pretty. Who do you suppose she was? A starlet, maybe?"

Maybe Aggie had her act together, but I was still trembling, leaning against the squad car, sucking on the cigarette. They could speculate all they wanted, *but I knew who the dead girl was*—and, yes, she had been pretty—only, to do my civic duty and inform police and press that this was Elizabeth Short, of Medford, Massachusetts, would be to reveal myself as a prime suspect. This woman had, after all, tried to hit me up for abortion money, less than a week ago. A child belonging to me was probably still inside her, right now, a tiny Heller every bit as dead as she was.

On the other hand, if I kept quiet now, and the cops found out about the connection between us later, I could wind up breathing in more than a Camel cigarette, namely cyanide fumes at San Quentin.

Still . . . despite the jam I was potentially in—and the murdered girl's attempt to shake me down—I felt my eyes welling up and throat getting lumpy, and I wasn't catching cold, either, despite the nippy wind under the gray sky. I had liked this girl—she'd been nice to me, and not just sexually; sure, she'd been troubled, with more ambition than common sense, one of the legion of pretty girls who came west daily, looking to trade beauty for fame, hoping to be discovered—just not in a vacant lot.

More cops (from neighboring divisions), more reporters (from all five Los Angeles daily papers), arrived, as did numerous plain citizens; this desolate stretch of wired-off lots—previously populated chiefly by weeds and telephone poles—was suddenly teeming.

The circus had come to this neighborhood once again, just not Ringling Bros. and Barnum and Bailey this time. Onlookers, kept back by cops, stood on top of their parked cars to get a gander.

Oddly, for such a mob, a quiet settled over the scene. People were talking, sure, but with voices low, respectful, as if this were visitation at a funeral home.

Before long, a plainclothes dick from nearby University Station—Lieutenant Haskins—took charge, casually informing Aggie that this would be his case. That proved to be wishful thinking.

Aggie had moved away from the crime scene and was interviewing a little boy on a bike from the neighborhood when an unmarked midnight-blue Chevy sedan arrived and parked, barricade-style, to help block traffic.

Even before they climbed out, I pegged them as homicide dicks from Central Division; no great deduction on my part: it happened I knew one of them a little—again from the Peete case—and this was not a lucky break for me. Aggie, distracted by the extreme nature of the slaying, had glossed over the presence of a private detective at this crime scene; Detective Harry Hansen would not.

On the force for over twenty years, better than half of them working out of Homicide Division, Hansen stepped out from the rider's side and just seemed to keep coming: tall, tanned, lanky, in his late forties, he had an oblong, deeply grooved face with deceptively sleepy eyes, a long blunt nose and a pursed kiss of a mouth. The big redheaded Dane—who supervised most significant L.A. homicide investigations—had a reputation as the most dapper cop in the department, which his wardrobe this morning lived up to: tailored dark blue suit, white-and-shades-of-blue-striped silk tie, and dark-banded powder-blue snapbrim fedora.

The fedora—probably a fifty-dollar number—was his trademark, and he was seldom seen out of one, even indoors—in part, it was said, because he was balding. The newspapers liked to call Hansen "Mr. Homicide," a sobriquet rumored to have been suggested by Hansen himself; but what he was called on the street, by both cops and crooks, was Harry the Hat.

I didn't recognize his partner, who'd been driving. Whoever he was, this plainclothes dick was not the second most dapper cop on the force: a prematurely gray, thirtyish, round-faced, chunky character in an off-the-rack slept-in-looking brown suit with red-and-white-dotted tie, with a rumpled brown fedora shoved back on his head, revealing a hairline that had receded to the next county.

The Hat scowled, glancing down and around at the cigarette butts and spent black flashbulbs littering the street and sidewalk. Maybe because his eyes were lowered, he didn't notice me, as he and his partner were ushered to the bisected body by that University Station lieutenant who, seeing Hansen, almost certainly realized he had just been usurped of his case.

Along the way, Lieutenant Haskins—slender, nondescript, his gray suit flapping in the breeze—introduced himself to the city's most famous homicide detective.

"I'm the one who called Captain Donahoe and requested backup," Haskins said.

Hansen's sleepy eyes snapped awake at the suggestion that he was "backup."

"I don't much care who called Captain Donahoe," Hansen said, his tone as gentle as his words were sharp, nodding toward the white shape in the weeds. "What I do care about is, who called *this* in?"

"An unidentified female."

"That makes two unidentified females we have on our hands."

The lieutenant shrugged. "The anonymous woman caller just said somebody was lying in the weeds, and needed attending to."

"I would call that an understatement," Hansen said, and ambled to the edge of the sidewalk. His chunky partner followed him, and when Hansen squatted to regard the corpse, the partner squatted beside him, as if their entire relationship were a game of Simon Says.

Like Aggie Underwood, Harry the Hat had seen damn near everything; but even from my vantage point in thc street, I could see his stony mask slip. The chunky cop at Harry's side was scowling in disgust.

"Christ, Harry," he was saying, waving away the flies.

"Somebody spent his sweet time on her, Brownie," Hansen said to his partner. "Ever see a face cut up like that?"

"Hell no."

"That grin carved in her face? Cut clean through the cheeks. . . . Somebody made a real hobby out of her."

The Hat rose; so did "Brownie."

Lieutenant Haskins said, "I already called in the lab boys. They should be on the way."

The Hat shot him a look. "Who did you talk to?"

"Lieutenant Jones—Lee Jones."

"Call again. Get Ray Pinker over here."

Pinker was chief of the LAPD crime lab.

"Yes, sir," Haskins said, and went off to use the police radio.

The Hat called out to him. "Don't use the radio! We got enough bystanders and meddling cops and damn reporters, already. Where's the nearest pay phone?"

"There's one on Crenshaw."

"Good. . . . Hurry back."

The lieutenant paused, as if trying to find the sarcasm in Hansen's words; but the Hat was a deadpan comic and you couldn't always tell.

Gazing with what might have been mild disgust at the lieutenant, who was climbing into his squad car to go make his phone call, Hansen finally noticed me.

Initially, surprise tightened the Robert Mitchum eyes; then his tiny mouth puckered into a smile. "And I thought this already was interesting. . . . Come say hello, Nate."

I nodded at the Hat as I made my way to the sidewalk.

"We have a celebrity at the scene, Brownie," Hansen was saying. "This is Nate Heller, that Chicago private detective you've heard so much about."

"I have?" Brownie asked.

"Fred Rubinski's new partner. The one who helped me break the Peete case."

Actually, I had broken it by myself, but never mind.

"Good to see you again, Harry," I said, and offered my hand.

The Hat grasped my hand with one of his, using the thumb of his other hand to indicate his partner. "This is Sergeant Brown—*Fine*-us Brown . . ."

That was spelled Finis, I later learned.

Shaking Brown's hand, I said to the Hat, "I thought you worked exclusively with Jack McCreadie."

"They split us up. Share the wealth—spread the expertise. I'm known for my skills as a detective, you know—like right away, my nose is twitching, finding a Chicago private dick at an L.A. crime scene . . . and what a crime scene."

I gave a quick explanation of how I came to be here.

"I don't know what became of Fowley," I said, looking around, not hiding my irritation. "Son of a bitch stranded me here."

"I can tell you," the Hat said. "Doesn't take Sherlock Holmes to deduce he drove over to the *Examiner* to fill Richardson in, in person. This is going to be a big case. Ever see the like, Heller?"

"Well, actually . . ."

The Hat snapped his fingers; the sleepy eyes popped awake. "You have! You worked that Butcher case in Cleveland! When was it, '38?"

That floored me. "How the hell do you know that, Harry?"

The Hat shrugged. "You turned up in the middle of the Peete case, Nate. I researched you. I know things about you that you've forgotten. . . . Brownie, Mr. Heller here is thick with Eliot Ness."

"Who?" Brown asked.

"Ness—he ran the Capone squad in Chicago, then made all those headlines in Cleveland, running the Mayfield Mob out of town. Youngest safety director in these United States, Ness was."

"Oh," Brown said. But it was obviously all news to him.

Under their lids, the Hat's eyes fixed on me like gunsights. "You think I should talk to Mr. Ness about this, Nate? That case was never solved, was it?"

"What case?" Brown asked.

"The Mad Butcher of Kingsbury Run. Thirteen torso killings . . . like this one, here."

"Not quite like this one," I said. "The Butcher usually dismembered his victims, and usually decapitated them, just for good measure. . . .This is a similar M.O., but—"

"Why don't you call Mr. Ness for me?" the Hat asked genially. "He's not safety director, anymore, I realize . . ."

"That's right. He's in private business."

"But it would be nice to get his read on this. Would you mind?"

"No! No, not at all."

That was Harry the Hat for you. His whole style was low-key—no intimidation, no rubber hoses from the Hat; he had a gentle touch, using psychology and subtle manipulation, to get confessions out of suspects.

"Mr. Heller here is a true detective, in the best sense, Brownie. We're lucky to have him with us . . . a lucky coincidence."

"I, uh, don't see anything so coincidental about it," I said.

Brown was frowning, eyes disappearing into slits on his basketball-shaped head. "You don't think it's a coincidence? A private dick at a murder scene?"

"Who worked another torso slaying," Hansen added pleasantly. "That is, slay-*ings*."

"Listen, boys, I'm just waiting for my ride. You've got a lot to do. Let me just get out of your way. . . ."

The Hat put a gentle hand on my shoulder. "Why don't you pitch in? A man of your expertise. What have you noticed?"

So I shared my observations with them, as I had with Bill Fowley, pointing here, pointing there: the lack of blood, the clean nature of the bisection itself, the discarded cement sack, the bloody obscured footprint on the driveway, the tire marks.

"You see, Brownie? A master detective, our friend from Chicago."

We were still on the sidewalk, near the corpse.

"You've hardly left anything for us to do, Nate." The Hat leaned over the corpse, touched the white flesh of her thigh, near where a chunk had been carved away. "She's cold. . . ." He eased his hand underneath her, just a little. He looked up at me in surprise. "Ground's wet."

I frowned. "Dew?"

Brown frowned. "Do what?"

Hansen nodded at me. "She was left here before dawn, when the ground was still wet with dew. . . . I'd say this body was washed, perhaps soaked in water, possibly scrubbed. . . ."

I'd forgotten to mention the bristles; I pointed those out.

Hansen, still kneeling, nodded. "Possibly an effort to remove latent prints."

Brown—who, of course, was also kneeling—said, "Maybe she was strangled . . . Look at those ligature marks on her neck."

"I'm not so sure she was strangled," the Hat said. "That large wound to the head could have caused a fatal concussion."

I was staring at the girl's face; I didn't want to—but I was compelled, as if I were trying to find the pretty features somewhere there, despite the battered forehead and the carved clown's grin.

The Hat, standing, brushing off his expensive suit, picked up on that: he didn't miss much.

"What is it, Nate? There's something personal, here. My nose is twitching again."

"It's just the flies, Harry."

"Don't kid a kidder, Nate. What is it? What were you seeing when you looked down at her?"

And what I told him, as far as it went, was the truth: "It's . . . she looks like my wife, is all. A little like my wife . . . and it shakes me up, looking at her. You mind if I . . . ?"

"No. You can move away. Say—where I can reach you?"

"At the Beverly Hills Hotel."

His eyebrows rose. "Very nice. You and Fred must be doing well."

"Maybe so, but my suits still aren't as nice as yours, Harry."

The tiny mouth grinned, a hole in his face filled with teeth. "It isn't just about money, Nate—it's also about good taste. . . . Ah! Lieutenant Haskins!"

I turned as Haskins, back from his mission, strode up, giving me an excuse to fade back to the street. That fucking Fowley—where the hell was he?

"Ray Pinker is on his way," Haskins said.

"Fine job, Lieutenant," the Hat said. He looked toward where the vacant lot yawned at the backyards of distant, finished homes. Several uniformed officers were picking through the weeds and grass. "And what are those gentlemen up to?"

"I thought we should get started, going over the ground," Haskins said. "If anything turns up, we'll have it ready for the lab boys."

A smile twitched on the Hat's tiny mouth. "Call them off, would you? At this rate there won't be anything for the lab to find."

Haskins, embarrassed, nodded, and was turning to take care of that when the Hat clutched him by the shoulder, saying, "Send them out to do something useful—let's canvass the neighborhood for the woman who made the phone call, and perhaps locate someone else who may have seen something, anything . . . hmmm?"

"Yes."

"And once you've done that, I want you to find some newspapers and cover up that poor girl's body. With the sun coming out, we need to preserve the body from discoloration, for Ray Pinker and the coroner."

Haskins looked up at the sky—the sun indeed was starting to poke its streaky fingers through the clouds—then nodded and scurried away.

Sighing, Harry the Hat—holding up a hand to freeze Brown in place (Simon says *Stay!*)—wandered over to where I was standing, in the street.

Sidling up me, the Hat said, "I don't think the lieutenant understands the sacred nature of a crime scene."

"The what?"

"Nate, it's sacred, this ground . . . sacred and profane, yes . . . but mostly sacred. Murder is a marriage between victim and slayer—it's a bond formed between two people that ties them together. It's more binding than marriage, though . . . you can divorce a mate, you can even remarry a mate . . . but you can only murder somebody once."

Was he needling me, with this marriage metaphor, after I mentioned the corpse reminded me of my wife?

But I said only, "That's, uh, hard to argue with, Harry."

He nodded toward the vacant lot, reached out a hand as if in benediction. "On that sacred ground, murderer and victim were together, one last time—even if he didn't kill her, even if he only deposited the remains. And that nasty tableau, Nate, it's a work of art, in the killer's mind . . . and, frankly, in mine . . . it's a reflection of his mind, his personality. . . .That sacred ground contains all the clues and evidence we might need to solve this murder, or at least it did before that boob from University allowed reporters and cops and God knows who else to trample around on it."

"That was some speech, Harry—but how do you know it's a 'he'?"

That made him wince in thought. "What do you mean, Nate?"

"You keep referring to the murderer as 'he' . . . Couldn't it be a 'she'?"

"Look at that display, Nate—it's a sex crime."

"Lesbians kill people, too. You see any sign of semen?"

"She was washed clean of it."

"How do you know? And, anyway—ever occur to you that that smile cut in her face might mean something nonsexual?"

The hooded eyes blinked. "Explain."

I shrugged. "Back in Chicago, a corpse dumped with its mouth gashed, we'd read that as somebody who got rubbed out for talking too much . . . and left as an example."

Now his eyes were wide; they stayed that way for a while. Then he said, as if bored to tears, "Interesting. . . .You know, I really do respect you as a detective, Nate—these insights, I appreciate them."

I couldn't detect any sarcasm in that; but maybe I just wasn't a good enough detective to do so.

He touched his hat brim in a tip-the-hat gesture and said, "Don't forget to make that phone call to your friend Mr. Ness for me, now, hear?"

"Sure. I'll call you."

"I wish you would. I may have my hands full."

He was just about to amble back to his partner when Fowley's blue Ford rolled in. The little reporter in the tight hat and loose suit parked in the street and came over and grinned at Hansen.

"Not surprised to see you, here, Harry," Fowley said. "This is gonna be a big one."

"Really?"

"Oh yeah. Richardson approved an extra."

Hansen frowned. "You're putting out an extra edition on a simple homicide?"

"You saw her—this is one homicide that ain't simple. We're gonna run with this, Harry . . . Don't tell me you'd mind seein' that popular feature 'Mr. Homicide' in the papers again?"

The Hat thought about that, just momentarily, and then stepped away from us and—in an uncharacteristic move from someone so softspoken—called out in a booming voice, "Would the members of the press mind converging? Thank you, gentlemen . . . thank you, Aggie . . ."

About a dozen representatives of the press—reporters and photographers—gathered around the Hat, the tired eyes in his hound-dog countenance almost shut as he made an announcement.

"Thank you for your cooperation," the Hat said. "I wanted to inform you of two facts. First, you're all about to leave this crime scene; I don't want the crime lab to have to conduct their investigation with you good people peeking over their shoulders, or making further contributions of flashbulbs and cigarette butts. . . ."

A general rumbling of discontent passed through the little crowd.

"How are we supposed to get our information, Harry?" Aggie demanded.

"Through me," the Hat said. "Exclusively through me. And if any of you attempt to go over my head, and get it from my boss, Captain Donahoe, or from the Chief himself, as some of you have been known to do . . . well then, I promise you, I will cut you off from any future information on this or any case. . . . Good afternoon."

The reporters dispersed, grumbling as they went; me, I was happy to be climbing into the Ford with Fowley behind the wheel.

"What took you so long, you prick?" I demanded.

He just grinned at me, a happy bulldog. "When I called Richardson, he told me to get the hell in and develop those negatives. That's a switch, huh? Heller pictures in the paper, and no Heller in the pictures!"

That was just how I wanted it.

"You guys are really going with an extra on this?" I asked him, as he swung his car around, giving me a view of Lieutenant Haskins and a patrolman taking apart newspapers and covering the halved corpse.

"You bet your lily-white ass," Fowley said. "The *Examiner*'s gonna be all over this baby."

I looked at the overlapping peaks of newsprint, covering her entirely, except for red-painted toenails—like Peggy's—sticking out from under the pages.

"You already are," I said.

# 4

Elizabeth Short—who I knew as Beth—had come into my life the previous October. I would be lying if I said she meant much more to me than any number of showgirls, waitresses, and secretaries with whom I'd had short-lived affairs. Beth was memorable chiefly because she resembled Peggy Hogan; otherwise, she was just another pretty young starry-eyed thing filled with dreams but no real plans.

As I attempt to share my memories of this ill-fated girl, please keep in mind that the several months prior to Peggy and me reconciling (and marrying) are something of a blur. Like many a spurned lover, I wallowed in self-pity, and when I got sick of that, I would turn to a bottle, and drink myself into a stupor.

Even my work, which I always relished, had become a mind-numbing bore. Due to extensive Chicago press coverage of my roles in such high-profile cases as the Lindbergh kidnapping, the Cermak assassination, and the Sir Harry Oakes murder, I had acquired a certain minor celebrity. This made it advisable for me to take initial meetings with clients—who sometimes wanted an autograph, and always wanted an assurance that the president of the A-1, Nathan Heller himself, would be handling their oh-so-vital retail-credit-check/divorce-case/personnel investigation, personally.

So I took these meetings, and my half a dozen operatives did the work. Most of them were, like me, ex-Chicago cops; the senior man was Lou Sapperstein, who took on the more challenging, which is to say rewarding and interesting, jobs.

Closing in on sixty, Lou—with bald pate, graying temples, bowtie, and tortoiseshell eyeglasses—looked more like an accountant than a private cop. Useful in shadow jobs, his appearance was deceiving: he was one lean, hard op, and little slipped past him—including my state of mind and lackluster performance.

"This finnan haddie has more color than you," Lou said, pointing to his plate.

We were having lunch at Binyon's, a dark-paneled businessman's bastion just around the corner from our offices at Plymouth and Van Buren.

I said, not really giving a shit, "What's your point, Lou?"

Shifting in the hard booth, Lou flinched facially and said, "Every day you come in hungover, half the time you forgot to shave, you fall asleep on your couch, you barely stay awake through client conferences, and look at you, a guy who's never really been much of a tippler, drinking your damn lunch."

I shrugged. "I wasn't hungry. And this is only my second one."

By that, I meant rum and Coke.

He pointed his fork at me. "Maybe you need to get back out in the field. Get back to some investigative work."

"Fine. Something lively comes in, I'll take it on myself."

"Do I dare let you? Better you fall asleep in the office than on surveillance, or the middle of an interrogation. Has your malaria kicked back in or something?"

I sipped my lunch.

"Listen, Nate, we've known each other for a long time . . . but I'm not a hired hand now."

A while back, I had given Lou a percentage of the business—not a big one, just a taste, to repay him, and motivate him, so he didn't get stolen away by the Hargraves Agency, or go out on his own.

"You're also not my boss," I said. "And it's been a long time since you were."

That he'd been my boss on the pickpocket detail had long been a source of friendly kidding between us, but my remark came out sounding not all that friendly.

"I'm also not your conscience, Nate, or your fairy fuckin' god-mother . . . but I would say you need to get over this."

"I don't know what you're talking about."

"I'm talking about Jim Ragen's niece. I'm talking about Peggy Hogan."

I just looked at him.

He glanced away, embarrassed. "I know. I know. I'm way out of bounds. Your personal life is nobody's business but yours. . . . Forget it. Forget I said anything."

He had a bite of his fish; then he had another.

I swirled my drink and looked into its blackness. Without looking up, I said, "What do you suggest I do?"

"Are you asking?"

"What, you want me to ask twice? If you think my . . . if you think I'm adversely affecting the business by my, I don't know, fuck, attitude . . . go ahead. Tell me what to do."

He thought about that for a second.

"I never thought I'd hear myself have to say this," he said, "considering you're just about the randiest son of a bitch I ever knew . . . but, Nate, really, truly—you need to get laid."

That remark caught me by surprise, and actually made me laugh—first time I'd laughed in weeks. But there was truth in his remark: Lou knew I hadn't been out with a woman since Peggy dumped me. I hailed a passing waiter and ordered a steak sandwich and French-fried potatoes, which—along with not asking for a third rum and Coke—was my way of telling Lou I was going to try to rejoin the human race. Thus ended this rare personal chat between Lou and me.

In light of the housing shortage, I had held on to a "suite" (a living room with kitchenette and a bedroom) on the twenty-third floor of the Morrison, Chicago's tallest hotel. I'd stayed off-and-on at the Morrison—which was at Madison and South Clark, a few blocks from the A-1 offices—for almost ten years, and the fact that I still resided in a hotel seemed emblematic of the sorry state of my life. I should have been married by now, preferably to

Peggy, and—assuming my connections and money could get past that aforementioned housing shortage—either living in a Gold Coast apartment or a suburban bungalow, pursuing the glorious postwar life I'd fought for.

The Morrison was also home to the Boston Oyster House, which dated back to just after the Great Fire and rivaled Jim Ireland's as Chicago's premier seafood restaurant. It was an elegant yet informal basement dining room refreshingly free of the usual cornball nautical trappings, other than a scattering of marine landscapes. I ate there several times a week, as it was both convenient and good, and—unlike, say, the Berghoff, another of my haunts, which ran to no-nonsense, rather grizzled waiters—orders were taken and delivered by waitresses, many of them attractive and young.

This is not to say that I was trolling for female companionship, after Lou Sapperstein's pep talk: I was just hungry. For food. No kidding. I swear.

The aquamarine uniform with the white collar and cuffs was designed to look primly attractive, not alluring, but her slender, shapely figure had an agenda all its own. I spotted the new girl when I first came in, but it was from a distance, and all I got was the general effect of that classy chassis topped off by a china-doll face and lots of dark curls, shoulder length and yet piled high.

That and the way she walked: a sensuous, swinging sway that would have done a runway model proud.

I slipped a fivespot to the maîtresse d'—the warm friendly, unfortunately named Pearl Kuntz, the head waitress now for several decades—for the privilege of having the new girl wait on me.

"All right, Nate," the fleshy, perennially blonde Pearl said, eyeing me suspiciously. She wore a black uniform, and was tucking the five in a side pocket. "Just don't make a madam out of me."

"I have nothing ungentlemanly in mind."

"It's not your mind that worries me, Nate."

She was showing me to my small table against a wall, where a gilt-framed whaling oil painting awaited to keep me company.

"You've never forgiven me for that pass I made at you in '32, have you, Pearl?"

"Sure I have, Nate. What I haven't forgiven is you not making one since '38."

We grinned at each other, and she handed me a menu and trundled off.

It wasn't until the waitress arrived to take my order that I got my first good look at her, which knocked the wind right the hell out of me.

"Is something wrong?" she asked, her voice low, rich, husky. Her eyes were clear and cool and the same aquamarine as her uniform; that china-doll effect was due to a bright red lipstick and a light shade of pancake over a naturally pale complexion.

"No," I said, lowering my menu. "It's just . . . you remind me of someone."

Amusement twitched her full lips; her pencil tapped rhythmically on her order pad. "An old girl friend, by any chance?"

"Not very original, is it?"

"Not very."

I was shaking my head, astounded. "But I'm not kidding. You really are a ringer for her."

The amusement disappeared and the translucent eyes fixed on me, and she stopped tapping the pencil. "That isn't just a line, is it?"

"No. It isn't."

Dark eyebrows—thick, unfashionably so—tightened over the gorgeous, limpid-pool eyes. Her voice was soft—private. "You really cared for her."

"Yeah. I really cared for her."

"She isn't . . . please excuse me for asking . . . she isn't dead, is she?"

"No! No. She's fine . . . it's just 'us' that's deceased."

She smiled a little. "I get you. . . . Now, what can I get you?"

I ordered a long-standing menu favorite, Pearl's Special—surprisingly, not a seafood dish, but a porterhouse steak with baked potato—back on the menu now that ration books were ancient history.

In Chicago, the coffee was usually served, like the salad, with the meal; but I asked this lovely waitress to bring mine right away. I took it with cream and sugar.

"Tough guy like you?" the waitress asked, a twinkle in those aquamarines, now.

"What makes you think I'm a tough guy?"

"Miz Kuntz says you're a private eye, Mr. Heller. A famous one, at that."

"Make it 'Nate,' and there's no such animal as a famous private eye; or if there was it would be bad for business."

"Why?"

"Because when people recognize you, it's darn hard to spy on 'em."

She laughed at that. "Okay. Cream and sugar, it is."

"Anyway, don't you think the world tastes nasty enough, without voluntarily swigging something bitter?"

"You're right. I don't even like coffee. Not even with cream and sugar."

Pearl, from her post at the front of the restaurant, was giving me the evil eye.

"You better pay attention to some of your other customers," I advised her.

"Maybe I don't want to," she said regally, and glided away. That walk; what a walk—like sex on springs . . .

I glanced over at Pearl, who was frowning at me, and blew her a kiss; she turned away before I could see her smile—she thought.

"So what's your name?" I asked the lovely waitress, as she delivered my grilled-onion-topped porterhouse, sour-cream-slathered baked potato, and Russian-dressing-crowned head-lettuce salad.

"Well that depends," she said, placing the plate before me, brushing nicely close, her Chanel Number Five blotting out the rising aroma of the steak; her full lips somehow managed a pixie smile.

"Depends on what?"

"Whether you like Betty or Beth. I'm Elizabeth Short, and both Betty and Beth are short for Elizabeth."

A silly little joke, which she'd probably told a couple thousand times, but I found it amusing and chuckled accordingly. Goddamn, it felt good to flirt again! I felt human—I felt like me.

"You're much too poised and chic for 'Betty,' " I said, and she was—inordinately so, for a waitress, to where I wondered if it was an affectation or a put-on. "So I'll go with 'Beth.' "

"Good choice," she said, obviously pleased. "That's my preference, too." She nodded toward my steaming steak. "The chef said I should mention that's really, really rare. If you want it cooked some more, just say the word."

"Much as I'd like the excuse to talk to you again," I said, carving into the porterhouse, seeing a deep, satisfying red, "this will do nicely—far as I'm concerned, the only way a steak can be too rare is if it's still grazing."

Now she chuckled at my silly little joke, and sashayed away.

I was pretty well stuffed from the porterhouse and trimmings, but—looking for an excuse to prolong my relationship with the waitress (and telling myself that her striking resemblance to Peggy had nothing to do with it)—I ordered dessert. The house specialty was a mocha layer cake, one of the restaurant's fabled slabs of which would probably knock me into a coma.

"Ooooo, I just love chocolate," Beth said, writing down my order.

"Hey, wait a minute—why don't you cancel that, and let me take you out for dessert, when you get off? When is that?"

She was frowning, but not in displeasure. "Well, uh . . . it'll be fairly late, we're open until eleven, you know. . . ."

"What's your favorite dessert?"

"Oh . . . banana split, I guess. Maybe cheesecake."

"They've got both at Lindy's. What do you say?"

Eventually, she said yes; and when—just after eleven—she met me in the Morrison's plush, high-ceilinged lobby, I did a double-take: this lowly waitress was wearing a smart black dress with a pattern of pink roses on the bodice and a leopard fur coat and hat, plus dark nylons and black clutch purse. This was what she'd worn to work?

Maybe her regal, refined manner hadn't been a put-on.

I offered her my arm and she beamed at me—God, she was stunning . . . Jesus, she looked like Peggy—and ushered her out into the nippy fall night. She shivered, snuggled close, and covered a cough, so I decided to flag a Checker cab and spare her the walk over to Lindy's, on West Randolph. Also, I wanted to impress this classy little dame, which I think I did.

We sat in one of the booths under the mezzanine and had a banana split—we shared it, at her insistence—and those blue-green eyes, seeming more blue than green now, were wide with the celebrities and near celebrities frequenting the theatrical restaurant. At a neighboring booth, Eddie Cantor and Georgie Jessel were deep in some noncomical conference over chop suey and cigars; Martha Raye, a frequent Chicago nightclub attraction, was having cocktails with that young singer, Dean Martin; and at a table in the bar, that genial tank of a woman, Sophie Tucker, loud and laughing, was holding court with a trio of fawning young men, eager to light her latest cigarette or fetch her a fresh drink.

Beth hadn't wanted a drink: her lips touched neither liquor nor tobacco, she informed me rather proudly. She felt both activities were unladylike and "could make a girl look hard before her time."

She had no such reservations about banana splits, however, and admitted to being "addicted to ice cream," though her slender if busty figure didn't betray that.

Already I was mildly smitten with this girl who so resembled Peggy. Dipping my spoon into her dish, sharing the sundae with her, was at once innocent and sensual.

"Am I the only one here impressed by all these famous people?" she asked, as she sipped tea and I stirred cream and sugar into my coffee, our empty sundae dish cleared away. "Nobody's asking them for autographs, or even looking at them. . . ."

I shrugged. "That would be gauche. You can see celebrities and would-be celebrities in here any time of day and night, show-biz types and newspapermen and big-time politicians . . . Joint never closes."

She made a cute face. Those luscious full red lips in the Kabuki mask of her face were startling—would even have been clownish, if she weren't so beautiful. "I guess I don't know much about Chicago."

"Your first time here?"

"I stopped over, a few times before. This is the first I've stayed for any real length of time. I came because I had an opportunity to do some modeling."

"Not surprising, with your looks and grace. What kind?"

"For newspaper ads—hats, gloves, coats."

I sipped my coffee. "With what agency?"

"Sawyer Agency."

"*Duffy* Sawyer?"

She nodded, seeming vaguely embarrassed.

"Let me guess why you quit—Duffy expected you to entertain his male clients."

With a tiny humorless smirk, she said, "He put me up in a hotel—the Croyden—and had me go to dinner with him and various . . . business prospects. He said he wanted me to 'lay the charm' on these businessmen."

Emphasis on "lay," I thought.

She was saying, "It wasn't so bad, at first; we went to a lot of hep jazz clubs. But, uh . . . Duffy got mad at me, because—"

"You weren't charming enough."

"Something like that. So I quit, and moved out of the Croyden—I'm bunking in with some girls at the St. Clair Hotel . . . know where that is?"

"Sure." It was over on East Ohio; both hotels she'd mentioned were home to a good share of showgirls and models. "You still interested in modeling?"

"Oh yes—legitimate modeling, and acting. I sing, too."

"Well, honey, Chicago isn't what it used to be. Vaudeville's dead, most of the radio shows have moved east or west, and not much national advertising's done here, anymore."

"I can also dance."

I smiled, shook my head. "Afraid there's only one chorus line in town, and that's the Chez Paree—measly six girls, and those positions are golden. Oh, sometimes the Palmer House and the Sherman put on productions, but . . . pretty slim pickings, unless you're willing to work burlesque."

"Stripteasing."

"Yeah. Lots of that in this burg . . . but I don't think you'd like that any better than dispensing 'charm' to businessmen."

The aquamarines widened. "You are so right . . . though I do have the figure for it, don't you think?"

"No argument there, and I'm not judgmental about the profession. Some of my best friends are strippers."

That news didn't seem to put her off. "Well, anyway, I'd never stoop to . . . stripping."

"Good. It's a hard life—and if you aren't Sally Rand or Gypsy Rose Lee or Ann Corio, you're lucky to make fifty bucks a week."

"I'm better off waiting tables."

"Yeah, and it's warmer."

She lifted her chin as if offended—but maybe kidding on the square. "Is that what you think I should stick to? Waiting tables?"

"Hey, I'm not trying to discourage you—that's just the reality of it. Tough as that town is, Hollywood's a better bet for you."

She nodded, saying, "I've been there—several times."

"Any luck?"

"I've done some extra work, and a little radio."

"It's a start." I waved a waitress over for more tea and coffee. "Look, there is some modeling to be had in Chicago—I know people at the agencies. Plenty of local advertising, and the big mail-order companies do their catalogue work here. . . ."

"I might take you up on that. But I probably will head back to Southern Cal. I only came to Chicago for the modeling job, and . . ."

"And what?"

She shrugged. "A serviceman I know had a stopover scheduled here. An Army Air Corps lieutenant."

"Boy friend?"

"Nothing serious. I met him last year, at the Hollywood Canteen. I was a junior hostess, there. Met a lot of stars—Franchot Tone, Arthur Lake, all kinds of celebrities."

"What about that Air Corps lieutenant?"

"What about him?"

"If you and he weren't serious, why did you come to Chicago to see him?"

Another shrug. "Like I said, I came for the modeling job, and just took the opportunity to connect with Gordon again. I'd been writing him letters . . . I have a lot of servicemen friends. I write to several, I like to build their morale. . . ."

"Sure. Guys you met at the Hollywood Canteen."

*Was that her story?* I wondered. Was she one of those "Victory Girls," who had a thing for servicemen?

"Yes," she said, as if answering my unspoken question. "I've kind of bounced around back and forth from Florida to California, and I met quite a few nice boys both places."

"California to Florida is quite a commute. Where are you from?"

She sipped her tea, looking out at the Lindy's clientele, probably seeking celebrity faces. "I'm not really from anywhere."

"Everybody's from somewhere. I'd almost swear I heard a little New England in your voice. . . . Or maybe I'm imagining that, 'cause we met at the Boston Oyster House."

She laughed lightly; I had her attention again. "You *are* a detective. . . . I grew up in Medford, Massachusetts. But I never really felt like I lived there."

"Why not?"

"I don't know, exactly. For a long time, even in high school days, I wintered someplace warm, because of my health—asthma . . ."

That explained the cough.

". . . and maybe that's why I've never felt like I belonged anywhere, except maybe—don't laugh—Hollywood."

"I'm not laughing, Beth. You look like a movie star."

Beaming, she said, "Everybody says I look like—"

"Deanna Durbin."

"That's right." She was obviously proud of that. "And I sing like her, too, only my voice is lower."

I didn't suppose it had ever occurred to her that Hollywood already had a Deanna Durbin, name of Deanna Durbin.

Beth was saying, dreamily, "I've always known, deep down inside of me, that I was different . . . special . . . that I was going to be famous someday."

How many pretty, ambitious, restless girls had thought that same thing? Every day of every month of every year, buxom babes like Beth left farms and small towns, forsaking family and friends and sweethearts for the lure of bright lights, boarding a bus or hitching, diamonds in their eyes and cardboard suitcases in their hands. It was one of the most standard, enduring, and little-realized American dreams.

And yet I said, "I wouldn't be surprised if you did become famous, Beth. You're a lovely young woman, with a nice speaking voice, and a refined demeanor."

"You really think so?"

"I really think so."

She spent the night with me in my suite at the Morrison. We sat on my couch and talked and talked into the night, and I heard all about her hopes and dreams and enthusiasms. She went on and on about how much she loved music—Benny Goodman, the Andrews Sisters, Kate Smith, Glenn Miller, Jo Stafford, both Bing and Frankie—and when I told her I knew Sinatra personally and that maybe I could introduce her someday, she had given me a great big kiss.

And then we necked, like schoolkids, and for a change I was drunk not with rum but with a girl's beauty and her perfume and those clear blue-green eyes that you wanted to dive into and splash around. We petted, and I caressed her perfect breasts—they were full and firm and more than a handful—and finally she let me undo the back of her dress and it folded down around her waist like flower petals and her skin was a remarkable alabaster, smooth and flawless, with a beauty mark on one shoulder. I kissed the buds of her breasts and she moaned with pleasure and I kissed them some more, buried my face in their soft firmness, but when my hand, stroking the suppleness of her thighs, tried to edge up between them, she took me by the wrist and drew my hand back, shaking her head, her expression almost sad, as she said, "No, no, not yet, it's too early," and I could understand that, since this was only our first night, so when her hand undid my zipper and her head dipped into my lap, that pile of curls bobbing up and down, working expertly, I was stunned, I was shocked, I was delighted. . . .

I saw her three more times. Whether I picked her up at the hotel where she was freeloading off model friends, or simply met her at the Morrison, she would be dolled up in expensive clothes—either that leopard fur coat or a white fur, and black outfits with dark nylons, her white-powdered face glowing angelically in the night, red lips like a lovely scarlet wound—looking like a movie star, not a would-be actress waiting tables. She borrowed money from me every time we were together—as little as twenty, as much as a hundred—but she was not a hooker, at least she didn't see herself that way, and I refused to see her that way.

We would talk about each other. She described herself as Black Irish—"lace curtain, not shanty!"—and wondered why a man with a Jewish last name looked so Irish, and I explained that my father had been an apostate Jew, a leftist bookseller on the West Side, and my Irish mother, who died when I was born, had given me my red hair and Mick mug. She said she barely knew her father, that he had been an entrepreneur who had had a small chain of miniature golf courses that failed in the early years of the Depression, and disappeared, only to turn up years later in California, where she had tried to get to know him, and failed.

Because she was so soft on servicemen, I found myself telling her how I'd been in the Marines and on Guadalcanal, since after all I had to compete with these kids in uniform she was writing her letters to; and she even wormed it out of me that I'd been awarded a Silver Star—something I never mentioned to anybody; I never talked about the war—but, what the hell, she could know anything, she could take anything, considering what she was giving.

And I told her about Peggy, and she told me about her late fiancé, Matt, a major in the Flying Tigers who had been killed on his way home from India, in a plane crash, earlier that year.

"That's why I haven't . . . you know, gone all the way with you," she explained on my couch, the second night we were together. "I didn't date while Matt was away, keeping true to him . . . and now that he's gone, I'm having to start all over again, just taking little tiny baby steps."

No, she wasn't going "all the way" with me; she was just putting her head in my lap—some little baby steps! Yet for some reason, I didn't feel like pointing out this glaring, illogical inconsistency.

Anyway, there was more to her reluctance to perform intercourse than the memory of her dead pilot: on the third evening, she had requested a loan of one hundred dollars because she needed to see a "female-trouble doctor" in Gary.

"You're not pregnant, are you?" I asked.

"No! It's . . . something personal. Please don't ask."

Maybe it was V.D. of some kind, in which case I really wasn't anxious to change our pattern of sexual activity.

Still, female trouble or not, I was becoming quite taken with Beth Short. She was filling the Peggy void quite nicely, and her enthusiasm for orally servicing me was—I am neither proud, nor particularly ashamed to say—intoxicating.

On the fourth and final night we were together (she had the evening off from the Oyster House), we dined out at Henrici's and came back to my Morrison suite, where she announced that she had indeed decided to return to California.

"Why don't you try staying on in Chicago, awhile?" I asked her, fixing her a Coke on ice and myself a rum and Coke on ice. "I talked to Patricia Stevens this morning—I can get you an interview."

That was the number-one modeling agency in town.

"No, Nate, I appreciate it. I appreciate everything you've done . . . but just this morning, I spoke on the phone to a famous movie director, and he wants me to come to Hollywood, right away, to take a screen test."

This sounded like a pipe dream if I ever heard one. I handed her the Coke and sat next to her on the couch. "What famous director?"

"I can't say. He asked me not to."

"That's bullshit, Beth—he's just another asshole who wants to get in your pants."

"Don't be crude, Nate—don't be mean."

I was a little owly at that, at the thought of having those exquisite "baby steps" vanish from my life. "I was kind of hoping . . . I mean, I thought we were getting along pretty well. . . ."

"We are, we are," she said, and she put her arms around me and we began kissing, and petting, and then her head was in my lap and I was giddy, I was in heaven.

Which made it a hell of thing to have to accept her leaving. So, as the evening progressed, I did my best to talk her into giving Chicago a go of it, and along the way I had another rum and Coke, and another, and another. . . .

I don't remember much more of the evening except Beth saying, "Let's just forget our problems and enjoy this last night together. . . . Live for today, I always say. . . ."

At some point in the night I woke up, needing to use the bathroom, and noticed Beth in bed next to me. So—we had finally made it from the couch to the bed. A light was still on in the outer room, filtering in enough that I could lift the covers and have a peek at her busty little frame. She was nude, slumbering peacefully, though snoring a little, something bronchial stirring in her chest. She had washed the lipstick and white pancake away and her high-cheekboned beauty, framed by the mane of black, was even more striking unadorned.

I remember wondering—as I staggered in to take a pee—if I had finally fucked her, only to have forgotten in my drunkenness; and I remember thinking, if she did have the clap or something, I probably caught it—and deserved to.

Then, class act that I am, I stumbled back to bed and fell asleep next to her.

When I awoke, she was gone; and the next time I heard from her was in January, on the telephone, from a pay phone at the Biltmore Hotel in Los Angeles.

And the next time I saw her, she was nude, just as she'd been in my bed, only this time she was in two pieces, in a vacant lot on South Norton Avenue.

# 5

Fowley parked his blue Ford in the lot across from the gloomy-looking, five-story cream-colored stucco building at 11th and Broadway. The sun had finally banished the clouds and burned off the smog, making a reflective blur of the *Examiner* building, a huge American flag flapping above the main entrance, adding a splash of color and just the proper hint of hypocrisy.

Feeling shaky and sick and trying to hide it, I had suggested—as we'd rolled along Olympic Boulevard, heading to the *Examiner*—that we postpone our meeting with Fowley's city editor, Richardson, since this hot new story had dropped in their laps.

"Not a chance in hell," Fowley had said, grinning, cigarette bobbing. "Richardson says he's more anxious than ever to talk to you. Hell, you're our star photographer!"

Now we were crossing Broadway, on foot, navigating traffic, stepping over trolley tracks, the newspaper's massive black printing presses looming through the big plate-glass windows that took up much of the *Examiner*'s ground floor. Those presses, silent now, would soon roar to life with an extra edition, newsprint threading through at sixty miles an hour, headlines screaming of the "werewolf" killing.

I had made this appointment with the *Examiner* in hopes of

getting myself some ink; but WEREWOLF SUSPECT IN CUSTODY—PRIVATE EYE KNEW VICTIM wasn't what I had in mind.

Lavishly corniced brown-marble columns did their best to dominate the impressive lobby, competing with a vaulted ceiling across which strode gilded centuries-ago heroic figures—nobody ever accused publisher William Randolph Hearst of a light touch. After all that ostentation, a single, comically insufficient wrought-iron cage elevator awaited us. The two of us and the operator made a crowd.

"Why aren't you out in Leimert Park," I asked Fowley, the elevator grinding its way up to the third floor, "knocking on doors, looking for leads?"

"Richardson already sent out his foot soldiers," Fowley said. "I think he's got something else in mind for us."

I didn't like the sound of that: by "us" did Fowley mean himself and the rest of the city-room crew? Or did he mean . . . us?

Not anxious for the answer, I just followed the little reporter through a low-slung swinging gate across a nominal reception area, where he went in a door whose opaque glass window bore the black block letters CITY ROOM. The world beyond was a big, bustling one: thirty or more plastered-over steel bearing beams kept things open, despite the countless desks (often paired up and facing each other) where reporters and (with phone receivers cradled at their necks) rewrite men banged away at ancient machines that looked more like coffee grinders than typewriters. Against one wall, a pair of telephone operators spoke into horns sprouting from their chests, as they fielded constant incoming and outgoing calls at a red-light-flashing switchboard; teletypes machine-gunned out wire-service copy, only to be ripped free by attentive copy boys, while—in the midst of all this controlled chaos—blue-pencil-wielding proofreaders sat engrossed at their copy, like monks doing calligraphy. Cutting straight down the center was an aisle, a copy boy's gauntlet ("Boy! Copy boy!") from the news desk to the city desk which sat in front of a big window, on either side of which were wainscoted, glassed-in offices.

I knew city editor Jim Richardson a little, from the Peete

case—he was feared by cub reporters, and respected by the veteran newshounds, a chainsmoking, mostly bald, bullnecked, self-proclaimed son of a bitch.

He was also wall-eyed. Richardson's left eye had a weak muscle, and when he looked at you, it took half-a-second for the left eye to catch up with the right. The effect was no more eerie than seeing Karloff as the Frankenstein monster for the first time.

Richardson rose behind his desk and waved at us to follow him into a glassed-off editorial chamber. He barked at several other reporters, seated in the nearby bullpen, who trailed after him into the conference room. Fowley and I were the last ones in.

Everybody had taken a chair around the big, scarred table except Richardson himself, who was expectant-fathering at its head, lighting up a fresh cigarette off the butt of his previous one. While Fowley and the three other reporters were wearing their suits and ties and, in several instances, their hats, Richardson had long since removed his tie and the sleeves of his suspendered white shirt were rolled up over Popeye-powerful forearms.

"So we're stuck with that fucking prima donna Hansen," Richardson said, as if this were the middle and not the beginning of the discussion.

Fowley, not missing a beat, said, "The Hat made that clear at the scene—we try to go over his head to Donahoe, he'll freeze us out. And you know what a weak sister Donahoe is."

One of the reporters said, "Hey, this crime beat stuff is new to me, boss. What's the story on Donahoe?"

"He just got transferred from Robbery," Richardson said, grimacing, cigarette dangling. "Before that he was in Administration, doing what he does best—pushing paper. He doesn't have a clue about pushing people—captain or not, Jack Donahoe's no match for that hotdogging Hansen."

"Too bad," Fowley said, and the other reporters looked at him for more. Fowley gave it to them: "The boss here has done favors for Donahoe . . . could easily play him, if Harry the Hat was out of the way."

"Well, he's not gonna be out of the way," Richardson said. He cast his eerie gaze around the room at us, the right eye leading, the left one eventually swimming into place. "But, goddamn it, this is *our* story. We found it, and we're going to keep it, and turn it into the fucking crime of the century."

"What if the victim turns out to be a hooker?" another of the reporters asked. "How do we make *that* the crime of the century?"

"Okay—let's say she died a whore," Richardson said, gesturing with open hands. "You don't think she started out that way, do you? She was a good little girl once upon a time, some daddy's sweet little girl, before she started banging for bucks, and suckin' off sailors."

Inside, I groaned.

"I still think it's a hard sell, boss," Fowley gently insisted.

"Boys," Richardson said, slapping the table, making them jump, "Jack the Ripper killed whores back in a day when a whore was considered less than human. And look at the ink that crazy bastard got."

Behind us, the door opened, and a guy with a black rubber apron, rubber gloves, and a distasteful expression came in carrying by his thumbs a dripping-wet print, a big one—11" by 14". Grinning, eyes gleaming, Richardson pointed to the table like he was showing a bellboy where to put the room service tray.

"Put it down—lay it right down there," he instructed the guy, who obeyed, and left.

The print lay there, dripping moisture like tears.

"Jesus," somebody said.

It looked just as bad in black and white: the bisected body of a once beautiful girl, on grotesque display, in the weeds and grass.

The reporters had stood, gathering 'round to get a closer look—though Fowley and I kept our seats, having already had our share of close looks at this grim subject matter—and, hardened though they were to every disaster a major city might visit upon a human being, several gasped and they to a man sat back down, faces white as blistered skin.

"Take a good look, boys," Richardson said, arms folded, rocking a little on his heels. "This is what you're going to be working on, till I say different. . . . Pretty photography, don't you think?

Nice work, Heller. Guess you bedroom dicks get a lot of practice shooting dames in the raw."

Richardson was trying to snap his boys back to attention, with the gallows humor so typical of reporters and, for that matter, cops.

But his boys—seated here and there around the big table—were staring at the grisly body, still in shock.

"What about the Mocambo, boss?" Fowley asked, the only reporter not unnerved. He was referring to a heist at the famous nightspot that had made recent headlines.

"Wrap fish in it," Richardson said with a snort. "The heisters are behind bars, and this murderer, this wonderful fiend, is very much at large." He sighed smoke admiringly as he surveyed the photo. "Ain't she a pip?"

No one disagreed; no one said anything.

Sensing the pall, Richardson affected a football coach tone: "Are we going to let that prick Hansen take this away from us? Are the cops gonna control this story, or are we?"

"We need something on them," Fowley said.

The other reporters nodded, one chiming in with, "Yeah, yeah we do."

But their editor was shaking his head, the coach disappointed in his boys.

"Naw—pull your heads out of your asses. That fucking Hansen is as clean as he is press hungry." Richardson spoke with authority: he had helped take down more than one local crooked administration.

"I don't mean corruption," Fowley said. "We give them something—so they owe us."

"Such as?"

"I don't know. If we're out there in force, we may turn something big up before they do. It's like you always say, boss—the cops in this town couldn't find a horse turd in a box of chocolates."

That got a few nervous laughs from the boys, but not from Richardson. "Yeah, that's what I always say, and it's true of most of the cops—but not the Hat."

I had been trying to just fade into the woodwork, but I couldn't let this pass.

"What's this nonsense about Hansen being 'clean'?" I asked, the Chicago cop in me offended. "Put him on the damn payroll, already!"

Next to me, Fowley shook his head. "The boss is right, Nate—the Hat's a straight arrow, so clean he squeaks."

"Yeah? And where'd he get those fancy threads?"

"Paid for them."

"On a cop's salary?"

Fowley shrugged. "Harry's wife has money, plus he earns income off the textbooks he's written. He's also sold his life story to Hollywood two or three times. . . . The guy has solved hundreds of murders."

"What, like the Peete case?" I looked at their city editor, standing at the head of the table like a patriarch getting ready to carve a turkey. "Come on, Richardson—you were there back in '44—you saw that pompous prick steal my thunder."

Richardson waved at me dismissively. "What's the difference whether Hansen solved those cases, or just convinced the world he did? He's put himself up on a pedestal like no other dick in town, but I'll be goddamned if we let him take our story from us."

"You know, boss," Fowley said, something sly in his voice, "the Hat ain't partnered with McCreadie anymore."

"No?" This perked Richardson up. "Who's Hansen's new Watson, then?"

"Finis Brown," Fowley said.

"Fat Ass Brown?" one of the other reporters said. "Well, he's no fuckin' straight arrow."

"Hardly. As of a few months ago, he was Mickey Cohen's bag man."

Cohen, who I'd met, had taken over for Ben Siegel in Los Angeles when Ben shifted his base of operations to Vegas. The bagman role Fowley was referring to probably meant Sergeant Brown was the local mob's payoff conduit to scores of bent cops.

Shifting in my hard chair, I said offhandedly, "So him you could put on the payroll."

"Yeah, for what good it'll do us," Richardson said.

"What do you mean?"

"Hansen's no fool—if we know Brown is bent, don't you think the Hat does, too? He'll likely use Fat Ass as an errand boy and keep him in the dark as to what's really going on."

"If we could identify her before they do," Fowley said, drumming his fingers on the scarred table, "that would put Donahoe in our pocket, and give us leverage on the Hat."

And, of course, a man who could have identified her sat among them—and I was starting to think that by keeping it to myself, I was just digging myself a deeper hole.

"What are you planning to do, Bill?" one of the reporters asked Fowley, flipping a finger toward the still moisture-shiny blowup of the bisected corpse. "Show this around and see if somebody can identify *that*?"

Fowley had no answer, but his boss did.

Richardson said, "I'm already on top of that. I have a staff artist working with Heller's photographs to see if he can come up with a sketch."

"Good," Fowley said.

Another of the reporters asked, "Which staff artist, boss?"

"Howard Burke."

The reporter nodded. "Yeah, well, Howie's a good artist, all right—but do you really expect him to be able to come up with a representation of what she looked like before her face got carved up and beat to shit?"

"Yes, I do—the bone structure, the eyes, even the general shape of the mouth, despite that gash . . . plenty for an artist to go on." Richardson leaned on the table with his palms and his smile was almost as ghastly as the corpse's. "And then we could give that sketch to the cops, to show Captain Donahoe and Detective Hansen just how helpful we're trying to be."

"Boss, I'm with you on this," Fowley said, "but they got their own artists, remember. If Howie lucks out and comes up with a good likeness, I say screw giving it to the cops—we run with the pic in this extra edition and encourage phone calls from our loyal readers and see if we can identify her before the cops can. We hand them a *name*, they'll start cooperating all the way down the line."

A name. They wanted a name *Elizabeth Short* and the only guy in this town who could give it to them *Elizabeth Short* besides the killer was sitting right beside them. I knew who she was *Elizabeth Short* and the cops didn't, which gave me a head start if I wanted to try to crack this thing *Elizabeth Short* before they made me as a suspect, which couldn't happen till they figured out who the hell she was *Elizabeth Short* but first I had to shake loose of these newshounds. . . .

One of whom was saying, "Bill, you can forget that. The Hat's probably identified the dame by her fingerprints, already—that's where he made his reputation, in the Records Bureau. They say he could trace fingerprints faster than a team of ten."

"You're almost right, Ed," Richardson said, and he finally sat down. He folded his hands, prayerfully. "I just had a call from Sid Hughes, who tailed the Black Maria over to the morgue."

So they had the same slang for the black morgue wagon in L.A. as in Chicago. And when they arrested you, they probably threw you in a paddy wagon, here, too. . . .

"Sid's sticking to the coroner like toilet paper to a shoe," Richardson said, panning his gaze around on his boys, the slow eye taking its sweet time catching up. "And word is Hansen's already eliminated this girl from local fingerprint files."

"That's impossible!" Fowley said. "They haven't even had time to autopsy the body!"

"That's a fact—the coroner took one look at her and said, 'This can wait till after lunch!' " Richardson was lighting up a new cigarette off the old one. "But they did take time to print the half of her body that had fingers on it . . . and a card's winging its way to the FBI for identification right now."

The FBI had 104 million Americans on record in their neatly cataloged, cross-referenced files. Would Elizabeth Short be in there? I wondered.

"You're assuming the girl was in trouble," I said quietly.

Richardson's wall-eyes settled on me, one at a time. "Well, we know she was in trouble at least once, Heller—when some bastard decided to take her on a date that was so lousy, she just went to pieces. . . . Anyway, she may have worked at a war plant, or some other defense-related—"

"Boss!" Fowley was sitting up, like a kid in bed who woke from a bad dream. "Are you saying they sent the prints *airmail* special delivery, to the FBI—in Washington, D.C.?"

Richardson exhaled smoke, impatiently. "They didn't send 'em Pony Express."

Now a slow grin began to form on Fowley's pleasant bulldog puss. "That's what you think, boss. You got any idea what's going on out on the East Coast right now?"

"Is the East Coast my business? I'm city desk."

"Snowstorms are grounding planes all along the Atlantic seaboard. Washington, D.C.? They're buried to their ass in two feet of snow."

Richardson's eyes were narrowing, even the wall-eyed one.

Fowley was saying gleefully, "They'll be lucky to get to Chicago. It'll take days, maybe even a week to get those prints to Washington for identification."

Dragon smoke poured out of Richardson's nostrils. "Then why are you grinning like the cat that ate the canary?"

Fowley was damn near bouncing on his chair. "You want to get the cops on our side? Let's offer them the SoundPhoto machine! We can send the prints over the goddamn wire!"

I felt sick; I thought I might puke . . . maybe I could do it right on that blowup and cover that grotesque picture up. . . .

"Prints over the wire?" Richardson was on his feet again. "Can that be done? Has it *ever* been done?"

Fowley shrugged, grandly. "I don't think it *has* been done, but I don't see why it couldn't be—if it works for a pic of Betty Grable's gams, or DiMaggio's ugly mug, why wouldn't it work for fingerprints?"

Nodding slowly, sucking smoke, Richardson smiled and said, "Why wouldn't it. . . ."

It wasn't exactly a question.

"And," Fowley pointed out, "the SoundPhoto is something we got that the cops don't."

"Yeah . . . yeah." Richardson pointed with his cigarette between thumb and forefinger. "And I could call Ray Richards at our Washington bureau and have him deliver them to the FBI."

Fowley was nodding, grinning. "And we share it with the cops on the condition that the other papers don't get the info until we've run our morning edition."

The wall-eyes bugged again. "Fowley, there's only one thing wrong with that idea."

"Yeah? What?"

"*I* didn't think of it. . . . Back to your desks, check if our boys in Leimert Park have phoned in with anything. We should have Burke's sketch in a few minutes, and you can start showing it around."

"Where?" one of the reporters asked.

"She was a good-looking piece, before she got turned into two pieces. Show the sketch at the studios, the casting agencies, up and down Hollywood Boulevard—do I have to do all the goddamn fucking thinking around here? Go, go, go!"

They went, went, went . . . but when I started to rise, Richardson held up a hand in a "stop" motion.

"Nate," Richardson said, and he came over and looked right at me, hand settling on my shoulder just about the same time his left eye caught up with his right. "Stick around—we'll talk."

"We can hash out this p.r. business later," I said, "when it's not so frantic around here—"

"Yeah, yeah . . . but just sit back down, give me a few minutes. I gotta call the Hearst Washington bureau, gotta phone the FBI. . . . Want me to get you some coffee?"

"No—no, that's okay."

"Sit, sit, sit."

I sat, sat, sat. Alone in the editorial chamber, I wondered what the hell I was still doing here, right smack in the middle of an investigation into a crime for which I might momentarily become a suspect. My head start had evaporated, or likely soon would, thanks to Fowley's wirephoto brainstorm and the FBI's 104 million sets of fingerprints.

All the while, the grisly photo of that poor butchered girl glistened on the table, taunting me . . . and then, as if Elizabeth

Short herself had whispered in my ear, it finally dawned on me that right smack in the middle was still the best place for me. With the jump Richardson had on this case, I could be in a position to know whether Beth's murder was in any way leading back to me.

And if Fowley's slant on sending those prints via wirephoto really did i.d. the corpse as Elizabeth Short, the cops would owe them bigtime—meaning most everything the cops had would be shared with Richardson and his boys.

Much as I wanted to flee the *Examiner*, like Stepin Fetchit exiting a haunted house, I knew the best way not to be a suspect in this murder would be to solve the fucking thing—to find the maniac responsible. If I could lend my skills to the investigation, help bring it to a quick resolution, I could clear myself before I needed clearing, before anybody had even tumbled to my connection to the girl.

After all, I had known her in Chicago, hadn't even seen her in L.A., the only contact being that single phone call.

So what I needed to do now was find some way to stay a part of this . . . to stay on the *Examiner*'s team. . . .

I was pondering that when Richardson came back in, as usual lighting up a new cigarette off an old one. He shut the door, unintentionally slamming it a little, glass rattling—and rattling me.

But then the city editor settled in next to me and again placed a friendly hand on my shoulder.

"We have a singular opportunity, Nate," Richardson said, and smiled, and looked at me sideways—of course, he always looked at you sideways, even when he was looking at you frontways.

"What would that be . . . Jim?"

"This whole notion of ballyhooin' your agency in the *Examiner*? It's blossomed from a nice little mutually beneficial arrangement into a once-in-a-lifetime golden opportunity."

"Really."

"Oh, yeah. I believe this 'Werewolf' case is gonna be the biggest thing since the Lindbergh baby. Fifty years from today, they'll still be talking about the L.A. 'Werewolf' slayer."

"It really ought to be 'Vampire.' "

The wall-eyes flinched. "Huh?"

"She was drained of blood. That's not a werewolf—it's a vampire. Also, 'Werewolf' slayer sounds to me like somebody's going around slaying werewolves. . . ."

Richardson patted his chest. "Leave the wordsmithing to us, Heller—your job is investigating."

Perfect—this was going to be *his* idea. . . .

Playing reluctant, I said, "But this isn't my case. And you know how the cops frown on private detectives working an active murder."

"I'm putting every man I can spare on this thing." He swiveled to look right at me—one eye at a time. His smile was just slightly crazed. "Nate, I've just talked to the Chief on the phone . . . and he's as excited about this story as I am. Sees the full potential."

By "the Chief," Richardson meant Old Man Hearst himself.

"We'll run circles around every other paper in town," Richardson was saying, "and the cops, too—we've got expense accounts that make their allocations look silly."

"Are you saying you want to hire me, Jim?"

"You're goddamn right I want to hire you."

"I'm not a reporter, you know—and you're damn lucky those pictures turned out halfway decent. . . ."

So to speak.

"Listen, Nate, the difference between a reporter and a private detective is no wider than a gnat's eyelash. Hell, when I was in between reporting jobs, I worked as a private eye myself."

"I didn't know that."

"Some of my best friends are private eyes—Harry Raymond, remember him?"

"Got blown up in a car, helping you try to bring down Mayor Shaw?"

"That's the one. Hell of a guy."

This was all so reassuring.

Richardson sucked on his cigarette, then said, "Considering the possible scope of this thing, me sending out crews of reporters and photogs, I'm gonna be shorthanded as hell—stay and help investigate this thing, Nate. You and Fowley'll be the guys who were in on it from the start. You stick with Fowley, and keep playing photographer."

"I told you, I'm no photographer, Jim."

"Well, pretend you're peeping through a window—we can always hang drapes on a Speed Graphic, to make you feel at home." He laughed, raspily, and it turned into a cigarette cough, after which he continued: "We're gonna solve this damn case, Nate, and hand the murdering son of a bitch to the cops on a platter . . . and when we're done, we'll be the only paper that anybody in this town bothers reading, and you'll be the most famous private eye in America."

One way or the other.

"Okay, Jim," I said, never more sorry to get what I wanted. "Get out Mr. Hearst's checkbook."

# 6

On Temple Street, between Broadway and Spring, the Los Angeles County Hall of Justice engulfed a block's worth of prime real estate, its fourteen limestone-and-granite stories making it one of the taller edifices in this earthquake-mindful downtown. The rusticated stonework, massive cornices, and two-story crowning colonnade seemed a little grand for a building whose top five stories housed the county jail—granted the municipal courts, sheriff's department, and D.A.'s offices were here as well.

So was the county morgue—in the basement. Murderers could await trial in the upper reaches of this fine Italian Renaissance-styled building; their victims had to settle for the sweating pale yellow brick halls of a cramped, squalid warren of fogged-over glass, leaky water pipes, and electric-fan-circulated formaldehyde fumes.

Late afternoon, we had come in the back way, through the wide entry that Black Marias backed up to, to deposit the various questionable deaths, unidentified corpses, and murder victims who made up the morgue's client base. Fowley—having parked next to a sign that said NO PARKING AT ANY TIME—went up three cement steps, past a sign that said POSITIVELY NO ADMITTANCE.

I followed.

Just inside the hot, humid hallway, Fowley lighted up a cigarette (next to a NO SMOKING sign) and offered me one.

I declined and tagged after him down the hallway, our footsteps echoing like small-arms fire.

"They keep threatening to shut this shithole down," Fowley said, striding past several gurneys bearing covered, unattended bodies. "But there's only so much money, and lots of pockets that need filling—and the corpses never bitch about the accommodations, so what the fuck?"

We moved by several rooms whose doors had moisture-frosted glass panels, creating a haze through which could be made out stiffs stacked on steel tables, like so much firewood.

"Local funeral parlors have been raising a stink, though," Fowley said, just making conversation. "Half the time the bodies sent over from here ain't been sewn back up . . . you know, some poor bastard's face, folded back up over his skull, with the wife and kids waiting on the other end."

Fowley paused at an open doorway, which revealed a lounge of sorts, where deputy coroners in blood-splotched white sat at tables drinking Cokes or coffee and eating doughnuts or candy bars, laughing, talking, their patients in no hurry.

One of the deputy coroners looked up—a pudgy, balding, rat-faced little guy with dark, squinty, yet glittering eyes behind wirerim glasses—and frowned at Fowley, who crooked his finger, like a parent summoning a child. The little man sighed heavily, pushed to his feet and left his half-eaten doughnut and paper cup of coffee behind.

"Hiya, Doc," Fowley said, moving down the hall, away from the open door.

The round little guy trailed after the reporter, but his eyes—blinking like a mole seeing sunshine—were fixed on me.

"Who's this? Who's this?" he asked, pointing at me. His voice was a high-pitched whine.

"My photographer," Fowley said, blowing smoke. "He's new."

"We have to talk in front of him?"

"Yeah."

Tight lips twitched a grimace; then he shrugged. "Well . . . doesn't matter, anyway. I don't have anything for you."

Fowley frowned. "Haven't they done the autopsy yet?"

The deputy coroner nodded. "Just. I assisted. Jane Doe Number One. Down in room four. Newbarr and CeFalu."

Fowley whistled, impressed. "First string. Important homicide to you boys?"

The little man looked furtively about. "Unusual. Unusual."

Nodding, sucking on his cigarette, Fowley said, "Getting cut in half, you mean."

"That, and— I can't say any more."

"You haven't said anything yet."

The squinty eyes somehow managed to narrow behind the wirerims. "I can tell you she was disemboweled. Certain organs were missing. There were . . . other irregularities."

Shaking his head, grinning, cigarette bobbling, Fowley reached a hand in his pants pocket; but the little rat-faced man held up his hands, as if in surrender.

"Skip it. Skip it. . . . I can't say anything. This time I can't say."

"Why not, Doc?"

"Certain facts are being withheld. Facts only the murderer and his victim could know. If I leak what I have, I could lose my job. Obstructing justice, it's called."

"Doc . . . you can trust me. . . ."

"Forget it. Forget it! We'll do business some other time."

And the little round ratman clip-clopped back down the hall and slipped inside the lounge to finish his doughnut.

"What the hell could they have found out?" Fowley asked.

*That she was pregnant when she was killed.*

But I just shook my head, like I was wondering the same thing. "It's not like she was keeping any secrets, lying there naked, cut in half."

Fowley squinted in thought. "Something inside her, maybe. Something she swallowed. Or something in her pussy . . ." He snapped his fingers, eyes wild. "Maybe he fucked her in the ass!"

Only Fowley could make a foul-smelling morgue like this even more distasteful.

I said, "Come on, Bill—we're not going to find anything out, down here."

"Don't give up so easy, Nate," he said, and dropped his cigarette to the cement floor, grinding it out with his heel. "What kind of detective are you? Let's check out room four."

I followed Fowley down several more dank hallways, past more unattended corpses on gurneys.

"Sometimes they do the autopsies right on the gurneys," Fowley told me, lightly, "when things get bottled up. Rims around the gurney edges are too shallow to catch fluids, and blood and guts just spill on the floor, and they just wade in the shit. It's the fuckin' Middle Ages around this joint."

"Spare me the tour-bus chatter, will you, Fowley? And remind me not to die in Los Angeles."

The door to room four—which lacked any glass panel to peer through—was closed. Fowley stood there, studying the doorknob, apparently trying to decide whether to just barge in, when the door opened and two men ambled out: Harry the Hat Hansen trailed by his pudgy Watson, Finis Brown.

I got just a glimpse of her on the shining steel table, the two halves of her, pelvis tipped obscenely up; her head was to one side, staring at me, teeth showing through the gaping wound across her mouth. The flesh of her scalp had been cut and pulled away, the top of her head had been sawed off, for the removal of her brain.

Then, thankfully, the door was closed.

Harry—his powder-blue fedora snugged in place, still natty in his dark blue tailored suit despite a brutally long day—looked at us blankly. He was the kind of premeditated man who had to decide whether or not he was pleased or pissed off.

Brown—his rumpled fedora in hand, his suit looking more slept-in than ever—didn't need time to know how he felt.

"What the hell are you shitheads doing here?" the chunky cop exploded, moving forward, putting a flat hand against Fowley's chest. "Get the fuck out. This is restricted!"

Hansen, however, was smiling. He rested a hand on Brown's shoulder. "Brownie—relax. These are the men who found the body, remember? Perhaps they're just here to volunteer their formal statement."

"We can go down to Central Homicide, if you like," Fowley

said, obviously a little cowed from having the beefy Brown in his face.

Gazing sleepily at us, the Hat spoke as if in benediction. "That's not necessary. Brownie here can take your statement, Bill—and we'll send over a typewritten version to the *Examiner*, for your approval, and signature."

Fowley didn't quite know what to make of that.

"Brownie," the Hat said, "go see to it that police guards are posted at the ambulance entrance of this fine facility, would you?" To us, the Hat added, "That *is* how you got in?"

We nodded.

"Do that, Brownie, please, and then get right back here, to take Mr. Fowley's statement."

"Sure, Harry," Brown said, flashing us a couple of dirty looks that would have seemed silly if the fat S.O.B. hadn't been such a nasty piece of work.

Once Brown had bounded off, the Hat looked from Fowley to me and back again, clapping his hands together. "First, do you boys have any questions? We're going to cooperate, after all—the *Examiner* and the LAPD, that is. Two fine institutions with the public's welfare at heart." This son of a bitch was so dry, you could never tell when he was pulling your chain.

"Any surprises in there, Harry?" Fowley said, nodding toward the closed door to room number four. He got out his notepad and a pencil and waited for an answer.

It finally came.

The Hat's tiny mouth puckered a smile. "Of course there are . . . 'surprises.' I'm sure your source in the coroner's office has already told you that . . . and I presume he's also refused to share those surprises with you, or you wouldn't still be standing here."

Fowley grinned, tapping his notepad with the pencil. "Fair enough, Harry. What *can* you give me?"

"Let's back up a little. Your extra edition has been on the street, what, two hours?"

"Something like that."

The Hat lifted an eyebrow and the blue fedora rose a tad. "We've already had six confessions."

Fowley smirked. "I guess that's no surprise—something this splashy . . . and this friggin' weird . . . it's gonna bring 'em out of the woodwork."

Nodding, the Hat said, "I anticipate more Confessin' Sams than you could shake a stick at, making all kinds of work for us, pointless work that can get in the way of actually solving this thing."

I asked, "What can be done about that?"

Harry held up three fingers. "Let the public know that Detective Hansen is withholding three pieces of information—three things that only that poor dead girl and her killer could know. That may help minimize the false confession problem."

"Or," I said, as Fowley jotted that down, "present your 'Confessin' Sams' with a challenge, a guessing game."

"It will also tell the real killer that we are already breathing down his neck. That we have three pieces of evidence just waiting to put him in the gas chamber."

I said, "Is this a sex crime, Harry?"

Irritation flashed through the sleepy eyes. "She was mutilated and tortured and left naked, and cut in half. If we're not dealing with a sex crime, what are we dealing with?"

"I told you at the scene, Harry—her mouth is cut the way mobsters send a warning to squealers."

"It's a sex crime. Half the department is interviewing known sex offenders, and our dragnet's going to be spread statewide by tomorrow morning. Within twenty-four hours, hundreds of sex degenerates and suspected sadists will have been thoroughly interrogated."

Fowley wrote that down.

I asked, "Was there semen in her vagina?"

Hansen frowned. "Let's just say it's a sex crime and leave it at that."

"I knew it!" Fowley said, slapping the pad with the pencil. "He fucked her in the ass, didn't he?"

Hansen looked at Fowley a long time; buried in the blank grooves of the cop's face were ribbons of contempt.

"What?" Fowley asked, wide eyed.

Echoing footsteps announced Sergeant Brown's return.

"It's took care of, Harry," Brown said. "I got a couple sheriff's deputies to help out."

"There, you see, gentlemen?" the Hat said to us. "Cooperation."

"I may advise Richardson to put out another extra," Fowley said, smirking. "That's a first for the sheriff's department and the LAPD."

With a small, insincere smile, the Hat said, "Mr. Fowley, give your statement to Sergeant Brown, would you? . . . Mr. Heller, Nate—a word in private?"

Hansen took me by the arm—gently—and walked me down the hallway and stopped; the yellow brick walls and the Hat's tanned complexion were strangely compatible.

"Nate," the Hat said, his tiny mouth pursed in its kiss of a smile, "I understand you've gone to work for the *Examiner*."

"Not as a reporter, just providing some investigative backup. They're gonna be shorthanded."

"Richardson is going all the way with this one."

"Yes."

"Well, that's fine. You tell Jim I'll be glad to cooperate with him . . . as long as he cooperates with me."

I shrugged. "Richardson is his own man, Harry. If you want to know the truth, I think he plans an end run around you boys."

"That's not surprising news. Nate, can I trust you?"

"Can I trust you?"

He put a fatherly hand on my elbow. "We worked well on the Peete case, together, wouldn't you say?"

"Sure."

Now the hand rose to my shoulder and settled there. "I know you feel I . . . took credit where perhaps it wasn't due."

"I didn't give a shit—what good would California publicity do me back in Chicago?"

He removed the hand from my shoulder, gesturing as he did. "Yes, but now you're doing business here, and that changes things. . . . Nate, I want to work out an arrangement with you."

"What kind of arrangement, Harry?"

The pouchy eyes tightened. "You keep me abreast of what the *Examiner* is up to, and I'll do the same for you, where my efforts are concerned."

"And the point of this is . . . ?"

"To find the fiend who did this awful thing!" Oddly, he was smiling as he said that, revealing just enough teeth to make him look like a big well-dressed rabbit. "And to be the detectives who solved the most notorious murder in the history of California."

"It's a little early to be calling it that, Harry, don't you think?"

"Not really—not considering the crime . . . not considering the noise Jim Richardson and Old Man Hearst are making, and will make. . . . What do you say, Nate? Is it a deal?"

"All right."

He offered his hand—it was smaller than a frying pan—and I shook it, firmly.

The Hat sighed, contentedly, as if he'd just finished a big, fine meal. He folded his arms and said, casually, "Now, let's move on to that other question."

"What other question?"

"The one about trust. Can I trust you, Nate?"

"I don't know why people even bother asking that question, Harry—an honest man and a liar will give you the same answer."

"What about this, Nate, as a show of trust?" He nodded toward coroner's room four. "I'm going to share one of those three 'surprises' with you."

"Why?"

He raised a lecturing finger. "Because if you tell anyone, if it gets in the *Examiner*, I'll know I *can't* trust you . . . and I'll still have two surprises left." Yes, sir, the Hat was one crafty son of a bitch.

Grinning in spite of myself, I said, "Okay, Harry—surprise me."

He glanced down the hall—both ways. Then, very quietly, he said, "That girl . . . whoever she is . . . she ingested fecal matter before she died."

I winced. "What the hell?"

"To put it more coloquially—in words your friend Mr. Fowley could understand—she ate shit, Heller. Someone made her eat shit before killing her. . . . That's the kind of man we're dealing with."

"Holy Christ."

"Why, Nate—you've turned pale on me. Hardcase like you?"

"It's just . . . some sick fucker needs to be cured."

Nodding, the Hat said, "Cyanide pellets would do nicely. Now—do you have anything you can give me, from the *Examiner*'s side?"

"Yeah, actually, I do," I said, and I told him about Richardson using the SoundPhoto to wire the prints to Washington.

"If she's on file with the FBI," I told him, "Richardson will be calling you or your boss Donahoe with the girl's name, in the morning . . . and using that to get leverage."

"At this very moment, we have dozens of men going through hundreds of missing persons files," the Hat said thoughtfully, "and they're going to work straight through the night . . . maybe we'll get lucky and come up with her name before Richardson does."

"Maybe. And I hope you do. Because a case where a newspaperman like Jim Richardson controls the evidence is bound to become a travesty of justice."

I failed to add that in a town with a police force as corrupt and incompetent as L.A.'s, a travesty of justice would be no big change of pace.

The Hat studied me—perhaps reading my mind—and then he said, "Come along, would you? Give your statement to Brownie."

I followed him back to where Fowley and Brown were winding things up. Then, there in the hot, humid hallway of the basement morgue, I gave Fat Ass Brown my statement, as well.

The Hat thanked us, and dismissed us.

"What did he want?" Fowley asked me, as we made our way out, past forgotten bodies on wall-hugging gurneys.

"Credit," I said.

# 7

In a perfect world I might have been able to confide in my wife. In this imperfect place I inhabited, I didn't feel like discussing with my new bride the fact that I'd known the once-lovely victim of the "Werewolf Slayer," much less share the news that the dead girl had (like my bride) been carrying a child of mine.

When in the early evening I returned to our honeymoon bungalow at the Beverly Hills Hotel, Peggy was napping on the double bed, in a black slip, legs bare, atop the floral spread, somehow having found a place to do so amid the array of boxes and sacks (Sak's Fifth Avenue, Christian Dior, Van Cleef & Arpel's) that were the spoils of her day of shopping.

Hanging my suitcoat in the bedroom closet, getting out of my tie, I gazed at the pretty young woman to whom I was so freshly married; she was in more or less the same position Elizabeth Short had been, in the vacant lot, except in one piece. I bent over and kissed her freckled nose—freckled under her makeup, anyway—and she smiled a little, groaned sexily, and turned over on her side.

Looking at her, I had a terrible pang—guilt, sorrow, shame, regret—a whole series of emotions all mixed together, emotions most people (including me) figured I was immune to. But I loved Peggy, loved her dearly and deeply, and I had today been subjected to the sight of another woman—of whom I'd been at least a little fond, primarily because she reminded me so of Peg—butchered and dumped like two sides of beef in a vacant lot. Beneath the sentimental twinges, a slow rage was burning in my belly; I knew it would kindle, and finally ignite, and blot out those other emotions.

Even with everything I had at stake—my marriage, my business, my freedom—the thing I wanted most was to find the sick son of a bitch who had done this and drain him of just enough of his blood to drown him in.

Leaving the door cracked, so I could see her a little from the living room, I fixed myself a rum and Coke from the bungalow's wet bar, and plopped onto the couch and sat there trembling. Watching Peg's slumbering form, I wondered if I dared confide in my new A-1 partner, Fred Rubinski. After turning it over in my mind a few dozen times, I decided *no*. Fred and I were good friends, and business partners. But he was not one of the two or three people I considered my closest friends, my best friends.

Funny thing was, one of my best friends was in Hollywood this very minute—Barney Ross, the former lightweight (and welterweight) champ. We went way back—I'd grown up on the West Side of Chicago with him, and we'd worked together as kids as "pullers," hustling goods outside Maxwell Street shops; I was even *Shabbes goy* to his Orthodox folks. Starting in the mid-twenties, Barney had run a speakeasy on the ground floor of a building he owned at Van Buren and Plymouth; when I left the cops, and was just starting out as an independent investigator, Barney traded me office (and living) space in exchange for keeping an after-hours eye on his building. He was that kind of friend.

We had even got drunk and joined the Marines together, one ill-advised evening in 1942, two overage idiots with patriotic hard-ons; and we had fought side by side, notably in a muddy shell hole on Guadalcanal where we had somehow managed to get dozens of Japs killed and not ourselves.

And, yes, we had both been wounded on that foul island, but my scars were mostly the kind that didn't show, which is to say I was honorably discharged on a Section Eight, Mental Instability

Due to Combat Trauma. On the other hand, Barney had left the military with all his marbles, as well as a morphine habit that turned a good-natured, sweet-hearted guy into a lowlife junkie. By pulling strings with my friend Frank Nitti, I managed to dry up Barney's street sources—in Chicago anyway—which ultimately sent the former champ, however reluctantly, into rehabilitation.

According to the *Examiner* and other local rags, Barney had just been released from the U.S. Public Health Service addiction hospital in Lexington, Kentucky, and was making his first post-rehab stop in Los Angeles as a part of a public-relations attempt to win back his wholesome reputation with the public. I had a hunch it was in part for the benefit of his ex-wife Cathy, who lived out here, a beautiful former showgirl who had walked out on him when the monkey on his back started meaning more to Barney than she did.

So my best friend in the world—one of my two best friends in the world, anyway—was staying at the Roosevelt Hotel, maybe ten minutes away, and I couldn't talk to him about this. I couldn't talk to him about anything, because he hadn't spoken to me since March of 1943, when I pulled the plug on his Chicago connections.

I knew only one person I could confide in, and that was my partner back in Chicago, Lou Sapperstein. Maybe Lou and I weren't as tight as Barney and I once had been, but I knew I could count on Lou—and, anyway, I simply had to clue him in on this. Using the endtable phone, keeping my voice low, I called Lou at home; he didn't say much as he listened to my sad tale, and when I finally stopped talking, an endless, crackling long-distance silence was all I heard.

"You still there, Lou?" I asked, almost whispering, the sleeping Peg in view through the cracked door.

After another long staticky pause—a pregnant pause, if you will—Lou's baritone, a sort of tone-deaf Crosby, purred, "Are you sure you want to go this direction?"

"I've already gone. What choice do I have, Lou? These damn coincidences make me look dirty as hell."

"Time of death on the girl?"

"With a corpse drained of blood, that's no easy thing to pinpoint. The coroner estimates within twelve hours of the body's discovery."

"You got an alibi for last night?"

"Just Peggy—we spent a quiet evening here at the hotel. Even had a room service supper . . . went to bed early. She starts that picture at Paramount tomorrow and is trying to get herself on an early schedule."

"Well, a wife's alibi is better than nothing."

"Tell it to Bruno Hauptmann. Anyway, who's to say I didn't get up in the middle of the night, leave Peg sleeping, and go play mad doctor on that poor kid?"

Lou's sigh was world-weary enough for both of us. "Even if the cops clear you, you know, your name and reputation will be dragged through the slime."

"Hell, that's the least of my worries—I already got a shady reputation, which in our business isn't all bad."

"Shady is one thing, Nate. But immoral? Evil? Not so good . . . even in our business."

I sipped my rum and Coke. Shook my head. "I'm not arguing, Lou. You've just confirmed what I been thinking."

"Which is?"

"Which is, I have to try to crack this thing, before somebody lays it on my doorstep."

"That's a lousy idea, Nate. . . . How can I help?"

"First of all, we never had this conversation. I don't want you to face aiding and abetting after the fact."

"Be quiet. How can I help?"

"First things first. Keep an eye on our esteemed Chicago press—this thing is going to get major play out here . . . I need to know how much space it gets back home."

"That's easily enough done."

"Pretty soon the cops and reporters will have the girl identified. Maybe in Chicago, all that'll rate is a few column inches, inside. But if Beth Short's picture is splashed on the front page—like it will be out here in sunny Southern California—then she's going to get recognized."

"Was Elizabeth Short that distinctive looking?"

Gazing at the sleeping Peggy, I said, "Think of Deanna Durbin, Lou, but sexy—jet-black hair, pale pale skin, dark dark lipstick, lovely lovely smile, figure like Lana Turner."

"Yeah," Lou said dryly, "kid like that just mighta got noticed."

I cautioned Lou to keep a close eye on the *Herald-American*, because the Hearst papers were the most likely to play it up big. I explained that a handful of people—at the Morrison Hotel, the St. Clair, Lindy's, Henrici's—could possibly link the Short woman and me.

"And eventually," I told him, "even these dumb L.A. coppers will figure out Beth Short spent time in Chicago, and they'll send somebody to start poking around."

"Christ, Nate . . ."

"If that girl's name and picture do start showing up in the Chicago papers, cut her mug out and show it around the Morrison, and see if she gets made."

"I get you—just staying ahead of the game."

"Just staying ahead of the game." I had another sip of rum and Coke. "Now, in the meantime, Beth Short told me she was going to see a doctor in Gary, a gynecologist most likely . . . She said she had 'female trouble.' Lou, I want you to track that doctor down."

"Should I use her name?"

"No! Beth may not have used her real name, anyway. Just give 'em her description—it would have been late October of last year. See, I been thinking, and it may be wishful thinking at that . . . but if she saw a doctor in Gary, 'cause she was *already* pregnant—"

Even over the wire, I could hear Lou snap his fingers. "Then she wasn't pregnant by you!"

"That's right. Maybe she was looking to get an abortion, thanks to one of these war heroes she had such a yen for—so you'll need to be sure to check up on the less savory quacks in the Gary area."

"No shortage of rabbit pullers in that neck of the woods . . . but, Nate, if you didn't knock her up, why would she call you from the Biltmore, looking for abortion money?"

"Maybe she was just trying to shake me down. To her, I must've looked like a well-off mark—big-shot private eye, opening an L.A. branch. Maybe she wanted to buy some more fancy black threads, or maybe she had some other medical problem she was raising dough for."

"Y'know, she might have had an ongoing ailment; maybe she was seeing that doc in Gary 'cause of a venereal disease."

"Yeah? Then why didn't I catch it?"

"Why didn't you?"

"See, Lou, that's just it—I don't have any memory of actually having intercourse with the girl. Of course, that was when I was drinking heavily, and—"

"You get around, Nate, but I would assume you usually remember having sex."

"Usually."

"If the Short girl wasn't really pregnant by you, that would give you less of a motive. Or anyway, we could play it that way."

"Yeah, and it would also indicate I wasn't necessarily the only person she was trying to shake down."

"Right! Which means somebody else has a murder motive."

"Maybe several somebody elses, Lou. Hansen and Richardson and the rest of these chowderheads, they all see this as a sex crime—me, I keep seeing a woman's mouth slashed the way a gangster does an informer . . . or a blackmailer. And one of the few things we know for sure in this case is that Beth Short was capable of blackmail."

"You're hoping the cops and reporters are going down the wrong road."

"Hoping like hell—that's my best shot at coming out of this cluster-fuck breathing air and not cyanide fumes. If the cops and reporters are looking for a sex maniac, when the killer is really some disgruntled ex-boy-friend or some gangland type Beth got misguidedly involved with—"

"Then you'll see things that they won't," Lou said, something hopeful in his voice. "You'll look at evidence, at clues, that they're dismissing, when you're seeing the significance."

"Exactly. I have an in with both the *Examiner* and the lead police detective . . . and if my take on this murder is on target and theirs isn't . . . I might come out of this with my ass *and* business intact."

"And maybe even your marriage."

I gazed at Peggy, still on her side, snoring softly. "Maybe even that."

Lou grunted. ". . . I guess this is my fault, really."

"How do you figure that?"

"When you were mooning over bustin' up with Peggy? I encouraged you to get back in the saddle again."

"So to speak."

"Next time I give you advice, take it from me: don't."

We signed off, and I placed another call, to a friend who was even closer to me than Lou, and just as close as I had once been to Barney—my other best friend in the world, actually. . . . Only I couldn't risk coming clean with this guy. This guy was too straight an arrow for that. This guy was Eliot Ness.

I had known Eliot since we were both students at the University of Chicago in the late '20s. When I was a cop and, later, a private detective, I had found Eliot to be my most reliable source within federal law-enforcement circles, back in the days when he and his Capone squad—the so-called Untouchables—had helped put Big Al away.

After Prohibition, Eliot had gone on to a well-publicized, highly regarded six-year stint as Cleveland's (and the nation's youngest) Public Safety Director, cleaning up one of America's most corrupt police departments, busting the notorious Mayfield Road Gang's numbers racket, and exposing numerous crooked unions. In several instances I had worked for Eliot in Cleveland, particularly during the period when the cops there couldn't be trusted.

One of the cases I'd helped crack was that of the infamous Mad Butcher of Kingsbury Run; from 1935 through 1938, the torso killer had killed at least thirteen men and women, mostly indigents, and possibly as many as seven or eight more. Officially, this case remained unsolved. But Eliot and I knew otherwise.

"This killing does sound as if it has some of the earmarks of the Butcher," the celebrated gangbuster said from his home in Cleveland. We had a long-distance connection as strong and clear as Eliot's voice. "A number of the torso slayer's victims *were* bisected at the waist."

"And washed and drained of blood."

"Yes, Nate . . . but our friend Lloyd also liked to collect heads, remember. That was his signature."

The Butcher was Lloyd Watterson, a former medical student, the son of a well-to-do Cleveland physician. The prominence of the family had made it a political necessity to sweep the Butcher's capture under the rug, and for Watterson himself to be committed to a Sandusky, Ohio, mental hospital.

"I realize Watterson almost always decapitated his victims," I said, "but this girl's face was mutilated in such a distinctive fashion—"

I could sense Eliot nodding. "Like an informer, a 'squealer.' "

"My thinking, exactly. The killer obviously left the girl's head attached because the slashing of her face was a part of a message he was sending."

"A message to whom?"

"That's the key question, isn't it?"

"I don't think Lloyd Watterson would vary from his signature, particularly when sending a message . . . *if* he were at large."

"You're probably right, Eliot. Still, with these striking parallels, I thought you should know about the murder. Since the Butcher case is officially open, and so few people actually know the score about Watterson, you could be getting a phone call from the LAPD, any time now. Harry the Hat specifically asked me to call you on this."

"Nate, I haven't been Public Safety Director of Cleveland for a long time."

Eliot left the Public Safety post in March 1942, under a cloud, after he was in an icy-roads auto accident that involved drinking and even an accusation of hit-and-run on his part. It was mostly trumped up, by some of the crooked cops he'd been in the process of rooting out, but the scandal had damaged his otherwise Boy-Scout-flawless reputation.

During the war, Eliot had regained much of his good name by heading up the federal government's Division of Social Protection, which was a fancy way of saying he'd been the nation's top wartime vice cop, battling the spread of V.D. on military bases and near defense plants.

Currently, Eliot was chairman of the board of directors of the Diebold safe company, where he was apparently doing a good job, getting a glowing write-up in the current issue of *Fortune*.

"I know you're a private citizen, now, Eliot, but you were *the* famous face on the Butcher investigation . . . and you may want to keep an eye on this 'Werewolf Slaying,' since there *are* parallels . . . and, considering the way the Butcher case was ultimately handled, well . . ."

"It was a cover-up, Nate—don't sugarcoat it."

"Just as long as Watterson is still having his jacket buttoned up for him, in the back, by valets in white, I'm satisfied."

"I can assure you our man is still in a padded cell. I even get the occasional postcard from him."

"Really?"

"Oh yes, that's one of Lloyd's hobbies—taunting me with his threatening gibberish."

"I would think they'd keep the lad away from sharp objects, including pencils."

"It's a mental hospital, Nate, not a prison."

"All the more reason to check up on him, Eliot."

"I will. . . . What's wrong, Nate?"

"Wrong?"

"I sense something in your voice. I'm reading a . . . personal involvement in this thing."

"I just happened to be with the reporter who stumbled onto the corpse, is all. . . . She was a pretty girl, Eliot, and some twisted bastard butchered her . . . It's sickening."

"I know. I know all too well. I was called to enough vacant lots and the like to view the Butcher's handiwork. . . . I'll make sure Lloyd is still inside, Nate. You'll hear from me tomorrow."

"Good."

"Don't let this get to you. I had my share of sleepless nights myself, thanks to that fiend. We should have put his ass in jail."

"We should have killed him."

Eliot said nothing.

"Anyway—thanks, Eliot."

When his voice returned, the tone had lightened. "You're still willing to be my best man?"

"What? Oh, sure! When is the wedding, again?"

"January thirty-first, right here in Cleveland. Big church ceremony, the whole shooting match, family, friends. Can you and Peggy still make it?"

"We'll be there with bells on. I can't imagine anything keeping me from standing up for you." Except maybe a jail cell.

"Betty and I are counting on the both of you. . . . Speaking of which, how's married life treating you, so far?"

"So far, so good," I said, leaving out a few details.

"Peggy's a great gal."

"So's Betty. I know you two will be happy, Eliot."

His laugh had a little embarrassment in it. "Well, you know what they say—third time's a charm."

This would indeed be marriage number three for Eliot. He was a hardworking, hard-drinking guy and was no doubt not terribly easy to be married to. Wife number one had been his secretary, during the Capone Chicago years, and that marriage had burned out during his tumultuous Public Safety run. I had thought his second marriage, to a terrific girl named Evie—a fashion designer up for the high-flying social life Eliot relished so—would have stuck. But nobody knows what's really going on inside somebody else's marriage.

Hanging up, I looked toward Peggy, who seemed, finally, to be stirring. I went in and kissed her neck and her ear and her face, gently rousing her.

"Where have you been?" she asked me, sleepily, violet eyes half-hooded.

"All your life? Or just today?"

"Today's a start."

I was seated on the edge of the bed, next to her. "Actually . . .

it was long and kind of unpleasant. I'll fill you in, but I think we oughta grab supper, first."

"Ooooo. . . . That unpleasant?"

"Oh yeah."

Neither one of us was terribly hungry, so we just had sandwiches and iced tea at the Fountain Coffee Shop, which was tucked away under the Polo Lounge stairway. Dressed casually, in a snappy white blouse with brown-white-checked boyish slacks, Peggy chattered about the wonderful buys she'd found, at the after-Christmas sales. I politely listened and did not point out that bargain-hunting in Beverly Hills was a contradiction in terms.

Her hair was down, tonight, brushing her shoulders. All I could think of was how beautiful she was—and how much she and Beth Short looked alike.

Over a piece of strawberry cheesecake we shared off a single plate, Peg began to babble about how excited she was, tomorrow being her first day on the Bob Hope picture.

"I'll be working with Dorothy Lamour, too," she said. "And Peter Lorre. I'll tell you a funny coincidence."

Not finding coincidences all that funny today, I managed, "What?"

"It's a private-eye spoof. Isn't that a riot?"

"Four alarm," I said.

As we walked hand-in-hand back to our bungalow, enjoying a cool breeze riffling the trees, she frowned up at me. "Here I've been babbling on and on about my fun day, and how I'm looking forward to tomorrow . . . and poor you, you've had such a long, hard day . . . How did you describe it?"

"Unpleasant," I said.

"Unpleasant," she nodded. "Tell me about it, darling."

I waited until we'd made a fire—and had dragged pillows off the couch, to make a cozy nest for us, where we fell into each other's arms—before I told her.

Told her what I could, that is: that I'd been with that reporter Fowley when the bisected body of a beautiful unidentified woman had been found, and that I would be working with the *Examiner* on the case.

She knew immediately what I was talking about. Even on Rodeo Drive, newsboys had been hawking the *Examiner*'s extra edition, and the case had been all over the radio, as well.

"I heard the grisly details in the car," she said, sitting up. She was in panties and bra and looked like a bright-eyed girl at a slumber party; I was in T-shirt and boxers and socks, like a pervo pop peeking through a keyhole at his daughter's girl friends at that same slumber party.

"You don't seem, uh . . . bothered at all," I said.

"Are you kidding? This is a big story! This is going to be the biggest thing since the H-bomb. And my husband's in the middle of it!"

"I'm glad you're pleased."

"This is going to make our business, out here."

"Our business?"

"Our business, your business! You'll be the most famous detective in town, you big lug, if you take full advantage. Do you and Fred have a press agent?"

"Not really—that's why we teamed up with the *Examiner*."

"Well, you two may want to think about getting a press agent. God, this is exciting! What a wonderful break!"

"Yeah, I'm, uh, pretty thrilled myself."

Her brow tensed and she raised a palm, like somebody was swearing her in at court. "Don't get me wrong . . . I'm sorry for this poor girl. She was probably no different than me, just another beauty queen looking to make it in the movies or something. But she wasn't lucky, like I was."

"How do you mean?"

"She didn't have you in her life."

Then she kissed me. Long and hard, her tongue tangling with mine.

The fire cast a glowing, flickering pattern on her creamy-white flesh, as if someone were projecting a film onto her body. The dark bushiness of her pubic triangle teased through the white panties. She sat up and reached behind her and undid her bra; it slipped to her lap, where she brushed it away like a pesky insect.

Her breasts weren't large—they were merely perfect, delicately veined, pertly symmetrical, hard-nippled. I kissed them, I touched them, I helped her scoot out of the panties and she climbed on top of me, sat on me, riding me slowly, eyes half-lidded, smiling in that distracted way that precedes orgasm, until the smile finally blossomed, her eyes closing, hips accelerating. . . .

The sweetness of it lingered well after she was again in my arms, turning bitter only when she asked me once more if we couldn't "wait" to have our first child. Things were going to be so perfect here, she assured me dreamily, with her landing her first film role, and me landing such an incredible, important case.

I held her face in my hands and I looked into those lovely violet eyes and I said, "We're going back to Chicago, as soon as you've shot your little movie and I've solved my big case. We're going home and we're having our kid, and then we'll decide where we're going to live and work. . . . I promise you I will abide by your wishes on that score, Peg. If you want to come back here and be in the movies, well, I'll work here, too, and we'll hire a nanny or whatever the hell and we will have it all—yes, we will. But if you ever suggest aborting our child again, I will fucking kill you."

With a yelp of fright, she bolted from my arms and ran naked to the bedroom, where she shut the door, though that didn't keep me from hearing her crying in there, as I tried to sleep on the reassembled couch.

Dumb little bitch.

Stupid bastard.

# 8

The prints the *Examiner* sent by wire to the FBI were too blurred to be identifiable; but one of Richardson's staff photographers suggested sending 8" by 10" negative blowups. Within minutes the prints were identified as those of Elizabeth Short, who had—four years before—applied for, and landed, a civilian job at an Army base near Santa Barbara, working at the post exchange at Camp Cooke.

A description derived from the job application was as follows: weight, 115 pounds; height, five feet five; race, Caucasian; sex, female; hair, brunette; eyes, blue-green; complexion, fair; date of birth, July 29, 1924; place of birth, Hyde Park, Massachusetts.

In addition, the FBI had cross-referenced an arrest in 1943, Santa Barbara, California; a minor, Elizabeth Short had been picked up for drinking in a bar where she'd been with a girl friend and two soldiers. To her description were added these telling details: an I-shaped scar on her back from a childhood operation, a quarter-size brown birthmark on her right shoulder, and a small tattoo of a rose on her outer left thigh. The girl had been sent by bus back home to Medford, Massachusetts, to be given over into the custody of her mother, Mrs. Phoebe May Short.

"Look at this little beauty," Richardson said, gesturing to a police mug photo, side and front, of Elizabeth Short. With her dark hair tousled, translucent eyes sullenly blank, wearing none of the China doll makeup at all, under the unyielding gaze of a police photographer, she was as lovely as a movie queen's soft-focus, airbrushed glamour portrait.

Richardson was standing at the head of the scarred wooden conference table; he and I and Fowley were in the glassed-off editorial chamber where we'd confabbed yesterday with a whole gaggle of reporters. This morning it was just the three of us.

"She does look better than in the shots Heller took yesterday," Fowley said. Wearing a light brown checkered sportcoat and a darker brown tie with yellow horses prancing across it, he was seated to Richardson's right and I was across from the reporter, on the editor's left.

"A living doll," Richardson said, managing to fix both his eyes on the photo, "or at least she used to be—and that gives us a genuine star for our 'A' picture."

The editor—in shirtsleeves and suspenders—was giddy as a schoolgirl. Yesterday, when the competition's afternoon editions appeared with the "Werewolf Slayer" story, it was two hours after the *Examiner*'s extra hit the street, in a sold-out press run second only to VJ Day.

"You want us to hit Camp Cooke, boss?" Fowley asked.

"Sid Hughes is already on his way up there," Richardson said, lighting up a cigarette, waving out a match.

"We could check out that Santa Barbara arrest," I suggested.

"I got two men on that." Glee was coming off Richardson like heat off asphalt. "Right now we're so far out in front of the pack—they're never gonna catch up. I've had crews out digging since five o'clock this morning, and the other papers didn't even know Elizabeth Short's name till they read it in our morning edition."

Fowley shifted in his hard chair; his tone vaguely irritated, he said, "So what's left for the first string, if you've emptied the bench covering every lead the FBI gave us?"

"The best lead of all. . . . Get your notepad out, Mr. Fowley." Richardson turned his eerie stare on me, his slow eye playing catch-up. "Nate, you're the best interrogator in house at the moment."

I frowned. "Gee whiz, thanks—but what are you getting at?"

His left eye was still swimming into place as he fixed his gaze on me. "Plus, you were a cop for a lot of years."

"What's on your mind, Jim?"

"You've had to break bad news before, I mean."

I'd grabbed a bacon and eggs breakfast at a diner on my way over here; the greasy remains were turning in my stomach. "What exactly do you have in mind?"

"Also, you know how to work a phone."

That was self-evident: private detectives spent most of their working day on the phone. "What the hell do you—"

"Just a second . . ." Richardson went to the door, opened it, and yelled for a copy boy to bring him in two phones. Then he looked at me again, one eye at a time, and unleashed a smile almost as ghastly as his gaze. ". . . I want you to locate Mrs. Phoebe May Short, in Medford, Massachusetts."

"That's the news you want me to break? Her daughter's death?"

He strode back to the head of the table, nodding. "Unlikely she's heard yet, unless the cops got right on it . . . and I don't think Hansen even gets in till nine or nine-thirty."

I sighed. "All right. It's gotta be done."

"Yeah . . . but gracefully . . . you know, let her down easy. First, tell her that Elizabeth won a beauty contest."

"What?"

He shrugged elaborately, held his palms up. "If you just flat-out tell the poor woman that her little girl's dead, she's gonna go to pieces on you, Heller—you know that. We need to get all the background, before you inform her of, you know, the tragic event."

"You are one sorry son of a bitch."

"True, but if you don't make this call for me, Heller, you won't be working for this sorry son of a bitch any longer. You and Fred Rubinski will be on the outside of this case, as well as this newspaper, and you can pony up some real dough for a real press agent, which you will sorely need, considering the bad ink we will drown you in."

"How do you sleep at night?"

"Like a dead baby. Anyway, you got the skills for this, Nate. You can do it. I know you can."

"That show of confidence just sends me soaring. Why don't you have Fowley here do your dirty work? He oughta be used to it by now."

Fowley leaned back in the chair, raised his eyebrows, and his hands, like he'd just touched both burners of a hot stove.

Richardson, his left eye floating, said kindly, "He's going to be taking notes while you work your magic."

"Fuck you."

"By 'fuck you,' I take that to mean, yes, you'll do it."

"Yes, fuck you. Yes, I'll do it."

Soon two phones on long wires had been plugged into the wall, one each in front of Fowley and me. The switchboard connected us, so that Fowley could listen in.

It took a while to track the woman down. No Medford telephone was listed for the Shorts, but by sweet-talking an operator, I was able to find my way to the next-door neighbor, who told me the Shorts rented out a flat upstairs in their house and that the flat did indeed have a phone. I got ahold of the tenant, and, before long, Mrs. Phoebe Short was on the line. I identified myself as a reporter with the *Examiner*.

"Why yes, I have a daughter named Elizabeth." The voice was medium pitched and touched with a New England accent, and its pleasantness indicated that news of her daughter's death had surely not reached her yet.

"Is your daughter by any chance in California?" I asked.

"Yes, she is. She's been out there some while, off and on, trying to break into the moving pictures."

Richardson was seated next to Fowley, listening in as the reporter jotted down notes; the editor's eyes—including the slow one—lighted up like a candle in a jack-o-lantern. The Werewolf's victim was a starlet! What more could a sleazebag editor ask?

"Mrs. Short," I said, "your daughter has won a beauty contest out here—Miss Santa Monica."

"Oh! How wonderful . . . I can't say I'm surprised. She's such a pretty girl—she's won these sort of contests before, you know, starting with right here in Medford. And when she worked in the PX at Camp Cooke, during the war? She was selected 'Cutie of the Week.' "

Fowley was scribbling and Richardson was grinning.

"She's such a wholesome young woman," the excited mother was saying. "She doesn't smoke, or drink. . . ."

She was just arrested for underage drinking, and had a tattoo on her left thigh.

"How long has Elizabeth been in Hollywood, Mrs. Short?"

Now a little embarrassment seemed to creep into the proud parent's tone. "Well, you have to understand, everyone back here was always telling Elizabeth how beautiful she was, that she was born to be a movie star."

"Is that right?"

"She dropped out of Medford High in her junior year. Of course, pursuing her acting dreams is only part of why she left school. Hard to imagine, healthy as she looks, but she's always suffered from asthma, and other lung conditions. So that sunny weather is good for her. She's spent some time in Florida, too."

I didn't want to get into Elizabeth Short's travel habits—since they included "sunny" Chicago—so I moved the mother back to Hollywood.

"Has your daughter appeared in any movies since she's been out here?"

"She's had some small parts—what do they call it, when you're in the background of a scene?"

"An extra?"

"Yes, an extra. She's appeared as an extra."

"Has Elizabeth always been interested in acting?"

"I'm afraid my daughter's always been kind of movie struck," the mother bubbled, "and I'm afraid I have to take credit, or maybe blame."

"Are you a movie fan, too?"

"Oh yes, I've always loved the movies. From when they were little girls, I always took Betty and her sister Muriel to the picture show, two or three times a week. Everyone says Betty looks like Deanna Durbin, you know."

"There is a striking resemblance."

"Betty's sister, Ginnie, is very talented, too, studying opera, and the two girls would just battle over the radio—Ginnie wanting to listen to that long-hair stuff, and Betty just loved the popular songs. Was there a talent competition for Miss Santa Monica? Did she dance? Betty's a wonderful dancer."

"Well, I wasn't at the competition, Mrs. Short—I'm trying to get in touch with Betty. Would you happen to have her most recent address?"

"I don't understand. If she won the beauty contest, why don't you have—"

"We got Elizabeth's name from the Chamber of Commerce," I said glibly, feeling like the goddamn liar I was, "who sponsored the contest, but they neglected to give us her address, in their press release."

"I don't know if I have her most recent address—she was staying in San Diego, at least until two weeks ago."

Richardson was nodding at me, mouthing, "Good, good."

"But it doesn't surprise me she's back in the Hollywood area," her mother was saying.

"Why is that, Mrs. Short?"

"Well, Elizabeth said she only went down to San Diego because of the movie union strikes—she said everything in the film industry was kind of shut down. But I know she had to get back to Hollywood before too long."

"Why is that?"

The pride in Mrs. Short's voice was palpable. "Betty had a screen test coming up."

"Really? Do you know for what studio?"

"It wasn't a studio, I don't think. She said it was a director, some famous director."

"Well, that's swell. Did she say what director?"

"No—just that he was very, very famous. It's someone she met at the Hollywood Canteen."

"Oh, she worked at the Canteen?" Actually, I knew that already—Beth had mentioned that, and the "famous director"—but I hadn't shared the information with anybody.

"I don't think she did, officially. But she said she was on the list to be a junior hostess, and got meals there, free, sometimes."

"The Hollywood Canteen, that's a wonderful thing, supporting our servicemen like that."

Mrs. Short laughed, lightly. "I don't mean to speak out of school, but my daughter does have a soft spot for a man in uniform."

"Well, a lot of girls do these days, Mrs. Short."

"They certainly do. . . ." And now her tone turned somber. ". . . Elizabeth was engaged to a major in the Army Air Corps, oh, for almost three years. But he died in action."

"I'm so sorry. Do you, uh, happen to know where she was staying in San Diego?"

"I told you, I don't think she's still staying there. . . ."

"Have you heard from her since she left San Diego?"

"Well, no—but maybe the nice people she was staying with would have a forwarding address for Elizabeth . . . Let me see if I can find that letter for you . . . Do you mind hanging on? I mean it is long distance, and this must be terribly expensive for you."

"No, please, do see if you can find that letter."

"All right."

As she put down the phone, I could hear Mrs. Short excitedly telling her tenant the good news about Elizabeth winning a beauty contest in Hollywood.

"Heller," Richardson said, "you're doing great."

"Kiss my ass," I said.

"I just might, if you land that address."

Finally Mrs. Short came back on the line, and said, "I found it! Let me just read through this letter, refresh my memory. . . . She was working part-time at a Naval hospital in San Diego, staying with a girl friend named Dorothy French, at the home of the girl's mother, Mrs. Elvera French—in Pacific Beach. I believe that's a suburb of San Diego. Do you have a pencil?"

"Yes," I said, and she read off the address.

I glanced over at Fowley and Richardson. Covering the mouthpiece, I said, "You got your goddamn address."

"Now," Richardson said.

"What?"

"Tell her now."

"What a sweet bastard you are. . . ." Into the phone, I said, "Mrs. Short, I'm afraid I haven't been entirely honest with you. Are you sitting down, ma'am?"

"Why, yes, I am—what is it? Is something wrong?"

"Forgive me for the pretense. I had to make sure I was speaking to the right person . . . that you were in fact Elizabeth Short's mother, the right Elizabeth Short. . . ."

"Something's happened to her, hasn't it?"

"Forgive me—yes. A young woman was killed, probably Tuesday night."

"Oh God . . . oh dear God . . ."

"Her body was found Wednesday morning."

"Do you mean . . . murdered? My Betty was murdered?"

"This young woman, who we believe to be your daughter, was murdered, yes."

"Are you . . . are you sure it's Betty?"

"This girl had black hair, weighed about 115 pounds, was five feet five, a lovely girl with blue-green eyes and a fair complexion."

"That could be a lot of girls in Hollywood, couldn't it? Did this girl have a scar on her back? Elizabeth had a scar on her back from a lung operation—she was sick with pleurisy, when she was small, and had to have a rib removed. If this girl didn't have that, then—"

"I'm sorry, Mrs. Short. She did have such a scar."

"Oh dear . . . oh dear . . ."

She was weeping.

"Mrs. Short, I know there's nothing I can say except that I'm sorry, and I apologize for the deception."

Suddenly Richardson was behind me—I hadn't noticed him move from Fowley's side: it was startling, like a jump cut in a movie.

Clamping his hand over the mouthpiece, Richardson leaned in and whispered harshly into my ear, machine-gunning the words, "Commiserate with the woman—cry along with her—tell her the

*Examiner* feels for her, tell her we'll pay for the funeral, we'll bring her and her daughters out here, all expenses paid. . . ."

"You tell her." I yanked the phone free from him. "Mrs. Short, once again, my sincere apologies—the city editor of the *Examiner* would like to speak with you."

And I handed him the phone, got out of the chair, and gestured for him to sit.

He sat, not missing a beat as he smoothly spoke. "Mrs. Short, this is James Richardson of the Los Angeles *Examiner*—if you will stay on the line, we want to help you in your time of grief . . . please stay on the line. . . . Thank you." Richardson covered the receiver. "Heller, you and Fowley get your asses down to San Diego, toot sweet." To Fowley, who was already getting up, notepad in hand, Richardson said, "Leave your notes with a rewrite man—just take the address. . . . That a good enough lead for the first string, Bill?"

"Not bad," Fowley said, and I followed him out of the editorial chamber as Richardson, in a voice that would have melted butter, soothed and consoled and manipulated Elizabeth Short's mother.

As we walked through the bustling city room, Fowley said, "If Richardson can convince that dame to let him fly her out here, we can keep her away from the cops long enough to wring Christ knows how many leads out of her. The boss is something, isn't he?"

"One of a kind," I said.

Then I excused myself and went into the bathroom and puked up my breakfast.

The outskirts of Los Angeles blended into the bleakness of derrick-flung oil fields, which quickly gave way to vegetable farms and citrus groves. Soon Highway 101 slipped down to the ocean, whose shimmering blue beauty contrasted nicely with the brush-dotted hills of a barren coastline occasionally broken by farming and resort communities.

The morning was sunny yet cool, and the surf-level ride to San Diego—with Fowley behind the wheel of the blue '47 Ford—was pleasant enough, considering the company.

"Some way to spend your honeymoon, huh, Heller?" Fowley said, hat pushed back, cigarette dangling, windows down, wind rushing by.

"Peg knew I was going to do a little work out here," I said.

"Beautiful girl, you lucky bastard. Seems like a nice gal, too. Understanding, is she? About the screwy nature of what you do for a living, I mean?"

"She understands," I said.

She'd even forgiven me, in the middle of the night, when I cuddled in next to her. And I'd forgiven her. We'd even made love again, passionately, desperately, bawling like babies when we climaxed, as might be expected from a pair of newlyweds trying to make up for the wife wanting to abort their child and a husband who'd threatened to kill her.

I'd seen Peggy off early this morning, with some flowers I'd bought at the hotel gift shop, wishing her well on day one of her first Hollywood shoot. No makeup on, turbaned, in a boyish cotton T-shirt and gray slacks, she looked goddamn gorgeous.

"Let's not hurt each other anymore," she suggested.

"It's a deal."

I gave her a big kiss and walked her to the studio-provided limo.

"So, tell me, Nate," Fowley was saying, working his voice above the wind and the staticky sound of Frank Sinatra singing, "The Girl That I Marry"—great guy to be giving marital advice.

"Tell you what, Bill?"

"What does your partner Rubinski think about the A-1 Detective Agency falling into the biggest crime since Papa Hitler's rubber broke?"

I grunted. "Fred thinks we better be in on the *solving* of this crime, if we want the right kind of publicity."

"We'll solve it. Hell, you don't think the cops are gonna beat us to it?"

"No, not the way the *Examiner* is withholding evidence, and doling it out to the cops like a kid's allowance."

"Ah, you're overstating."

"In future I'll strive for the subtlety expected of *Examiner* staffers. Anyway, Harry the Hat knows what he's doing, at least."

"Yeah, the Hat's smart enough to know to look over our shoulders, you mean. But he's the exception." Fowley lighted up a fresh cigarette off the dashboard lighter. "Half the LAPD is in Mickey Cohen's pocket, the other half's in Jack Dragna's. Besides which, these LAPD detectives are the biggest bunch of boobs this side of the Mississippi."

"You may have heard, we have our fair share of bent cops in Chicago."

"Ah, yes, but not idiot bent cops!" Fowley raised an authoritative finger. "There are more unsolved murders in Los Angeles per capita than any other major American city."

"With guys like Finis Brown in the department, I'm not surprised."

Fowley grinned over at me. "Ever hear of Thad Brown?"

"Isn't he Chief of Detectives?"

"That's right—Fat Ass is his brother."

"No! Thad Brown's supposed to be a good, honest cop!"

"That's right, Nate. And his brother is a Mickey Cohen bag man. You figure it. Funny thing is, the uniformed officers in L.A. are pretty fair cops; it's just the detectives that couldn't find their ass with two hands."

"Why is that?"

"Well, take your motorcycle cop for instance. Those cycle jockeys got a rigorous exam to take, tougher than hell. And the department encourages the uniformed boys to take university extension courses, and major in criminal science, really improve their efficiency in police work. That's the rank-and-file . . . but to become a big-shot detective? There's no definitive exam—you just get appointed."

"Based on what?"

Fowley shrugged, both hands on the wheel. "Based on your ability to fit in with the Old Boy network of detectives, the ones that have ongoing deals with bailbondsmen and criminal attorneys. It's the same dicks who are in Cohen's pocket—him or Dragna."

Cohen and Dragna again. Funny Fowley bringing them up. When I'd called my L.A. partner Fred Rubinski at home, last night—to give him the censored version of our agency's involvement with the *Examiner* and the "Werewolf Slaying"—Fred had mentioned the same two notorious names.

"You may be on to something," Fred had told me, "where the wound to that girl's face is concerned. These cops and reporters aren't from Chicago, like us—they don't know how to read the signs."

"Getting slashed ear-to-ear means you're talking too much. How hard is that to read?"

"Well read this, Nate: that vacant lot where this girl was found is only a couple blocks from where Jack Dragna lives."

"What? No shit?"

"None. He's a well-known Leimert Park resident."

Jack Dragna was the so-called "Capone of California." Born Anthony Rozzotti, Dragna had been a typical Prohibition-era mob boss, operating bootlegging, gambling, and prostitution out of L.A.'s Italian ghetto; Nitti had done business with him in the early '40s, when Willie Bioff and George Browne infiltrated the movie unions.

I gathered that Dragna—whom I'd never met—had resented the intrusion of Ben Siegel, a few years before, into the Los Angeles scene. East Coast mob bosses Meyer Lansky and Lucky Luciano had simply foisted Siegel upon Dragna, unapologetically muscling in on the California Godfather's territory; and in recent months—after Ben began focusing his attention on the Flamingo hotel/casino in Las Vegas—Siegel's L.A. rackets interests had been turned over to his former bodyguard, the diminutive, dapper, if somewhat goonish Mickey Cohen.

"Are Cohen and Dragna business partners," I asked Fred, "or business rivals?"

"Yes," Rubinski said. "Rumor has it Dragna is working against Mickey, but it's all *sub rosa* stuff. You know Mickey a little, don't you?"

"A little is right—I remember him from Chicago. And Ben Siegel reintroduced us a few months ago, on Tony Cornero's gambling ship."

"Ah, the late lamented *Lux*," Fred said. "Well, you know Mick is a regular at Sherry's. He's an affable little guy, for a roughneck. He'd be good for you to get to know better."

"I don't mind Mickey Cohen frequenting your restaurant, Fred, but I'm not sure we want him for an A-1 client. We're already trying to collect bad debts for Ben Siegel, and I've got enough p.r. problems over my so-called Capone/Nitti associations."

"Cohen's not that kind of gangster. He's just a bookie."

"Yeah, and hasn't he been bumping off his rival bookies?"

"That's none of my business, Nate. As long as they don't go shooting up Sherry's, what do I care?"

"What does it mean to you, Fred, a woman murdered, wearing the slashed mouth of an informer, being dumped on Dragna's doorstep?"

"Could be Cohen warning Dragna—or maybe Dragna warning Cohen. Plays either way."

"Maybe I do need to talk to Mickey Cohen."

"Nate, I can make that happen."

"Fred, I'll let you know."

Fowley and I had just passed Doheny Park, with its bougainvillea-terraced sea cliffs, when the reporter suddenly began sharing his insights on Elizabeth Short.

"We got the perfect Hollywood story here," Fowley was saying, as Perry Como sang "Prisoner of Love" on the radio. "Small-town girl, beauty contest winner, comes looking for fame . . . gets it the hard way."

"I'm not so sure being a movie star was her goal," I said.

"Are you kidding? You heard her mom—this was a typical movie-struck kid, the time-honored see-her-name-in-lights, stars-in-her-eyes routine."

"Stars and stripes in her eyes, you mean."

"Huh?"

"Elizabeth Short had a thing for men in uniform," I said. "You heard her mom say that, too."

Fowley shrugged. "Yeah, well lots of would-be actresses were Victory Girls, during the war. You were in the service, right, Heller? Marines?"

"Yeah."

"I was in the Coast Guard. Hey, it wasn't the Marines, but we sank two German submarines on two convoys. And even that sorry Coast Guard uniform of mine—why, it was like a license to steal. I got more nookie than a Mormon on his honeymoon."

"Is there a slide show that goes with this?"

"You know what I'm talking about; and these little Victory Girls—like Elizabeth Short—all they had to do was see a uniform, maybe a medal or two, or hear a sad tale about shippin' out tomorrow, and they'd be on their backs, making the 'V' for victory—"

"That's my point, Bill. I think this girl spent more time laying soldiers and sailors than trying to break into the movies. Everybody told her she was pretty enough to be a movie star—but maybe what she really wanted was a husband."

"House, picket fence, passel of kiddies . . . maybe. We can run with that, if the Hollywood angle gets old." He shook his head, grinned goofily. "Reminds me of this Mocambo deal."

"Mocambo deal?"

"Yeah, the robbery at the swanky nightclub. It's what we were playing up, before the Werewolf Slayer came dancing into our boring lives."

"I didn't follow that story. Fill me in." What else did we have to do? We were gliding by the white stucco and red roofs of the Spanish Village–style city of San Clemente.

The heist had gone down a week ago, Monday, January 6. The notion of the glittering Mocambo—a prime haunt of almost every Hollywood star—being victim to an armed robbery summoned images of men with guns rushing in from (and back out into) the night, terrorizing beautiful women in furs and handsome men in tuxedos, lush surroundings echoing with harsh commands.

In reality, the job had taken place in the morning, at 10:30, a "daring daylight robbery" by three armed thieves wearing slouch felt hats and raincoats. The trio had come in the back way, rounded up four employees (three of them women) into a small office, and calmly emptied the safe of $15,000 in cash and another ten grand worth of jewelry. The cash represented the nightclub's weekend receipts, the jewels were part of a display for a Beverly Hills jewelry store. One of the thieves stood six foot four and his face was badly acne scarred, although that description fit none of the four men the cops had recently arrested.

"The ringleader is a guy named Bobby Savarino," Fowley said. "Three other guys got nailed, too—apparently they're part of a pretty active heist string—the cops are looking at them for some bank robberies, too, including one where a teller got shot."

"How did these L.A. cops you're so dismissive of manage to make the arrest?"

"Well, Savarino and his partner, I forget his name, were brought in on some unrelated petty theft charge, and got put into a show-up, where the Mocambo witnesses made 'em."

"This is fascinating, Bill, don't get me wrong—but why do Victory Girls screwing soldier boys remind you of this Mocambo heist?"

Fowley grinned, sitting up, leaning over the wheel. "It's this guy, Savarino—he's half genius, complete idiot. When he was arrested, looking for sympathy, he tells the judge he's a war hero—not just any kind of war hero, but a Congressional Medal of Honor winner."

"Yeah?"

"Yeah! He has documents with him, too—his 'Separation-Qualification Record,' which states he's the most decorated enlisted man in the ETO."

"Has Audie Murphy been informed?"

Fowley snorted a laugh. "Get this—the documents say our armed robber was not only presented with the Congressional Medal by Harry-Ass Truman himself, he also got the Distinguished Service Cross, the Silver Star, the Bronze Star, oh hell, I forget what all."

"And he was a phony?"

"Fourteen karat. Yours truly made a simple phone call to the War Department in D.C. They never heard of the bum."

I laughed. "Well, I hope he got some mileage out of it before you came along and spoiled his fun."

"I should say he did. He's got a curvy little redheaded wife, who bought the story, and when I interviewed him, he started laughing and admitted he had his share of girl friends, too, who liked gettin' close to a bona fide war hero . . . which kinda rubbed me the wrong way."

"Since when are you against a guy getting a dishonest piece of tail?"

"Hell, Nate, even I got more conscience than this guy. I mean, Savarino's wife—she's a doll, and seven, eight months pregnant, to boot—and he's out chasing quim!"

I shrugged. "He's a thief by profession."

Fowley sighed. "The guy does have his balls. Day before yesterday, he tries to trade the cops some info to get his ass out of jail. You shoulda heard the yarn he spun."

"Do tell."

"This crazy fucker claims that several weeks ago he was offered twenty-five hundred bucks to bump off Mickey Cohen."

That snapped me to attention. "What?"

"Yeah, Savarino claims him and his partners turned these guys down . . . I mean, our boy Bobby may be a liar and a thief, but him and his pals ain't no Murder, Inc."

"Are you saying this . . . Savarino wants to trade the cops the names of the guys who wanted Cohen rubbed out for—"

"For consideration or leniency or whatever. Although I understand yesterday he changed his tune, clammed up, getting smart after the fact. I mean, in the first place, if somebody wanted Cohen whacked, it's probably Jack Dragna—and why would a guy like Dragna use smalltime, nonmob guys like Savarino and his boys?"

*Because Dragna was supposed to be working on the same team as Cohen, and having outsiders do the hit might protect him from the wrath of the East Coast Combination—Meyer and Bugsy and Lucky and* their *boys.*

"And in the second place," Fowley was saying, sending his smoked-to-the-butt cigarette sparking out the window, "what sort of idiot would try to trade info on Dragna to the L.A. cops? Don't these clowns know half the badges in this burg are in Dragna's pocket?"

"Maybe they don't. Are they local?"

Fowley gave me a one-shoulder shrug. "They're from back East originally, I guess. But they been out here long enough to get wise, surely."

"Maybe you're right—maybe he's just an idiot."

"Hey, Savarino's a cocky, good-lookin' guy—take a look at him—he's in the-day-before-yesterday's paper . . . check the morgue, if you're interested."

The morgue Fowley was referring to was not in the basement of the Hall of Justice, rather his own backseat, where he kept a stack of recent *Examiner*s as a sort of traveling reference file for ongoing stories.

Soon I was thumbing through the January 14 edition, where (on page three, lined against a Central Station wall) tall, dark, cleft-chin handsome Bobby Savarino grinned smugly at me, a study in underworld black: black shirt under a black sport-jacket, black trousers, black curly hair, black glittering eyes. Next to Savarino was his accomplice, a little guy in a rumpled light-color sportcoat and a dark wrinkled tie loose around an askew collar: Henry Hassau, who looked like an Arab camel trader yanked out of his tent in the middle of the night, his dark eyes startled in a narrow, sharp-cheekboned hook-nosed face set off with just the right trashy touch of wispy mustache and scraggly goatee.

"From the looks of him," I said, tapping Bobby's matinee-idol countenance, "Savarino shouldn't need to play war hero to get laid."

"Yeah, he's got the tools, all right, but he's greedy, a regular ass bandit. Reminds me of a guy I knew in the Coast Guard—son of a bitch was hung like a . . ."

And as chatterbox Fowley changed the subject (if not the subject matter), and Dinah Shore sang "Shoofly Pie and Apple Pan Dowdy" on the radio, I tuned them both out.

I was busy reading between the lines of an *Examiner* story (BOOKIE DEATH OFFER BARED) that indicated self-styled lover-boy war hero Bobby Savarino had been threatening mob boss Jack Dragna on Tuesday . . .

. . . knowing, as I did, that on Wednesday, the very next day, a beautiful woman would be found murdered in a vacant lot, a few blocks from Dragna's house—wearing the mark of the informer.

# 9

Pacific Beach—a tiny farming and resort suburb just north of San Diego—was home to the Bayview Terrace Navy housing project, a sea of anonymous tract prefabs assembled during the war for shipyard workers and their families. The best you could say for the premeditated neighborhood was that its lawns were as green as they were flat, and that the little white crackerboxes—like the one at 2750 Camino Pradero, where Mrs. Elvera French resided—appeared sturdier than cardboard.

Fowley rang the bell; as we stood on the small cement stoop, we could hear the barely muffled roar of a vacuum sweeper. A second ring of the bell was only drowned out by the continuing Hoovering, so I stepped forward and rapped on the door several times, hard enough to be heard, I hoped, but not so hard as to knock the place over.

The vacuuming ceased, and the door opened; through the screen we saw a slender honey-blonde woman of perhaps forty-five in a white cotton blouse and blue denim pedal pushers, her medium-length hair ponytailed back. Though she wore no make-up, she was attractive, even though she was frowning at us—blue-eyed, apple-cheeked, brow flecked with sweat.

"Didn't you gentlemen see the sign?" she asked, pointing to a handlettered NO SOLICITORS card stuck in the wood frame of the screen.

"We're not selling anything, ma'am," Fowley said. "We're from the Los Angeles *Examiner*."

"Oh!" Now her frown turned thoughtful. "And I don't suppose this is about a subscription, either . . . It's about the Short girl?"

"Yes, it is. My name's Fowley and this is Mr. Heller."

She sighed sadly, shook her head. "Come in, gentlemen, come in, please."

She opened the door for us, and we were immediately in a small, tidy living room. Moving the vacuum cleaner out of the way, she gestured to the rose-color, nubby-upholstered sectional sofa and seated herself in a nearby matching chair. The furnishings were as blonde as she was, and as starkly modern as the cream plaster walls.

"Dorothy and I thought the description in the paper fit Beth," she said, still shaking her head, hands on her knees. "Dorothy's my daughter. . . .We thought somebody would show up sooner or later, but frankly, I expected it to be the police."

Fowley nodded. "You will be hearing from the police, soon, Mrs. French—the *Examiner* and the L.A. homicide squad are hand in hand, working together to find the maniac responsible, as soon as possible."

"Anything I can do to help in that effort, anything. Either of you fellas have a cigarette?"

Fowley rose, shook a Camel out of its deck, and she plucked it out, Fowley firing it up for her, and depositing the waved-out match in a geometric glass ashtray on the blonde endtable.

Sighing smoke, she said, "You're lucky to have caught me—this is my day off. I'm a widow. My husband died in the war, and we get a small government check, but it's not enough. I work at the Naval hospital, clerical. . . . Our days off float, you see."

"Yes," Fowley said. "I understand Beth Short worked at the Naval hospital, too."

Mrs. French laughed, then caught herself. "I'm sorry. . . . I'll tell you right now, I have no intention of speaking ill of the dead—I liked Beth, for all her faults. But I wouldn't be surprised if that girl never worked a day in her life."

"She wrote her mother that she was working at the hospital."

Mrs. French laughed again, smoke trailing out her nostrils. "That wouldn't surprise me, either. You see, my daughter is an even softer touch than I am—and I'm plenty soft—but we invited that girl in off the streets, just to spend the night. That 'night' was a month long."

Fowley had his notepad out and was scribbling furiously.

In early December, Beth Short had turned up at the Aztec Theater, where Mrs. French's daughter, Dorothy, worked as an usherette and cashier.

"Dorothy felt sorry for the girl," Mrs. French said. "The Aztec, until recently, was an all-night theater . . . you know, the kind of place you can duck into and find a spot to sleep for the night, for the price of a movie ticket? Dorothy could tell the poor kid needed a place to stay . . . and Beth looked so pretty, and she had the air of somebody who'd been successful, but was down on her luck."

Fowley nodded. "How did you react when your daughter brought home a stranger?"

"I didn't think much of it. What with the housing shortage, so many girls losing their jobs to returning servicemen, prices going sky high . . . and us lucky enough to live in a rent-controlled house . . . why shouldn't we help a nice girl get back on her feet?"

"And that's how one night turned into a month."

"More or less. The story was Beth had missed her ride and was kind of stranded, and would just 'camp out' on our couch for the night. That first night I sat and drank coffee with the girl and made her a sandwich and gathered quickly that she was hungry and homeless and broke. She looked so pale, and she coughed, like she had some kind of congestion. Like I said, I guess I'm a soft touch myself, and when it turned out she'd lost her husband—Major Matt something, died in a plane crash, in India—I guess I kind of identified with her."

"You invited her to stay for a few days."

"Yes . . . my son, Cory—he's thirteen. I think had a kind of a crush on Beth—she sweet-talked him, after school, to take the bus down to the Greyhound station and pick up her suitcases. Cory said her bags were so heavy they mighta been filled with rocks . . . but it was clothing, expensive clothing too, silk, satin, all those exotic black outfits she wore."

I said, "I guess once you saw her moving in her suitcases, you figured your overnight guest was planning to stay awhile."

Mrs. French nodded, smirking just a little, drawing on the Camel; she exhaled as she said, "Beth assured me she wouldn't stay longer than a day or so, just until some money she had wired somebody for had arrived. And she said she'd pay us for our inconvenience. . . . Of course I said, 'Don't be silly—you're our guest, our welcome guest.' Welcome was right."

When Mrs. French came home for lunch on the second day of Beth's stay, she found the girl still asleep on the couch, with the living room turned into a virtual showroom of fancy clothing and underthings—including black lacy lingerie and black silk stockings.

"There was a strong, sickly sweet scent everywhere, from her perfume—as if she covered not just herself but her clothing in the stuff. She woke, when I came in, and she apologized for sleeping so late—she'd been out till two in the morning, the night before, she explained, a date with her prospective employer . . . supposedly she had applied for a job at Western Airlines."

The late nights, followed by sleeping till noon, became a pattern for their houseguest. Every night, it seemed, Beth was out with a different man—"For a poor lost soul, this girl had gathered quite the circle of admirers!"—and the following morning, she would sleep till noon, then lounge through the afternoon in her black satiny pajamas and/or a black Chinese flower-and-dragon-bedecked robe, sipping coffee, raiding the icebox, writing letters, reading magazines, fiddling with her clothes, laying them out and looking at them, occasionally ironing them, putting on her makeup, painting her toenails red.

"I asked her to dress a little less casually when my son was in the house," Mrs. French said. "Cory's at that impressionable age—a beautiful half-naked girl wandering about the house, flaunting herself in front of a teenage boy, well . . . it's hardly ideal."

Unless you were a teenage boy. Hardly.

"She turned my living room into her bedroom," Mrs. French said, shaking her head. "Then Beth tried to sweet-talk Cory into giving her *his* bedroom, suggesting he sleep on the couch, which he was more than willing to do . . . but I forbade that—things would've never got back to normal! That girl was treating my son like a damn coolie—pardon my French—sending him out after scented stationery and movie magazines and, excuse me, sanitary napkins. My son!"

"If you don't mind my asking," I said, "why didn't you just throw her out on her pretty behind?"

She sighed more smoke. "Beth and Dorothy had become good friends, and Cory just loved her; she did these imitations of stars on the radio that made him laugh . . ."

Plus she walked around half-naked.

". . . and me, well, the two of us would sit at the kitchen table and talk about our husbands who'd died in the war. She still loved her pilot, she said, so much so that it had kept her from falling in love again, no matter how many men she dated. She said if 'fate had been kinder' she might be living with her major in a little house somewhere, right now . . . a nice little house like ours."

"She never did get a job?" Fowley asked.

"No, not at the Naval hospital or that airline office or anywhere else—she took a certain number of interviews, or at least pretended to. But that's all. I started to get fed up, toward Christmas— I mean, here I am, tiptoeing around my own house, getting ready for work, not wanting to wake this lazy girl, who should have been up and dressed and out looking for her own job. I mean, particularly when you consider how badly she said she needed money."

"Considering the low overhead," Fowley said, "what did she need money for?"

"She didn't say—just that she needed to save up for 'something special.' "

Like an abortion. Going rate, in Hollywood—for a first-rate rabbit-puller, anyway—was five hundred bucks.

"All I know is," Mrs. French was saying, "Beth never said no to somebody else paying her way, and while she was with us, she kept wiring people, boy friends and family, for money. She got a one hundred dollar money order from one of her servicemen boy friends, right before Christmas, and another twenty-five dollars from some actress friend in Hollywood."

Fowley asked, "And she didn't spend any of this money, that you know of?"

"No—she hoarded her cash. Well, she did give us small presents at Christmas—trinkets to 'repay our kindness.' Dorothy thought Beth might have been saving for some special wardrobe for her screen test."

"What screen test is that?"

"Oh, probably *no* screen test. She was full of big Hollywood talk, how when the strikes were over she'd go back and move from 'bit parts' into bigger, better movie roles. She claimed a Hollywood celebrity had promised to help her—some famous director."

Fowley sat forward, perked by this concept. "She didn't mention anybody by name?"

"No—well, maybe. She referred to this celebrity as 'George,' or 'Georgie,' a few times."

"Again," I said, "why didn't you just ask her to leave?"

Her eyebrows hiked. "You can't tell someone to go away, once you've asked them to stay! Finally I gave her the address of a temporary employment agency, and she said she'd call them, but I told her it would be better to apply in person . . . Eventually she got dressed and went out, but she looked more like she was going out on a date, in gloves and a hat with a veil. That was one of the few times she went anywhere by herself, and not with Dorothy, or one of those men of hers. It was almost like she was afraid to leave the house, alone."

"Afraid?" I asked "Really afraid?"

Mrs. French nodded. "I didn't think much of it at the time, but now . . . now that she's suffered this awful fate . . . it does seem to me Beth was . . . skittish. Whenever anyone came to the door, she'd act . . . nervous."

"Nervous?"

"Frightened—she didn't say anything very specific, for as much as we talked about her late husband and her Hollywood aspirations and all, Beth could be . . . secretive. Always polite, but private. I did ask her what she was frightened of, and she said there were a lot of crazy, dangerous people in 'Tinsel Town.' As an example, she told me about a woman chasing her down Hollywood Boulevard, threatening her life."

Fowley asked, "When was this?"

"Right before she came down to San Diego, I gathered. Oh yes, and she made reference to having an 'Italian boy friend,' who she seemed . . . if not afraid of, wary of. I even wondered if maybe she hadn't come down to San Diego to get away from him, even to hide out."

I asked, "Did she mention this Italian boy friend's name?"

"No. But there was this one unusual incident—right before she left." She blew out some smoke, gathering her thoughts. "A tan coupe pulled up outside our house, and two men and a woman came up to the door, and knocked, and waited. Beth peeked out the front window at them, careful not to be seen. They knocked again, and—waking me, I'd been napping—I stumbled out of my bedroom and over to answer the door, but Beth stopped me, wild eyed, and shaking her head, no, no, no."

I asked, "Did you get a look at these people?"

"Not a good one. One of the men was taller than the other one—they were in topcoats, what-do-you-call-them, trenchcoats, with hats snugged down. Like gangsters in a movie. The woman was a blonde—I barely glimpsed her, but she was in a fur coat and seemed to have a nice figure, but her face was kind of hard looking."

"How old were these people?"

"Late twenties, early thirties. I didn't get a good look, to be honest—I could never identify them, except maybe the woman. Anyway, when they didn't get an answer to their knocking, they ran back to their car . . . Isn't that strange? Ran back to their coupe and squealed off."

"Did Beth say who they were?"

"No—she was terribly upset, and refused to talk about them."

"When was this?" Fowley asked. "Can you give us even an approximate date?"

"Oh, I remember exactly. It was the day before she left—that would make it January seventh. You see, finally I just got fed up and asked her to leave—as you can see, our place is small, and I said to her it was just getting too crowded."

"How did she take it?"

"Graciously, I must say. And, actually, to be fair—she did give me a gift before she left. Would you like to see it?"

"Sure."

The slender housewife arose, leaving her mostly smoked Camel in the glass ashtray, and went to a closet near the front door. From a shelf above the hangers she plucked a hat—as she stretched for it, the denim pedal pushers were nicely tight across her firm fanny. She walked over and displayed the hat to us.

"It's a Leo Joseph number," she said. "I'd admired it, and Beth gave it to me, as a way of thanking me for letting her stay. You see, she used to work as a hat model in Chicago."

Fowley perked again. "Chicago?"

Oh shit.

"Yes, she'd been there in the fall, I believe. So that's one job, at least, that she held. Oh, and you'll want the name of the man she left here with."

Fowley might have been goosed, he sat up so straight. "What? Yes!"

"Do you have another cigarette, Mr. Fowley?" she asked, as she sat, crossing her legs. She was, in her quiet way, a real dish. Her husband had been a lucky man—except for the part where he died in the war.

Of the blur of men Beth had dated, while she stayed with them, only one had been a "repeat admirer," as Mrs. French put it.

His name was Robert "Red" Manley, and he'd been to the Frenches' home picking Beth up, several times; he worked at Western Airlines (he said) and had met Beth when she applied for that job she didn't get. They had dated every night for about a week, in mid-December; then, when Mrs. French had informed Beth her stay at the little house on Camino Pradero was drawing to close, he had come around to pick her up in the late afternoon.

I asked, "And you remember the date?"

"It was a red-letter day around here, the day I got my living room back—January eighth. He picked her up at six p.m., loaded her two suitcases and a hatbox in his light-colored coupe."

"What does this Red Manley look like?"

"Kind of cute—lanky, red-haired as you might guess . . . little jug-eared, maybe. Maybe twenty-five. Sharp dresser—he was wearing a brown pin-striped suit when he picked Beth up."

Fowley asked, "What was she wearing when she left?"

"What she called her 'traveling clothes'—a black collarless suit, nicely tailored, a white frilly blouse and white gloves . . . oh, and she had a black clutch purse and black suede shoes and, of course, seamed black stockings. Beige camel's-hair coat over her arm. . . . Is there anything else I can tell you?"

Mrs. Elvera French had told us plenty. Fowley asked if we could take her picture, and she consented, if we would wait for her to put on some makeup.

"Frankly," I said, "you look like a million bucks without it."

"Give me two minutes," she said, with a tiny smile, "and I'll give you an extra million."

So I took her photo in the kitchen, at the table where she had so often shared coffee and sandwiches with her houseguest.

"We'd like to talk to your daughter," Fowley said, as we were heading out, "if we could."

"She's working," Mrs. French said, "but I'm sure she could spare a few minutes. . . ."

The Aztec Theater was a second-run house on Fifth Street in San Diego; the Mission-style building, with its Mexi-Moderne touches, must have been the cat's meow in 1924. The marquee boasted an Alan Ladd double bill: *O.S.S.* and *Blue Dahlia*, two pictures I'd managed to miss first time around.

Dorothy French—trimly shapely in her red bolero jacket, white blouse, and blue slacks with a red stripe down the side—was working the concession counter. She was a pert, pretty blonde in her early twenties, very much the image of her mother, perhaps even prettier, her eyes bigger and lighter blue, her lips more full and brightly red-lipsticked. Her hair was a well-organized tumble of curls set off by a little red usherette's hat, more suitable for an organ grinder's monkey than a doll like her.

It was midafternoon and halfway through one of the features, and the half hour we spent talking to Dorothy was uninterrupted by any patron. Throughout our conversation, she leaned casually against the glass top of the display case of candy bars, and chewed (and occasionally snapped) her gum; nonetheless, she answered our questions solemnly, giving the tragic death of her friend the grave respect it deserved.

She had been expecting us: her mother had called ahead.

"I don't know if I'll have much to add to what my mother told you," she said.

When the Aztec's houselights had come on, at 3 A.M. on the morning of December 9, Dorothy had found the black-haired sleeping beauty in one of the theater's threadbare seats. Confused when Dorothy awoke her, Beth Short had stuttered that the sign outside said the moviehouse was open all night.

"We'd just had a change of management," Dorothy said, "and the sign hadn't been painted over, yet. I apologized, and Beth said that was all right, and started coughing. I got her a paper cup of water and we began talking, and she told me how she'd come from Hollywood and was supposed to meet a friend, but they hadn't connected up . . . and she was really in a jam, starting with, she was out of money."

"Did she hit you up?" Fowley asked.

"No." White teeth flashed as she chewed her gum. "She did say she'd been an usherette and a cashier, in moviehouses back east, and wondered if we needed any temporary help here at the Aztec. Funny thing is, later, after she'd been staying with us a few days, I tried to get the manager to hire Beth . . . and that's a funny one in and of itself."

"What is?"

"She came by for a job interview and ended up going out on a date."

Fowley frowned. "With the theater manager?"

"Yes. They went out on a couple of dates, and Beth claimed he'd gotten fresh, and refused to hire her because he was in love with her and didn't want other men looking at her!"

I asked, "Do you think that's true?"

"It's probably malarkey, but I'm not positive. Not that it would be hard imagining Beth making a boy friend jealous."

"Why do you say that?"

"Beth was a beautiful girl." Dorothy said this wistfully, as if longing to be that beautiful herself, seemingly unaware of her own comeliness. "When we'd ride the bus together, guys would just sit and stare at her. She had a sort of . . . glamour quality she radiated, partly the way she dressed, partly the way she was always all made up, and how she kind of . . . preened. Guys were always trying to date her."

Fowley asked, "How close did you and Beth get?"

"We were friends. She would kind of swing between being very talkative, and gay, with her Hollywood stories, and melancholy, in a sort of—I don't know, calculated way—when she was talking about her war-hero husband dying, especially. Like she was in a movie, acting. Other times, she'd be real quiet. There was a sadness about her, like deep down she was somebody with nobody to turn to."

Dorothy had been impressed with Beth's expensive, elegant wardrobe.

"She had these sweaters with such delicate embroidery work, tiny loops and circles around sequins and beads and pearls. She'd dress up for dates and twirl for me, saying, 'What do you think?' What I thought was, I could never wear clothes like that . . . but she sure could."

Fowley said, "Your mother mentioned a screen test. . . ."

"Yes. She was looking forward to that. Some big director."

"But she never mentioned a name?"

"No. I don't know if there *was* a name to mention. All of this Hollywood talk, I don't know if there was really anything to it—she'd go on and on, like she was trying to believe it herself, like if she said it enough times, it would be true."

I asked, "You don't think she really worked in the movies—that it was just a pipe dream?"

Her brow furrowed. "You know, I'm not convinced she really cared about Hollywood. For all her movie talk, what really seemed to matter to her was finding the right man . . . *That* was her dream, far as I'm concerned. You know what she said to me once? 'If I could only find some handsome Army officer, or sailor, or Marine, or airman, who would love me like I know I could love him . . . then tomorrow could be something wonderful.' "

Fowley smirked. "That sounds like acting, too."

"No—it was how she really felt." Chewing her gum, Dorothy gazed dreamily at nothing. "You could see it in her eyes. Those beautiful blue eyes."

This was coming from a girl with eyes as blue as a summer sky.

Dorothy smiled—the first time since we'd begun talking about her late friend—and it was a bittersweet smile, at that.

"Funny, isn't it?" she said, snapping her gum. "Funny coincidence, I mean."

"What is?" I asked.

"You coming to talk to me when *The Blue Dahlia* is playing."

"Why's that?"

She blinked, batting long lashes. "Don't you know? Maybe you haven't heard . . . I guess maybe Mother didn't know, or didn't think it was important enough to mention."

"What?" Fowley asked.

"Beth had this nickname, some guys in Long Beach gave it to her, she said, 'cause of her black hair and lacy black dresses, and 'cause she was . . . this is so silly . . . in 'full bloom.' And, anyway, *The Blue Dahlia* was playing at the moviehouse around the corner from the drugstore where these guys and Beth hung out, so it was a takeoff on that."

"What was?" I asked.

She batted her eyelashes again. "Her nickname—'The Black Dahlia.' "

Fowley looked at me and I looked at him. Then Fowley jotted that down in his notepad. I had a strong suspicion the days of "The Werewolf Slayer" tagline had just ended.

"The only other thing I can think of," Dorothy said, "is her memory books."

"Memory books," I said. "Scrapbooks, you mean? Or diaries . . . ?"

The usherette shrugged and her blonde curls bounced. "I dunno for sure—I never saw them. Beth just said, one day, she was sorry she'd left them behind, her memory books, wishing she could show us pictures of her late husband, and maybe paste in a few new pics of Mom and me."

Fowley pressed. "Left them behind where, did she say?"

"In her trunk."

"Did she say who she left it with—a friend, maybe?"

"It was in storage."

"She say where in storage?"

"Los Angeles—the American Express office."

If a trunk had been sitting awhile, unclaimed, it might be in a nonpayment warehouse by now. That should be easily tracked. I wondered if Beth Short's "memory books" had any entries about a private detective she'd met in Chicago.

"What can you tell us about Robert 'Red' Manley?" Fowley asked.

"Not much," she said, shaking her head, chewing her gum dejectedly. "I really wish I had something more to tell you. Oh, I do know the name of the motel where Red took Beth, after he helped her move out of our place."

My mouth dropped open, and two words managed to tumble out: "The motel?"

"Yes, where he and Beth stayed, the night before he drove her to Los Angeles." Lashes batted; gum snapped. "Would that help?"

# 10

Maybe Red Manley was new at cheating on his wife. Or maybe he needed a receipt, to make a claim against an expense account. Or maybe he was just a goddamn idiot.

Whatever the reason, Robert Manley had broken the first rule of philandering: on the evening of January eighth, at the Pacific Beach Motor Camp, he had signed his own name on the motel register; and so, incredibly enough, had his companion for the night, Elizabeth Short. Manley's address was listed—8010 Mountain View Avenue, Huntington Park—as was his automobile license number.

Elizabeth Short had given only "Chicago" as her address. The lack of anything further—say, the St. Clair Hotel, or the A-1 Detective Agency—was small consolation.

"Chicago again," Fowley said, as we looked at the register at the motel check-in counter. He grinned at me wolfishly. "Sure this 'Dahlia' dame ain't some old girl friend of yours?"

"You never know," I said, and grinned back at him, back of my neck prickling.

Huntington Park was five miles south of downtown Los Angeles, in the midst of an industrial district, and while Mountain View Avenue may not have lived up to the scenic promise of its name, the quiet residential street was a sizable step up from the tract housing of Bayview Terrace. At dusk, bathed in the dying sunlight Hollywood moviemakers called "magic hour," the little Manley home seemed California idyllic: a modest green-tile-roofed pale yellow stucco in the Spanish-Colonial style with a well-tended lawn, a cobblestone walk bordered by brightly flowering bushes, and thorny shrubs that hugged the house like prickly bodyguards.

Fowley rang the bell, and—almost supernaturally fast—the door opened and a lovely young woman was standing there, raising a "shush" finger, the fingernail painted the same candy-apple red as the lipstick glistening on her full red lips. She was a honey-blonde with a heart-shaped face, big blue eyes, upturned nose, peaches-and-cream complexion and a trim, shapely figure wrapped up in a red-striped white seersucker sundress that left her smooth shoulders bare.

"Please be quiet," she said, her voice hushed. "My baby's sleeping." I glanced at Fowley and he glanced at me—we each knew what the other was thinking: what kind of lunatic runs around on a dish like this?

"Sorry, ma'am," Fowley said, almost whispering. He held up a badge—an honorary deputy's badge the L.A. County Sheriff issued to certain reporters, which those reporters often used to imply they were law enforcement officers. "Are you Mrs. Robert Manley?"

After barely glancing at the badge, the big blue eyes blinked at us. She must have been about twenty-two, a kid herself—her pretty face still had a pleasing baby-fat plumpness.

"Yes, I am," she said, alarm swimming in those big blue eyes.

I said, "Is your husband home, Mrs. Manley?"

"No, he isn't. He's in San Francisco on business—he's a traveling salesman. In hardware."

There was a joke in there somewhere, and it wouldn't have taken much looking to find it, but I didn't bother.

"Could we ask you a few questions, ma'am?" Fowley asked. "Would it be possible for us to step inside?"

Her eyebrows tightened and a vertical line formed between them, a single crease in an otherwise perfectly smooth face. "This is about that girl Robert picked up, isn't it?"

Again, Fowley and I glanced at each other.

Nodding, I said, "Her name was Elizabeth Short."

"I know," Mrs. Manley said wearily. "I read the papers. . . .Why don't we sit in the kitchen? I have some coffee made. Just please be quiet—Robert, Jr., is sleeping, and believe me, you don't want to wake him."

She led the way through the sparsely but nicely appointed bungalow, venetian blinds throwing slashes of shadow across gleaming hardwood floors. A playpen scattered with stuffed toys sat amid a wine-colored angora mohair living room suite, and vaguely Spanish, mahogany-veneer furnishings—everything looked new, suggesting a young couple buying on the installment plan.

The kitchen was a compact, streamlined affair of white and two tones of blue; a scattering of the latest appliances lined the countertops, as did baby bottles. Another baby bottle warmed in a pan on the gas range, and a red telephone on the wall was like a splash of blood against the white tile. We sat at a white-trimmed blue plastic-and-chrome dinette set and sipped the coffee she provided.

"My name is Fowley," the reporter said, his notepad out, "and this is Mr. Heller."

"I'm Harriet Manley," she said, sipping her coffee, her eyes wide and rather glazed—and, I noticed, slightly bloodshot. She had a lovely speaking voice, a warm alto, but—right now at least—her inflections were negligible, emotionless. "Bob is due home tonight. He and his boss, Mr. Palmer, are on their way back right now, from San Francisco. . . . Did I say that already? I'm sorry."

"Mrs. Manley," Fowley asked, "what do you know about your husband and Elizabeth Short?"

"Bob phoned me from San Francisco this morning," she said, in that same near-monotone. "He saw the story in the papers up there, and said he recognized the girl's picture. Of course, I'd read about the, uh . . . read about it myself—it's all over the front page."

Fowley gave me a look that indicated he would take the notes, and I should ask the questions.

So I asked one: "What did Bob say about this girl?"

She was staring into her coffee. "He had given her a ride back from San Diego—just as a favor, he said. Nothing between them."

"I see. And what did you say to this?"

"I'm . . . I'm ashamed to tell you."

"Please."

". . . I asked him if he'd done it."

"Done it?"

"If he'd killed that girl."

"And what did he say?"

"He said, 'Of course not, honey. Whatever made you think I did?' "

I searched for sarcasm in her tone but couldn't find any. "And what did you say to that?"

She looked at me; it was like staring into the glass eyes of a doll. "Do I have to answer?"

"Of course not."

Now her gaze returned to her coffee; her lips were trembling, just a little. "I said . . . because of your nervous trouble."

"What nervous trouble was that?"

"Bob . . . Bob was discharged from the Army. What you call a 'Section Eight.' "

I knew what that was, all right.

"Was he in combat?" Fowley asked, looking up from his notepad. "Did he have battlefield trauma—"

She was shaking her head. "No, not exactly. He was *near* combat, when he was overseas, on USO tours."

Frowning, I asked, "USO tours?"

"Bob's a musician—he was in the Army Air Corps band. Saxophone."

"Really. Does he still work as a musician?"

"Sometimes. He's in the union. He gets a call for a weekend job now and then: bars and nightclubs."

So this guy was a traveling salesman and a weekend musician who played in bars. That a guy in those twin trades might pick up a little poontang here and there might come as no shock—unless you were, as I was, seated across from the striking beauty he was married to.

I asked, "What did your husband say when he called you from San Francisco?"

The full lips twitched in a nonsmile. "He said he figured the police would be around, sooner or later, and he didn't want me hearing about this from anybody but him. I suggested he go talk to the authorities himself. I figured that would . . . look better."

"You're right," I said. "What did your husband say to that?"

"He said he didn't want to go looking for trouble. He had accounts to call on, and he was with his boss, and it would just be too embarrassing. . . . He represents a pipe and clamp company, you know."

Another easy joke to be found, had I been in the mood.

I asked, "How long have you and Bob been married?"

"Fifteen months. Robert, Jr., is four months old."

Robert, Sr., was a hell of a guy.

"The day your husband drove back from San Diego with his passenger," I said, tactfully, "that was last Thursday, just a week ago. Would you happen to remember what time he got home that night?"

She was already nodding. "He made it home for supper—probably six-thirty. We had some friends over, for bridge that evening—neighbors. I can give your their names."

"Please," Fowley said.

"Mr. and Mrs. Don Holmes," she said, rather formally, and gave the particulars as the reporter scribbled.

Then I asked, "What about the next several days?"

"Bob was at home every day, working, calling buyers on the phone, until he left for San Francisco with Mr. Palmer—that was on Monday."

If that were true, Manley had been out of town when the murder was most likely committed.

The phone's shrill ring jolted all three of us. Harriet Manley was up like a shot, probably to make sure the thing didn't jangle again and wake her baby.

"Hello," she said.

Then her eyes tightened, and immediately softened.

"Hello, baby," she said.

Fowley and I looked at each other: her other baby.

Covering the mouthpiece, eyes huge, the pretty housewife whispered, "It's Bob . . . Do you want to talk to him?"

Shaking his head, Fowley patted the air, whispered back, "Better not tell him we're here."

Though her voice remained calm, her eyes danced; she obviously was torn, wondering whether to warn him.

"No, I'm fine. . . . I love you, too. . . . I believe you. . . . I believe you. . . . I believe you. . . . I know you do. . . . I know you do. . . . I do, too. . . . I miss you too. . . . 'Bye."

Hanging up the phone, she said, "He was calling from a pay phone, at a diner. He said he should be home by ten or eleven tonight. . . . He has to stop at his boss' place first. That's where he left our car, before he and Mr. Palmer drove up to San Francisco."

I asked, "Where does Mr. Palmer live?"

She was leaning against the counter, near the baby bottles. "Eagle Rock. I can give you the address, if you'd rather . . . rather pick him up there. Instead of here."

"Would you like that, Mrs. Manley?"

"I think so."

"Did Bob say anything else?"

"Yes. He said he loved me more than any man ever loved a wife."

Her lip was quivering and I thought she might break down; but she did not. I believe she had made a decision that she would maintain her dignity in front of us.

Rising from the little plastic-and-chrome table, Fowley asked, "Would you happen to have any recent photos of your husband that we could borrow? For identification purposes?"

And publication purposes.

"We just had some taken," she said, "by a professional photographer. . . . If you'll wait here . . ."

She exited the kitchen and returned moments later with a triple frame, from which she removed a grinning photo of her husband, a young, handsome if jug-eared fellow. "Do you want these, as well?" She indicated the other two photos—one of herself and Robert, beaming at each other, and another of the family with Robert, Jr., in his mother's arms, mom and dad looking adoringly at junior.

Fowley said, "If you don't mind."

"Take them."

I took them from her. Harriet Manley looked radiant in the photos, which were beautifully shot.

"We would appreciate it," Fowley said, as we headed out through the living room, "if you didn't talk to anyone else about this, especially if newspaper reporters should start coming around."

"Oh, I won't talk to any reporters," she said.

Fowley, having no shame, stayed at it. "And if your husband calls back—"

"I won't say anything. I know he has to . . . face up to this."

"If he's innocent—"

"He didn't kill that girl, Detective Fowley. But he's not 'innocent,' is he?"

"Are you going to stand by him?"

We were at the door, now.

"I'll have to think about that. We have a son, after all, and I do love my husband very much. Bob has his flaws, his problems, but I never thought he was . . . stepping out on me. I never imagined—"

I said, "You don't have to go on."

Harriet Manley swallowed, her big blue eyes hooded. "Terrible . . . terrible."

"Yes."

"What happened to that poor girl, I mean."

"Right."

"She was . . . very pretty, wasn't she?"

"Elizabeth Short? Yes. But if you don't mind my saying so, not compared to you. Not nearly as beautiful."

She managed a slight smile. "You're kind, Mr. Heller."

"Hardly. It's the truth. Your husband's a damn fool."

"I know . . . I know. But I still love him, anyway."

On the way down the cobblestone walk, "Detective" Fowley said, "Jesus Christ, she's gonna forgive the bastard! What a woman. . . . Where do I go to find a dame like that?"

I glanced back—it was after dark now, and the beautiful mother of Robert Manley's son was watching us go, haloed in the doorway of the precious little bungalow on Mountain View Avenue. Red Manley had everything any man could ever hope for, and—whether a murderer or not—had risked it all for a piece of tail.

Then she disappeared, and I could hear the muffled sound of crying—Robert, Jr.'s. I had a hunch he wouldn't be crying alone.

With Manley due back in town around ten tonight, we took time to grab burgers at a greasy spoon on Colorado Boulevard.

"Well, even if Red Manley isn't our murderer," Fowley said, dragging a french fry through a river of ketchup, "he's how Elizabeth Short got from San Diego to L.A."

"*Six days* before her body was found," I reminded the reporter, across from him in a booth.

"Yeah," he said, chewing the fry, "but once we know where Bob dropped her off, we'll know where to pick up her trail. And, anyway, who's to say his alibis are gonna hold up? Maybe the little woman's covering for him, and after she has time to stew over hubby straying, she'll change her story."

I nibbled at my cheeseburger. "If Red and his boss were in San Francisco when the coroner says Elizabeth Short was killed, then Manley's biggest problem is going to be holding his marriage together."

Fowley shook his head. "I can't wait to see this sap. I'd kill the Pope in the May Company window for a night with that wife of his."

"Not if I got my hands on the wop, first," I said.

The Eagle Rock district was high on the foothills between Glendale and Pasadena. Manley's boss, Mr. Palmer, lived on Mount Royal Drive, another quiet, if more exclusive residential street, in another Spanish-Colonial number, only this was no bungalow. The glow of a streetlamp mingled with the ivory wash of moonlight to illuminate the sprawl of red-tile-roofed, off-white stucco, a patio to one side, a two-car garage under the main floor, the rest of the house spilling up an elaborately landscaped slope with palm trees, century plants, and cacti. Lights were on in the place, a few anyway.

The night was chilly, almost cold. We left the '47 Ford at the curb, across the street and down a ways, and Fowley peeked in the garage windows while I climbed the curving cobblestone path to the front door.

A heavyset Mexican maid in a pale green uniform answered my knock. I asked her if Mr. Palmer was home, and she said Mr. Palmer was not, but that Mrs. Palmer was. I said my business was with Mr. Palmer, excused myself, and walked back down the path.

"Only car in the garage is Manley's," Fowley reported. "Same license number he gave at the motel—a light tan Studebaker, prewar model."

"Palmer isn't home yet. His wife is, but I ducked her."

"Okay, then—we wait."

We waited, sitting in the Ford with the windows down while Fowley smoked one Camel after another. After a while, I got the old urge and smoked a couple, myself—I think it was right after Fowley said he was going to advise Richardson to call the *Herald-American*, Hearst's Chicago paper, and get a crew out there sniffing around after the Short girl.

"Maybe we oughta send you, Heller," Fowley said.

"What, and interrupt my honeymoon?"

Now and then headlights swept across us, as the occasional car made its way up quiet Mount Royal Drive—little or no through traffic, just neighborhood residents. Just after ten, a pair of powerful highbeams blinded us, as a big automobile swung into the driveway, the headlights flooding the red garage door.

We got out just as the driver—a tall, horse-faced man in a suit but no hat, revealing a balding dome—climbed out of the Lincoln Continental, a dark blue vehicle that blended into the night.

"Freeze!" Fowley called out, flashing the deputy sheriff's badge.

Fowley gave the driver just enough time to glimpse the badge before he straight-armed the guy in the back, shoving him against the garage door, barking at him to assume the position.

On the rider's side, Robert "Red" Manley was getting out onto the cement driveway, or rather was sneaking out, trying to slip away as Fowley was occupied with the man I figured was Palmer, Manley's boss.

Manley—eyes wide and wild, mouth open—was maybe six foot, wearing a snappy brown sportjacket and tan slacks. He had the build of a defensive end, and was taking off like one, too, dashing across the lawn, tie flapping, weaving around exotic plants.

He hadn't seen me; but I, of course, had seen him.

I cut around a cactus and threw myself at him, bringing him down in a hard tackle, and we both rolled down the slope of the lawn, dropping off the curb into the street. I hit the cement pretty hard, scraping the skin along my right hand, and yelped in pain, letting loose of him reflexively, which allowed him to scramble up and out of my grasp, and then he was running down the street, arms churning, like a Zulu trying to outrun another Zulu's spear.

I didn't have a spear and I didn't have my nine-millimeter, either.

But I didn't feel like chasing the fucker, so I just took off my shoe and took aim and hurled it.

The heel of the Florsheim caught the heel of the Manley household in the back of the head; the sound, in the quiet night, was like the popping of a champagne cork. It knocked him off balance, and he yiped like a dog getting its tail stepped on, as he tripped over his own feet, tumbling to a stop against a curb.

I walked over and collected my shoe, put it on, and then I walked over and collected Robert Manley.

"First you trip over your dick, Bob," I said, "and now you trip over your own feet."

As I hauled him by the arm to those feet, he blurted, "I know what this is about!"

"Swell," I said, and patted him down for a weapon. Clean.

He put his hands up without being asked. His hair was a tousle of red curls, his face pale except where it was shadowed from not having shaved since morning. "Listen, I knew Beth Short." His voice was youthful, breathy. "I turned sick inside when I read the paper in San Francisco, this morning."

"You just hadn't got around to calling the cops about what you knew."

"Are you kidding? Think of the publicity! I got a beautiful wife and four-month-old son! What would *you* have done?"

"Kept my pecker in my pants," I said, and yanked him back toward the house.

Manley's boss professed to know nothing about Red's connection to the already notorious "Werewolf" slaying, and generously—if nervously—turned over his kitchen for the questioning of his employee. I got a glimpse into the living room of the Spanish-appointed home, through a dining room archway, where Manley's balding boss was hurriedly explaining the situation to his wife, a pleasant if distressed-looking fortyish brunette in a house robe, then herding her off, away from the "police" who had taken Robert Manley into their custody.

Like the one in Manley's home, the Palmer kitchen was streamlined and white and modern—but about three times the size, and touched with two tones of green, not blue. We sat at a green-and-white chrome-and-steel dinette, one of us on either side of Manley, who we allowed to smoke. He had taken off his brown sportjacket, slinging it over the back of his chair, and sat in his shirtsleeves, suspenders, and a green-and-brown tie that, oddly, seemed perfectly coordinated with the kitchen around us.

"I'm just sick to my stomach," he said, and he did look pale enough to puke. "My poor wife. What have I done to her? Jesus, my wife."

Again, Fowley took notes and I took the lead, where the questioning was concerned.

"Where and when did you meet Elizabeth Short?"

"It was a late afternoon in December—couple weeks before Christmas. She was just this pretty black-haired dish, standing on the corner near the Western Airlines office. Just standing there, not crossing with the light or anything, kind of . . . distracted. I went around the block, and she was still there, so I pulled over and offered her a lift. She played hard to get awhile, and I told her I was in town on business, could use a little help getting to know my way around San Diego, and . . . finally she let me give her a ride home."

"Home."

He nodded, breathing smoke out his nostrils. "To Pacific Beach, those people she was staying with, the Frenches. We went out a couple times—nothing happened. Kissed her a few times."

"Did she know you were married?"

"Yeah. But I told her my wife and me were at a sort of crossroads, that it didn't look like it was gonna work out. And, anyway, I thought at first Beth was married, too, 'cause she wore what looked like a wedding band. But then later she said her husband, this Matt she talked about all the time, was killed in the war. Officer in the Army Air Corps. I think she liked that I had been in the Air Corps, too."

"You didn't tell her you were discharged on a Section Eight."

He winced, flicked ash into a green Bakelite tray. "You *know* that? How do you know that?. . . . Anyway, it was an honorable discharge. Lot of guys got out on a Section Eight."

"I know. Me, too."

That perked him up; I'd made myself a little more likable. "You, too? You're a vet?"

"Yeah. Marines. I understand you were in the Army Air Corps band."

"Yeah, yeah, I was. Loved it—I mean, I couldn't fit in with the Army ways, you know? All that discipline, regimentation."

"You're a free spirit."

"Well, I'm a musician. Sax man."

"Still?"

"Weekends and such. It's pretty hard to do as a profession, music—you've got to have something special. I'm good, but . . . not special, not really."

"What were you doin', Red, running around on that pretty little wife of yours?"

"How do you know she's pretty? She's pretty, all right, but . . . how do you know?"

"We spoke with her."

He hung his head, shook it. "Oh, Christ. Oh, Jesus." Now he looked up. "Is she all right?"

"She didn't break down on us or anything."

"No . . . no, she wouldn't."

"But, Red—do you figure she's 'all right' with her husband chippying on her?"

He sighed smoke, gestured with the cigarette. "Look . . . I don't expect you to understand, but . . . I was just trying to give myself a little test."

"A test?"

"Yeah—see if I could resist a good-looking dame like Beth Short. See if I still loved my wife."

"How did you do?"

He twitched a grimace. "I said you wouldn't understand. We just had a baby. You married?"

"Yes."

"Any kids?"

"One on the way."

"You'll see, you'll see. Nobody talks about it—nobody ever talks about it . . . your wife won't want to have relations, you know, after she has the baby. Not for a while."

"It's called recuperation, Red. Giving birth to a kid is no picnic."

"I know, I know . . . and then . . . when your wife does want to have . . . relations again . . . you may find you don't feel the same."

"The same?"

"She just didn't seem . . . like the same person. Harriet was a real sexy baby, when we dated. But now she's a . . . she's a *mom*. . . . A kid came out of her, down there. And the baby, crying all the time, up all night, baby made me . . . nervous. I got nervous trouble anyway, you know—that's why I got Sectioned Eight. Don't think I don't feel guilty about it. You think I don't feel like a rat?"

"I wouldn't know."

"Well, I do. I talked to doctors over at the veterans hospital, a couple times, and they gave me some pills, for my nerves. I told them that putting my . . . you know, putting it into my wife, after a baby came out of her, made me feel queasy, and they— Aw, shit. I sound like a fucking creep, don't I?"

"Yeah."

"Well, fuck you, Charley. You'll see. There's a readjustment period, for a guy, after his wife gives birth. And Beth Short . . ." He shrugged, drew on the cigarette. ". . . she was just part of my readjustment."

"She was the test you gave yourself."

"Yeah. And I didn't have relations with her, understand? Never! I took her out for dancing and drinks and a few meals, and that was it. Usually this place called the Hacienda Club. This was during about a week when I was in San Diego, seeing my accounts. I'm a hardware salesman—did I tell you that?"

"Palmer's your boss. You deal in pipe."

He studied me, trying to find the sarcasm in that; he didn't look hard enough.

"Anyway," he said, "I was going back and forth about my marriage—mentally, I mean. Loving my little son, not attracted to my wife anymore. I told the doc at the veterans hospital I thought I was having a nervous breakdown, and he said I was doing fine and gave me some more pills. And also I couldn't stop thinking about that girl."

"Beth Short."

"She was so damn pretty. So different from Harriet . . . Oh, Harriet's pretty, real pretty, but Beth was sort of . . . I don't know, exotic, with those spooky clear blue eyes and all that black hair and those black clothes and stockings and white flowers in her hair and all. Did you know she was called 'the Black Dahlia'?"

"I heard that."

"And Beth seemed so . . . worldly. So much older than her years. You know, she was in the movies, had all these big friends, like that famous director that was gonna give her a screen test."

"Did she mention his name? This director?"

"No. She just smiled and laughed and said I'd be amazed, like as if it was gonna turn out to be Alfred Hitchcock or John Ford or something . . . which is all the movie directors I ever heard of, by the way. So I decided to see her again, when it was time to go back to San Diego, and service my accounts."

The jokes were just too easy to bother making, with this guy.

"The Frenches don't have a phone," he was saying, "so I wired Beth I'd be down. Then when I got there, she said she was wearing her welcome out with the Frenches, and could I drive her back to L.A.?"

"This was on January eighth?"

"I guess. It was last Wednesday, I mean a week ago Wednesday. Was that the eighth?"

"Yeah."

"Then it was the eighth. I couldn't take her back that night, 'cause I still had some accounts to see, in San Diego, the next morning. So we went out, again. Funny thing, for all her worldliness and fancy clothes, she was a cheap date. Preferred drive-in joints to posh restaurants."

"Is that where you took her, that night, a drive-in?"

"To a little burger joint called Sheldon's, not far from the Frenches. I did take her to the U.S. Grant Hotel—that's about as fancy as we ever got—'cause they had a hot band playing that night, and I wanted to hear it."

"But you wound up staying at the Pacific Beach Motor Camp, right?"

"Right. And we did some club-hopping . . . She drank a little more than usual; she wasn't really a drinker, got a little sick, a little moody. When we finally landed at the motel, and she got undressed, I noticed something that, you know in retrospect, might be important."

"Yeah?"

"She had red scratch marks on her arms. Forearms. I asked her about them, and she said she had a jealous boy friend. Which is a disturbing thing to hear a girl undressing in a motel room say."

"She mention a name?"

"No—just that he was Italian, and 'cute,' but 'not a very nice guy at all.' "

"Were these recent scratches?"

"I thought they were, 'cause they were bleeding a little; but she claimed the guy did it, her boy friend, before she came down to San Diego. That she just had a nervous habit of picking at the wounds."

"And you spent the night?"

"Yeah—but we didn't sleep together! She was feeling punk, actually. I made a fire—it was a cozy little cabin; it would have been perfect for romance, but it didn't go that way."

"What way did it go?"

"She was shivering, like she had the flu or something, coughing. She was sitting in a chair by the fire, bundled up in blankets. I offered her the bed, said I'd sleep in the chair, but she said no."

"So you took the bed."

"Yeah, and in the morning when I woke up, she was next to me in bed, or on top of it, pillow propped behind her, wide awake. I asked her if she'd slept at all and she shook her head no. I looked at my watch and saw I was late for my first appointment, and took a powder out of there—advising her to catch a few winks before I got back at noon, which was checkout time."

"And that's when you got on the road?"

"My morning calls ran late—we didn't hit the road till twelve-thirty, quarter to one. I made a few calls on the way back to L.A. She had no objection. In fact, she was real friendly on that drive—wanted to know if she could write me letters, offered to make it sound like business so my wife wouldn't get wise. Still wanted to get to know me—said I was sweet."

"How many stops did you make?"

"Three business calls. Once for gas, again for food. She said she was planning to hook up with her married sister, who lived in Berkeley and was coming down to L.A., and that she intended to head home to Boston after that."

"What about her screen test?"

"She said nothing about that. Or how these travel plans would fit in with seeing me, again. You got to understand, with Beth Short, you never knew what was a plan, and what was a daydream . . . and I'm not sure she knew the difference herself."

"How was she dressed, that day?"

"Like a page out of a fashion magazine—black tailored cardigan jacket with a skirt that matched, an expensive-looking white blouse with a lacy collar, black suede pumps . . . light-color coat over her arm. And those black stockings with the seams up the calf?"

"You were kinda taken with her, weren't you, Red?"

"Hard not to be—that hubba-hubba figure, those clear blue eyes . . . her perfume, man, she got inside you. . . ."

Even if he hadn't gotten inside her.

"When you got to L.A.," I asked, "where did you drop her off?"

"Well, first I took her to the Greyhound Bus Depot, on Seventh Street. Kind of a rough neighborhood, so I went in with her, helped her put her suitcases and hatbox in a locker, there."

Fowley glanced up from his notepad. Those suitcases should still be there, tucked away in a bus-station locker—what a prize they would make to an industrious reporter.

"Then I took her to the Biltmore Hotel, over on Olive Street. . . ."

Where she had called me, from the lobby, with her unsettling news of a not-so-blessed event.

". . . and I parked around the corner, on Fifth, walked her into the lobby. She said she was supposed to meet her sister there, and had me check at the desk for her, but the sister hadn't checked in and didn't seem to have a reservation, either. Anyway, it was getting late . . . almost six-thirty . . . so I just said goodbye and she smiled—sort of thanking me—and touched my arm, squeezed it a little. It was real . . . affectionate. Her eyes were so beautiful, bright and shining and so clear and blue, looking right at me, looking right through me . . . and I gave her a little kiss on the cheek and took off."

"And that's the last time you saw her?"

"Well, going out the door, I glanced back at her, just to wave one more time, and she was getting change at the cigar stand. I saw her heading to the telephone."

Was I the only call she'd made?

I asked, "Can you think of anything else pertinent, Red?"

"No. I have to tell ya, fellas, I'm beat. Beat to hell. I feel like I could sleep forever."

If he was lying, that would be arranged by the state of California.

I glanced at Fowley, who had closed his notepad. "Why don't you go find Mr. Palmer and ask to use the phone?"

Fowley's eyebrows rose. "Time to call Harry the Hat and Fat Ass? Share the wealth?"

"I think so."

Fowley grinned like a greedy child, and damn near scampered out of the kitchen.

"Got another cigarette?" Manley asked.

"No. My associate's got the pack—he'll be back and fix you up, in a minute."

"You think I'm a jerk, don't you?"

"Yeah. But most men are."

"You, too?"

"Sometimes."

He laughed. "Funny what a guy'll do for a little head."

"What did you say?"

". . . Nothing."

I sat up. "You said you didn't have sexual relations with Beth Short."

"I didn't."

"But she sucked you off, didn't she, Red?"

He wouldn't look at me, now. "I didn't say that."

"Yes, you did. Oh yes, you did."

From the dining room, Fowley called to me. "Heller!"

I went to the archway between rooms. "What is it?"

"The Hat and Fat Ass are on their way. . . . Go out to the car and grab your camera . . . Somebody's here to see our boy."

Fowley had barely said that when Harriet Manley—blonde hair tucked up under a flowered kerchief, shapely frame tied into a dark topcoat, pretty features delicately made up—rushed in, brushing by him, dashing desperately toward the kitchen.

When I returned with the Speed Graphic, Red and Harriet

were in each other's arms. She was looking up at him, her red-lipstick-glistening lips quivering, her blue eyes moist, touching his face with red-painted fingertips, her expression a mixture of tenderness and hurt. They held hands, they embraced, they kissed, and I caught it all on film.

"He's gonna get away with it," Fowley said, shaking his head.

He meant Manley, getting back into the good graces of his lovely wife; but I wondered if the same might apply to whoever had killed the Black Dahlia.

# 11

The next morning was a big one for the *Examiner*, with its exclusive coverage of the arrest of Robert "Red" Manley. This made up, some, for getting beat to the punch by the *Herald-Express* on the Black Dahlia nickname, which their reporter Bevo Means had unearthed in time for yesterday's afternoon edition, thanks to a Long Beach druggist.

Outside the Palmer home, we had staged some photos for Harry the Hat, showing the cops making the capture; those—and my shots of Red trying to make up with his lovely, hurting bride—made the competing papers' coverage look sick. At the scene, Fowley had suggested to the Hat that he and Sergeant Brown take Manley over to the Hollenbeck Station, instead of downtown, since a swarm of reporters who'd been monitoring police calls would no doubt be waiting. And that's what the Hat arranged—lie detector, relay teams from Homicide, and even the police psychiatrist were soon waiting at the neighborhood station. But we weren't invited to the party.

"You boys have done a nice job," the Hat said, a tiny kiss of a smile puckering, his eyes gazing sleepily in the shadow of his pearl-gray fedora's brim. He had one hand on my shoulder, and the other on Fowley's. "But I think you have all the coverage you need to make the morning edition."

"Bull fucking shit, Harry," Fowley said, "I'm going over to Hollenbeck!"

That had been the point, after all, of leaving the rest of the press stranded downtown.

The Hat lifted one shoulder in a shrug. "You can come sit in the press room, if you like . . . and I'll give you a report or two, as things progress—but that's all you get."

Fowley sighed and nodded. That was better than nothing.

The Hat slipped an arm around my shoulder and walked me inside the Palmer garage, where Manley's tan Studebaker was still parked. He apparently wanted a quiet moment.

"Is there anything you've picked up on," the Hat asked, nodding toward Fowley, out in the drive frowning at us like a kid who didn't get invited to play ball, "that may have eluded that esteemed member of the fourth estate you've been tagging along with?"

I tried to think of a bone I could toss Hansen—and promptly told him he needed to talk to Mrs. Elvera French and her daughter Dorothy down San Diego way. Manley would soon spill those names, anyway, so it didn't hurt anything.

The Hat jotted that information down, nodding, saying, "You were a good boy, Nate—you didn't give up that piece of information I gave you."

He meant that nasty piece of business—that Elizabeth Short had eaten, or been fed, human feces before her murder—which was one of the three pieces of key evidence he was keeping up his sleeve.

"I may be dumb, Harry, but not dumb enough to cross you."

"Good."

"So how about another? You could give me one more, you know, and still have one left."

He puckered up another smile. "Think it would help you in your investigation?"

"Who knows? Sure couldn't hurt."

I didn't expect this request to work, but the Hat surprised me.

"All right, Nate . . . here's another evil morsel for you. A piece of skin was carved out of Elizabeth Short's outer left thigh . . . it had a tattoo of a rose on it."

"I guess I knew that already," I said, scratching my head, "or should have. I noticed at the crime scene some flesh had been cut away from her thigh. And I suppose you learned she had a rose tattoo there, from her Santa Barbara arrest record."

"Well, yes and no. Actually, we found the missing piece of flesh with the tattoo on it."

"Found it? Where in hell?"

"That's the second piece of undisclosed evidence I'm going to share with you, Nate, and you alone."

"Where you found it?"

"Yes, where we found it. That is, where the coroner found it."

"Where, goddamn it?"

"Stuck up that poor girl's ass."

I was thinking about that when the Hat tipped his hat, said, "You go on home, Nate—there'll be no pictures over at Hollenbeck. . . . By the way, thanks for calling your friend Ness for me."

"Oh—have you talked to him?"

"Yes, you'll probably be hearing from him, soon. He's coming out by train tomorrow, to consult with us on the case."

"Your idea or his?"

"Sort of mutual. . . . Good night, Nate."

So I had gone home—that is, to the bungalow at the Beverly Hills Hotel—and my wife, already in bed and half-asleep, had the same news for me: not the rose tattoo stuck up Beth Short, no—that Eliot had called and wanted me to pick him up at Union Station tomorrow evening at 7 P.M. He'd left no further message.

Peggy told me her long and busy first day as a Hollywood bit player had been wonderful—she did not seem to have any residual animosity from our argument, yesterday—then rolled over in bed and began to softly snore. And, for the first time, on this bizarre honeymoon of ours, a day (and night) passed without our making love. The next morning, she was up and off to the studio before I woke, courtesy of a car Paramount sent around.

So now I was again sitting in the *Examiner* conference room, sipping coffee, just Fowley and me and the wall-eyed, eagle-pussed Richardson.

Word from Hollenbeck Station was not promising, where

Robert "Red" Manley was concerned; as a human being, Red stunk—as a suspect, he also stunk. Ray Pinker had administered a polygraph, which he deemed "inconclusive." A second test, with which Harry the Hat himself helped Pinker (presumably probing about those three undisclosed items), tended to substantiate Manley's story. And Manley's alibis were looking solid.

But that was fine with Richardson; he didn't want this case solved that quickly, anyway—it was selling too many papers.

"Those bags you boys led us to were a gold mine," Richardson said, referring to the two suitcases (and hatbox) at the Greyhound Bus Station that Manley had told us about.

I said, "You got to them before the cops?"

"Fowley called me with that tidbit from Hollenbeck Station. I sent Sid Hughes over." Richardson grinned as he matched a cigarette. "It's amazing what you can buy in this town for ten dollars."

Shifting in my hard chair, I said, "I don't mean to be a stick-in-the-mud, but just how much of this tampering and withholding of evidence can you get away with?"

The city editor waved that off. "I called Donahoe over at Homicide, first thing this morning, and he was tickled pink to get the stuff—Fat Ass Brown picked it all up half an hour ago."

I sipped my coffee. "After you went through it all."

He leaned both hands on the table, beaming at me, slow eye swimming into place. "Little elves at the *Examiner* workshop sat up all night, gleaning info out of that junk."

"What kind of junk?"

His cigarette bobbled as he spoke, spilling gray ash on the scarred tabletop. "Lots of that satiny sexy black clothing she liked to wear, and sheer lingerie and silk stockings—but that ain't all, fellas and girls. Yesterday all we had for art on this story were those ghoulish vacant-lot pics and that mug shot from the Santa Barbara bust. Now? Now we got glamour photos, cheesecake yet, her in playsuits and bathing suits and sittin' in nightclubs with sailors on her arm and white flowers in her black hair."

I grunted. "Don't drool, Jim—it's not becoming."

"Plus, we got a list of names a mile long of ex-boy friends and former roommates. . . .We're swimming in goddamn leads."

Fowley said, "So how about giving us one?"

Richardson ripped a page out of a notepad. "I saved the best one for my best boys—the Florentine Gardens."

"Hog dog," Fowley said. "Not bad!"

Fowley's reaction was understandable: the Florentine Gardens was a nightclub whose current floor show, *The Beautiful Girl Revue for 1947*, was the nudest in town—unusually so, considering the Mills Brothers were headlining, a mainstream (if colored) act for that kind of venue.

For many years, the Gardens had played second fiddle to Earl Carroll's luxurious deco nightclub at Sunset and Vine, where nearly naked showgirls and most of the celebrities in Hollywood converged. But ever since Ziegfeld's personal pulchritude picker—the legendary starmaker Nils Thor Granlund—had taken over as impresario, the nitery was flourishing.

"Seems till late last year," Richardson was saying, "the Short dame was one of Mark Lansom's harem living in that castle on San Carlos Street, behind the Gardens."

"Who's Mark Lansom?" I asked.

"Lansom owns the Gardens," Fowley said. "Also, a buncha moviehouses and some dime-a-dance halls."

I said, "I thought the Florentine was N.T.G.'s spot."

N.T.G. was one of Nils Thor Granlund's two well-known nicknames; the other was "Granny."

"Granlund's the manager of the Gardens," Richardson said. "But Lansom owns the joint, and it's his baby as much as Granny's."

"What's this about a 'harem,' and a 'castle' behind the nightclub?"

"Lansom's a regular ass hound," Fowley said. "A lot of the chorus girls and waitresses live in this big house of his—fancy place, with a pool and everything."

"A dormitory of babes," Richardson said, leering, "and Lansom's the housemother."

Fowley gave me the rundown on Lansom: the former bootlegger was now a respected member of the Hollywood community, even a sponsor of the Junior Philharmonic. He was separated from a wife tied to him by mutual ownership of real estate; she lived in Beverly Hills, alone, and he lived on San Carlos Street, with all those girls.

"Jim," I said, "I know Granny a little bit, from when he brought his revue to Chicago."

"Yeah, so?"

"Well, nobody knows his way around publicity—good or bad—like Granny. If I go there alone, and let him stay off the record, we might get further."

Fowley bolted upright. "Don't be a pig, Heller! Aren't you getting enough pussy on your honeymoon to hold you?"

I gave Fowley a long unfriendly look. "Is it true you're Noel Coward's ghostwriter?"

Richardson was pacing, nodding, smoking. "You got something there, Heller. Tell Granlund we'll keep his name away from the cops if he talks to us on the q.t."

"Can we do that?"

"What's stopping us?"

"Well, this lead came from the stuff you turned over to the cops this morning, right?"

"It might have."

"Jesus, Jim! What are you withholding?"

"Your paycheck, if you keep asking *me* the nosy questions." He turned to Fowley. "I got a good little lead left for you, too—a roomful of girls at the Atwater Hotel in Long Beach. . . . Here's the address."

Scowling, Fowley scribbled it down, then took the names of the girls.

"Right before Short moved in at Lansom's," Richardson said, "she bunked in with these babes—they're B-girls and would-be singers and actresses. Short was one of five dolls jammed into one little hotel room."

"Sounds like the stateroom scene in *Night at the Opera*," Fowley said, his attitude toward the assignment improving visibly, "only with titties."

"Well," his boss said, ignoring this astute observation, "grab a camera, and don't take all morning. I'm sending you up to Camp Cooke this afternoon."

"I thought Sid Hughes was covering that."

"Yeah, but Sid got busted, flashing a badge and pretending to be Harry the Hat. Irritated Harry, when he found out, and didn't make the U.S. Army love the *Examiner*, either."

Fowley pointed at himself with a thumb. "What makes you think I'll do any better?"

"Say you're with the *Herald-Express*. All in the family."

Fowley and I went our separate ways, he in the *Examiner*'s Ford and me in the A-1's Buick.

The Florentine Gardens was at 5955 Hollywood Boulevard, just a few blocks from its main competition, Earl Carroll's. In the morning sunlight, the building was blinding white, a massive structure with modern lines and classical trim, including neon-lined columns. Spanish-style wrought-iron front doors were positioned between a pair of palm trees, and a banner advertising the Mills Brothers flapped above the club's boldly neon-lettered name.

The place was closed, but the doors were open. The lobby walls were rounded and powder-blue, trimmed in gold, the carpet a luxurious floral number; to my left the hat- and coat-check window was unattended, and to my right an entryway revealed the black-and-white jungle of the Zanzibar Cocktail Lounge, also unattended. Straight ahead double doors closed off the ballroom; but I could hear a piano, seeping through, echoing across the big room beyond, playing "Don't Fence Me In," Cole Porter's improbable cowboy tune.

When Nils Thor Granlund took this place over, a few years back, he had jettisoned the exotic motif designed to invoke ancient Florence (Italy), and went for an art moderne look, invoking Florenz (Ziegfeld). Still, the main room retained an open, airy feel, powder-blue rounded walls mirroring a central round dance floor with two tiers of spacious, high-backed golden-upholstered booths on either side, and private nooks recessed in the walls.

As I strolled in, down a wide gold-carpeted aisle that emptied onto the dance floor, I was facing the stage, way across the yawning room—a bandstand designed to look like a big top hat, with a window cut in it, its brim surrounding the stage. The tiered seating for the orchestra was empty, but a bored bald heavyset cigar-chomping guy in his shirtsleeves was playing piano, while strung across the stage, a dozen pretty girls were rehearsing a dance number.

The chorus girls were in various casual leg-baring outfits—sunsuits, halter tops, short-sleeve blouses, shorts and short skirts—and their hair was either ponytailed back or in pincurls under a kerchief; they also weren't wearing any makeup. And yet they seemed much sexier looking to me than if they'd been all dolled up.

"No, no, no! You impossible cows!" The choreographer, down on the dance floor in front, was a guy about forty in a short-sleeve white sweater, frayed dungarees, and moccasins.

The girls froze in midkick, the pianist stopped, taking time to relight his cigar. The girls relaxed as the choreographer began performing all of their steps ("Land, lots of land!"), admittedly with more grace than the girls, and comparable femininity, for that matter.

The chorus line nodded, acknowledging his superiority, and soon they were back at it, better than before. The guy knew his stuff.

I was just watching them, forgetting my troubles, enjoying their athletic beauty, thinking about how goddamn many beautiful women there were in the state of California, wondering why California couldn't get along without the beautiful woman I was married to, when a gravel-edged voice called out to me.

"Are you still alive?"

I turned and noticed, nestled in one of the booths, the Florentine Gardens' resident impresario, N.T.G. himself.

"Hiya, Granny," I said, on my way over to join him.

Granlund was a big lumpy-nosed Swede who wouldn't have looked out of place at a plow in the middle of a field, if he hadn't been dressed in tailored gray sharkskin with a silk black-and-white-patterned tie. Smiling in his avuncular manner, gray hair slicked back, eyes a dark twinkling blue, Granny—who was in his late fifties—leaned his chin on a hand bedecked with gold rings, exposing gold cufflinks and a gold wristwatch no more expensive than a new Plymouth.

"I heard you were in town," he said, gesturing for me to sit next to him in the booth. "You and Fred should do well."

Granlund knew both Fred Rubinski and me primarily from his stay managing the showroom at Chicago's Congress Hotel in the mid-'30s, where I'd handled security.

"Thanks, Granny. Nice little joint you got here."

"Not mine, exactly, but thank you, Nathan. How do you like my girls?"

"You still know how to pick 'em."

"Yes, I do." Gazing almost dreamily at the chorus line as the choreographer whipped them into shape, he said, "The Short girl wasn't in the chorus, by the way. She was strictly a waitress—Mark hired her."

That caught me like the sucker punch it was. I said, "You don't fool around, do you, Granny?"

He beamed at me like a big Swedish elf. "You're mentioned in the *Examiner* coverage, fairly prominently. I assumed someone from the press or the police would show up—rather relieved it's you."

"To my knowledge, the cops haven't connected Beth Short to the Gardens."

With a smile and a contented sigh, pleased by the array of pulchritude he'd assembled, Granny leaned back in the booth, withdrew a gold cigarette case from his inside suitcoat pocket, offered me a smoke, which I declined, and then lit up.

"The police will connect her with us," he said offhandedly, "if the *Examiner* runs a story."

"The *Examiner* is prepared not to mention the Gardens—not until, or unless, the cops make that connection."

Raising an eyebrow, he said, "Really. Why? Has Jim Richardson come down with a sudden bout of compassion?"

"It's on the assumption that you could provide a few exclusive leads on the girl."

"Off-the-record tidbits?"

I nodded.

He sat and smoked and watched his girls dance, for maybe a minute—a long one. The bored piano player kept grinding out "Don't Fence Me In."

Then Granny said, softly, "I only spoke to the girl a few times. As I say, Mark hired her. She was strictly a waitress, albeit a very decorative one, but then all of the waitresses here are beautiful. . . . You don't come to the Florentine Gardens to see plain janes."

"Having beautiful waitresses encourages drinking among male patrons."

Half a smile dimpled one cheek. "Nathan . . . I know you too well. You're trying to suggest that our waitresses are B-girls. That's not the case. There's no prostitution here. We did have a bad incident last year—"

"Those underage twins."

Both eyebrows arched this time, smoke trailing out his nostrils. "You know about that?"

"I know you've always hired underage girls when you could get away with it, Granny."

He shrugged. "What's prettier than a pretty fifteen- or sixteen-year-old? And what's wrong with displaying their charms, in a tasteful fashion? It's just that one of the girls got involved with a customer, and . . . well, we were prosecuted for placing a minor in an 'unsavory situation,' and we've been most circumspect ever since."

"How circumspect is it, this Lansom having your girls rooming over at his own house? Right behind the Gardens?"

Granny twitched a smile. "How off the record is this, Nathan?"

"All the way off—level with me about Lansom. This is for me, not Richardson."

The dark blue eyes narrowed. "You have a . . . personal stake in this?"

"Yes."

"Which is the extent of what you'll reveal to me?"

"Yes."

He gazed at his girls as they bounced to the piano. "I'm considering leaving the Gardens."

"Really?"

"Yes. I'm not entirely . . . in tune with my employer."

"And why is that?"

Granny's thin lips formed a faint sneer. "Let's return to the subject of Elizabeth Short, shall we? She's rather a case in point. You see, Mark hires these girls as waitresses, implying that this is the next step to their being discovered by yours truly."

"And placed in the chorus line."

"Yes, or for the aspiring actresses, that I'll put them in the movies."

None of this was far-fetched. As a starmaker over the years, Granny numbered among his discoveries Joan Crawford, Barbara Stanwyck, Ginger Rogers, Martha Raye, and Alice Faye; and more recently, here at the Florentine Gardens, N.T.G. had hired and showcased Betty Hutton, Yvonne DeCarlo (another of his underage finds), and Marie "the Body" McDonald.

"Granny, no offense, but you've been known to . . . work closely with your 'discoveries.' "

The choreographer was chewing the girls out again.

Granny said, "You're not an angel, Nathan, nor am I. Mark generously provides me with an apartment, over his garage, where I can . . . provide guidance to my discoveries."

Away from his wife, with whom he lived in a near-mansion near the Greek Theater.

"Granny, I'm not seeing the problem, here. Lansom's hiring pretty girls and giving you a home-away-from-home to check out the merchandise."

He frowned at me, and his voice had a sudden cross edge. "Nathan, I do not make false promises to these young women. Nor do I take advantage of their friendship . . . and it *is* friendship. I'm a big brother to them."

Frequently committing incest, but a big brother.

"Granny, you're making some fine distinction I'm just not grasping."

He grimaced in irritation. "I don't use who I am to fool young girls into giving themselves to me—that's not who N.T.G. is. I am a judge of feminine beauty, a connoisseur, if you will . . . and I don't use my position to deceive the fairer sex into rewarding me for something I am not prepared to give."

I managed not to laugh, finally getting it. Banging Granny wasn't the audition to get into the chorus line: the girls had to pass the audition, first—then Granny banged them. Funny, the different ways people learn to live with themselves.

"I simply don't like being used to put girls in another man's bed," he said, quietly self-righteous. "Owner or not, Mark damn well knows my contract specifically grants me full casting—these were empty promises on his part. He'd screw them, and they would audition, miserably, and they would wind up in one of his dime-a-dance halls, downtown."

"Did Beth Short audition, miserably or otherwise?"

"That girl was a case in point—Mark promised her a part in my revue—a featured role, of the sort I'm currently giving Lily St. Cyr."

"And only you do the casting."

"Precisely. Oh, the Short girl was a pretty thing, even glamorous . . . and perhaps, in a g-string, and high heels and ankle straps, she would have dressed up the stage."

Undressed up the stage.

"I understand Elizabeth Short was fairly talented," I said. "I've heard she was a decent singer and dancer."

Granny was leaning on his hand again, watching the girls dance, the piano relentlessly grinding through the Cole Porter "cowboy" tune. Almost absently, he said, "I wouldn't know—I never did audition her. Mark simply cast her, without approval, or permission. Foisted her upon me."

"And what did you do?"

"I fired her."

"That's a little harsh."

"Mark's misconduct wasn't the only factor. She contributed to her own dismissal."

"How so?"

He gazed at me; the avuncular mask was gone—there was a lumpy, unforgiving quality to those previously pleasant features, now. "The Short girl did not have what it took to make it in this town. Oh, she had the beauty, the sex appeal; and she had the ambition, or said she did. But she . . . wasn't discriminating in the friends she made, the companions she chose."

"Like Mark Lansom?"

"That's not who I'm referring to."

"Who are you referring to?"

"She had a hoodlum boy friend."

I frowned. "An Italian, by any chance?"

"I believe so, yes. At any rate, I think you may recall, from Chicago days, my attitude toward my girls cohabiting with gangsters."

Granny—like anybody in show business, particularly in the nightclub game—had worked for his share of underworld figures. But ever since one of his Ziegfeld girls got notoriously involved with Legs Diamond, Granlund had let his chorines know that if they got in bed with a hoodlum, they would be asked to leave the show.

"Who was this boy friend?"

Another shrug. "I don't know his name. But I received the information from a source I trust, a source close to Mark."

"Who would that be?"

"One of the actresses living in Mark's house. Don't ask for her name. Why don't you walk over there, and ask around? You should find Mark on the premises."

"All right—I'll do that." I shifted gears. "Word is you and Lansom encourage your girls to entertain celebrity guests, and special customers."

Granlund gave me a sharp look. "I won't deny that's done . . . but it's *not* prostitution!"

"I didn't say it was . . . exactly. Who did Beth Short 'entertain'?"

"If by 'entertain' you mean a euphemism for sexual intercourse, I don't know that she 'entertained' anybody. But she was friendly with Mark Hellinger, the producer."

Hellinger had passed away a few months ago, heart attack.

"Who else?"

"Franchot Tone, the actor—I believe he went out with her a time or two. Also, Arthur Lake."

"Who, the guy that plays Dagwood in the movies?"

"The same." He pressed his cigarette out in a powder-blue tray. "And, of course, she was particularly friendly with Orson."

I blinked again; he was pitching fast, and they were all landing like beanballs. "Welles?"

"Oh yes. Apparently they'd met before—several times. Orson was generous with performing his magic act on army bases—she was working at one, I understand. I believe they knew each other from the Hollywood Canteen. She was a waitress there; it was one of her references."

Welles certainly fit the bill for that "famous director" who'd been promising Beth Short a screen test. I asked, "Did they date?"

"I don't know. They were friendly."

I was trying to make this work in my mind. "Jesus, Granny, Welles is married to Rita Hayworth."

"Married men have been known to stray, Nathan."

"Married men married to Rita Hayworth?"

He was lighting up another cigarette. The girls were moving on to their next number, stretching, getting limber. "Orson and Rita have been on-again and off-again, over the last year or so. Of course, you know . . . no, that's probably nothing."

"What?"

The choreographer counted off, and the piano player started up "Ac-cent-tchuate the Positive," to which the girls bounced delightfully.

"Well," Granny was saying, "it just occurred to me—in his magic act, the one Welles would perform for servicemen, Rita was often part of it. Magician's assistant sort of thing, usual corny routine."

I took my eyes off the girls and looked at Granlund. "Yeah?"

"Yes—he sawed her in half."

# 12

Round windows glared through exotic foliage and grillwork grimaced as I approached the off-white two-story Spanish Colonial behind the Florentine Gardens. The big house on San Carlos, a residential street between Hollywood Boulevard and Sunset, was a sprawl of towers and intersecting wings and tile-roofed verandahs, protected by palms and column evergreens and pepper trees. Richardson hadn't been kidding when he described Mark Lansom's digs as a castle.

I could also see how the near-mansion could serve as a sort of apartment house, and—I discovered when I made my way through an archway back to a walled-in pool—those wiseguy reporter remarks about Lansom's harem turned out to be the real stuff, as well.

On rattan beach chairs and loungers, on spread-out towels on the brick patio that the shimmering blue of the pool interrupted, half a dozen young women in bathing suits sunned themselves. Three blondes, two brunettes, and one redhead—their straps undone, in pursuit of a more perfect tan—lay stretched out, as perfectly arranged as Elizabeth Short in that vacant lot, and almost as nude.

The Black Dahlia had been one of these girls, not so long ago, alive and lounging here . . . and in one piece.

My shadow fell across the brown-as-a-berry back of the nearest brunette, and I was just admiring the way tiny beads of sweat were pearling along the tiny wispy hairs of her neck, when she turned to look up at me, her breasts spilling out of the white-with-red-polka-dots bikini top, the whiteness of the pink-tipped flesh against the brown rest of her almost as startling as their swollen perfection.

And me on my honeymoon.

Her eyes were hidden behind white-framed, orange-lensed sunglasses, her hair pinned up in a bun, her lipsticked mouth making a scarlet O. "You're not Mark," she said.

"No, I'm not," I said, taking off my hat.

She was just a little prettier than Susan Hayward.

Casually, with neither indignation nor shame, she returned her breasts to their polka-dot sheath, like a western gunfighter his sixguns to their holsters. She tried to tie the strap behind her, but had trouble.

"Do me," she said.

That was the best offer I'd had all day.

I did her—that is, I got down and fastened the bikini and then she rolled over and looked up at me, kneeling over her. She was a shapely five foot five (lying down) with just enough plumpness to give her a ripe lush look.

"You have a nice face," she said.

"Yours wouldn't stop a clock."

"You're not an actor, though."

"No?"

"You're not in show business."

"Not a flashy enough dresser?"

She took off her sunglasses and showed me her mahogany eyes and her well-tweezed ironically arching eyebrows and chewed the earpiece with tiny perfect teeth. "You dress all right. That's a nice enough sportcoat."

"Gee thanks."

"You're not an actor because you don't look stupid."

"Thanks again."

"And you're not an agent or a studio exec or anything, because that smile of yours?"

"Yeah?"

"It isn't aimed at anybody. You're just smiling 'cause you feel like it."

I looked at her, then glanced around at the other sunning beauties, none of whom were paying us any heed. "It's easy to smile here."

"Easy for you. I'm Ann Thomson."

"I've seen you in something."

She tugged her bikini top into place, smirked a little. "You saw me in nothing, a minute ago. I've been in half a dozen movies . . . with about as many lines."

"My name is Nate Heller." It was warm, the sun really beating down, though not unpleasantly. "Does anybody ever go in for a swim, around here?"

"On rare occasions. Are you a cop?"

"Sort of. Does it show?"

"I thought I was starting to hear it. Why, 'sort of'?"

"Private. Work with a fella named Fred Rubinski."

"Ah! Sherry's restaurant guy, who used to be a cop."

"That's right." I glanced toward the other sunning beauties. "How many girls live here, Ann?"

"Varies. Sometimes as many as a dozen."

"Do you pay rent?"

"Me in particular, or us girls in general?"

"Let's start with you."

"No. But I'm . . . close to Mark. Some of these girls pay Mark a minimal rent check."

"Did Elizabeth Short?"

Her only reaction to that bombshell was to tilt her head. "I've been wondering when somebody would come around. Why do you want to know, if you're a private dick?"

I liked the way she said "dick"—the simple pleasures. "I'm working for the *Examiner*. I was with the reporter who found the body."

"Shit, sure! I saw your name in the paper. Give me a hand."

I helped her up and I followed her over to a rattan liquor cart. She was a pleasure to follow, having a lovely well-rounded rear end, with deep dimples that peeked over the bikini bottoms, and legs like Betty Grable.

"What's your pleasure?" she asked, pouring herself a martini from a pitcher.

"Rum and Coke," I said, leaving the double entendres to her. She was testing me—not so much flirting, or being seductive, as to see if I was easily distracted . . . and to see how seriously I was taking her.

We sat on rattan chairs at a round rattan table under a yellow canvas beach umbrella and she sipped her martini and I sipped my rum and Coke.

"I'd rather not be quoted," she said.

"I'm just doing background research." I took off my hat, set it on the table. "I'm not a reporter."

"Can you leave me out of it? By name I mean?"

"Sure. What can you tell me?"

"Not much, even though Beth roomed with me."

"Roomed with you here, you mean?"

"Yeah." She pointed to the second floor. "Beth dated a lot of guys, talked a lot about getting in the movies, maybe singing on the radio. I mean, Mark has all the right contacts, and she wanted to be in the floor show at the Gardens, of course . . . but other than that, I don't think she tried that hard."

"To make it in show business, you mean?"

"That's right. Beth was . . . she was a loafer . . . lounging around the house, writing letters, reading movie magazines, painting her nails, futzing with her hair."

"She didn't lounge out here?"

"No—she came out for a dip, now and then, but she didn't sunbathe. She liked to keep that skin of hers nice and pale and creamy."

"When did she stay here? For how long?"

"A month or two . . . some time in August, till early October, when she took off for Chicago."

I didn't want to explore that any further.

"Who did she date, Ann?"

"Guys—any good-looking guy. A few famous ones."

"Granny says she and Orson Welles were an item."

She frowned over the rim of her martini glass. "You talked to Granny already?"

"Yeah, we're old friends. He sent me up here."

"Oh! All right, then."

"So what about her and Welles?"

"Were they an item, you mean? Don't know if I'd go that far. They were friendly, went out a few times. Did Granny tell you any of the names of the other actors she dated?"

"Yeah—Franchot Tone. Dagwood." Suddenly I flashed on Elvera French mentioning an actress friend sending Beth Short some money. "You sent her money, didn't you, Ann, around Christmas? Twenty-five bucks, wasn't it? When she was staying in San Diego?"

Eyes expanding with surprise, she said, "What crystal ball are you looking in? How'd you know that?"

"Why was she borrowing money?"

"She just needed cash, that's all."

"It was for an operation, wasn't it?"

The girl nodded, not looking at me.

"For an abortion?"

"She didn't say . . . but that's what I gathered."

Going down this road was dangerous, but I had no choice. "Do you know what doctor she was using?"

"No—she said something about an old family friend, some doctor from where she was from, you know, New England."

"How desperate was she for money? Was she turning tricks, Ann?"

"No! You're getting the wrong idea—Beth may have been a little lazy, but she was a good girl—didn't smoke, and barely drank . . . and you know, for all the dating she did, I don't think she put out. I think that's why Mark allowed Granny to fire her."

"Granny fired her over her Italian boy friend, right?"

"Yeah. Good-lookin' hood she had the hots for."

"What's his name?"

"*Excuse me*," a mellow yet knife-edged male voice interrupted.

The actress turned quickly toward the sound, alarmed, and I

wheeled in my chair, to look at the source of the syrup-thick voice, myself.

He was perhaps five nine, a pear-shaped hundred and eighty pounds tied into a knee-length terrycloth robe with a gold ML monogram. Despite his access to the sun, Mark Lansom had that pasty look endemic to the perennial nightclub denizen, white hair slicked back, half-lidded blue eyes circled dark, a beaky nose, a weak chin and puffy, jowly face. He positioned himself beside Ann and looked witheringly down at her.

"Mark, this is Mr. Heller," she said, a bit nervously, knowing she'd overstepped playing hostess.

"Nathan Heller," I said, offering my hand. "I'm Fred Rubinski's new partner."

He turned his half-lidded gaze my way, and did not shake my hand. "I know who you are—you're helping the *Examiner*."

"On the Short girl's murder, yes. I understand she lived with you."

"Not *with* me—she rented a room here. I try to help out aspiring actresses. . . . Ann, get me a screwdriver, would you?"

"The orange juice is in the house."

"Yes—go after it, and Ann . . . no rush."

She nodded and went inside.

"This is not the kind of publicity the Gardens needs right now," Lansom said, taking the chair Ann had vacated.

"Actually, Granny suggested I speak with you. I cut a deal with him—you boys feed me a few leads, and we don't run anything about the Black Dahlia's stay at the Florentine Gardens, or at la casa Lansom, for that matter—unless the cops tip to it, of course."

He smiled faintly, shook his head. "The cops won't bother us."

"Yeah? Low friends in high places, Mark?"

A smirk lurked in the puffy face. "Does that offend your sensibilities, Nate? I thought you were from Chicago."

"Not offended in the least. I figure, if you're running a call-girl operation out of the Gardens, then you'd need some police pro—"

He interrupted sharply: "The Florentine Gardens is not a brothel." The indignation in the mellow voice surprised me.

"Well, some people seem to think Elizabeth Short was a hooker."

He snorted a laugh. "They didn't know her, then. She was a manipulative little bitch, yes—hooker, no. She'd have to give it up to be a hooker, wouldn't she?"

"You're saying she never paid her rent on her back?"

The smirk curled into a sneer. "She was a conniving little prick tease. Oh, she'd put her face in your lap, but that's as far as it went. She stole money from me, and she stole my address book, too—has that turned up?"

This seemed to worry him.

"Not that I know of," I said.

"If that fucking thing gets in the wrong hands," Lansom said, eyes darting in thought, "like your boss, Richardson, well . . ."

"You'd be royally screwed, Mark?"

Lansom's gaze settled on me like a rash. It took so long for him to speak again, I thought one of us was going to fall asleep first. "I don't think I have anything else to share with you, Nate . . . about the Short girl or otherwise."

"What about her and Orson Welles?"

He shrugged, looked out at the sun glimmering on the surface of the blue water in his white pool.

"What was her Italian boy friend's name?" I pressed. "The hood she got fired over?"

He shook his head. The interview was over.

"Well, thanks for the refreshment, Mark," I said, and had one last sip of rum and Coke. Rising, I nodded toward the girls. "Quite a collection you've got there. I'm in the wrong business—next life, I'm gonna be a landlord."

I was walking around the table, heading for the archway between wings of the house, leading out to the street, when I noticed a familiar figure ambling through that same archway—not a shapely one, either.

In a baggy brown suit and a crumpled fedora that would have looked fine on a horse, Sergeant Finis Brown was heading toward the pool area. No sign of his partner, Harry the Hat—just Fat Ass, shambling on over.

"Maybe the police have caught up with you after all," I said to Lansom, who was frowning as Brown approached.

"What are you doing here, Heller?" Brown growled at me, his round face splotchy.

"Following a lead," I said.

The chunky detective thumped my chest with three thick fingers. "You stay away from Mr. Lansom."

Lansom was sighing, shaking his head. "Sergeant Brown, Mr. Heller was just leaving. Let's not make a scene in front of the girls."

Ignoring that, Brown thumped my chest again. "You get me, Heller?"

"Oh, I get you, Brownie—this explains why you coppers haven't traced Beth Short to the Florentine Gardens . . . Thad Brown's brother is Mark Lansom's boy."

The splotches disappeared in a flush of red, in the midst of which bloodshot brown eyes glowed like coals.

"This ain't your town, Heller," he said, his nose almost touching mine. "And it ain't your case."

I smiled in his face. "So what's the story, Brownie? Mark here is running girls, and maybe Mickey Cohen gets a taste, and you're the bag man?"

Brown grabbed me by the lapels and was lifting me up when I kneed him in the balls.

The girls around the pool were gathering their tops, their towels, their lotion, their things, scurrying inside.

While Fat Ass was rolling around down there on the patio brick, clutching himself, howling in pain, I turned to Lansom and said, "In the weeks before she died, Beth Short was trying to raise money. She stole some from you, Mark—money and an address book."

"Get outa here, Heller," Lansom said, not looking at me.

I had to raise my voice to be heard over Brown's cries of agony. "Beth Short was trying to shake you down, wasn't she, Mark? She knew you were running hookers out of the Gardens, and she stole an address book filled with your best customers."

"You're wrong. Go away."

I leaned a hand on the table, looking right at Lansom; he wouldn't meet my eyes. "But was that worth killing her over? You couldn't have done that yourself, could you, Mark, not that grisly piece of surgery. How about Fat Ass here?"

And as I gestured at Brown, I saw him getting to his feet, recovering faster than I thought he would, or could, and I heard a cry of pain and anger, a deep wounded roar like a gored rhino, and then the chunky cop was charging right at me, tackling me, taking me down onto the brick patio.

I hit hard, on my back, the wind whooshing out of me, and I was helpless for a while, long enough for Brown to try to take his revenge. Instead of just staying on top of me and beating the shit out of me, like any sensible son of a bitch, he clambered to his feet so he could rear back and kick me, kick me in the balls like I had him . . .

. . . was the point, but it didn't take. I had my wind back and rolled to one side and caught Brown's brown shoe as the kick swished by me, and grasped his ankle and yanked, setting him down, hard, on his ass.

He cried out, "Fuck me!"

Then I jumped on top of him, as if I were accepting his offer, and instead slammed my right fist into his face three times, turning his nose into a sodden red mass, blood streaming out his crushed nostrils. He was barely conscious when I took him by the collar and belt and dragged him to the pool and threw him in.

Well, shoved him in—he was too fat and heavy for anything else, and I was strong, but not strong enough to make that grand a gesture.

Fat Ass flapped around in there—it wasn't deep—swearing at me, but not coming after me, streaky ribbons of blood from his shattered nose destroying the pool's perfect blue.

"Do you think that was smart?" Lansom asked, as I collected my hat.

"Tell him the next time he lays a hand on me," I said, trembling, "I'll kill him."

Lansom studied me. His blue eyes were hard in his puffy face. "I believe you would."

"Mark, you're a good judge of character."

I was dusting myself off, breathing hard, moving through the arched passageway toward San Carlos Street when Ann Thomson—still in the polka-dot bikini—bounced out a front door and up to me.

"I saw everything from the kitchen," she said, eyes wide and flashing, smiling like a happy kid. "You're really something."

"You're not exactly chopped liver yourself, kiddo."

She touched my arm. "You want to know the name of that Italian boy friend of hers?"

"Is it Savarino?"

She blinked in surprise. "Why, yes! He was involved in that Mocambo robbery. She met him in a cafe just a few blocks from here. . . . If you knew his name, why did you ask?"

"Because until you told me," I said, nodding goodbye, "it was just a hunch."

# 13

Aggie Underwood and I both ordered the corned beef hash, one of the Brown Derby's specialties. We shared a booth in the bustling restaurant, complete with framed movie-star caricatures and signature derby lampshade throwing soft yellow light. It took connections to land a booth here at the height of lunch hour; but my diminutive red-haired companion—schoolteacherly as ever in a white-dotted blue dress—was feared and respected in Hollywood.

We were in the Brown Derby #2, the non-hat-shaped one on Vine Street, and Aggie had already pointed out the irony that two of the four caricatures sharing our booth were Alan Ladd and Veronica Lake, stars of *The Blue Dahlia*.

"I would have sworn Bevo Means cooked that 'Black Dahlia' moniker up," she said, between bites of hash, "really too good to be true—but it keeps turning up."

"Yeah, we heard it from the French girl down in San Diego," I said, just poking at my food.

"Tell me why I should have accepted this invitation," she said, eyes hard and glittering behind jeweled, dark-framed glasses, tiny mouth with tiny teeth smiling like a small predator, "when you're working for the competition."

I shrugged, sipped my Coke—no rum this time. "The *Examiner*, the *Herald-Express* . . . it's all in Mr. Hearst's family."

She laughed humorlessly, spoke through a mouthful of hash. "Have you guys interviewed the father yet?"

"Elizabeth Short's father? No. Have you?"

She nodded. "This afternoon's edition—guy's a fourteen-carat crackpot. Was an entrepreneur of sorts, back in the late twenties, building miniature golf courses; then when the depression hit, he went bust, like everybody else. So guess what Cleo Short does when times get hard?"

"That's his name? A man named Cleo?"

"Yeah, Cleo." Jaw jutting, she pointed her fork at me. "Guess what he does? Fakes his own suicide, and disappears!"

"Jesus—how'd he manage faking his death?"

"Left his car running on a bridge, with a suicide note, next to those icy waters. Years later, he writes his family and says, 'Surprise, I'm not dead,' and invites his daughters to come visit him."

"Did they?"

"Over time. The mother was less than charmed, never spoke to the son of a bitch again."

"How about Beth?"

"His daughter Elizabeth came to see him, in '43, when he was working in the shipyard at Mare Island, and she stayed with him for a while . . . Deal was, she would keep house for him, and he'd help her look for work. In a few weeks, he threw her out."

"Why?"

The little reporter waved her fork like a wand. "If I can remember his quote from my article, something like, 'She was a lazy, greedy, boy-crazy little tramp.' "

"Seems pretty broken up about losing his daughter."

"Says he hadn't seen her since he tossed her out on her behind in '43, and had no desire to ever see her again. 'She went her way, I went mine!' Even refused to identify the body. Officially Beth Short's still a Jane Doe."

I shook my head, pushed my half-eaten plate of hash aside. "The mother can do the unenviable deed—she's arriving this afternoon."

"Yeah, I heard—Jim Richardson's flying her out." She smiled

like a pixie, eyes narrow and twinkling behind the jeweled frames. "You know where the father turned up, Nate?"

"No, Aggie—where did the father turn up?"

"In an apartment house on South Kingsley Drive, near Leimert Park."

If I'd opened my eyes any wider, they'd have fallen out. "What?"

She was smiling smugly. "Fifteen minutes from that vacant lot."

"Christ, he's sounding like a suspect."

Aggie shrugged. "Harry the Hat's treating him that way. I don't buy it, though. Cleo's a pipsqueak, a mousy little bastard."

"Yeah, well, still waters run wacky . . . and as screwed-up as Elizabeth Short was, Aggie, how surprised would you be to have incest show up in her family history?"

"Not very." She pushed her plate—cleaned—to one side, lighted up a cigarette. "But it's one thing for a loving papa to sex up his baby girl, and quite another for him to carve her up. . . . You having dessert?"

We ate cheesecake and Aggie asked the obvious.

"So why take me out on a date, Nate, when I look like a munchkin in a Harpo Marx wig, and you're in a townful of beautiful dames, one of whom you're newly married to?"

"Well, in the first place, I think you're a beautiful dame."

"Right answer."

"And in the second— Hell, Aggie, you know why. I need the kind of information only the best crime reporter in town might have."

She grinned, flicking ash onto her cleaned cheesecake plate. "That's a lovely compliment, you lying son of a bitch, but you could talk to Sid Hughes or half a dozen others at the *Examiner*, and get what you need, and not come to a rival reporter."

"Hell, I'm not a reporter—I'm doing some investigative work for the *Examiner*, yes, but I'm going down some private roads."

Aggie's eyes narrowed and she began to look at me differently. "Care to be more specific?"

"Not to a real reporter, I don't. Look, everybody in town is pursuing the sex-crime angle . . . understandably . . . but I'm chasing down a few stray rumors that put Beth Short next to some hoodlums. Nobody but me seems to be looking at that girl's slashed mouth and coming up with 'informer.' "

This time her smile was like a tiny, enigmatic gash in her face, which opened as she asked, "You do understand why, don't you, Nate?"

"I think so. The papers like the sex-crime angle—it's a better story that way. And the cops are so thick with the hoods that they'd rather not look under certain rocks."

"You're not wrong." Aggie was nodding. Her firm jaw lifted and, short though she was, she nevertheless seemed to gaze down at me. "You ever hear of the Georgette Bauerdorf murder?"

"No."

"Socialite killed a couple years ago—pretty, apple-cheeked girl, kind of wild . . . she was strangled and raped and her body was found facedown in her bathtub."

I frowned, leaned toward her. "Are you saying there are similarities to the Dahlia murder?"

"A few. It's widely assumed Beth Short's body was dismembered in a bathtub . . . Perhaps the Bauerdorf girl's killer was planning to do the same thing, but got interrupted."

Leaning back again, I mused, "Beautiful dead nude girl, strangled . . . I can see it. But it doesn't jump out at me."

Cigarette in her fingers, she gestured emphatically. "How does this grab you? The Bauerdorf girl and Beth Short were pals—they hung out at the Hollywood Canteen together."

For a few moments I just sat there, trying to absorb the words; this entire conversation—about grisly murders and their aftermath—seemed oddly abstract in the soft-yellow glow of the subdued Derby lighting.

"Aggie," I said finally, "that's major—is that in the afternoon edition, too?"

"No. That story got killed deader than the Dahlia." She flicked ash onto the plate, adding casually, "As a matter of fact, I'm off the Dahlia story."

I sat forward. "What in hell . . . ?"

"Got my ass yanked right off. The order came from upstairs—way upstairs."

"No! Old Man Hearst?"

"William Randolph himself. Seems the girl's father, George Bauerdorf, is a close friend of the Old Man's, and Bauerdorf doesn't want his daughter's death, and her loose ways presumably, splashed all over the papers again, further soiling the good family name. Then there's the Dagwood situation."

"Arthur Lake, you mean—Dagwood in the movies. He knew Beth Short. That I've heard."

"That's right. But have you heard this, cutiepie? Lake knew the *Bauerdorf* girl, too. Met both murdered girls at the Hollywood Canteen."

My eyes were about to roll out of my head, again. "Shit, is Dagwood Bumstead the Black Dahlia slayer?"

She laughed, once, pointing at me with the cigarette in hand. "Exactly the headline everybody wants to avoid. Lake has an alibi, and I've spoken to him—he's a harmless, good-natured semilush. But he's also married to the niece of Marion Davies. . . ."

"Hearst's mistress."

"That's right. Hearst doesn't want Dagwood's name dragged through the mud, and he doesn't want the Bauerdorf family to suffer through any more nasty publicity—their daughter's tragic death was enough, after all."

"And so you're off the Dahlia story?"

She sighed, pretended to smile. "Starting tomorrow, I'm sitting at my desk with my embroidery hoop and needle. Nothing else on my docket . . . so, Nate, if there's anything I can help you with, why not? Just don't bother taking Dagwood and the Bauerdorf murder to Jim Richardson . . . the one man Jim doesn't cross is Hearst."

Aggie had a cocktail—a stinger—and I had another Coke, still with no rum. My head was spinning enough from Aggie's revelations.

Finally, I got around to what I'd brought her here to ask her: "What do you know about the accused Mocambo robbers?"

"Well," she said, with a shrug, "four of them have been arrested—first, this Bobby Savarino and that Hassau character. Then a couple days later, Al Green and Marty Abrams. But it's a bigger group than that—probably another half dozen stellar citizens in that gang."

"It's a heist crew?"

"Yeah, they pull down medium-size scores all over town. Operate out of Green's bar and grill on North McCadden—the McCadden Cafe, it's called. Green is short for Greenberg, by the way—you oughta ask Mickey Cohen or your pal Ben Siegel about him . . . He's an old Murder, Inc., guy from back East."

"What do you make of Savarino's yarn about being approached to hit Cohen?"

Wincing, she shook her head. "I don't know what to make of it . . . and he clammed up, almost immediately. Are you trying to make some connection to the Dahlia?"

The waiter delivered the check and I took it.

"You're not on the story anymore, Aggie—remember?"

She reached across the table and patted my hand. "Whatever this is really about, Nate . . . good luck."

I didn't say anything—Aggie Underwood had a nose for news. I was just glad she was my pal—and off the Dahlia case.

Before I left the Derby, I ducked into a phone booth and called Fred Rubinski. I wanted him to get out his black book of celebrity addresses and set up a meet for me.

"Orson Welles?" Rubinski said.

"That's right—Martians *have* landed."

"He's shooting a picture at Columbia, with his wife, only they're kinda shut down, 'cause of the strikes. I'll try to track him down."

"Today, if possible. This afternoon."

"And Orson Welles will just drop everything to talk to Nate Heller?"

"You did a job for Welles a year or so ago, didn't you, Fred?"

He drew in a surprised breath. "Yeah—how did you know that?"

"Who do you think referred that aging Boy Wonder to you?"

"You do get around, Nate. Orson Welles—what do you want from that crazy egomaniac?"

"Not a screen test," I said.

Spitting distance from the busy business district of North Highland Avenue, on a dead-ending side street just off Yucca, stood a freestanding stucco building with a gravel parking lot in back. Mine was the only car in the lot, and a sign in the door said CLOSED—OPEN AT FOUR.

But through the front window, between the neon beer signs and the painted letters spelling out McCADDEN CAFE, I could see—cutting through shadows cast by the blades of ceiling fans—a tall, cadaverous guy in an apron going around the room, cleaning off tables with a rag. He had a cigarette going, and moved with a pronounced limp.

I knocked on the front door, hard enough to rattle it, peering around the CLOSED sign, and the skinny guy saw me, and scowled and shook his head, yelling, "Can't ya read, buddy?"

But apparently he could, numbers anyway, because when I held up a fivespot to the glass, he limped over—twig-thin but towering—and unlocked the door, poking his pockmarked face out at me.

It was a long, narrow, high-cheekboned Indian-ish face, with brown eyes peeking out of slits, a wide yet pointed nose, and a balled, dimpled chin. His hair was dark brown and widow's peaked and greased back, and his breath reeked, as if he'd puked last week and hadn't brushed his teeth since, a notion their yellowish tobacco-stained hue affirmed.

"What do you want for that fivespot?" he asked, his voice as reedy as he was.

I had to look up at him—he weighed about as much as a box of kitchen matches, but the bastard must have been six foot four. "Just want to ask a few questions."

Somehow those slitted eyes slitted further. "Cop woulda showed me a badge not a fiver. Reporter?"

"My name's Nate Heller—I'm a private detective, doing backgrounding for the *Examiner*."

An Adam's apple worthy of Ichabod Crane bobbled. "What did you say your name was?"

"Heller. Nate Heller. This fivespot has a brother, if you give me a little time."

Frowning in thought, and temptation, he said, "I gotta clean up 'fore we open again—lunch hour was a friggin' zoo. And I got prep to do in the kitchen—I'm the cook, you know. This about that Short girl?"

"Yeah. Was she a customer here?"

He didn't answer. Instead, he said, "You got a double sawbuck in that pocket of yours?"

"I might, if you have something worth that much."

He swallowed and the Adam's apple bobbled again. "I don't want my name in the papers."

"It won't be—you're what they call a 'confidential source.' "

Heaving a sigh, he said, "Okay . . . come in."

He locked the door behind us and pointed to one of the booths along the left wall. The McCadden Cafe wasn't exactly the Brown Derby—the walls were knotty-pine, the bar with stools was at the right, the serving window onto the dinerlike kitchen was straight ahead, tables with no cloths and mismatching chairs were scattered about the central area. Like a fat man in a colorful coat, a jukebox squatted in front of the window. The air was about an even mix of stale beer and tobacco smoke, and the floor was piss-yellow, scuffed, cigarette-butt-burned linoleum.

My instinct: any heist gang operating out of here would be smalltimers. On the other hand, maybe this was just a clever front.

He brought both of us beers and sat across from me in the knotty-pine booth. The apron was food stained and under it was a threadbare blue-and-white-striped shirt, sleeves rolled up, and faded dungarees.

Then, suddenly, startling me, he thrust out his knobby hand, saying, "Arnold Wilson, Mr. Heller."

I shook his hand—his grip was surprisingly strong, if slimy.

"Pleased to meet you, Arnold. Ex-serviceman?"

The acne-damaged face beamed as he nodded. "Got the gimpy leg in the Pacific. Friggin' Jap bayonet."

Obviously his proudest moment.

"I was in the Pacific myself. Marine."

"Army." He shook his head, grinning. "Best time of my life. Listen . . . bein' as we're both vets and all . . . to be honest, I don't know if I got a double sawbuck's worth for ya, about Beth Short."

Interesting that he referred to her as "Beth" and not "Elizabeth," as the papers were wont to do.

"Let's start with her being a customer, Arnold. When was that?"

He had a gulp of beer—with that Adam's apple, it looked like he was swallowing a baseball—and he shrugged. "Well, calling that kid a 'customer' is maybe stretching it. I don't remember her ever spending a dime in here, except maybe on the jukebox—she had a way of finding some guy or other to buy her a Coke or a sandwich or both. She thought I made the best grilled cheese sandwiches anywheres—see, my secret is, I grill a couple slices of tomato right in there with the cheese—"

"When was she frequenting this place?"

"In the fall, though there was this stretch, around October, when she was back East or something. See, she lived right here in the neighborhood."

"Where in the neighborhood?"

"Two places—around August, September maybe, she was in this hotel over on North Orange; then in November she was at the Chancellor Apartments, over on Cherokee."

I sipped my beer. Smiled. "Arnold—okay I call you by your first name?"

"Sure, Nate." He raised his beer glass to me, then had another gulp. "One vet to another, after all."

"Arnold, was Beth Short a pro?"

"Naw, she wasn't hooking. Al—the proprietor—he wouldn't put up with that . . . Al likes to steer clear of the cops."

If Al Greenberg and Bobby Savarino were using the cafe as their heist crew's clubhouse, that made sense.

"But it didn't hurt," Wilson was saying, "having a good-looking piece of tail like that sitting on a bar stool. Wasn't exactly bad for business."

"One guy was buying most of her drinks, though—right, Arnold?"

The Adam's apple bobbled again. "You mean Bobby."

"That's right—Bobby Savarino."

Thin lips twitched in the ravaged mask of his face. "I don't think I should get into that."

"For that double sawbuck, Arnold, I really think you should."

A big bony hand pawed the air dismissively. "Bobby was filling her with all that Medal of Honor bullshit—dago bastard, he was never even overseas! But good-looking guy like him, line of bull like that . . . hell, he gets more ass than Sinatra."

"I understand he's a married man."

Wilson shook his head, disgustedly. "Yeah, with a nice wife, nice-*lookin'* wife, kid on the way . . . I like Bobby, man. I mean, he's a regular joe, but, shit—that's friggin' low."

"Did Beth Short know Bobby was married?"

"Not at first . . . and Bobby told her he wanted to marry her, too. Can you believe this, before she found out he was married, they were engaged for a while—he even gave her a ring."

"A diamond?"

"Yeah. Bobby's connected to these jewelers—ice is never no problem for the group."

"The group?"

Wilson paused, his deer-in-the-headlights expression indicating he'd spoken too freely. But he continued, anyway, saying, "Yeah, uh—the McCadden Group. It's a bunch of guys that hang out here at the cafe."

Sort of like the Elks or Kiwanis, except for the part where they went out on heists with guns.

"What happened to her diamond ring?"

Wilson shrugged. "I heard she hocked it. She was raising money."

"Do you know why?"

"I dunno. . . . I think maybe she had Bobby's bun in her oven."

"Fertile fucker, isn't he?"

"Yeah. He's a fucker, period—but I like the guy, don't ask me why. . . . Listen, she wasn't in here since November, first week of December at the latest. I mean, you could ask Henry's wife, her and Beth were tight . . . Maybe she could tell you something."

"Henry's wife? Mrs. Henry Hassau, right, the guy who was arrested with Bobby?"

Now Wilson knew he'd spoken too freely. "Oh—so you know about that."

"It was in the papers. It's no secret, Arnold—or that your boss Al Greenberg is in county lockup, too."

Too casually, he said, "Yeah, for that Mocambo robbery."

"How tall are you, Arnold?"

The slitted eyes blinked, several times. "I dunno. Six four maybe."

"Funny—that's just how tall the witnesses said one of the thieves was. He had bad acne scars, too."

Wilson thrust out a big hand, palm up. "Let's have the double sawbuck—I'm through talkin'."

I gave him a pleasant smile. "Look, Arnold—I have no interest in turning your skinny ass over to the cops. . . . By the way, how the hell did they miss you, if they're arresting guys left and right out of this joint?"

The Adam's apple jumped again. "I was in San Francisco for a week. Al called me and asked me to come watch the joint while he was in stir. He'll be out soon—the Ringgolds'll post bail."

"The Ringgolds. And who are the Ringgolds?"

The eyes widened and rolled and he shook his head, apparently pissed at himself. "I already said too much. . . . How about that double sawbuck?"

"There's a Ringgold Jewelry Store in Beverly Hills, isn't there? Wouldn't happen to be the jewelry store whose display merchandise at the Mocambo got taken in that robbery?"

A shooing hand waved the air. "You better get on outa here, now—I got work to do 'fore four."

So the Mocambo heist had been primarily an insurance scam: steal jewelry for its owners who can claim the loss and keep the stones. I wondered how many other jewelry robberies the Mc-

Cadden Group had pulled for the Ringgolds. This little heist crew was definitely more impressive than these meager surroundings.

"Arnold, a whisper from me in Harry the Hat's ear would land you in the cell next to your boss."

Wilson jerked back, almost hitting his head on the wooden booth. "Are you threatening me?"

"I wouldn't do that, Arnold—you and me, fellow vets and all. But this conversation—this private conversation, which goes no further than just the two of us—ends when I say it ends. Understood?"

He sighed. And nodded.

I swirled the last of the beer in its glass. "I just want to ask you a question—simple question, obvious question, that just happens to be one nobody's asking. . . ."

I looked right at him—hard.

"Arnold, do you think Beth Short was murdered to send a message to Bobby?"

Wilson didn't answer right away, and when he did, it was pitiful: "How would I know?"

"Just looking for an informed opinion, Arnold."

Words tumbled out: "Bobby was blabbing to the cops and the papers about Jack Dragna trying to muscle him into hitting Mickey Cohen. Next day, Bobby's girl friend turns up dead in a vacant lot in Dragna's backyard with her mouth slashed, informer style. What the fuck do you think?"

"You think Dragna did it?"

Wilson shrugged one scarecrow shoulder. "Had it done. Who else but Dragna?"

Dragna was the answer I kept coming up with, myself.

"Arnold, I don't get this. Why would Jack Dragna go to Bobby Savarino to do this?"

Wilson shrugged both shoulders this time. "Maybe 'cause Bobby was friends with the Meatball."

Benny the Meatball Gamson was a renegade bookie who had been bumped off, not long ago, reportedly at Mickey Cohen's behest.

"Still," I said, "why would a savvy mob boss like Dragna try to enlist the help of somebody in Al Greenberg's gang?"

"Which don't make sense to you," Wilson said, nodding, "because Greenberg is an East Coast guy and a crony of Ben Siegel's, whose boy Cohen is."

"Yeah!"

"Well, for one thing, Bobby coulda got close to Cohen . . . Mickey wouldn'ta suspected one of Greenberg's group. And Al, well him and Siegel were friends, sure, but Al did a stretch in Sing Sing, was one of the handful of them Murder, Inc., guys unlucky enough to do time. Al don't owe any of those guys nothing."

"But in the end, Savarino didn't want anything to do with hitting Cohen."

Wilson was shaking his head, but it was an affirmative gesture. "Bobby's no hitman. He's just a thief, knockin' over scores."

I took the last sip of beer, and said, "I'd like to talk to Bobby. You think the Ringgolds'll post his bail?"

"Maybe. You want me to set up a meet, if they do?"

I reached in my pocket and withdrew the twenty and held it up. "There'll be another one of these in it for you."

Wilson took the twenty. I told him where he could find me, and I got out of the booth, thanking him for the beer.

"Arnold, you got a phone I can use?"

"Sure—behind the bar."

I called Fred.

"You won't believe this," he said, "but Welles *wants* to see you. How do you know this guy?"

"He got his start in Chicago."

"Well, he's anxious to meet with you. And it seems he is out at Columbia, strike or no strike. Write down these directions. . . ."

I did.

Moments later, ceiling fans churning the stale air, the cadaverous Arnold Wilson was walking me out, the limp not slowing him down appreciably. Perhaps our conversation had got him excited—or that double sawbuck.

"You know, if Jack Dragna's the one that had the Black Dahlia butchered," Arnold said, unlocking the door, "the cops won't touch it. Nobody'll do a damn thing about it, a Mafia guy like that responsible."

"Arnold," I said, already halfway out the door, reaching back to pat him on his bony shoulder, "don't count on it."

# 14

Horse operas, crime melodramas, horror pictures, comedies, and every other stripe of B-movie were still churned out by the independent studios on Sunset Boulevard, near Gower Street. Despite the ongoing strike by the CSU—the Conference of Studio Unions—the usual parade of featured players was crossing Sunset in full makeup to grab a bite at a hamburger or hot-dog stand; Brittingham's, the popular eatery in Columbia Square, at the corner of Sunset and Gower, was servicing its usual clientele of actors and extras, including western gunfighters with empty holsters (prop men having confiscated their sixshooters) and starlets in sunglasses and white blouses and dark slacks, freshly waved hair tucked under colorful kerchiefs.

This lack of support for the strike came as no surprise to me, and was in fact why a bit player like Peggy was getting chauffeured to the studio, daily. The CSU was a militant leftist coalition that included carpenters, painters, and machinists; they were an alternative to the International Alliance of Theatrical and Stage Employees, IATSE having been organized by Nitti racketeers Willie Bioff and George Browne, both currently still in stir. Under the leadership of new Screen Actors Guild president Ronald Reagan, however, the CSU had been left twisting in the wind, and SAG actors—among other union and guild members—were crossing the picket lines.

Which was how Peggy could be working at Paramount, during a strike, and I could be keeping an appointment with Orson Welles at the giant of Gower Gulch, Columbia. A Poverty Row weed that had blossomed under the firm hand of Harry Cohn, Columbia was now a major force in Tinsel Town, and had been ground zero for the strike last October, when fifteen hundred picketers laid siege to the studio, with nearly seven hundred strikers arrested on charges ranging from unlawful assembly to assault with a deadly weapon.

But now, several months later, sold out by Dutch Reagan and SAG, the picketers were a halfhearted, signs-on-their-shoulders bunch, a sea of Reds who quickly parted to allow me to check in at the guard gate. My unionist pop would have been ashamed of this lackluster picket line—and ashamed of me, for crossing it.

I parked and strolled past surprisingly ramshackle-looking offices onto a typically bustling backlot—workshops, cutting rooms, projection rooms, soundstages. But—despite following Fred Rubinski's detailed directions—I soon found myself wandering amid chattering extras in costume and bored grips and gaffers in work clothes, ducking cars and trucks transporting people and equipment. Finally I was just standing there, scratching my head, a detective who could have used a detective, when I felt something—or somebody—tug at my sleeve.

I glanced down and a large adult male face was looking up at me.

"You're Mr. Heller, ain'tcha?" the hunchbacked dwarf asked. His accent said New York, Lower East Side.

"Uh, yes."

He grinned up at me; he had a pleasant, well-lined face—blue eyes, high forehead, gray hair, late fifties.

"The boss is expectin' ya." He shuffled around in front of me and extended a hand. He was wearing white pants and a white shirt and white shoes, and looked like a little ice-cream man—the shirt, however, was spattered with red. "Shorty Chivello, Mr. Heller—I'm Mr. Welles' chauffeur and personal valet."

I shook his hand, which was of normal size, his grip firm and confident. "Chauffeur, huh?"

He laughed, saying, "Hey, I'll save you the embarrassment of askin' how I manage that, Mr. Heller—I got these special wooden blocks strapped to the pedals."

"Cut yourself shaving, Shorty?" I asked, as I followed him toward a nearby soundstage.

"Aw, it's just paint, Mr. Heller."

"Make it 'Nate.' "

"Naw, that's okay. I'm 'Shorty,' but you're 'Mr. Heller.' The boss likes certain respect paid. . . . He says you're an old friend."

"That may be overstating, Shorty. But he was barely out of that prep school in Woodstock when I first met him in Chicago."

"Jeez, was the boss the boy genius they say he was?"

"Shorty, he still is."

Shorty opened the door for me and I stepped into the mostly darkened soundstage, and what I saw gave me a start: out of the gloom emerged another giant head—not another hunchbacked dwarf's, something even better, even stranger . . . the profile of a wild-eyed, vaguely Chinese dragon, hovering above me, perhaps forty feet off the floor, the head itself thirty feet high, angled skyward, a shiny slide extending from its open mouth like an endless silver tongue snaking its way up into the darkness where the ceiling presumably was; disturbingly, the silver slide also exited the back of the beast's head, emptying into a vast pit.

"Christ!" I said. My eyes adjusting to the near dark, I could see that the whole preposterous serpentine affair was constructed on roller-coaster-style scaffolding.

Shorty was shuffling around in front me, saying, "Watch your step, Mr. Heller. The boss had 'em dig that pit right through the cement. . . . Ya shoulda heard them jackhammers!"

We skirted the edge of the mini-abyss, which was a good eighty feet long, and half again as wide, perhaps as deep.

"The boss made the cameramen slide down that thing on their stomachs," Shorty was saying. "Put the camera on a mat. So you could get a whaddayacallit, objective view."

I figured he meant "subjective," but I never argue with hunchbacked dwarfs, particularly on soundstages dominated by dragons. Just as a general policy.

Moving past the towering slide, I followed the little man, the movement of his body seeming more side-to-side than straight ahead, to a door in the midst of portable walls that were clearly the back of a set—about a third of the soundstage was blocked off behind these "wild" walls, which could be moved to facilitate filming from varied angles.

Shorty opened the door and revealed a black-haired man in baggy black trousers and loose white shirt and loosened black tie, a big man at least six two and easily pushing two hundred and fifty pounds, standing at a small work table, dabbing red paint onto the wide grin of a grotesque clown mask which lay like a shield on the table. The lighting—provided by occasional work lamps hanging like fruit from extension cords vanishing up into the same darkness that swallowed the ceiling—was harsh and spotty and shadow inducing. The walls were decorated with a scratchy black-and-white mural replete with nightmarish, violent images—medical-text anatomical diagrams and grinning clown faces juxtaposed with the death smiles of dancing skeletons.

The black-haired man smiled over his shoulder at me, puckishly, dark hard eyes melting in a soft baby face where strong cheekbones struggled to be seen, dark slashes of eyebrow expressed constant irony, and an upturned nose seemed to thumb itself, all punctuated by a dimpled chin.

"Nathan, darling," he said, in that sonorous voice radio listeners all over America adored, including many who disliked the young man who possessed it, "what do you think of my Crazy House?"

"What was that remark that got you in so much trouble?" I asked, moving next to him as he reddened the clown's grin with a Chinese brush. "Something about a movie studio being your personal train set?"

"Well, now it's my personal erector set." He flashed me that raffish smirk of his that seemed to invite you in on every private joke. "Did you know that the definition of one word has kept our two noble unions from coming together? And what is that single word over which our carpenters and painters and set dressers and other skilled artisans have, shall we say, come to blows? *Erection*, my dear." He sighed and smiled and lifted his eyebrows as he bent over the clown mask, touching it up skillfully.

"Erection?"

"Yes, they can't make up their minds—does it mean, the building of sets, or does it refer to simply assembling that which has already been built?" He gave me an amused pixie look. "Perhaps I should point out to them that, in my experience, a woman who is 'built' can cause an erection to quite naturally occur. Wouldn't you agree?"

Shorty had moved in between Orson and myself, paint can in hand, tending his master like a medieval apprentice.

"I think Mr. Heller and I may require some privacy," Welles said gently to his factotum. "Would you mind terribly leaving us alone?"

Shorty set the paint can on the table, gestured "o.k.," then trundled off.

"Why's that little guy a deaf mute, all of a sudden?" I asked. "He was talkative as hell, all the way in here."

Welles twitched his tiny smile. "Yes, Shorty's loquaciousness—even his bluntness—can be something of a problem. That's why I've instituted my docking procedure."

"Your what?"

"I dock Shorty ten dollars every time he speaks around any guest or business associate I'm entertaining." He carefully set the brush across the open paint can. "Care for the nickel tour?"

The pudgy, congenial, vaguely arrogant man showing me around his film set had, at thirty-one, already made history in theater, radio, and film. His dynamic Broadway productions for the Federal Theater Project and his own Mercury Theater had made him famous; his *War of the Worlds* radio broadcast, duping thousands into thinking Martians had invaded earth, had made him infamous. His Hollywood achievements included directing and cowriting three movies—two of which were already acknowledged as modern classics, if not box-office favorites—as well as condescending to star on occasion in films for other directors. He was widely considered a genuine genius—and, in the executive suites of the movie industry, a genuine pain-in-the-ass, starting with his ill-advised, barely veiled attack on press lord William Randolph Hearst by way of his film *Citizen Kane*.

How Welles had come to be directing a movie at Columbia could be explained only one way: his wife, Rita Hayworth, was Harry Cohn's biggest star . . . and she was starring in this picture.

For perhaps ten minutes, Welles guided me through his "Crazy House," a fully operable carnival funhouse, with sliding doors, tilting floors, slanting walls, and a seemingly endless hall-of-mirrors maze. The latter was equipped with plate-glass mirrors seven feet by four feet, one after another, dozens and dozens of them, and several more dozen of the distorting variety, turning Welles razor-thin and making a short fat fool of me.

"I discovered at an early age," he told me, leading me mischievously through the labyrinth, "that almost everything in this world was phony—done with mirrors."

Images of each other seemingly blocking our every path, I asked him how in hell he could shoot in here, with all this glass.

"They're mostly two-way mirrors," he said, "and those that aren't have tiny peepholes drilled for the camera operators. Not that way, dear! This way . . . follow me. . . ."

Welles' funhouse had a distinctly macabre flavor—he led me gleefully through rooms of flimsy canvas walls and spongy plywood floors that were weirdly angled, painted with skewed faux windows, creating a warped *Caligari* perspective. He grinned like a naughty child as he ushered me through hanging beads and drooping chains and gauzy half-shredded curtains, past black-and-white murals with STAND UP OR DIE lettered in the quaint fashion of turn-of-the-century circus posters, into areas decorated with papier-mâché skeletons and cattle skulls and grotesque grinning clown heads.

Something sprang out at me, and I jumped—a blonde mannequin head on a bobbing spring was suddenly staring right at me; she had the bottom of her pretty face rotted away, and a cigarette in her skull teeth, through which Welles' booming laughter seemed to emanate.

In the next chamber, dismembered female legs dangled from

the ceiling—shapely mannequin limbs, in high heels and sometimes seamed stockings—with further ghastly images painted directly over the fake brick walls, including a trio of handle-bar-mustached gents in old-fashioned bathing attire that revealed where sections of their flesh and musculature had been cut away from the bone.

"We've worked our way to the front," Welles said, gesturing me through a passageway, "which in true movie-magic tradition is in the back."

The entrance was papier-mâché rock, with plywood stairs painted gray to match, as if the "Crazy House" had been fashioned within a cave, and all around the doorway, mannequin hands and reaching arms poked out from the walls, a frame of disembodied limbs. On one wall had been painted a cartoon of a woman, cut in half, a screw protruding from her left breast and dripping blood, lying atop a cow that had been flayed to the midsection.

Welles sat on the steps and fished out a cigar from his suitcoat pocket; just above him a decapitated clown's head grinned from within a baroque bird cage. "You don't care for one, do you, Nathan?"

He meant a cigar, not a clown's head.

"No." I sat next to him. "No, thanks."

He fired up the Havana and got it going, waved out his match, and I noticed for the first time that the dark eyes in that cherubic puss were bloodshot.

"You know, I just can't seem to finish this set. It was the first thing I began on this picture, back in late September . . . before we went to Mexico, for location shooting. . . . I'm responsible for this strike, you know."

"How are you responsible?"

He gestured to the gruesome images around us. "By doing all this painting myself, with the help of a few friends. I couldn't turn over something this . . . intensely personal . . . to the hacks in the Columbia art department. I would have had the same artisans who bring their masterful touch to the Three Stooges."

"And that's what started the strike?"

He sighed dark, richly fragrant smoke. "It did, when members of the Motion Picture Set Painters Union . . . local 279 . . . came to this soundstage and discovered that their work had been completed by 'nonunion' hands."

"And here I thought you were such a flaming liberal."

"Oh I am, my dear, with a notable exception—in matters relating to my art, I am slightly to the right of Genghis Khan."

"You haven't asked why I wanted to see you."

The rosebud mouth twitched a tiny smile. "Did I thank you for recommending your friend, Mr. Rubinski, to handle that piece of business last year?"

"No. You're welcome. I take it Fred handled that matter . . . discreetly."

"Oh yes . . . of course I had to pay the girl twenty thousand to keep it out of court, and out of the papers. I didn't rape her, you know—that was utter nonsense."

"None of my business."

"My darling, if you had seen her—she was such an ugly thing. I would simply never rape an ugly girl. And I never seem to have to rape the beautiful ones."

His irony was strained, and as relaxed as that baby face was—so unformed looking, almost fetuslike—his forehead was tight and between his brows was a deep crease of tension.

He leaned toward me and touched my arm. "Have I apologized for snubbing you?"

"When did you snub me?"

"At La Rue, a week or two ago . . . I was dining with my soon-to-be-ex-wife."

So he *had* noticed me.

"You see," he was saying, "we've been making some silly attempts at reconciliation, not the least of which is this film, and if I'd introduced you—my friend the famous divorce detective from Chicago—Rita might have misunderstood."

"That's all right. No offense taken."

"And I was in a particularly black mood, further acerbated by alcohol. Who was your lovely companion?"

"My wife."

"Really! Congratulations! When did this happen?"

"Not long ago. We're sort of on our honeymoon."

"I was given to understand you were out here consolidating your business with Mr. Rubinski—did I read something to that effect in the *Examiner*?"

"You read the Hearst papers?"

"I'm keeping a particularly close eye on them right now."

"Why is that?"

Welles ignored the question, exhaling Havana smoke. "I hope your marriage is more successful than mine. I'm sure you wonder how even a 'monstrous boy' like me . . . that's what Houseman likes to call me . . . could fail to make a go of it with a beautiful, kind, sensitive, intelligent woman like Margarita Carmen Cansino Welles."

"You have a child together."

"Becky. Lovely girl—she is as wonderful a child as I am a beastly father."

"You don't have to sound proud of it. Some people would think you had it made."

"Some people are imbeciles. I'm sure you think I was running around on her—married to Rita Hayworth, and not satisfied with what he has at home. That Welles *is* a glutton!"

"Not my business."

"Well, I wasn't unfaithful, not at first, not for the longest time. But she constantly accused me of infidelity—you see, she is mentally unstable, that lovely child . . . She has an inferiority complex, largely due to the fact that that fiend of a father put her on stage, not in school, and that's the least of what that son of bitch did to her. . . . She's an unhappy woman, my darling Nathan, and a pathologically jealous one. She wept every night of our marriage, and yet, just last week she told me that our marriage was the happiest time of her life . . . Can you imagine?"

"You're saying, she accused of you cheating so often, you finally went ahead and did it."

"As did she. I'll always love her . . . and I think she will always love me." He sat smoking the cigar, then shook his head and said,

"You know what she always called me? George. That's my first name, you know—detestable, ordinary first name—that's what she always called me."

"Rita always called you George?"

"Not Rita, my dear—the Short girl. This 'Black Dahlia' you think I may have murdered."

Orson Welles liked to present himself as a harbinger of high culture, bringing Shakespeare, Conrad, and Kafka to the masses; but never forget that this glorious ham was also the Shadow. Melodrama was his metier.

Nonetheless, I was struck as dumb as Shorty, reeling from Welles' cliffhanger-before-the-commercial punch to my mental solar plexus.

"I told you I've been following the Hearst papers especially closely these last few days," he was saying. "I noted, with no small interest, your involvement in the investigation. I have to say I'm relieved to be talking to *you*, and not some Hearst reporter—or worse, one of the Los Angeles gestapo."

"Did you—"

"Know her? Of course I knew her. Perhaps not in the true biblical sense. . . . She was a lovely girl, one of those absolutely black-haired girls, with skin as white as Carrara marble, and eyelashes you could trip over. She rather reminded me of another Betty, Betty Chancellor, also a dark-haired, fair-skinned beauty . . . my first love, at Dublin's Gate Theater, back in '31. As for Betty Short, I met her at Camp Cooke, when we were touring the army camps with my 'Mercury Wonder Show,' and again at the late lamented Canteen, then most recently at Brittingham's, where she mooched the occasional meal."

"What I was going to ask was if you killed her."

Welles sighed. "If I knew, darling Nathan, I would tell you."

I studied that baby face and the haunted eyes staring out of it. "You mean to say, you don't know where you were, the night she was murdered?"

His smile in response was seemingly guileless. "Not a clue. A blank . . . It's a classic pulp premise, my dear—the man wakes up in a room, covered in blood, with a dead body next to him . . .

and no memory of having done the dastardly deed . . . or for that matter, not having done it."

"I'm guessing you didn't wake up in that vacant lot next to that butchered corpse."

"No . . . I was in my wife's house in Brentwood."

"Was your wife with you?"

"She was in the hospital. Exhaustion and dysentery from our Mexican location shooting. And Shorty had the night off, as did my secretary."

"So you have no alibi."

"None, my darling. Nor memory. In a cheap thriller, a blow to the head would have granted me the blessing of amnesia. I, however, earned my loss of memory, every missing moment of it."

"How?"

"It may come as a shock to you—I know it does to me—but my youth is fading fast, and my energy is no longer boundless. To work for days, without sleep, requires certain pharmaceutical assistance. Similar assistance is necessary to help me maintain my boyish figure, to better perform my leading man duties. And, as you know, I do take the occasional drink."

"Okay—so we're talking booze and amphetamines."

"Did you know that my family tree includes Horace Goldin—the legendary celebrated magician who invented the 'Divided Woman' illusion, the trick of sawing a female in half?"

"And that means you bisected Beth Short's body?"

As if the cigar were a wand, he gestured to the dismembered limbs framing the Crazy House doorway, and to the painting of a woman cut in half, her corpse flung on a flayed cow carcass. "I needed you to see these terrible images, Nathan—these images which were, by the way, created prior to the Short girl's murder." He tapped his temple with two fingers; his eyes bugged out. "They were in this mind. Nightmarish visions that I sought to exorcise in this harmless fashion."

A few terrible moments dragged by, and then he rose, without looking at me, saying, "Let's continue this in a more reflective setting."

He almost bolted from the hideous, hellish self-created surroundings, disappearing into the funhouse. I found him in the hall of mirrors, seated on a folding chair, staring blankly at perhaps eighty images of himself. Another folding chair, next to him, awaited me, and I took it.

"Could I have committed this act, Nathan?"

He was asking my reflections; I answered his.

"Orson, I don't think so. Just because you're a megalomaniac doesn't make you a homicidal maniac."

He continued to meet my gaze in the mirror; and almost the entire conversation that followed was delivered through the buffer of glass. The cigar had disappeared. As we spoke, it was as if I were speaking not to Welles, but his image, projected on a screen, dozens of screens.

"These Bosch-like grotesqueries," he said, "could they have been unfulfilled wishes? Worse, images I did fulfill on a black, forgotten night?"

"With *your* bad back?"

That halted the melodrama and made him laugh. "Yes, that did occur to me. I've been wearing that damn metal brace about half the time, lately—when I'm under stress, these genetic anomalies of the spine of mine, which my weight hardly helps, make me as helpless . . . and as harmless . . . as a kitten. But what if drugs and alcohol combined to blot out the pain? And to unleash some murderous rage in me, and then blot out the memory?"

I looked at him, not his reflection. "I don't think you killed her. But you may be able to help me figure out who did, by answering a few questions."

"By all means."

"Was Beth Short a hooker, Orson?"

"Not to my knowledge."

"When did you see her last?"

He stole a look at me, then spoke to my image. "At Brittingham's—I hadn't seen her since October. I bought her a sandwich and a Coke. It must have been . . . a week prior to the . . . grisly discovery."

"You just ran into her . . . ?"

"I don't think it was a coincidence—she was looking for me, hoping to see me—she admitted as much."

"What did she want?"

"Money. She said she needed an operation."

"An abortion?"

"That would be a reasonable assumption, considering she mentioned she was going to see a certain Dr. Dailey."

The back of my neck was prickling. "Why? Who is he?"

"Wallace A. Dailey—a former L.A. County Hospital chief of staff, a retired, respectable physician . . . and, I'm told, Hollywoodland's current abortionist of choice."

Sensing I'd struck gold, I scribbled the name down in my notepad, asking, "Would this Dailey happen to hail from New England, originally?"

This line of questioning seemed to make Welles uncomfortable, and a certain irritability, even impatience, colored his tone, as he replied, "I wouldn't know. Nor do I have an address on the man, though I presume he would be listed in the yellow pages, though probably not under 'abortionist.' "

"She tried to shake you down, didn't she, Orson?"

"Not precisely. There . . . may have been an implied threat of . . . embarrassment. I gave her what I could—fifty dollars. The child she was carrying was obviously not mine."

"You weren't intimate with her at all?"

"Define *intimate*."

"I would consider having your dick sucked intimate."

He winced at that, but admitted, "She did have a gift for fellatio. Children are seldom conceived in that fashion, you realize."

"She have any other gifts? Did you promise her a screen test?"

"I did. Not a false promise, either—she was very attractive, as I've said, lovely, really, and I understand she had a pleasant singing voice. How did you link me with her?"

"Florentine Gardens."

He nodded and dozens of him nodded in the mirrors. "N.T.G.?"

"Yeah, him and that actress, Ann Thomson. I don't think they'll mention you to the cops. The cops don't even know about her working at the Gardens, yet. And there were a lot of celebrities she came into contact with there—you'd be on a long list. I got a feeling the same is going to prove true of the Hollywood Canteen."

Now he looked at me—he seemed very young, like a big child with that helpless baby face. "I'd like to engage your services, Nathan."

"To cover this up?"

Still holding my gaze with his, he said, "I need to know that I was not responsible for this ghastly act. I need to *know*, Nathan."

"And if you are responsible?"

Now he spoke to me in the mirrors, again. "One calamity at a time. Let me just say, there is schizophrenia in my family, Nathan—if I in fact suffer from these agonizing Welles clan strains, then the next 'Crazy House' I inhabit may not be on a soundstage."

"You didn't do it, Orson."

His most charming smile beamed at me from dozens of mirrors. "Nathan, darling, there is in even the most humane of men an irrational drive to do evil."

I could only think of the opening of his old radio show: "*Who knows what evil lurks in the hearts of men?*"

Now he swiveled on the chair and looked right at me, placing a hand on my shoulder. "The only cover-up I ask is that you not breathe a word of this to the *Examiner*. If Hearst gets wind of my connection to the Black Dahlia, I'm finished—I might as well have done the crime."

Welles was right: Hearst would take immense pleasure in finally having his full revenge for *Citizen Kane*.

"I'll help you, Orson."

"Nathan, darling, there's one other small problem."

"Another problem?"

"I'm broke."

"Directing and starring in a Rita Hayworth picture, you're broke?"

"Dead broke. As a magician, my best act seems to be making money disappear. A horde of creditors, including the IRS, are hounding me, daily." He gestured to his hall of mirrors. "I'm doing this to repay a fifty-grand advance Harry Cohn wired me when I desperately needed money to pay the costume rental bill for *Around the World.*"

Orson had recently staged a Broadway show of *Around the World in 80 Days*, a lavish production with Cole Porter music that had nonetheless tanked. Rumor was Welles had sunk every cent he had into it, and was in hock for hundreds of thousands.

"You can charge me your standard hourly rate against an interest in my next production," he suggested, as he walked me out onto the soundstage.

"Which is?"

"I'm talking to Herbert Yates about a project over at Republic."

"Where they make all those B-westerns? You are running out of studios to alienate."

He was ushering me through the near-darkness of the vast chamber past the endless dragon slide.

"Don't be cynical, darling Nathan—I'm going to be doing Shakespeare on the same soundstages where Roy Rogers and Gene Autry bring badmen to justice. There is something delightful about that! I'm mounting it as if it were a horror movie, you know, like Universal used to make with Karloff and Lugosi."

"Which play?"

"*Macbeth*—murder in the night, followed by nightmares, guilt and rampant paranoia."

"Well," I said, stepping out into the light, "at least you got the research out of the way."

His expression was blank. "I only hope I haven't been researching *Othello.*"

And he slipped back into the darkness.

Then I turned and bumped into Shorty, waiting to show me the way out of Columbia's backlot, a maze rivaling Welles' hall of mirrors.

# 15

The Bradbury Building, on the southeast corner of Third and Broadway in downtown Los Angeles, was only slightly less bizarre than Welles' Crazy House. The five-story turn-of-the-century building's unremarkable brownstone exterior concealed a baroque secret life: ornamental wrought-iron stairwells and balconies, globed fixtures illuminating the open brick-and-tile corridors; caged elevators, their cables and gears and rollers exposed, like contraptions out of Jules Verne; and an enormous greenhouse-style skylight that bounced an eerie gold-white light off the glazed floor of the huge central court that was the Bradbury's lobby.

Our offices were on the fifth floor, near an elevator, behind a frosted glass door that said *A-1 Detective Agency, Fredrick C. Rubinski, Chief Investigator* (both our names, however, were listed on the building directory—we were the only detective agency in a world of doctors and lawyers). In the outer office sat our receptionist—an attractive gum-chewing, nail-filing blonde—who worked for free, because Fred allowed her to sit at a switchboard, running her own answering-service business. In addition to the inner office, which was Fred's alone, an adjoining, cubicled-off office accommodated four operatives.

Late in the afternoon, I sat across from Fred and filled him in on my day's activities.

"Assaulting a police detective," Fred said archly, leaning back in his swivel chair, the dwindling stub of a once-fine cigar in a corner of his mouth, "that should be good for business. . . . Why so reckless, Nate?"

A hard round ball of a man, Fred looked like a bald, slightly less homely Edward G. Robinson, typically natty in his gray suit and blue-and-gray patterned tie.

"Fat Ass isn't a cop," I said, sipping a cup of water from the outer office cooler. "He's just a thug on the city payroll. Anyway, there won't be a peep out of him—he won't tell a soul."

"Because he was at Lansom's, playing bag man, you mean?"

"That's right. I think they're running hookers out of that nightclub."

Fred lifted a thick dark eyebrow. "If so, I haven't heard about it. Ever since that underage-chorus-girl shit hit the fan, Granny's been keeping the Garden squeaky clean."

"Yeah? Then why is Granny quitting?"

"The hell you say!"

"Granlund told me as much today. Seems Lansom's up to something that's rubbing our esteemed road-company Ziegfeld the wrong way."

"That's pretty goddamn interesting . . ." Fred pressed out the stub of his cigar in a brass tray on his tidy desk. ". . . but I still don't think it's hookers. Did you break Brown's nose?"

"Probably. Fat Ass won't fuck with me—he thinks I'm a Chicago Outfit guy."

"Aren't you?"

I wadded up the empty Dixie cup and tossed it in a corner wastebasket. "Not in any major way, but I'm not going to burst his bubble, on that score. Listen, what can you tell me about a . . ." I checked my notepad. ". . . Dr. Wallace A. Dailey?"

Fred rocked in the chair, fingers tented on his belly over his silk tie. "Just that he's everybody's favorite rabbit-puller, these days."

"Abortionist to the stars."

"Yeah, and the social set."

"And how does a physician achieve such distinction?"

Fred laughed, shrugged. "We're not talking about some back-room abortion mill, Nate—Doc Dailey is, or anyway was, a prominent member of the medical community, out here."

According to Fred (who confirmed and expanded upon what Welles had told me), Dr. Dailey was a former chief of staff at Los Angeles County Hospital, and—until fairly recently—had been an associate professor of surgery at the University of Southern California.

"There was some kind of scandal that got hushed up," Fred said, "back in early '45 . . . a malpractice situation that got paid off and swept under the carpet. But serious enough that the doc had to resign both his positions."

"You don't know what the nature of that malpractice was?"

"Well, you gotta understand, the doc's in his late sixties, or anyway that's what I'd guess . . . and it's pretty well known he's not really functioning on all cylinders, these days."

"How so?"

Fred shrugged. "He's forgetful, turned into a regular absent-minded-professor type—hell, maybe even senile. He probably sewed a scalpel up inside somebody."

This wasn't tracking. "Then what makes a pregnant movie star want to go under his knife?"

"Dailey's respectable, with a spotless reputation . . . prior to those resignations, anyway . . . and, besides, I would venture to say he's not doing the cutting, himself. It's probably that amazon, doing it."

I leaned back in my chair, arms folded, shaking my head. "If you're under the impression I know what the hell you're talking about, partner, you're as batty as this doc sounds."

Fred selected a fresh cigar out of a carved wooden box—like Welles, Rubinski was strictly a Havana man. "I'm talking about this South American woman Dailey took in as a partner—Dr. Maria Winter. Big, handsome gal in her forties, some kind of war refugee."

"The war was in Europe, as I recall."

"Yeah, well," he said, puffing the cigar, getting it going, "she was over there studying, when the bombs started dropping, went to the University of Prague or some such—what landed her in that part of the world, how the hell should I know? . . . But eventually she wound up on Doc Dailey's doorstep, when he was still at the County Hospital. He took her under his wing, and she worked as his nurse while she took classes, till she could pass the boards for her California medical license."

"How do you happen to know all this?"

"I don't 'happen' to know it." He drew on the cigar, held in some smoke, blew it out, choosing his next words carefully. "I refer clients to them, in need of the Dailey clinic's particular medical specialty."

"Oh."

"Look, any number of people could have filled you in on those two characters—I mean, it's one of those only-in-Hollywood affairs."

"How so?"

Fred shook his head, grinned, cigar in his teeth now, like he was waiting for a circus marksman to shoot it out. "Respectable doctor, at the end of his career, happily married, kids, grandkids—and then this built-like-a-brick-shithouse hot tamale good-neighbor-policies her way into his life."

I frowned. "She's not just his business partner, you mean?"

"Naw! The doc is separated from his wife; maybe filed for divorce by now, for all I know. It's comical—Dailey's this proper little old man, suddenly in the clutches of this tall, curvy femme fatale—"

"And they're running an abortion clinic together," I said. "Right out in the open?"

Fred smirked. "That's not hard in L.A. It's a homicide bureau setup, y'know—a protected ring with Dailey and Winter up near the top of the list. The State Medical Board investigates any complaints or info that comes in, regarding abortions performed by doctors or chiros or midwives or whoever; but they turn their results over to the homicide bureau, who either shake down or crack down on anybody outside of the ring . . . and those who *are* in the ring, tip-offs are made, any arrests are smothered . . . you get the picture."

"Are we back to Fat Ass again?"

"He's a homicide dick," Fred said, nodding. "Now, Harry the Hat, he wouldn't touch this kind of crap."

"And you're saying, the A-1 has an existing relationship with Dr. Dailey and his partner—"

"Dr. Winter. Yeah. We get a referral fee."

"A kickback."

Half a smile dimpled Fred's plump cheek. "Why, does that offend your sensibilities, Nate? We swim in Hollywood waters—so what if it's a swimming pool, and not the Chicago River? That doesn't make the water any less scummy."

I sat thinking for a while, then asked, "Early this month, did you get a phone call from a girl—kind of a low, husky voice—wanting to get in touch with me?"

Fred's endless forehead clenched in thought. "Come to think of it . . . yeah—she was the daughter of an old friend, she said, wanted to say hello."

"And you gave her my number at the Beverly Hills Hotel."

"I think I did. Why? Shouldn't I have . . . ?"

I didn't answer. My heard was whirling. I was still trying to wrap my brain around the notion that Beth Short had chosen an abortionist who took referrals from my own detective agency! What the fuck was going on?

"I have to talk to this Dailey," I said, "*and* his amazon partner—sooner the better."

Fred was looking at me, funny. "Well, his office is probably open for another half hour or so. . . . What are you not telling me, Nate?"

"You don't want to know." I stood, digging my car keys out of my trousers. "Where is Dailey's office, Fred? Can I make it there before he closes?"

Fred blinked. "Are you kidding?"

"Do I look like I'm fucking kidding?" I yelled, leaning in, a hand against the desktop. "Where is Dailey's office, Fred?"

He swallowed and pointed to his left. "Just down the hall, Nate."

Down the corridor, around a corner, there it was, on the frosted glass: *Doctor Wallace A. Dailey, M.D., Surgeon; Doctor*

*Maria Winter, M.D., Gynecologist.* The Dailey practice seemed to engulf the equivalent of three or four standard Bradbury Building office layouts.

So.

Elizabeth Short had gone to see her doctor—that is, the abortionist whose fee she was trying to raise—and had noticed, either on her way to or from that doctor's office, the neighboring A-1 Detective Agency. She had recognized the A-1 as mine, remembered my talking about opening a California branch, and may even have checked the building directory, where my name was listed. Then she called Fred Rubinski and got my number at the hotel.

All of which led me to believe the baby she was carrying had not been mine: that seeing my name had simply reminded her of one more male acquaintance she could shake down in her effort to raise that five hundred dollars she needed to abort *somebody's* child.

But if I wasn't the father, then who was?

A man who tortured her and cut her in half and left her, drained of blood, in a vacant lot?

The chairs that lined the waiting room were empty, and the receptionist—a pleasant white-uniformed brunette in her early twenties—looked up and out from her window and informed me the office would be closing, momentarily.

I gave her my card, explained that I was the president of the A-1 Detective Agency, and would like the opportunity to briefly introduce myself to the two doctors.

Soon I was waiting in an office whose walls were decorated with framed diplomas, awards, and group photographs in both hospital and academic settings. I took one of two wooden, cushioned chairs across from a desk that was massive and mahogany and bare except for a blotter and family photos in standing frames—if any work had been done at this desk lately, it wasn't showing. Wooden filing cabinets hid in corners, and along the back wall a lighted cabinet displayed a considerable collection of carved jade—mostly Buddhas and dragons and other Oriental figurines, with a shelf of exquisite jewelry and an intricate Chinese fan.

The door opened and a man in a white jacket and green tie and brown tweed trousers stepped in, drawing his head back and blinking as he saw me sitting there. He was in his sixties, somewhat pudgy, with a salt-and-pepper mustache—neatly trimmed, as was his full head of gray hair—and regular features, including rheumy green eyes behind wireframed glasses.

He said, "Oh! Please excuse me."

And he went back out.

I sat there, looking at the closed door, and perhaps two minutes later, he came in and blinked at me again.

This time I stood, however, and stopped him before he could rush out. "Dr. Dailey?"

He looked at me carefully. "Yes? Am I interrupting?"

"No. I was waiting for you. My name is Nathan Heller. I just spoke to your receptionist, your nurse? I wanted a moment of your time."

"Certainly." He smiled, nodded. "Certainly."

He took his place behind the desk and folded his hands. "What can I do for you, Mr. Heller?"

I explained that I was the president of the A-1, that my Chicago agency had merged with Rubinski's.

"And I understand we've been sending you some referrals," I said.

The doctor frowned in seeming thought. "Have you?"

"Yes. But I wanted to ask you about a specific young woman—Elizabeth Short."

That name—the hottest topic on the lips of just about every newspaper reader in Los Angeles—got no visible reaction out of him. He just shook his head. "I don't recall that particular patient. I'm afraid I'm growing a bit forgetful, Mr. . . . uh . . . !"

"Heller. Elizabeth Short was her name—she may have been an old family friend."

Nodding, eyes narrowed behind the wireframes, he admitted, "Now that does sound familiar. . . . Not the name, but . . ."

"Did you practice medicine in New England, Dr. Dailey, before coming to California?"

He sat up straight. "Did I? I could have. . . ."

"Surely, Dr. Dailey, you can remember where you practiced medicine."

"Certainly. Medford Memorial Hospital."

This response had been crisp, immediate.

I said, "Then Elizabeth Short did come here to make an appointment."

"Did she?"

"Pretty girl, with black hair, fair complexion—she wore a lot of makeup."

"Like a geisha!" he said, snapping his fingers. He stood. The eyes seemed alert, suddenly. "Let me show you my jade collection."

"Uh . . . all right."

The little doctor moved quickly to the cabinet, where I followed him, and for several minutes he described the pieces in detail, in particular a tiny Fei Tsui jade dragon that was particularly valuable.

"Should be in a safe deposit box, I suppose," he said, shaking his head, "but I just couldn't bear to hide away such beauty."

Throughout this mini-lecture, Dailey was entirely coherent and focused; it was no great stretch to see that he'd been a professor. And his hands, gesturing confidently, suggested the respected surgeon he'd once been.

"What was your name?" he asked me, as he settled himself behind his desk again, and I took my chair.

"Yes, what is your name?" another voice asked—female, strong, sultry.

She stood framed in the doorway—unmistakably the amazon Fred had referred to—tall, perhaps as much as six feet, in white smock and pants that neither emphasized nor hid her generously well-shaped form. Not beautiful, exactly, Dr. Maria Winter was indeed "handsome," her oval face home to large, languid yet piercing dark brown eyes, her nose aquiline, her mouth thin lipped and touched lightly red, her jaw firm, like her expression. Brown hair sat in a bun atop the rather oversize head; her smooth, clear complexion had an olive cast.

"I'm Nathan Heller," I said, standing. "I gave your receptionist my card—I'm president of the A-1 Detective Agency . . . your neighbor."

I offered her a hand and she shook it, firmly, introducing herself.

"I'm afraid Sharon neglected to tell me you were here," she said. "We're closing for the day. Is this a business matter, or—"

"Since my agency is sending referrals to you, I thought I should pay a courtesy call."

"How kind."

"But I also have a few questions about one of your patients."

And I went back and sat down. "Dr. Dailey was just telling me about working in Massachusetts."

She was still framed in the doorway, staring at me as if from two glass eyes.

Dailey turned to her and said, "Would you mind if I showed the gentleman my jade collection?"

Her mouth formed a smile, as she gazed at him, but it didn't soften the hard, brittle mask of her face. She strode to him, put a hand on his shoulder—gently—and said, "You've had a hard day, a long day."

He touched the hand on his shoulder, beamed up at her lovingly. "Shall we go home, dear?"

"Soon." Her hand still on the doctor's shoulder, she stared at me coldly. "Mr. Heller, Dr. Dailey is a fine man, and a fine physician . . . but he has his good days and bad, and his sapient moments and his . . ."

"Not so sapient moments?" I offered.

"The doctor is suffering from encephalomalacia, cerebral and coronary arteriosclerosis, and threat of myocardial infarction."

"He's senile and at risk of heart attack."

"Yes."

Dailey was smiling at me, hands folded, seemingly oblivious to the conversation we were having about him.

"The doctor and I work side by side," she said. "He is often quite lucid, and—together—we are able to help many patients."

"I trust the doctor isn't performing surgery, any longer."

"He is not . . . and as for the, uh, procedure in question . . ."

"Abortions, you mean."

The eyes tightened in the terrible handsome mask. "Mr. Heller, I'm surprised a man in your line of work would be so indiscreet. Surely I don't have to tell you that a private office can easily be bugged with dictaphones?"

I smiled, shrugged. "My understanding is that you're protected."

She folded her arms over the shelf of her breasts; she looked like an annoyed genie. "Be that as it may, the procedure is performed either by myself or by a physician's assistant."

"Not a physician?"

"An assistant with sufficient medical training to safely perform this simple procedure."

"Skip the hard sell, Dr. Winter. I know you're good; otherwise you and Doc Dailey wouldn't be the film colony's favorite mistake correctors."

A frown disrupted the perfect smoothness of her face. "Is the referral fee we've been paying Mr. Rubinski in your view insufficient? I would hope you stand by the terms your partner and I negotiated, when—"

"No, that's fine. I'm here about Elizabeth Short. You know—the Black Dahlia."

Only the slightest twitch around her mouth indicated that what I had said had thrown her in any way. She said, simply, "I read the papers."

I leaned back in the chair. "Don't play games, Dr. Winter. I know the Short woman was a patient, or anyway a prospective one—she knew Dr. Dailey back in her hometown. She must've heard his name bandied about among her Hollywood girl friends, as the reliable quack to go to for 'the procedure' . . . and recognized the name as that of an old family friend."

Dr. Winter came around the desk, sat on the edge of it, looming over me. Dailey was smiling, giving no indication of whether he was following any of this or not.

She said, "Confidentiality between patient and doctor is a sacred pact, Mr. Heller."

"Get off your high horse, lady—this is an abortion mill . . . kindly old doc, respectable offices, and fancy jade collection don't change that."

"I'm not going to confirm or deny Elizabeth Short as one of our patients."

"This a murder case, get it? That alone should be enough to catch your attention; but it's also not just any murder case. If the Short girl gets connected back to you, and this office . . . and then the A-1 office . . . we're—"

The door opened. A tall, broad-shouldered man in doctor's whites leaned in and said, "Excuse me—am I needed any longer?"

"Dr. Dailey and I are done for the day, Floyd," Dr. Winter said, "but I'd like you to finish putting away those supplies, if you haven't already."

"Glad to," Floyd said. Though clearly in his early forties, he had a boyish look, his hair blond, his eyes ice-blue. "That'll only take a few minutes."

"Thank you, Floyd," she said. "Then lock up, would you?"

"Sure," he said, and slipped out, closing the door behind him.

"Your physician's assistant?" I asked.

"Yes," she said; impatience tinged her tone. "Now, Mr. Heller, if I can assure you that Elizabeth Short was not referred to us by the A-1, will that allay your trepidation?"

"Then you're saying she *was* a patient?"

Her gaze was withering, her sigh disdainful. "No, I am not. Is that all, Mr. Heller?"

I said for the moment it was, and shook the smiling Dr. Dailey's hand, complimenting him on his jade collection—he offered to take me over and give me a closer look, but I declined—and nodded to Dr. Winter, who nodded back, icily, and opened the door for me. After that, I found my own way out.

In the corridor, I leaned against the balcony railing, feeling dizzy: it wasn't vertigo; I wasn't even looking over the edge. I was still gazing at the frosted glass doorway of the Dailey practice.

Their physician's assistant, Floyd, had not seemed to notice me, when he interrupted my conference with the two doctors; but I had noticed him.

Only his name wasn't Floyd, not really: it was Lloyd.

Lloyd Watterson.

Also known as the Mad Butcher of Kingsbury Run.

# 16

Union Station's courtyard, with its peaceful patio of trees, bushes, benches, and flagstones, provided a less frantic setting for farewells and welcomes than most big-city train stations. With sunset approaching, cool blue shadows touched the low-slung sprawl of red-tile-roofed white stucco buildings, overseen by a formidable clock tower.

I was surprisingly relaxed, and not at all tired, as I moved through the immense ticket room, with its tall, colored-mosaic ceiling, whistling a tuneless tune as I fell in with the flow of the hurrying crowd, passing through the soundproofed elegance of the waiting room with its leather chairs where bums slept and passengers waited. The cavelike, well-lighted passenger tunnel, with its eight ramps feeding sixteen tracks, echoed with footsteps, conversation, and the jolts and screeches of trains lurching in and out of the station. I stopped at the ramp where the Union Pacific had just come in, and saw Eliot Ness in the process of tipping a colored porter who was handing him a single buckled bag.

Eliot looked both older and smaller than I remembered. His freckled, Scandinavian boyishness was largely obscured in a pouchy, puffy face; he was in his mid-forties, but—I was a little shocked to see—looked more like his mid-fifties. Eliot's gray suit was typically well tailored, with a gray-and-shades-of-blue-striped tie, and a snapbrim fedora of a darker gray, a trenchcoat folded over the arm.

Moving up the ramp, the aging Untouchable spotted me and smiled; but his gray eyes seemed troubled. He'd had a long train trip, which could take it out of anybody; still, I could tell this was more than that—something was wrong.

Me, I was jingling the change in my pocket and whistling my tuneless tune.

"You're in a pleasant mood," Eliot said, as we shook hands and I grinned at him.

"Yeah, I've had a productive day."

The troubled gray eyes tightened. "Well, I'm afraid I'm going to spoil it for you. Can we take a moment, before you take me to the hotel? We need to talk privately."

The best place to talk privately, of course, is in public. The station fronted Alameda Street and I guided Eliot a few steps west, to the Plaza, that beaten-down circular patch of grass, pigeons, and spreading magnolias where Los Angeles was born, with the neighboring shabby relics to prove it. To the east the curio stores and restaurants of old Chinatown lurked; to the north sprawled Olivera Street, where Peggy and I had explored the bazaarlike tourist-trap marketplace; to the west stood the adobe walls of the Old Mission Church, adorned with a marker of historic significance, as well as graffiti ("KILROY WAS HERE!"); and at the south loomed the twenty-story white tower of City Hall, the present presenting its middle finger to the past.

We sat on a bench with pigeons scavenging at our feet—I had bought some popcorn and a cold bottle of Coke from a street vendor, and Eliot was sipping a paper cup of black coffee into which he'd poured something from a silver flask. Around us, on nearby benches, elderly Mexicans in food-stained shirts and well-worn dungarees sat staring blankly, as if wondering how their city had managed to fall into Anglo-Saxon hands; a few others had abandoned such empty speculation and were curled up and enjoying a siesta. A stone bench, circling the park, seemed the province of bums and winos. Dusk settled a cool, soothing hand on the indigents and on two old friends, about to share secrets.

"My dad would have been comfortable here," I said.

Eliot blinked at that. "What?"

"Lot of the big labor demonstrations are held in this plaza. Pop would have been in his element."

"Do you still carry his gun?"

"Yeah—the nine-millimeter. Well, not at the moment . . . It's in my suitcase. I probably should be carrying it—this is turning into that kind of job."

I told him about punching out Fat Ass Brown.

"Christ, they're corrupt out here," he said, shaking his head. "Worse than when I took over in Cleveland."

"At least when the Chicago cops do want to solve a crime—as opposed to commit one—they can pull it off."

"What about Harry Hansen?"

"The Hat's a real detective." I sipped my Coke; the bag of popcorn was propped between my thighs and I alternated eating a kernel or two, and pitching one for the birds to fight over. "Hansen's one of the smart, honest ones, even if he is a glory hound."

Eliot sighed. "I'm almost sorry to hear that he's competent."

"Why?"

He watched the pigeons pecking the popcorn I was pitching them. He sipped his coffee. Then he looked at the darkening sky for several long seconds, and finally at me, and said, "Nate . . . I have terrible news."

"Personal or professional?"

"Both." He shook his head. "This is something we have to keep to ourselves . . . something we have to *do* ourselves, work on in a . . . *sub rosa* manner."

"Of course."

"Nate, you're the only one I can trust—"

"Eliot. Go on. Spill."

He shrugged, gestured with both hands—no way to soften this blow: "Lloyd Watterson is in California."

"Really."

His brow clenched and the gray eyes were confused at my lack of reaction; nonetheless, he pressed on. "After we spoke on the phone, I figured I should check out Watterson's status—personally. I went to the Sandusky Soldiers and Sailors Home, where Lloyd was in the psychopathic ward."

"I wasn't aware Lloyd was a veteran."

"He wasn't, but his father, Dr. Clifford Watterson, was. Anyway, I learned that because Lloyd was signed in as a patient voluntarily, he could be signed out the same way."

I frowned. "That wasn't part of the deal you cut."

"Certainly wasn't." Finished with his coffee, he wadded up the paper cup and pitched it perfectly into a nearby trash receptacle. He turned to me and the gray eyes had hardened into steel. "Lloyd was to be committed, kept off the streets, completely out of circulation—and now I've learned that from August 1938, when he entered the mental hospital, until September 1944, he was signed out by his father eight times, for periods up to three weeks."

"Jesus. . . . What about *after* September '44?"

He breathed in heavily, breathed out the same way. "His father died in August of that year. And then in September 1944, Lloyd signed *himself* out . . . and hasn't been back since."

Something wasn't adding up. "What about those taunting postcards you received, postmarked Sandusky?"

Eliot helped himself to some of my popcorn, pitched it to the pigeons. "I did some good old-fashioned poking around—asked orderlies and patients about Lloyd. Turns out the Ohio Penitentiary Honor Farm shares certain facilities with the Soldiers and Sailors Home. Seems Lloyd struck up a friendship with a guy named Alex Koch, a convicted burglar."

"Is this Koch still serving his sentence?"

"No. He's been out for some time. I tracked him down to a rooming house in Cleveland. He was afraid, at first, when he saw me—and he wouldn't cooperate unless I assured him he wouldn't be considered an accomplice after the fact."

"Accomplice to what?"

A wry little half-smile formed in the puffy face. "Sometime, in the course of their intimate friendship, Lloyd confessed to his friend Alex . . . bragged, it would seem . . . that he was indeed the Kingsbury Run butcher. Uh, as you may recall, Lloyd's sexual preferences are . . . unusual."

I shrugged. "His gate swings both ways. Plus, there's that little fetish he has—most guys like to get a little head; they just don't keep a spare one in the icebox."

Eliot merely nodded. "I would call bisexuality combined with necrophilia a rather distinctive 'fetish.' And, although Alex did not specifically admit to this, I gathered that he and Lloyd were more than just friends. In any case, they did each other favors."

I had a swig of Coke. "Like Lloyd having sex with Alex without hacking him to death, you mean?"

"There's that. But it would also seem that Lloyd could perfectly mimic his father's signature and would forge prescriptions for barbiturates for Koch, in return for his pal coming back on visiting days to smuggle liquor in to Lloyd. Since Dr. Watterson's death, of course, that came to a stop. Still—and this is why I suspect a deeper bond between Alex and Lloyd—over the last several years, Alex has received occasional envelopes from Lloyd containing unmailed postcards—"

I snapped my fingers. "Postcards with those razzing messages to you. Lloyd had Alex mail them to you, from Ohio!"

Eliot smiled ruefully, tossed a kernel of popcorn to the pigeons. "Not only Ohio—Alex would drive to Sandusky to mail them, to get just the right postmark."

"Did Alex tell you where Lloyd sent them from?" I asked, knowing the answer.

"California. Specifically, Los Angeles." He shook his head. "And as if that weren't disturbing enough, I made a chilling discovery. You see, I went down to the Cleveland P.D. and was up all night, combing through the three-thousand-some pages of the Torso file with Detective Merlo. You remember him? Martin Merlo?"

"Sure—he was obsessed with the Butcher case. Last I heard, he was still on it."

"He still is, although he was officially removed from the investigation, years ago. Of course, Merlo was never part of the small circle of men who knew about Watterson, and he kept insisting that the Butcher was still striking—not in Cleveland, but around the country. . . . Remember that murder in New Castle, Pennsylvania, that we thought might have been Watterson's work?"

"Yes," I said, nodding, "but you ascertained Lloyd was still institutionalized."

"Correct—before I knew his daddy was signing him in and out of that padded suite." He sighed. "Merlo volunteered to make this trip, but I offered my services, at my own expense, and of course Detective Hansen specifically requested me . . . so the police chief took me up on it."

"With all your responsibilities at Diebold, Eliot, how did you spring yourself loose for this?"

He shrugged. "I get three weeks of vacation."

"Some vacation."

"As I started to say, I found something very disturbing in the Torso file—"

"I'd kinda think there'd be a lot of disturbing things in the Torso file."

"Well, this one really sent alarm bells ringing. Back around 1939, Chief Matowitz and I got a letter postmarked Los Angeles from somebody claiming to be the Butcher. I dismissed it at the time, knowing—or thinking, that is—that Watterson was out of commission, tucked away inside rubber walls. And I'd forgotten it entirely, till I ran across the thing the other night—that letter said the Butcher's next torso would be found on Century Boulevard between Western and Crenshaw."

I was frowning again. "That's not precisely the vacant lot where Elizabeth Short's body was found . . . but it's goddamn close."

"Yes. Close enough to chill me to the bone, let me tell you. Los Angeles may have been one of Lloyd's visiting spots when he was getting Papa to sign him out, periodically . . . and California would seem to have been his permanent place of residence since around October 1944."

I wondered when, exactly, that bathtub slaying had taken place—that socialite friend of Beth Short's, that "Bauerdorf girl" Aggie Underwood had mentioned at lunch.

"And now, obviously," I said, "you're thinking Lloyd may have killed Elizabeth Short."

"I am. And I'm hoping the two of us can find that maniac before the police do."

That confused me. "Why *before* the police?"

Around us, the Mexicans stared and snoozed, and bums slumbered; the shadows had gathered into night, and the lights of Olivera Street winked at us. Somewhere over there, a cafe musician was singing a Spanish song, "*Ay yi yi yi,*" clear but strangely distant.

Eliot didn't answer my question. Instead he said, "I'll have to spend some time with the LAPD, doing my best to convince them the Butcher didn't kill the Dahlia . . . the difference in M.O. should make that simple enough."

"Why was there a difference in M.O., if Watterson did the murder?"

He didn't answer that, either. "I have a lead—not much of one, but a lead. This Koch character told me that Watterson has taken a job as a male nurse for some shady doctor out here."

"No kidding."

Eliot nodded. "Koch claimed not to know *what* doctor, or to have any address on Watterson. You know, Koch may not be the first time Lloyd paired up with an accomplice of sorts."

"Really? I always figured he was a loner."

"In the original investigation, we theorized it may have been necessary for the Butcher to recruit help—have a sort of apprentice—to help carry out the murders and dispose of the various body parts. We even had a suspect, a young homosexual who worked in the butcher shop of a St. Clair Avenue grocery . . . but it never panned out."

"If Koch is that kind of accomplice, and not just a jailhouse sweetheart, his information might be suspect . . . or he might have warned Lloyd by phone."

"No—you see, I still have friends at the Cleveland P.D. They booked Koch on vagrancy—he's being shuttled around from stationhouse to stationhouse, and should be off the streets till the middle of next week, at least. In the meantime, I'll to try to worm a list of known abortionists out of Detective Hansen, which I will then turn over to you, so you can go looking for Lloyd."

I tried the first question again. "Why aren't we working directly with the police on this, Eliot? Why are we keeping this investigation to ourselves?"

He gazed at me with hooded eyes. "Nate . . . if this came out . . . that I was party to this . . . that in 1938 I had the Mad Butcher in my hands and allowed myself to be fooled in this way . . . that the Short girl, and God knows how many others, died because of it. . . ."

He sat so slumped that his arms rested on his thighs, like a man trying not to puke. Then he touched a hand to his eyes. Jesus, was he weeping?

"Eliot . . . you couldn't have known . . ."

He shook his head. "No excuse. No excuse. And . . . Nate, what I'm going to ask you to help me do is unconscionable . . . but I just have no choice."

"No problem. We'll kill the son of a bitch and bury him in the desert." I shrugged. "Cutting his head off would be a nice touch."

He laughed at that, as if I'd been joking, then said, "No . . . that's not what I mean. It's . . . really, it's worse than that. I am desperately out of my element at Diebold, Nate—I need to get back into public life."

"I don't understand."

Drawing in a deep breath, Eliot Ness straightened himself, looked right at me. "Remember, years ago, when my boss Harold Burton stepped down as mayor, to run for congress? And I was asked to run in his place?"

"Yeah—you turned it down. You were satisfied with your job as public safety director."

"Declining that opportunity was the biggest mistake I ever made."

Burton had been succeeded by an opposition-party mayor who did not stand behind Ness as safety director, who in fact had forced Eliot from office after the unfortunate hit-and-run incident.

"Well," Eliot said, "I've been given a second chance—I've been approached to run for mayor of Cleveland, in the fall. Republican ticket."

Now it made sense: if this came out—the Butcher, the Dahlia—Eliot would be finished, politically—finished as any kind of public figure.

"I've spoken to Watterson's uncle," Eliot said.

"Congressman Watterson. I doubt you'll get his endorsement in your campaign."

Lewis M. Watterson, Lloyd's uncle, was a powerhouse in Cleveland's democratic party. Ironically, he had been Eliot's enemy in Cleveland, during the years Ness was public safety director, characterizing the Untouchable as being obsessed with rooting out even the most insignificant police corruption even as an "insane killer" was "stalking the streets of Cleveland."

This was, of course, before the congressman learned that his nephew *was* that insane killer—and before the congressman became part of that very small circle who knew that Lloyd Watterson had been committed to a mental hospital.

"I frankly asked the congressman what he thought I should do," Eliot said. "He pointed out what the scandal would do to all of our careers—his, mine, former Mayor Burton's . . ."

Who was a United States senator, now.

". . . and Congressman Watterson requested that I bring Lloyd back to him, and said he would go with me, personally, to make sure Lloyd was committed—permanently—to an asylum in Dayton."

"No more outpatient status."

"Locked up, key thrown away."

"I still like my idea better."

"You'll help me, then?"

"I'll help you. I can't promise I'll go along with the congressman's wishes."

The gray eyes studied me; Eliot shook his head. "Nate, your attitude . . . you're always kind of flip, but I don't get it—I tell you the Mad Butcher is at large—right here in California—and you barely bat an eyelash."

"Oh," I said, and took one last swig of Coke. "That's because he's tied up and locked in my office closet."

# 17

I drove Eliot over to the Bradbury Building, which was maybe eight blocks south of Union Station, and I filled him in—filled him in on everything. Fedora in his lap, the familiar comma of brown (graying) hair straying down his forehead, he sat quietly, taking it all in, occasionally lifting an eyebrow. Soon I was parking in the alley, near the service entrance. The building was locked up—no night man in the lobby, no book to sign—but I had a key to the tenants' door in back.

"You have a murder motive," Eliot said, his voice and our footsteps echoing through the brick-and-glass-and-iron cathedral, "and you were unlucky enough to stumble onto the corpse. . . . That's the kind of coincidence juries hang you over."

"Not in this state," I said cheerfully. "Here, it's the gas chamber."

We headed up the steep, wide iron stairway, with its heavy railings and ornate grillwork—the elevators were shut down, no attendants on duty, and self-service was discouraged. Only about a third of the streetlamp-like light fixtures were on, glowing globes in the ghostly stillness. As we climbed, I glanced around, looking for lights behind the frosted glass of office doors, seeing if anyone else was here after hours—not likely, on a Friday night.

"While we're talking coincidences," I said, pausing on a landing, "how about Lloyd Watterson turning up in Dr. Dailey's employ—in the same building as the A-1, yet?"

Eliot waved that off. "A good criminal lawyer can get rid of that—the A-1 and Dailey being in the same building is only natural, what with their referral system. And who else is Lloyd Watterson going to work for, but some shady character involved in abortion or other illegal medical practices?"

"So if I beat the murder rap," I said, starting back up the stairs, voice reverberating hollowly, "I face abortion charges? Sort of a consolation prize."

"You're just lucky Lloyd didn't recognize you."

Actually, Lloyd Watterson had only seen me once, almost ten years ago—granted it had been a memorable meeting, him coming in on me as I was sneaking around his house near Kingsbury Run, that modest bungalow in the basement of which Watterson had kept his so-called "murder lab." Decapitating living humans was messy, after all, what with the jugular vein spurting blood: privacy was needed to dispatch victims and tidy up after.

Lloyd's basement—painted a blinding hospital-white, open beams, block walls, concrete floor, white enamel examination table, white medical storage cabinets, counter arrayed with vials and tubes and beakers, including a jug ominously marked FORMALDEHYDE—was where he had tied me up, before coming at me with a cleaver that he had assured me was *not* used for butchery, for but amputation. Lloyd, you see, preferred the term "Mad Doctor of Kingsbury Run" to the less dignified, vaguely insulting "Mad Butcher."

I had insulted Lloyd more directly, kicking him in the balls—he had neglected to tie my legs to the chair—at about which time an associate of Eliot's, who'd been waiting outside, had the sense to barge in with a gun and make the capture.

"How did you manage to get Lloyd into your office closet?" Eliot asked, pausing to catch his breath on a landing, moonlight spilling down on us from the greenhouse-like skylight. My old friend—who had always been an avid tennis and handball player and jujitsu enthusiast—had a slightly paunchy, out-of-shape look that surprised me.

"Nothing too dramatic," I said. "I waited for him to leave the doctor's office—luckily, it was just late enough that no one else was around—stepped behind him, put a gun in his back, and walked him inside."

We started climbing again.

Eliot, somewhat winded, said, "I thought your nine-millimeter was in your suitcase."

"It is." On the next landing, I reached my hand in my sport-coat pocket and lifted the .38 snub-nose by the grip. "The A-1 is a full-service detective agency—Fred has a small arsenal in his bottom desk drawer."

"Fred know about about this?"

I was still glancing around, checking for any unwanted after-hours company in the surrounding offices. "No—he'd already gone home for the day, when I hauled in my guest."

"It's kidnapping, you know."

We were on the fifth floor now, just a few feet away from the A-1 door. Shadows cast by the ornate elevator spread across the polished tile floor and rust-brick wall like a spider's web.

"That's right, Eliot—and you're aiding and abetting."

He thought about that, momentarily, then shrugged. "Returning a mental patient to a concerned relative—that doesn't seem like much of a crime."

"Eliot, I abducted the son of a bitch at gunpoint." I put a hand on his shoulder. "How are you planning to get him back to Ohio with you?"

His reply was matter-of-fact. "On the train."

"On the train. And how will you get him on the train?"

"When I explain his options, Lloyd will do it voluntarily."

I shook my head. "This is no Boy Scout expedition, Eliot. You're in my world, now—where bad people sometimes just go away. Do you understand?"

Here in the open corridor, our voices echoed less; but my words hung in the air, just the same.

Finally he said, "That's one of the options."

As we approached the office, a muffled thumping seemed to be coming from behind the wood-and-frosted-glass door.

Working the key in the lock, I said, "Sounds like my guest is trying to order up some room service."

The thumping escalated into banging as I ushered Eliot into the barely illuminated outer office, not turning on the light. The noise clearly emanated from the secretarial supply closet, the door of which pulsed with each *whump*, almost as if the closet were breathing.

When I opened the door of the supply closet, a seated Lloyd Watterson—his ice-blue eyes wide and wild above the makeshift gag of sticky brown mailing tape—was scooting back on the casters of the walnut stenographic chair into which he was tied, rearing back like a bull about to charge a matador.

I'd cuffed his hands behind him and looped the cuffs through a rung of the chair, into which I'd tied him with heavy brown wrapping twine. Though I'd lashed his ankles together and looped the thick twine around the back of the chair, he'd been able to get enough traction with his feet to take a few hopeless runs against the heavy closet door.

Veins standing out on his forehead, cords taut in his neck, the blond, broad-shouldered, almost-handsome Watterson—a blizzard of a man in his male-nurse white pants and white shirt and white tennis oxfords with white socks, the heavy brown twine cocooning around him—had the expression of a kid caught masturbating.

"Oh, do you want out of there, Lloyd?" I asked obsequiously. "Sure thing."

I grabbed the front of his shirt and yanked him forward—the chair on its casters followed—and then pitched him careening across the office, where he crashed into the secretary's desk, whacking his back against its edge, and came to a stop. The chair, with him in it, almost toppled, wobbling on its rollers.

Watterson was trying to talk or cry out or protest or something, under the packing-tape gag.

"Oh, do you want to be heard, Lloyd?" I asked. "We can make that happen."

As if his face were a package I was trying to unwrap, I twisted the tape around his head, the final pass of the sticky stuff making itself known to Lloyd, who yowled at the hair-pulling, flesh-searing exercise.

"Kinda like taking off a bandage," I said sympathetically. "Fast is better."

I wheeled him around to face me. I had not turned on the lights in the office, and Eliot was just a figure in the shadowy darkness.

"Recognize me yet, Lloyd?" I asked.

The ice-blue eyes narrowed. He shook his head. His voice was oddly soft, gentle. "You . . . you were in Dr. Dailey's office . . . today."

"Think back, Lloyd . . . Notice I'm not calling you 'Floyd.' That's a hint. Here's another: the last time you saw me, you had *me* in this position."

The eyes widened again, but the rest of his boyish face tightened. "Wait a minute . . . wait a minute . . . I do know you. . . ."

"Hit the lights, would you?" I said to Eliot. "Just to the left of where we came in?"

The overhead light snapped on, flooding the office with illumination, and the Mad Butcher of Kingsbury Run saw Eliot Ness moving toward him.

"Oh shit . . ." Lloyd said.

"You and your daddy really fooled me, Lloyd," Eliot said pleasantly. He planted himself in front of Watterson, arms folded, his expression bland, even benign. "Really put one over."

A sickly smile formed on the perpetually immature face, the disturbingly sensual lips quivering. "I got help from the doctors, Mr. Ness! I'm better now."

"Is that right? From what I gather, you're back to your old bad habits."

Looking up at Eliot the way a child seated in the corner looks up at an approaching razor-strop-wielding parent, Watterson shook his head, and kept shaking it as he said, "No . . . no. I'm well. I'm cured of that sickness. I had therapy, Mr. Ness. I worked with the doctors. I don't have those urges anymore. I'm helping people now."

Eliot's eyes frowned and his lips smiled. "Performing abortions is helping people?"

Watterson nodded emphatically. "The women who want them, who need them, think so." Then he frowned at the unfairness of it all. "What other kind of work can I find? I'm not licensed."

It was damn near what Eliot himself had said.

Standing off to one side, I put in, "How did you wind up working for Dr. Dailey, Lloyd?"

Watterson turned his head to look at me, the rest of his body motionless, strapped to the chair. "He and Papa both went to Harvard. They were in the same class. After Papa died, I came out here and asked Dr. Dailey if he would take me in . . . let me be his physician's assistant. I went to medical school, you know."

Eliot said, "You flunked out, Lloyd."

Watterson looked up at Eliot again; his expression seemed almost embarrassed. "I had good grades till I started drinking too much. It made my hands shake. I don't drink at work."

"But you still drink?"

"I drink—I drink at night with friends, in bars, like everybody. But Mr. Ness, I don't have those unnatural urges, anymore. I don't get out of control."

Eliot leaned in nearly nose to nose with Watterson. "Cutting a woman in half, Lloyd, that isn't losing control?"

Watterson turned his head away, as if Eliot had bad breath. "I didn't do that."

"Do what, Lloyd?"

Now he looked at Eliot. "Kill that woman in the papers—that 'Blue Dahlia' woman."

Eliot sighed, stood straight again, rocking on his heels. "*Black* Dahlia, Lloyd. That kill has your fingerprints all over it—severed torso, body drained of blood, washed clean. . . ."

Watterson's expression was one of wounded indignation. "But she had her *head* on! The papers said she had her head on. That's not my style."

Eliot reached out and grabbed Watterson by the shirt, catching some of the twine. "Isn't it, Lloyd? Or did you leave that poor girl's head on her shoulders and carve that grin in her face so you could laugh at me, through her?"

"No!"

"Wasn't that death grin you cut in her face just the latest smart-ass postcard you sent me, Lloyd?"

"No! I didn't do that crime—you know it didn't fit my . . . what do you call it . . . modus operandi!"

Eliot let go of him, and began to pace slowly, in a very small area right in front of Watterson in his chair. "You never had a consistent M.O., Lloyd. Sometimes you left the bodies whole, after decapitation."

Watterson managed to shrug, despite his bonds. "That was the men."

"Yes, the men—who you also emasculated. It was the *women* you cut in two."

"And dismembered them, remember! Mr. Ness, that Dahlia woman was only cut in half—she still had all her arms and legs! And you know that's just not my style."

The surrealism of this discussion—Eliot Ness and the Mad Butcher of Kingsbury Run arguing over the finer points of mass murder—triggered images of Welles' bizarre Crazy House set with its dismembered mannequin limbs.

I moved in front of Watterson and Eliot stepped aside. "Lloyd, I can tell you something that is your style. One of your victims, in early '37, was a woman, never identified, her torso bisected. . . . She was probably around twenty-five with a nice figure, and a fair complexion and brown hair."

Eliot, wondering what I was getting at, asked, "The partial torso that washed up on the beach at 136th Street, you mean?"

"Yes," I said to him. Then to Watterson I said: "That victim on the beach had another one of your special, whimsical touches—you stuffed an object up the woman's ass . . . a pants pocket."

"I was sick, then," Lloyd said, with quiet dignity. "I'm well now."

"Happy to hear that," I said. "By the way, here's something that hasn't appeared in the newspapers, Lloyd: Elizabeth Short had something stuffed inside her, too—a scrap of flesh cut from her thigh, bearing a rose tattoo."

I stepped aside as Eliot moved in and pointed a finger at Watterson like a gun. "You did this crime, didn't you, you miserable son of a bitch!"

"No! I swear I didn't. I'm well. I'm better!"

I said to Eliot, "Get the door for me, would you?"

"The door?"

"Yeah, the door, Eliot. Open it."

Again, though he didn't follow what I was up to, Eliot went along for the ride. "All right," he said, went over and opened it and stepped aside.

I grabbed Lloyd by the blond hair on the top of his head and I dragged him by it out into the hallway—only it wasn't a hallway, really, but a relatively narrow corridor that bordered a five-story drop to the lobby floor. Casters screeching, the chair bearing the twine-tied Butcher did my bidding as I dragged it over to the central staircase and dragged his ass down the iron stairs, eight of them, jarring him, jolting him, shaking him, rattling him, thump, whump, thump. His wails of terror and pain echoed through the cavernous building, like memories of the cries of mercy he had ignored from his victims.

In the shadow-crosshatched moonlight, we were on the landing, Lloyd and me—still almost five stories up—and it was as if a little stage had been provided for our modest melodrama. Our intensely interested audience—Eliot Ness—walked slowly down the iron steps, making no move or even uttering a sound to try to stop me, as I pushed the tied-in-the-chair Watterson face first toward and then right up to the edge of the railing. The railing itself was heavy, and about waist high. I lifted the chair and the man in it by the back of the chair and held him up and over the railing so he could see the hard, shiny floor waiting far below.

I was barely breathing hard as I said, "Elizabeth Short was a patient at the Dailey clinic, Lloyd."

"Please don't kill me!"

"Don't say that again or I will. She was your patient, Lloyd, wasn't she?"

"No!"

"What happened? Did you botch the operation, accidentally, then find yourself with a beautiful young corpse on your hands? And did it just get the old juices flowing, Lloyd?"

"Noooo!" His cry reverberated through the vastness of the

Bradbury. "I didn't kill her! I didn't even operate on her! She was Dr. Winter's patient, not mine!"

I leaned him over some more, wondering if that twine would hold, not really caring. "You're saying Elizabeth Short, the Black Dahlia, just *happened* to be a patient at a clinic where you work?"

"Yes! Yes!"

"Yes, you did it?"

"Yes, it's just a coincidence!"

*Detectives do not believe in coincidence. Some of us believe in fate, a few even believe in God; but none of us believe in coincidence.*

I pulled him back, sat him down, in his chair, teeth-rattlingly hard, on the iron floor of the landing. Backing away from him, I found myself sitting on the stairs as Eliot moved in to take over.

"I don't care whether you admit to this crime or not, Lloyd," Eliot said, "you're going back to Ohio, with me."

Out of breath, shaking his head, eyes rolling wildly, Lloyd yelled, "I'm not! I'm well! I'm cured! I was legally released. I'm as sane as either of you crazy assholes! You have no right, no recourse to—"

Eliot stood calmly, arms crossed. "Your uncle requested I bring you home."

Watterson's face tightened, as if he was not sure he'd heard right. "My uncle . . . ?"

"It's either go home to your uncle, and sign in for some more therapy, Lloyd—or go to the police, and be identified in public as the Kingsbury Run torso killer . . . and the maniac who killed the Black Dahlia."

Lloyd thought about that for a while. And then, irritatingly, chillingly, he smiled. "You won't do that."

Eliot's eyes narrowed. "I won't?"

Watterson shook his head, confidently. "No. Mr. Ness, you would be disgraced, and I know you wouldn't want that. Besides, the police would never arrest me."

"Is that right?"

Now Watterson seemed openly amused—even smug. "It would

expose Dr. Dailey and his clinic and all the crooked homicide cops involved."

Eliot laughed humorlessly. "You want me to believe the LAPD would cover up a crime of this magnitude?"

"Why not? You did."

Eliot staggered back a step.

Then he grabbed Lloyd by the shirtfront and said, "Do you want me to turn you over to my friend, here? He wants to cut off your head and bury you in the desert. And I'm ready to bring the shovel."

"I didn't do this, Mr. Ness!" Watterson's smugness had evaporated, and the terror was back. "It's all just a coincidence, I tell you—a crazy goddamn coincidence!"

I stood. For a while I was just poised there, on the stairs, as if not sure whether to go up or down.

I thought of Orson Welles on that Columbia soundstage, wandering through a nightmare of his own creation, severed limbs and crazy shadows and clown grins. Was Welles the killer, or perhaps the mastermind manipulating some dupe, like Lloyd here? To me, that still seemed absurd on the face of it. And yet . . .

. . . *some* hand was directing this action. Not the director of *Citizen Kane*, perhaps—but some sure, sick hand . . . .

I said, "Eliot—a word."

Looking slightly shellshocked, Eliot followed me up the steps; we spoke at the mouth of the iron stairway, with Lloyd—tied in his chair—staring up at us with those empty blue eyes of his.

"He's right about the cops," I said softly. "Dailey is part of an abortion ring that's protected by the homicide bureau."

"Christ! I thought you said Hansen was straight."

"He is, but most of them are beyond bent—including the Hat's partner, Fat Ass Brown."

"So we avoid the homicide dicks—maybe get a statement and turn it over to the press—"

"Eliot," I whispered, "he may not have done this."

Eliot's eyes flared. "You have got to be kidding. The Mad Butcher of Kingsbury Run just happens to be working in an abortion clinic where the Black Dahlia was a patient?"

I was shaking my head. "Too many coincidences. One or two I can buy—that I was with Fowley when he caught that police call, okay. Just about everything else . . . no."

"What are you saying?"

"Somebody is stage-directing this. All of these things that we're trying desperately to write off as coincidences . . . we're being played for suckers. Hell, man, we're not even pawns on a chess board—we're just goddamn checkers."

He frowned. "Then who's behind it all?"

"I don't know. I don't think Lloyd does, either—although it's a good bet the person manipulating these events is someone in Lloyd's life."

Eliot twitched a nonsmile; he was taking me seriously, anyway. "What do you suggest?"

I took him by the arm and walked him down the corridor a ways—we could still see Watterson sitting on the landing.

"We continue investigating," I said. "I still look at that corpse in my mind's eye and see 'informer' carved on that pretty face—and I haven't even explored the Dragna avenue yet, or for that matter Mickey Cohen. You need to deal with Harry the Hat, and you could dig into the background of these abortion clinic players . . . see if anything turns up. Maybe Dailey isn't the senile dipshit he appears to be—maybe the Winter dame is the fucking Dragon Lady. We don't know yet. . . . Then there's this guy Arnold Wilson and the rest of the McCadden crew."

"Arnold Wilson?"

"Tall guy with a war-wound limp—he was in on the Mocambo heist, but unlike Savarino and Hassau didn't get nailed."

"Funny . . . Arnold Wilson—that name sounds familiar. . . ."

"Eliot, that's like saying 'John Smith' or 'Joe Doakes' sounds familiar."

His eyes were tight with thought. "No—I've seen it recently."

"Good, then that's something else you can check."

"What exactly are you suggesting, Nate?"

"I'm suggesting we tell Lloyd he's convinced us of his innocence."

"What the hell?"

"We apologize for roughing him up. Gee whiz we hope he understands, but we just had to make sure he wasn't involved. And we make him believe he sold us his bill of goods . . . which, incidentally, may not be a bill of goods at all. Elizabeth Short may have been cut in half so that smart sleuths like us would play pin the crime on the Butcher."

Now it was Eliot who looked wild-eyed. "Just let him go? Are you nuts? He'll run!"

"Of course I'm nuts. I got out on a Section Eight, didn't I? But I don't think our twisted friend here will run—*if* we convince him he's convinced us."

"Then what?"

I nodded toward the A-1 office. "We'll keep this guy tailed day and night—not too hard a job, since he works the fuck next door to my own detective agency. Fred and I have four ops working full-time, who we'll tap into."

Finally Eliot was liking this. "And we'll see who Lloyd intersects with."

"That's right."

Nodding, Eliot said, "Okay. No reason why I can't haul Lloyd back in a few days . . . but if any more butchered bodies turn up, I'm not going to sleep so good at night."

"How are you sleeping now?"

"Not so good."

Then we walked down the iron steps and apologized profusely to Lloyd Watterson, who wanted to believe us so badly—when (as we untied him) we said we believed him—that he did.

# 18

It was almost nine by the time Eliot and I made it to the Beverly Hills Hotel. We had followed Lloyd in his prewar Chevy to his rented room in a shoddy two-story wood-frame building on East 31st, and—having called Fred Rubinski to put the surveillance in motion—waited until a fresh-faced A-1 operative named Teddy Hertel showed up to take over for us. We warned Ted that Watterson was a dangerous subject, but I wasn't too worried—Hertel may have looked like a kid, but he had survived Bloodynose Ridge.

In the airy hotel lobby, with its lush plants and lavish floral arrangements, we seemed to have stepped into a decidedly different world from the one in which the Black Dahlia had been murdered. In the aftermath of our confrontation with the Mad Butcher, these soothing pastel surroundings seemed as surrealistic as Welles' Crazy House. We stood at the front desk as Eliot checked himself in; the desk clerk assured Eliot that a rental car would be delivered at the hotel, as prearranged, tomorrow morning.

Eliot accompanied me to the bungalow—taking in the well-manicured hedges, flowering shrubs, and colorful gardens of the grounds we wound through, on this cool evening—and I unlocked the door, cracking it open, calling, "Peggy! Are you decent? We have company."

"Come on in, darling," she called back, pleasantly. "And we already have company."

I stepped inside and found, sitting on the sofa, next to a less-than-roaring fire, Peggy—radiant at the end of her long day of filming, in a light blue T-shirt and trimly tailored darker trousers, legs crossed, red-painted toenails peeking through open-toed sandals—seated next to a guest.

"Your old friend Mr. Wilson dropped by," she said, gesturing to the man seated next to her, "and said it was important. I insisted he wait."

My "old friend" (who dated way back to this afternoon) was one Arnold Wilson—that cadaverous cook from the McCadden Cafe. In this elegant suite, the shabby short-order jockey was like the non sequitur object in a kid's "What's Wrong With This Picture?" puzzle.

"Mr. Wilson was telling me how you were in the war together," she said.

It was hard for me to believe Peggy had let the acne-scarred, Apache-looking Wilson in, considering he was still wearing the threadbare blue-and-white-striped shirt and faded blue jeans; he'd traded his apron for a ratty brown sportcoat, and was gaping at me with a grin displaying more shades of yellow than a paint-store color chart.

He must have sold her one hell of a bill of goods.

While I stood there giving Wilson a look that would have melted ice in a glass and maybe the glass, too, my wife bounded up, and went over to greet Eliot, hugging him.

They were making small talk—since Peggy and I had eloped, this was the first chance Eliot had had to offer congratulations and kiss the bride—and the tall, twig-thin Wilson was rising from the plush couch, trembling, his grin dissolving into an apologetic pout, his big bony hands open in supplication.

I had a hand on his wiry arm, squeezing, staring up into his narrow eyes, pointed nose poking at me, when he whispered, "Sorry I laid it on so thick, Nate . . . Mr. Heller. I just knew it was important to talk to you, right away."

"Why?"

"Bobby Savarino got bailed out—the Ringgolds were good for it, like I thought they might be. He's home right now, and he's willin' to talk—you said you'd give me another twenty if I set up a meet, remember?"

I let go of his arm. "I appreciate this."

Wilson sighed, relieved; his breath was like old gym socks. "Good. Good."

Placing a hand up on his scrawny shoulder, I smiled and said, "But, Arnold—I don't appreciate you invading where I live."

"Jeez, I'm sorry—it's a hotel. You said I could contact you here—"

"I like to keep what I do for a living separate from my private life—specifically, away from my wife. Do you understand, Arnold?"

"Sure, Mr. Heller."

"Call me Nate, Arnold. Now let's go talk to your friend Bobby Savarino."

Eliot's presence seemed to make Wilson nervous—I didn't know whether the cook had ever heard of Eliot before, but Ness was not hard to make as a cop (even if he wasn't one, anymore)—so I suggested to my old friend that he go ahead and get settled in his room. Peg and I would be going out for a late supper and he could join us later.

Eliot went along with this, but he knew what I was up to: Savarino was more likely to talk freely, one-on-one.

Soon I was behind the Buick's wheel, following Wilson up Sunset in his beat-up Ford, taking a right on North La Brea. The Savarinos lived on North Sycamore just off Hollywood Boulevard, near the Tinsel Town business district, tonight typified by a premiere down the block at Grauman's Chinese, complete with stars, searchlights, limousines, radio announcers, cops holding back fans behind roped-off carpeted aisles—the world of glamour so many clamored after.

But just a block or two away, around the corner, was the sort of quiet residential neighborhood others of us longed for, a bouquet of one- and two-story stucco bungalows—white, green, yellow, pink, blue—with driveways to two-car garages, and close-cropped lawns with the occasional palm or pepper tree. In the ivory of moonlight, daubed with streetlamp glow, these bungalows looked damn near idyllic to a returning combat veteran like yours truly. That a petty heist artist, pretending to be a war hero, had achieved this postwar paradise was a little grating.

I parked behind Wilson and followed the scarecrow-in-dungarees up the winding walk of one of the larger dwellings on the block, a pink, red-tile-roofed two-story stucco. On the little cement stoop, Wilson grinned down nervously at me as he punched the doorbell, making a tiny electric-chair buzz.

"Bobby may not like you being a reporter," Wilson said.

"I told you I'm not a reporter—just a dick doing some backgrounding."

"Oh yeah, that's a lot better—makes you a reporter with a gun."

Wilson had a good eye. I was in fact wearing the nine-millimeter under my left arm—I'd taken the time to sling it on, under a sportcoat supposedly tailored not to reveal its presence, before taking this little excursion into the home life of armed robbers.

The door opened to reveal a pretty, pretty hard bottle blonde in her early thirties with permed curls, dead blue eyes, and a painted-on beauty mark near an overly red-rouged mouth, from which dangled a recently lit cigarette. Her complexion was a mystery beneath layers of pancake, but her busty figure wasn't, in a light blue short-sleeved, V-necked angora sweater and form-fitting gray slacks. She had a glass of beer in one red-nailed hand.

"Hiya, Helen," Wilson said to her.

When she spoke, her voice was nasal and high pitched and as melodic as a car horn; she was a little drunk. "This is the guy wants to talk to Bobby?" she asked Wilson.

"Yeah."

She looked me over, then decided to smile—it wasn't half bad, even fairly white. "You're kinda cute."

"You don't make my eyes bleed, either."

"You know just what to say to a girl. Come on in, boys."

She made a sweeping gesture for us to enter. We were in the vestibule of a two-flat: steps to an apartment rose in front of us, and Helen was holding open a door at right. Wilson went in and as I passed her, Helen brushed the angora shelf of her bosom against me and gave me a promising look—which was the most fun I'd had all day.

The interior walls were stucco, too, same shade of pink as the exterior—you could turn this house inside out and nobody would notice. We were in a living room, which connected with a dining room off which a door fed a hallway to a bathroom and, presumably, bedrooms. The kitchen could be glimpsed beyond the dining room.

Everything was very nice, very new, and as mismatched as a Sears and Roebuck warehouse sale—a royal-blue mohair couch with walnut trim, a big flamingo-trimmed mirror over it; a mint-green button-tufted lounge chair; a console radio-phonograph in a mahogany cabinet, emitting the soft strains of a Benny Goodman platter; occasional pieces in stylings both modern and colonial, walnut and oak, dark and blond.

All of this—and the impressive array of gleaming white appliances winking at me from the kitchen—had either been boosted, or bought from (or the results of swaps with) one or more hot-goods fences. Bobby Savarino and the rest of the McCadden Group had discovered the way to achieve their postwar dreams: stealing.

The pleasantly trampy-looking blonde showed us her firm bottom, packed as it was into the gray slacks, as she headed toward the bedrooms, saying, "I'll get the kids for you."

As she disappeared, I said to Wilson, who had plopped himself in the lounge chair and was lighting up a Chesterfield, "Kids?"

"She means the happy married couple," Wilson explained, smoke streaming from his nostrils, dragon-style. "Bobby and Patsy . . . Patsy used to be Patsy Green, the stripper."

I blinked. "Not, 'No Pasties for Patsy' Green?"

"That's the one."

"Jesus, she played Chicago. The Rialto."

Maybe five years ago, I'd seen her perform—never met her—a bosomy jailbait redhead who was notorious for doffing her pasties right before she took her bow.

Bobby Savarino was holding his wife's hand as they walked through the dining room into the living room. The petite former stripper was still a beautiful woman, mane of red hair brushing her shoulders, her large, luminous, almond-shaped green eyes heavy with mascara and green eye shadow, her full lips brightly red-lipsticked, her famed bosom bigger than ever, which was not surprising, considering she was easily seven months' pregnant, in a blue-and-pink floral maternity top, blue-jean pedal pushers, and open-toed sandals.

I recognized Savarino from his newspaper pictures: good-looking kid with dark curly hair and dark long-lashed eyes, almost pretty. He was in a white shirt with the sleeves rolled up, a black tie loose around his collar, pleated black trousers. He had a slump-shouldered, vaguely embarrassed, air.

Trailing after Savarino was another guy I recognized from the papers: his accomplice, Henry Hassau, a hook-nosed little guy with a wispy mustache. It soon became clear Hassau had somehow managed to snag the bosomy blonde as his wife.

Seemed the Hassaus had the upstairs apartment, and the couples spent a lot of time together, mostly downstairs, in the Savarinos' quarters.

Introductions were made. I shook Savarino's hand and Hassau's, and took off my hat out of respect to the "little" woman, if any seven-months-pregnant dame can so be described. Somebody found me a hardback chair across from Mr. and Mrs. Savarino on the couch, with Wilson smoking in the lounge chair, nearby. The Hassaus sat at the dining room table, but the rooms were so openly adjacent, they could hear everything we said, and pitch in their two cents occasionally, as well.

Mrs. Hassau asked me if I wanted a beer, and I declined; she seemed to be the only one drinking.

As we got to business, Mrs. Savarino made the opening salvo in a Betty Boopish yet hard-edged voice. "Mr. Heller, we need to come to an understanding."

"All right. What do you have in mind?"

"Bobby will talk to you for one hundred dollars," she said, lifting her hand locked in his.

"That's kind of steep."

"We need to raise some money."

"Why don't you borrow some from your jeweler friends, the Ringgolds?"

She shifted uncomfortably on the sofa—not entirely due to the pregnancy, I gathered. "We, uh . . . have borrowed quite enough from them, getting Bobby bailed out."

"Okay, then. A C-note it is."

She raised a red-nailed finger. "And none of us can be quoted—not in print, not in private to the police. We'll help you gather some facts, but that's all."

"All right," I said. "Can Bobby talk now?"

"If you're going to be a wise-ass," she said coolly, "it's going to cost you more."

I raised my hands in surrender—this was no average housewife—then got out my billfold and handed her two twenties and a ten.

"That's fifty dollars, Mr. Heller," she said, handing the money to her husband, who folded it and slipped it in a trouser pocket.

"Fifty more after we've talked—after I know it's worth fifty more. Fair enough?"

She gave it a moment of thought, nodded.

"So, Bobby," I said, "who was it offered you twenty-five hundred to bump off Mickey Cohen?"

His wife answered, green eyes flashing. "That son of a bitch Jack Dragna!"

I said to her husband, "Jack Dragna personally? What, did he come here to the house?"

Which was about as likely as Louis B. Mayer dropping a film print off at a theater.

"It wasn't Dragna hisself," Savarino said. He had a husky, medium-pitched voice. When he spoke, he emphasized points with wags and nods of his head, making his curly hair bounce. "Three guys I never seen before come around, it was three weeks ago last night, Thursday night . . . I know 'cause we was listening to *Burns and Allen*. Henry and Helen and Arnie here was over, having beers and just listening to that daffy dame on the radio."

"That Gracie Allen kills me," Hassau said, smiling absently.

The blonde he was married to sipped her beer.

Taking no time to reflect on this cozy evening at home among felons, I asked Savarino, "And you never saw these guys before?"

"Don't look so surprised. We're not local. We come out from the East Coast, been here less than a year, knocking over scores. These guys offered me twenty-five hundred to take Cohen out."

"You're no torpedo, Bobby—why you?"

He shrugged, sighed, holding on to his wife's hand; the beautiful redhead was gazing at him supportively. "I was pals with Benny Gamson, you know—the Meatball."

So-called because he was shaped like a meatball, his legs like toothpicks stuck in it.

"When I knew Gamson in Chicago," I said, "he and Cohen were buddies—the Meatball was a card mechanic in Cohen's bust-out joint."

Savarino was shaking his head. "They weren't buddies out here. Cohen gets something like two-fifty a week protection payoff, each, from all the other bookies in town . . . only the Meatball tells him to go stuff hisself."

Gamson had been shot to death in October.

"How did you and Gamson get friendly?" I asked him.

"He was my bookie. He was willing to extend credit, no strongarm stuff, no leg-breaking. Hell of a nice guy. But I didn't love him—I wouldn't whack Mickey Cohen over him, even for that kind of money."

His wife said, rather proudly, "My Bobby's not a killer."

From the other room Hassau said, in his thin high-pitched voice, "These guys Dragna sent, they knew we was associated with Al Green, and that Al was pals with Benny Siegel, and that meant we had easy entree to Cohen, who is also pals with Siegel."

Apparently bored with this criminal flow chart, Hassau's wife got up to go into the nearby kitchen.

"Incidentally," I said to Hassau, "did your friends the Ringgolds bail out Green and that other guy from your string?"

"Marty?" Hassau said. "Marty Abrams? Naw, him and Al can

afford their own bail. The Ringgolds was helping us out, so that Al didn't have, you know, the whole financial burden."

The blonde in the angora sweater returned with a fresh glass of beer. She said to her husband, "Tell 'em about what happened after you turned those bastards down."

But it was Savarino who picked up on the story. "A couple days later, Patsy answers the door, and they push right past her—Christ, her pregnant like that, they coulda hurt her or the baby or something, just bulled right in."

"We were playin' cards," Hassau said, "with the girls."

Savarino, trembling with the memory, said, "They were big wops, three of 'em . . . One held a rod on us, and the other two started beating the shit out of us, one at time."

His wife was running her fingers through his curly hair, soothing him, settling him.

"Fuckers," Hassau said. "In front of our wives!"

Helen Hassau, unimpressed, sipped her beer, leaning so far over the table, her angora-clad breasts flattened out.

"They used a rubber hose on me," Savarino said, "and pistol-whipped poor Henry, there."

"I had a goose egg for a week," Hassau said, with the expression of a kid who had a bully steal his prize marble.

"They didn't want you to squeal to Cohen," I said.

"No," Savarino said, shaking his head. "See, Jack Dragna acts like he gets along with Cohen, but really he hates that little Jew like poison. Cohen and Siegel got shoved down Dragna's throat by the East Coast Combination."

"So you didn't warn Cohen about the hit?" I said.

"Hell no. Anyway, they musta called the thing off, 'cause nobody's thrown any bullets at Mickey, lately."

"I'd like to get my hands on those guys what roughed us up," Hassau whined.

His blonde wife was gulping her beer. She was the kind of broad you'd kill for to get in bed, and die if you woke up next to.

"Are you sure these goons were Dragna's?" I asked. "Cohen has other enemies, particularly among bookies he's muscled."

Wilson, who had just been sitting quietly smoking, said, "I

checked around on these guys . . . Dragna and this lieutenant of his, Jimmy Utley, have lunch every day at Lucey's."

I knew Lucey's—it was a movie-industry hangout on Melrose across from Paramount Studios.

Wilson was saying, "Two of the three guys who come here, and made that twenty-five-hundred-buck offer—I saw 'em walkin' Dragna outa the restaurant, after lunch."

"Bodyguards," I said.

Wilson nodded and winked, an action that made his gaunt face cartoonish.

"Tell me, Bobby," I said, turning to the hang-dog Savarino, "what made you decide to share this little episode with the cops?"

"I was tryin' to cut a deal—I figure, I give 'em a big fish like Dragna, they'll let me and my friends swim away."

"As in, they swam and they swam all over the dam?" I asked, referring to the hit parade's "Three Little Fishies."

"Somethin' like that," Savarino said, glumly.

"Only now you're wise to the fact that the LAPD is in Dragna's pocket," I said.

"Not all of 'em are!" Savarino said, somewhat indignantly. "Take that guy Hansen, f'r instance—he'd love to get Dragna by the short and curlies . . . and the papers, they'd eat it up, right?"

"Maybe." I said to the redhead, "After your hubby started squealing, did those three Dragna thugs come around again?"

She shook her head. "No, but we got all these threatening phone calls, both Helen and me, terrible, foul, frightening, awful. . . ." She covered her mouth, her eyes moistening.

Finally the blonde perked up. From the dining room, she said, "We got a threatening note in the mail, too—one of them cut-and-paste jobs."

"Not in the mail," Mrs. Savarino said, "the mail-*box*—somebody just walked right up and stuck that foul thing in." She shivered. "They were outside our door, on our front stoop."

"One of them threatened our baby," Savarino said.

"Yeah," the blonde said, "one said on the phone he had a baseball bat all picked out for Patsy's belly."

Still shivering, Mrs. Savarino cuddled close to her husband, who slipped an arm around her. That arm stiffened when I broached my next topic.

"Which brings us to Elizabeth Short," I said, wondering if that name would create fireworks between the Savarinos.

"She was a friend of Helen's," Mrs. Savarino said.

"Real good friend of mine," Helen chimed in.

All right—so that was the party line.

"So," I said to them all, "you figure Jack Dragna had this girl killed and her mouth slashed . . . informer-style . . . because by striking somebody within your circle, that would quiet Bobby, here."

"I have to admit," Savarino said, "hearing about these phone calls and that threatening note, that didn't mean shit to me. I didn't think they'd come near me or my family, with what I had on 'em. And, the spot I was in . . . still am in . . . I figured my best shot was, try to deal my way out. . . ."

"Then the next day the Short girl turns up cut in half in that vacant lot."

Everybody but me looked at the floor.

"Yeah," Savarino sighed, nodding, "and that's when I fucking zipped it—haven't said a word since . . . and Dragna hasn't bothered us. Not at all."

The former stripper hugged her husband's arm. "That's all we know, Mr. Heller. You got the rest of our money?"

"It's risky talking to me," I said, bothered. "Even without being quoted, if this gets in the papers, Dragna will put two and two together—"

Mrs. Savarino interrupted: "I think that gangster will have the sense to lay low, now that the woman he killed is the biggest story since the war."

Her chin was high and her eyes narrow and glimmering. She was a tough cookie, Mrs. Savarino—and a beauty. I had to know what kind of idiot would cheat on a woman this gorgeous, and this strong.

"I'll give you your second fifty, Mrs. Savarino, but only after I have a few minutes in private with Bobby."

"There are no secrets between us," she said.

But her husband was sitting there with a whipped-puppy look that told me otherwise.

"I met your terms, Mrs. Savarino—now, meet mine, or you're gonna have to settle for fifty bucks."

The ex-stripper said nothing, staring coldly at me for several seconds, then studying her husband, the same way. Then she shook her head.

I shrugged, and stood. "Your choice."

Savarino patted his wife's hand, which was gripping his arm. "Baby, let me talk to Mr. Heller, alone, for a minute. We really can use that extra fifty bucks."

She sighed and watching that impressive chest rise and fall was the second most fun I'd had today. Then she pouted, folded her arms, and gave her husband one quick nod.

We talked on the porch—sitting out on the cement steps in the cool evening, the sounds of Hollywood Boulevard wafting their muffled way across the quiet neighborhood. The little stucco bungalows had a quaint look, a very Hollywood look, like maybe Snow White's dwarfs lived inside.

"So was Beth Short really Helen Hassau's friend?" I asked him. "No bullshit, now."

"They were friends. I mean, I knew Beth first . . . met her at the cafe. She lived in the neighborhood, you know. I gave her the war hero routine, and she melted like butter—couldn't keep her hands off me. Anyway, when I started seeing a lot of Beth, that's when her and Helen really got to be pals—Beth and my wife barely knew each other, and, frankly, my wife don't really care for Helen that much . . . thinks she's a lush and a bossy little bitch, which is true, but we both put up with her 'cause Henry's my buddy and, well, partner in crime."

He said that last archly, like it was a joke and not a fact.

I asked, "Had Beth been here to the house?"

"Yes . . . no . . . not our apartment, except a few times when Pasty wasn't home—you know how it is . . . but Helen invited Beth over, now and then . . . Beth even stayed here, there, upstairs with the Hassaus I mean, till about the time she got, you know . . . killed."

"Beth was your girl friend."

"Yeah. You could say that."

"What were you doing with a girl friend, Bobby? You got a wife. A beautiful one. Pregnant with your kid."

He shook his head, dark curls bouncing. "I know, I know, you think I don't spend half my time kicking myself?"

"Just half?"

"Hey, you're a good-looking guy. Are you telling me that dames don't give you the come-on? And that you don't do something about it?"

"Not since I got married I don't."

"How long you been married?"

"Little over a month."

"Yeah, just wait! Your wife gets pregnant, and she's got a belly out to here, wait and see if you don't get tempted. Wait and see, then fucking judge."

"Is it true you gave Beth an engagement ring?"

"Yeah . . . that *was* stupid. But jewelry, half the time we're swimmin' in it, and Patsy and me, we'd had a bad fight and I really was thinkin' of leaving her, and . . . yeah, I gave her a ring, and it was stupid."

"Didn't Beth eventually find out you were married?"

"Yeah, of course. She took it surprisingly good, like she expected men to do bad, stupid shit in her life. Besides, I told her I was gonna break up with Patsy—though, you know, I told her I was gonna wait till after the baby came."

"Sure. You wouldn't walk out on your wife till after the baby came."

The pretty face frowned. "Hey, fuck you, what's your name? Heller? I'm trying to level with you. I was in love with Beth Short."

I managed not to laugh. "You weren't in love with your wife anymore?"

He shrugged. "I loved her, too. When I was with the one, I loved her; when I was with the other, I loved that one. Haven't you ever been in that situation?"

"Was Beth pregnant, too, Bobby?"

"I think maybe she was."

"You think?"

"It wasn't mine, if so."

"No?"

"No. I never fucked her."

"You never fucked her."

"No—she said she wanted to wait till after we were married."

"So that's why you got 'engaged' to her . . . thought she'd give it up that way. . . ."

"Fuck you! Anyway, it didn't work. She was still 'saving herself' for our friggin' wedding night."

I drew a breath, looked up at the sky where Grauman's searchlights were streaking across like a prisoner had escaped. "Let me get this straight. Your wife can't service you sexually because she's too far along . . . so you start dating a girl who's saving herself for marriage? And this girl, who talks like a virgin, also happens to be pregnant, just not very pregnant? Am I missing anything here?"

He sighed, shook his head. "You don't understand."

"Oh, and I forgot—you loved her."

"No . . . no, I'm talking about, you know . . . the blow jobs."

I didn't say anything.

"You can't imagine the mouth that girl had," he said, shaking his head, woozy with erotic nostalgia, "and what she could do with it."

Maybe I could.

"Well," I said, "she was pregnant—*somebody* fucked her."

"She never said she was pregnant. But I figured she was, since she needed money for an operation."

"Around five hundred dollars, the going abortion rate."

"That's right. Saving for it, hitting everybody up. And I told her, after this Mocambo score, I'd fix her up with whatever cash she needed. That's when she got . . . weird on me."

"Weird, how?"

Savarino shook his head, dark curls dancing. "She was an odd duck, man. She seemed so . . . worldly, is that the word? Like she'd been around, like she knew the streets, she was almost a goddamn hooker the way she'd work a guy for drinks. . . . I got a feeling I'm not the only guy she went down on, to buy her dinner."

"What's your point?"

"Still, there was this, whaddayacallit, naive side to her. Yeah, she wore black, and she was in show biz and hung out on the fringes of society, with lowlifes like me. Man, you should have seen her, dolled up in those black outfits, seamed black stockings, with that sweet, innocent face, glowin' in the night, like a fuckin' angel."

"Your point?"

"She had no idea what I did for a living—no clue that she was hanging out, there at the McCadden Cafe, in the middle of a nest of goddamn thieves. When I told her I'd give her the rest of the money she needed, outa my share of the heist, she wigged out—blew her friggin' top, man, scratchin' me, clawin' at me, slappin' me."

"And you got a little rough with her."

His dark eyes flared. "Well, I grabbed her by the arms and threw her ass offa me, yeah! Wouldn't you?"

"Is that when she took off for San Diego?"

He blinked in surprise. "How did you know—oh yeah, it was in the papers, wasn't it?"

"Yeah. You and Helen and Henry went down there, after her, didn't you? To the house where she was freeloading?"

"Sure we went lookin' for her . . . She'd sent a telegram to Helen, askin' for money . . . still trying to raise money. So we had the address."

"Why did you go all the way down there, Bobby? Why didn't you let sleeping dogs lie?"

"I guess . . . I guess maybe I was afraid, as bad as she needed money, she might sell what she knew to somebody . . . about the Mocambo score we was plannin'. You know, tip 'em off."

"But she didn't."

"No. And after the score, she come back, and she started stayin' with Helen. Hiding out."

"Why hiding out? Hiding from whom?"

"The cops. Beth figured she was an accomplice to the Mocambo score, since she knew about it, and didn't do nothing to stop it."

She'd been right about that: she would have been considered an accomplice.

"Anyway," Savarino was saying, "we fight, get back together, fight, get back, bust up . . . back and forth like that. I kept thinkin' I was gonna get in her pants, but I never made it past her mouth."

"And your wife never got wise?"

"Naw. Women believe what they want to believe. Anyway, I'm well rid of that crazy cunt. I'm happy with the one I got."

I savored the ambiguity of that for a moment, then asked, "You don't have any doubt, Bobby, that Dragna had Beth Short killed, as a warning to you?"

"None. Oh, that sex-crime angle, that's a good one—keepin' those dumb-ass cops busy. But when I heard about her face, how it was cut ear to ear, I knew what that meant. And I clammed, man—I clammed."

I stood. So did he.

I gave him the fifty bucks, and said, "Give this to your wife. If you don't, she'll come looking for me."

He laughed. "Yeah, she is a pistol."

"I saw her on stage, Rialto, back in Chicago. She was something."

Beaming proudly, he said, "She sure was. Amazing how she could make them tassels go in both directions."

"Bobby, you have any idea how lucky you are? Beautiful wife who loves you? Kid on the way?"

"I know," he said. He shook his head, curls flouncing, and his sigh started down around his shoes. "Now if only I wasn't facing no twenty years in stir."

And he went inside.

# 19

Of the jewels in the glittering bracelet of the Sunset Strip after dark—the Trocadero, the Crescendo, La Rue, and Ciro's, to name a few—the Mocambo was the brightest, and the gaudiest. The epitome of a Hollywood nightspot, with record-breaking attendance unfettered even by the post–VJ Day slump, the Mocambo sported a deceptively simple exterior. The two-story building's lower story was red with its name emblazoned in bold stylish white, the upper floor white with red-shuttered windows and a modest neon sign, with only the oversize canopy's red-and-white-striped awning to suggest anything remarkable might await within.

The club had a wildly eccentric South American motif, the inside of Carmen Miranda's mind as depicted by Salvador Dali. Oversize baroque tin wall sculptures of flowers and harlequins and dancing girls mingled with flamboyant terra cotta and soothing shades of blue, the latter perhaps intended to tone things down a bit in a room where striped patterns were everywhere, from draped walls to candy-cane columns wearing chrome crowns with oversize ball fringe dangling, invoking a demented gaucho's sombrero. An exotic aviary—a cockatoo, several macaws, a quartet of love birds, a couple dozen parakeets—added constant punctuation to the Latin music of house-band leader Phil Ohman (lured from the Trocadero).

The tariff at the Mocambo was steep—ten bucks a head—but a tourist's bargain, considering the parade of stars the joint attracted. With Eliot trailing after us like a high-priced bodyguard, Peggy and I were escorted through the packed club by maître d' Andre (stolen from New York's "21"). Along the way we passed Judy Garland and her escort, Myrna Loy and hers, Lana Turner with Tony Martin, Marlene Dietrich with Jean Gabin, and Rosalind Russell and an old gent my wife informed me via whisper was Irving Berlin. If a bomb dropped on this place, the only thing left of American show business would be the Ritz Brothers.

My wife and I were holding hands. I was in a dark suit with a black-and-gray tie and looked pretty snappy; Peggy was a vision in black crepe, her shoulders and midriff bare beneath misty black lace, her dark hair down and flouncing, mouth lushly red-lipsticked. She may have only been a bit player, but every male eye found her, as we wound through the tables. Partly it was her beauty—but some of it had to be her resemblance to the dead girl whose picture had been so prominently in the papers.

We had already had a fight, a little one back at the hotel, and had kissed and made up, after a bigger problem had taken center-stage.

The little fight had been over this late-night (our reservation was 11:30 P.M.) engagement to go dancing and drinking with several old friends. One of those old friends was Barney Ross, as Peg—without me knowing—had set this up with Barney's soon-to-be-ex-wife, Cathy, who was seeing him for the first time since his release from the drug rehabilitation hospital.

When Peggy informed me of this, I had already agreed to go out, and we were getting ready in the big bathroom in the Beverly Hills Hotel bungalow, me in my shorts, at the mirror, shaving, with Peggy in the tub, also shaving—face and legs, respectively.

"Barney's going to be there? Does he know *I'm* going to be there?"

"No. Cathy thinks it will be good for him."

"You can't spring me on Barney like this! We haven't spoken in years."

She shrugged and then returned her attention to her soapy, nicely formed calf, stroking it with her Lady Gillette. "I know he was a little put out with you. . . ."

"Put out! He was a dope addict, and I dried up his hometown street supplies!"

"But he's well, now," she said.

And all I could think of was Lloyd Watterson saying the same thing.

"Do you have any idea how few addicts make it?" I asked her in the mirror, royally pissed at her, loving the way the water made her breasts look so smooth and round and shiny. "Almost none!"

"You were friends since childhood. He's trying to make a new start. You have to help him."

"Surprising him like this is no way to do it!"

She began to drain the water, stood, and began adjusting the shower nozzle, so she could wash her hair. Over the tub gurgle, she said, "Then I'll just go without you and when Barney asks, I'll say you didn't want to see him."

And she turned on the shower, cutting off anything I might say in response.

My mirror began steaming up, and I was steamed too, rubbing a place on the glass for me to finish shaving, muttering to myself, watching her shower, cutting myself when I was paying too much attention to the way the water was streaming down her slender shapely frame, cascading over the tiny cliff of her perfect little breasts, a rivulet trailing through her dampened pubic tuft. . . .

I was in my underwear sitting on the bed when she came in with her hair wrapped up in a towel and her body tied into a terrycloth robe with the hotel's gold BHH monogram.

"I'm not going," I told her.

"You have to go," she said. "Besides, you told Eliot we were going out for a late supper."

She came over and sat next to me and sighed heavily, even dramatically, and announced, "Anyway . . . there's something more important than that we should, well . . ."

I frowned at her. "What?"

"Can we talk?"

Those three words again: now I was starting to know just how deadly they were in married life, trumped only by the fatal four: "We have to talk."

But I could tell something was really wrong. The violet eyes were troubled, the smooth brow managing a wrinkle.

Melting, I said, "Sure, baby."

"What I have to tell you is going to make you sad."

I slipped an arm around her. "What is it?"

"Oh, Nathan . . . I know you're going to be so disappointed . . ." She was tearing up; lips trembling.

"What, doll?"

". . . I got my friend today."

"Your friend?"

"My friend . . . you know—my period."

"You can't get your period—you're pregnant."

"No, I'm not. That's what I'm trying to tell you—it was a false alarm."

She explained that she'd always been as regular as clockwork with her periods (which of course I already knew—just as I knew the bad ones put her in bed for a day or two) and when she'd been late, a week and a half ago, she had assumed the worst. (Exactly how she put it: "The worst.")

"But you went to the doctor . . ."

She swallowed; looked sheepish. "No. I made an appointment, but I never kept it . . . didn't bother . . . I've never missed a period, never had one arrive so late—oh darling, I know how dearly you wanted a child, but we can have another."

I felt empty. The emotional roller coaster Peg and I had been riding lately, where this now nonexistent kid was concerned, had finally jumped its tracks; and this very long day suddenly caught up with me, and I flopped back onto the bed. For some reason, I began tearing up, too. Emotions getting away from me. . . .

Peggy crawled onto the bed and leaned over me; her face, with no makeup, at all, was lovely. "Nate, darling, when the time is right, we'll have as big a family as you want—I'll be your personal baby-making machine."

She was so earnest, hovering over me, making that silly statement, that I had to laugh. Smiling, she cuddled close to me.

"Are you all right?" she asked.

"Yeah."

"I'll make you better." She slipped her hand into the fly of my boxer shorts, found me, and brought me out for a look. "He's tiny."

"Just what every man hopes to hear from a beautiful woman."

"Let's see what I can do."

Then she knelt over me, making me grow, her head bobbing up and down, sliding up and down slowly, quickly, slowly, and it was dizzingly sensual, making me giddy with pleasure, and when I had to come, I warned her, but she didn't stop, wouldn't stop. . . .

It was the best I'd ever had.

Next to Elizabeth Short.

A man who has been paid that kind of attention will follow a woman anywhere, and so I was now in the Mocambo, hand in hand with her, Al Capone's nemesis trailing faithfully behind us, walking over to where my other best friend sat with his former showgirl wife.

My partner Fred Rubinski was there, as well, seated next to Barney in a spacious corner booth. Everybody had drinks already, and Fred was inflicting a Havana on them.

Just above and behind where Barney sat with Cathy at the linen-covered table, concealed lighting glowing upward, a huge tin sculpture seemed to float. The life-size figure of a South American native in a headdress of curled tin stood on a round pedestal, exotic fronds and flora at his feet, skeletal body festooned with webbing and ball fringe, arms outstretched, an elaborate electric candelabrum in one hand, a small iron cage in the other.

The tin figure would have been at home in Welles' Crazy House, or possibly in a dope addict's dream.

Though this surrealistic statue seemed to be springing from his head, Barney Ross did not look like a dope addict. In fact, he just looked like Barney Ross—a slightly pudgy bulldog-pussed brown-eyed ex-boxer in his late thirties, his hair prematurely stone gray, looking pretty spiffy for just getting out of rehab, in a brown-and-white-checked sportjacket and red bowtie.

I stood swallowing spit, feeling just a little awkward, no worse than the time I farted on the witness stand.

Cathy looked great—a Maureen O'Hara type with the flowing dark tresses to prove it. In her powder-blue dress with dark blue embroidered flower at one shoulder, she looked as chicly beautiful as the movie goddesses around us.

But Cathy's smile—which normally could make a man's knees go rubbery—seemed forced, and anxiety was doing a spastic dance in her usually flashing blue eyes.

She was holding on to Barney's elbow—he was looking up at me, pop-eyed—as she whispered to him: "It was my idea—I hope you don't mind, dear."

"Hey I'm sorry," I said to him, backing away a little, Peggy hugging my arm protectively. "I don't like surprises, either—Peg and me can just go."

Barney just looked up at me, frozen.

"Barney," Eliot said, ignoring the melodrama. He reached his hand across the table and Barney shook it, numbly. They were old friends, too—used to practice their jujitsu together. "Glad things worked out—you look good."

Barney was just sitting there as glazed as a glazed ham and with about as much expression.

Then he said to Cathy, "Let me out."

"Barney . . ."

"Let me out, would you?" His voice was flat.

She complied, getting out of the booth so that he could, too. Was he going to paste me one? Great—nothing like standing here waiting for a sucker punch from the former welterweight/lightweight world boxing champion.

"Barney," I said, holding out a palm, "take it easy—I couldn't stand what you were doin' to yourself; I had no choice, I had to do it."

Barney just stood there, looking at me, trembling, hands balled into fists, mouth quivering, eyes twitching—goddamn it, he *was* looking like a dope addict all of sudden. . . .

Then he hugged me.

And I hugged him back.

We held on to each other for a long time, and maybe we cried a little—that's what Louella Parsons claimed in her column the next day, anyway. Nobody minded: this was Hollywood, where people displayed their emotions openly, and a lot of men liked to hug each other.

This was followed by a round of congratulations for Peggy and me, on our recent marriage, including admonitions from Barney and Cathy (and, for that matter, Eliot) for not being included in the wedding, and we were told the impromptu Vegas nature of it was no excuse.

Cathy gave up her seat and I got in next to my childhood pal. She and Peggy sat next to each other, holding hands and giggling (which was okay—a lot of the women in Hollywood liked to hug each other, too), coconspirators who had happily pulled something off. Cathy had also had some bit parts in movies and the two women had a lot in common.

Eliot and Fred, who knew each other well from Chicago, sat and chatted and caught up with each other, as Barney and I did the same.

"Why the hell did you go to a government hospital?" I asked him. "You could afford a private sanitarium, and those guys never talk about their patients."

Cathy answered the question, or started to: "Barney didn't want to keep this a secret—he wanted to go public with it."

Barney shrugged, his smile rumpling his rumpled face further. "Best place to get the cure is a government hospital. They're the toughest—you need that military kind of iron discipline to beat this thing."

"What does Cathy mean," I asked, "you *wanted* this made public?"

He shrugged again, sipped his beer. "There's a lot of people, some of 'em just kids, who're hooked on dope, too afraid and ashamed to look for help. Maybe somebody like me comin' forward will help them get over that."

Blue eyes sparkling, Cathy said, "I bet you didn't know Eliot helped Barney make the original arrangements."

Eliot didn't notice himself being mentioned, he and Fred were so deep in conversation.

"No!" I said. "What's that about?"

Barney said, "The Public Health Service Hospital at Lexington is designed for addicts who got caught committing a crime—you know, it's one of those joints the courts order you to go to. Being admitted as a volunteer patient is a little trickier."

"And Eliot helped?"

"Yeah, with friends of his over at the Treasury Department. Set it up so I could surrender to their district narcotics supervisor."

I had a taste of my rum and Coke. I was trying to think of what to say, finally just blurted, "Listen, I'm not going to ask you how tough it was. I know it was tough. . . ."

And it was like I'd turned a spigot.

"I'll tell you this much," Barney said, words streaming out. "The withdrawal gave me the miseries, 'cause the reduced dose of morphine wasn't enough to kill the cramps and the sweats. I learned damn quick where that expression 'kick the habit' comes from, 'cause when they gradually cut down my dope, I got spasms in my arms and legs—I kicked like a chorus girl, without even trying. Then the nightmares, the delusions . . . I was back there, Nate. Back on the Island. I kept fighting the Japs in that muddy shell hole, over and over again. . . . But now? Now I don't have to go back there no more."

He was gripping my arm, just above the wrist. I patted his hand.

"No, buddy," I said, not quite sure whether he meant Guadalcanal or the rehab hospital. "No, you don't. How long have you been clean?"

"Three months."

"How come you aren't skinny?"

He grinned. "Most addicts come in skin-and-bones, so they feed you this high-calorie diet—meat and eggs and potatoes. Man, have I porked up. Gotta get back to the gym."

"Are you out for good? Are you sprung?"

Barney shook his head. "Officially, it's just a furlough. In two months, I go back—they check me for dilated pupils and needle tracks and runny nose and the whole megillah . . . three days of testing."

"But then . . . ?"

"Then it'll be over. I got my life back, Nate. Now all I got to do is get my wife back."

Cathy—who had been right with us through all of this, smiling, encouraging—suddenly stiffened, and turned away.

"I'm not supposed to talk about that," Barney said, with a pitiful grin. His voice was quavery. I knew he loved her like crazy. And I wondered why she seemed so supportive, yet insistent on going through with the divorce.

I learned the reason when Barney took Peggy out onto the dance floor.

Very quietly, Cathy told me, "Nate, you can't repeat this. You have to swear you won't share with this Barney."

"Hey, I'm the guy who took his dope away from him, remember?"

"It's the hardest thing I've ever had to do," she said, shaking her head, "telling Barney I wouldn't take him back. But his doctors at Lexington talked to me—they told me to let the divorce go through."

"What? Why?"

She glanced out where Barney and Peggy were dancing to "Come Rain or Come Shine." "I've told Barney he has to prove himself, to win me back. If I take him now, the way I'm dying to, the doctors say he could lose his incentive."

I was frowning. "Don't you think he already has 'incentive' enough, Cathy?"

Firmly, she said, "I've told him if he's still off that stuff a year from now, we can talk about remarriage. As for right now, the divorce will be final soon, and we won't be living together."

"Yeah, but if you were, you could watch him and—"

She shook her head again, dark tresses bouncing off her shoulders. "He has to do this himself, Nate—just like he checked into that hospital himself. If the disappointment of not immediately getting me back sends him reeling, reeling so bad that he starts back on the dope . . . then he isn't cured."

"Jeez—I don't know, Cathy. . . ."

"You promised me, Nate. You will respect my wishes on this."

I smiled at her, nodded. "All right. But if it's okay with you, I'm going to take the little bastard back in *my* life as of now."

She beamed and squeezed my hand.

Eliot was out dancing with Peggy, and Barney with Cathy, when Fred and his big Havana slid over next to me. "You get a load of the rocks in the lobby?"

"Actually, no—missed 'em somehow."

That Edward G. Robinson puss of his worked up a smirk; Fred was feeling pretty cute. "They're in a glass case recessed in the wall. You can take a gander on the way out—thirty thousand in diamonds."

Fred had told me earlier about the new Ringgold Jewelry display, which was making its debut tonight, replacing the ice that had been heisted by the McCadden Group.

"Just like I told ya they'd be, the brothers are here tonight, kicking off the new display—they're gonna get introduced by Phil Ohman, to take a bow. That's them, sitting ringside." Fred used his Havana like a director's baton, waving it toward distant tables. "That big bald guy with the glasses and the blonde—that's Sid. The little bald guy with the glasses and the brunette—that's Abe."

"What's the story on 'em, Fred?"

"Respected businessmen today, mob guys yesterday. Chicago boys, originally."

"Then why don't I know them?"

"Little before your time, Nate—the older one, Abe, was a Hymie Weiss bodyguard. Survived the hit on Hymie, back in, when was it, '26? Lost two fingers, which was a bargain considering it was machine-gun fire, and relocated to New York, and went to work for Luciano. Brother Sid was an accountant, worked with Lansky. Abe did two years or so on a gun charge, and the boys moved out here, decided to go straight, and went into the jewelry business."

"How straight?"

"Not that straight. Sid was fined two thousand dollars for perjury, couple years ago, over his questionable 'acquisition' of twelve grand in diamonds. Just a fluke—ran into an honest judge. The heist here at the Mocambo is probably the sixth time they've been robbed in the last ten years."

"Arranging the robberies, getting the insurance dough, and reselling the gems?"

"Yeah—and never 'inside' jobs, always working with guys like your McCadden Group, which puts the insurance companies in a position to have to pay."

Ten or twelve minutes later, Abe Ringgold was heading for the men's room just as Barney was ushering Cathy back to the booth.

Before Barney had a chance to sit down, I got up and grabbed his boxer's bicep and whispered, "I need your help. How soft are you?"

"I could take any of the pansies in this joint."

"What about the ones who aren't pansies?"

He shrugged. "Them, too."

The men's room was smaller than a Busby Berkeley set and decorated in the same demented manner as the rest of the Mocambo, red wallpaper trimmed silver and framed expressionistic paintings of South American dancing girls. No attendant on duty. At six urinals were two men: one of them Henry Fonda, the other a guy I didn't recognize. Only one of the stalls was in use, the feet and trousers down around them apparently belonging to Abe Ringgold.

I waited for Fonda and the other guy to finish pissing and wash up—Barney was already standing outside the door, informing patrons the restroom was temporarily out of service—and then I took a piss myself, because I was there.

Not being a complete prick, I allowed the bald little man with the glasses and dark well-tailored suit and the well-tanned, homely face to wash his heavily jewel-bedecked hands before I grabbed him and slammed him against a red-and-silver wall and placed the nose of the nine-millimeter against the side of his.

"Who the fuck are you?" Abe Ringgold demanded. His eyes were wild but his face tightened in the manner of a guy who'd been in tough spots before. He was the smaller of the brothers, but also the three-fingered one, the former Hymie Weiss bodyguard.

He was about sixty, and no real threat to me—at least I felt that way after I patted him down and found no weapon—but I wouldn't forget that when this jeweler was a kid he was a gangster shooting other gangsters in my hometown.

"I'm Nate Heller," I said. I placed the snout of the nine-millimeter right against his lips, like the automatic was giving him a kiss. "Maybe you know who I am."

"Frank Nitti's boy," Abe said matter-of-factly, as if the gun weren't pressing against his mouth.

I nodded, once. His description of me was an exaggeration I would let stand, in this company.

"Have you ever taken a Chicago lie detector test, Abe?"

"No," he said, gruffly, eyes settling down, "but I know what it is. Why don't you skip the shit and just ask me your fucking questions, and see if you like the answers."

"Fine," I said, and moved the snout of the gun so that it was just under his chin, creasing a jowl. "Did you have Elizabeth Short killed, Abe?"

Now the eyes went really wild. "What? No! Fuck no! Why the fuck would I do that?"

"To encourage Bobby Savarino to shut his idiot mouth."

"You're fucking crazy!"

"You really do know who I am," I said, and cocked the nine-millimeter.

The words came quickly: "Savarino was squealing on *Dragna*, you jackass, not me, not me and my brother. And if that dago did try to sell us out, what the hell good would it do him? You think we operate in this town without sanction? You really think we don't give the cops their taste?"

"You're saying Dragna did it?"

"How the hell should I know? He's capable of having somebody killed, sure, but this Black Dahlia deal, it don't sound like him. Too extreme—calls too much attention."

"None of that attention's on him. The cops and papers call it a sex crime."

"Yeah, that's a fascinating fucking insight. Why don't you take it up with Dragna, Heller? And listen, if I did wanna get at Savarino, I wouldn't hit at him through some goddamn bimbo—he's got a pregnant wife, for Christ's sake, that's his exposure."

I pressed the gun harder against his throat, making a deep

dimple. "You ever hear of a guy named Watterson, Abe? Lloyd Watterson?"

He winced, but his eyes gave no indication he wasn't telling the truth, when he said, "No. Means nothing to me."

I liked the way he was afraid, but not pissing-his-pants afraid. He was a tough little man.

Abe glared at me. "Stick that fucking thing in my mouth if you want, get me down on my knees, do the whole corny routine, Heller. You'll still get the same story."

I took the gun out of his neck, backed up a step.

"Yeah, I believe I would, Abe."

"But do you believe me?"

"Yeah. I do."

"Good."

The dapperly dressed homely little man straightened himself, smoothed out the front of his suit, went over and checked himself in the mirror. Looking at his reflection, not at me, he said, "Anything else?"

"No. Sorry for the rough stuff. No offense meant—I'm working against the clock here."

He glanced at me. "None taken. I been there."

I looked at him hard. "I don't have to sleep with one eye open tonight, do I?"

Abe shook his head. "Not on my account. I'll tell my brother we spoke."

I shoulder-holstered the nine-millimeter, and exited behind Ringgold, relieving Barney of his duties.

"I guess you have gone Hollywood," Barney said, as we walked back to the table, and the jeweler headed toward his.

"How's that?"

My old friend slipped an arm around my shoulder. "Wanting time alone with some guy in the john."

# 20

The next morning I accompanied Eliot to Central Homicide at City Hall. We took separate cars, because he would be linking up with Harry the Hat, while I would need to drive over to the *Examiner* building afterward, and check in with Bill Fowley and his boss Richardson; I planned to keep that headline-hungry pair at bay by giving them just enough information from my Florentine Gardens conversations to satisfy them.

After that I would again have to shake loose from Fowley, as I had looming before me the unenviable task of investigating the mob aspect of this murder. Fred Rubinski had confirmed that Jack Dragna held court at Lucey's at lunch each day—including Saturday, which this was—and it was my intention to beard the Sicilian lion in his den.

Right now, however, on this perfect, smog-free, sunny, blue-skied Los Angeles morning, I was showing an astounded Eliot Ness the entrance to Central Homicide: a ground-floor window you stepped through, going down a three-tier stairway consisting of piled-up cardboard evidence boxes.

Homicide had outgrown the antiquated facilities at Central Station, and moved its offices to the northwest main floor of City Hall. The side window had become an impromptu entrance, as the City Hall front entry was too far out of the way for the lazy dicks. Besides, Robbery and Burglary had transferred their offices here as well, with temporary offices set up in the hallway itself, which was no fun to wade through.

I had been here before, back when I was working the Peete case, and knew the way to where Detective Harry Hansen and his partner Finis Brown (the latter nowhere to be seen this morning) had two desks butted against each other, in a far corner—providing as much privacy as possible in the crowded bullpen.

As we approached, Hansen—seated at the desk with his pearl-gray fedora on, wearing a snappy three-piece gray suit (every other plainclothes copper in the bullpen had his suit jacket slung over the back of a chair)—was sifting through a stack of typewritten reports.

The big tall sleepy-eyed Dane rose endlessly from the desk, towering over both of us as I made introductions. The Hat gave Eliot a rare toothy grin—as opposed to one of those trademark pucker smiles—and pumped the Untouchable's hand.

A singular occasion, seeing the Hat impressed with another detective.

"A real honor, Mr. Ness," the Hat said, "meeting the man who put Capone away—not to mention cleaning up Cleveland."

"I had help in both instances," Eliot said.

"Let's go where we can talk privately," the Hat said, and led us through the bullpen out into the hallway, guiding us through the litter of desks and dicks. Our footsteps echoed off the marble floor. "I can't tell you how much I appreciate you coming out here to lend us a hand."

"How much help I'll be remains to be seen," Eliot said.

Soon we were in an interrogation room, little larger than a booth really, sitting at a small cigarette-burn-scarred wooden table, the walls lined with crumbling pale yellow soundproofed tile.

"Where's your partner?" I asked, wondering if the Hat was at all wise to the confrontation yesterday between Fat Ass and me.

"Well on his way to Chicago by now, I should think," Hansen said.

A spasm knifed through my belly. "Chicago?"

"Yes, he took a plane first thing this morning out of Burbank—

we know the Short girl was in Chicago for a few weeks in the fall. Brownie will do his best to trace her movements, there."

"Good idea," Eliot said, sitting back in a hardwood chair, arms folded, his expression blandly benign, not betraying his shared knowledge with me of just what lousy news this was.

"Poor bastard took a nasty spill, yesterday," the Hat said, shaking his head, working up half a smile. "Broke his stupid nose."

"How did he manage that?" I asked, studying the Hat's sleepy countenance for any sign he was playing with me.

"At home, slipping on his wife's freshly waxed floor." Hansen chortled. "Imagine that, the hazardous life of a homicide cop, and Brownie busts his beezer on the kitchen floor."

"Imagine that," I said, manufacturing a chuckle.

"Most accidents happen at home," Eliot pointed out quietly.

Of course, that one had happened at Mark Lansom's home, poolside.

"Well, I hope Brownie fares better in Chicago than we have here in the City of Angels," the Hat said, crossing a leg, ankle on knee, leaning back in his chair. He was seated directly across from Eliot and their postures mirrored each other's—except that Eliot had placed his hat on the scarred table, and Harry, of course, kept his on.

Eliot asked, "Any leads at all?"

"Nothing *but* leads—they just don't go anywhere. We have over seven hundred investigators working this case, Mr. Ness—"

"Eliot."

"Eliot. The sheriff has given us support by way of four hundred deputies, the highway patrol has two hundred and fifty men on the Dahlia. They've been searching storm drains, bridge basins, attics, cellars, looking for the killer's 'torture chamber,' as the papers call it. Sound familiar?"

Eliot nodded. "We went down the same road with the Kingsbury Run investigation. If that's what the sheriff's deputies and highway patrolmen are up to, what are you LAPD fellas doing?"

"Our lab man Ray Pinker and his boys have fine-tooth-combed that vacant lot a dozen times and they're still at it. Patrolmen going door-to-door in the Norton area are widening out into

Highland Park and Eagle Rock. We have sixty men scouring saloons in Hollywood and downtown L.A.—no easy task, as there's an endless supply of these seedy little bars."

Nodding, Eliot said, "Come up with anything?"

"The Short girl is known in any number of these joints—the Loyal Cafe, the Rhapsody, the Dugout. She was working as a B-girl at some of them."

I asked, "As a prostitute, or just coming on to patrons to buy drinks?"

"The latter. That's the fascinating thing about this girl—she seems to have been a professional tease. Nate, I can tell your friend here more, if you agree not to share it with the *Examiner*."

"Agreed."

"Not that even Jim Richardson could use it, without inventing a whole new lexicon of euphemisms."

"Why is that?"

"This girl was fairly promiscuous . . . and yet she seems never to have had, shall we say, conventional sex with a man." Hansen's mouth puckered in private amusement. "Take her stay at Camp Cooke, for example—where she was 'Cutie of the Week,' known as 'Miss Look-But-Don't-Touch' at the PX. She even lived with a certain sergeant for a while—and yet, if you'll pardon my French, boys, he never screwed her once."

Eliot sat forward, frowning with interest. "You've heard the same from other men who dated her?"

Hansen nodded. "The movie star, Franchot Tone—real ladies' man. Solid alibi, by the way. He described her as a 'siren luring sailors to their death.' "

"That's a little melodramatic," I said.

The Hat shrugged. "Guy's an actor. But I gathered Tone also dated but never slept with her. He indicated 'certain intimacies,' but as a 'gentleman' would say no more. All indications are Miss Short was an expert in the fine art of fellatio."

"She would go down on a guy," I translated, "but not fuck him."

The Hat winced at my crudity, but he affirmed my suspicion with a nod. "Of course another reason the gentlemanly Mr. Tone would not admit as much is that oral sex, which is to say sodomy, is a felony in this state . . . albeit one rarely enforced. I have taken to speaking to Miss Short's boy friends, off the record—assuring them no sexual charges will be brought, if they will be frank in their responses."

"Has this worked?" Eliot asked.

Again the Hat nodded. "A certain Hollywood Boulevard shoe-store manager, for example. He had an affair with Miss Short, last summer—another of these married men, with good-looking wives at home, and children, who nonetheless stray. For six weeks, he provided Miss Short with several purses, numerous pairs of expensive shoes, and, on one occasion, car fare. He did not consider her to be a prostitute, rather his girl friend—and they frequently parked, whereupon she would invariably service him orally."

"They never had normal sex," Eliot said.

"No—she always had an excuse. . . . It was her 'time of the month,' or she had an upset stomach."

"You're still following leads from her letters," I said, "the boy friends she wrote to. . . ."

"Yes, with no success as yet. Many of her servicemen paramours are out of state, with impeccable alibis. We have ruled out Red Manley, and her oddball father, Cleo, as well. Of course, we're still swimmin' in Confessin' Sams—none of 'em coming close to answering any of my three key questions."

"At least you can weed them out quickly," Eliot said.

The Hat sighed heavily. "It's still a royal pain. I'm going to start arresting these characters on obstructing justice, and see if that doesn't thin the crackpot crowd, some."

Casually, I asked, "Have you talked to Arthur Lake, yet?"

He frowned. "No. The actor? Dagwood actor?"

"Yes. He knew Beth Short at the Hollywood Canteen. He also knew the Bauerdorf girl who was slain several years before."

"Georgette Bauerdorf, bathtub slaying," the Hat said, nodding, digging out his notepad. "We're looking into that for possible connections. The Hollywood Canteen is a problem for us, now that it's been closed down, with the war over."

"Well, I didn't give you that lead," I said. Just trying to keep the Hat happy. "Lake is an in-law of Marion Davies, so the *Examiner* won't be going down that road; the only place you'll see Dagwood is on the comics page."

"I appreciate this, Nate," the Hat said, jotting down Lake's name. "Please do continue keeping your ear to the ground."

"Oh, I will—and if I hear hoofbeats, you'll be the first." I stood. "Now, I know you and Eliot have a lot to talk about, where the Kingsbury Run case is concerned. So I'll leave you boys to it."

Eliot said to me, "I'll catch up with you this afternoon."

"See you," I said.

The Hat nodded goodbye, and I exited.

My car was parked down the block, on North Spring Street. I was in something of a daze, wondering if I could crack this thing before my pal Fat Ass put the Short girl and me together, back in Chicago, when I realized someone had fallen in step alongside me.

He was a handsome Italian in a powder-blue suit and a pastel-yellow tie and brown moccasin-style loafers—fairly big guy, muscular, dark curly hair, with a tan so dark it verged on black. Almost too good-looking to be a hood.

Almost.

"Mr. Heller," he said, in a mellow baritone.

My car was within sight.

"Yeah?"

"My name's Stompanato. Johnny. We got a mutual friend."

We were just walking along, amid businessmen and clerks and lawyers and legal secretaries and tourists and other pedestrians, gliding by the Hall of Justice, Hall of Records, and State Building.

"What mutual friend would that be?"

"Mr. Cohen."

Now we were at the Buick.

"I know Mickey a little," I allowed.

Johnny Stompanato was smiling, a handsome guy, beautiful features, pleasant. I wondered whether that was a revolver or an automatic bulging under his left arm; the bulge in his trousers would have been of more interest to the females in the crowd.

"Well," Stompanato said, "Mr. Cohen thinks highly of you, and wondered if you'd had breakfast yet."

"Actually, I grabbed a doughnut, earlier."

"Mr. Cohen said to tell you he has fresh-squeezed orange juice and his cook makes a killer omelet."

That was an interesting choice of adjectives.

"Is this an invitation, or a demand?" I asked. I had my own bulges, after all.

"Simply an invitation." This guy was smooth. "Your partner Mr. Rubinski suggested to Mr. Cohen that you two might share a conversation, while you was in town."

"Where are you parked, Johnny? May I call you Johnny?"

"Sure, Nate. Right behind you—the Caddy?"

"Should have known. Can I follow you, or do I have to ride along?"

"Follow me, by all means. I'll keep the speed down, keep you in my rearview mirror."

I trailed the dark blue Caddy down Sunset to the exclusive suburb of Brentwood, adjacent to Santa Monica and the Pacific Ocean, home to many movie stars and other celebrities, including one Mayer Harris Cohen, AKA Mickey, the pint-size Capone who controlled bookie operations in Los Angeles.

Cohen did not live in a mansion, just a slightly oversize white Cape Cod cottage hugged by flowers exploding with color, surrounded by a wide, manicured lawn basking in the sunshine. This was the home every returning G.I. longed for, for his bride and himself, the postwar dream exemplified. Of course, Cohen's World War Two service had been limited to home-front black marketeering, since as a felon he couldn't serve.

No walls and no guard gate for celebrity gangster Cohen—though Stompanato stopped at a squawk box on a pole at the mouth of the wide driveway, checking in. I slid the Buick up next to the Caddy, parked right in front of triple garage doors. The only indication that this home belonged to a celebrity—particularly of the underworld stripe—was the floodlights on telephone-style poles surrounding the estate; after dark this place would be lit up like night football, and the lawn was big enough to field a game, at that.

I followed Stompanato to the front door, which opened as we got there, a middle-aged colored maid in full livery waiting for us. The maid peeled away and Stompanato did the honors, leading me across plush pile carpeting through a series of lavishly appointed rooms with gleaming woodwork and indirect lighting, each decorated in bold tones of a single color: a green room, a blue room, a mauve room, a pink room. From upholstery to the telephones, from the wallpaper to the fresh-cut flowers perched on the French Provincial furniture, one color at a time prevailed.

"Morning, Mrs. Cohen," Stompanato said to a petite redhead in the pink room, nodding to her, not introducing me.

Mickey Cohen's wife wore a pink top and blue slacks as she sat curled up on a sofa reading *Better Homes and Gardens*—the perfect little woman to go along with the dream cottage. And in that outfit, she could move from the pink room to the blue one with impunity.

"Morning, Johnny," she said in a distracted monotone. Her heart-shaped face had pretty, Shirley Temple-ish features, highlighted by huge dark green eyes; her expression was blank, in a stunned, recently poleaxed manner.

Before long, Stompanato led me into a bedroom that broke the pattern by risking two tones—tan and cream. This was apparently the master bedroom, though there was no indication a woman shared these conspicuously male quarters. From a large bathroom off to the left came the machine-gun tattoo of a shower-in-progress.

Stompanato stuck his head into the steamy room. "Boss! Mr. Heller's here!"

A raspy second tenor echoed back: "Great! Fine! Thanks!"

A few awkward seconds slipped by. Then, just making conversation, Stompanato said to me, "I, uh, understand you was a Marine?"

"Yeah. You too?"

He nodded, the curly locks staying perfectly in lacquered place. "Tarawa."

I said, "Guadalcanal."

"Semper fi, mac," he said, extending his hand, which I shook. "Pleasure."

I nodded, wondering if we'd be shooting on the same side in the next war.

The big double bed had a cream-color spread with a grandiose MC monogram; one wall was a mirrored closet, another had recessed shelving arrayed with more brands of men's colognes and creams than the May Company's men's toiletries department. Along one windowed wall, its exotic-plant-patterned drapes drawn, a comfy-looking love seat squatted next to a corner phone stand, over which staggered a few photographs of Mickey's fishing escapades . . . including the hood posing next to a marlin bigger than he was. Which didn't necessarily make it a very big marlin.

In one corner was a much smaller version of the double bed, duplicate mattress, duplicate monogrammed spread, except labelled TC. Stretched out on it, looking up at me suspiciously, was an ugly little bull terrier.

"That's Tuffy," Stompanato said. "Don't try to pet him."

"No problem," I said.

Stompanato said, "Mrs. Cohen has her own bedroom. Mirrors and walk-in vault for furs and jewels. Real feminine boudoir—you oughta see it."

Apparently he had.

Before long, the hairy, squarely built little Cohen, possessor of perpetual five-o'clock shadow, stepped from the shower stall, emerging from behind the moisture-streaked door with a towel wrapped around him, sarong-style. His black thinning hair flat to his egg-shaped skull, Cohen had the same broad forehead as his terrier, same pugnacious chin, similar flat blunt nose. The major difference lay in the eyes—the dog's big brown eyes radiated intelligence.

"Hey, Heller," Cohen said good-naturedly, giving me a glance, stepping up to the big mirror at a counter where a small army of toiletries stood at attention, waiting for commands. "Looks like we're both still alive."

"Luck on our part," I said, "bad marksmanship on theirs."

Cohen hacked a laugh, and began washing his hands in the

sink—apparently they'd gotten filthy in the shower. "Johnny, leave Heller and me be. We're old friends. He saved my buddy Jake Guzik's ass, couple years ago. Didn't you, Heller?"

"I'll do just about anything for money," I said.

Soaping his hands, he said, "Johnny, ya can even let him hang on to that roscoe he's packin', under his arm."

Those eyes may have looked stupid, but they didn't miss much. On the other hand, calling a gun a "roscoe" was fairly ridiculous these days.

Stompanato nodded to me, said, "Nice meetin' you," and slipped out.

I stood in the doorway of the bathroom as Cohen—finally convinced his hands were clean, all damned spots out, for now—used a handheld electric chrome hair drier on his wispy locks. The drier made a small roar that we had to work to speak above.

"I hear you're working for my pal Jim Richardson," Cohen said, "over at the *Examiner*."

"Yeah—background on the Dahlia murder."

"Great guy, Jim. I known him since I was a kid, hustling papers at Seventh and Broadway. Jim used to let me sleep in the *Examiner*'s men's john, waitin' for the presses to roll off on some red-hot extra."

"Why'd Jim give you such special treatment, Mick?"

Cohen grinned at me, his hair dancing under the drier's wind. "That was back in his drinkin' days. Richardson was a fuckin' lush, y'know, back then. I'd sober him up, walk him to his desk. . . . Brother, he's riding high on this Dahlia deal, ain't he?"

"It's a big story."

"I knew her, y'know."

"Really? News to me."

"At the Gardens. She was workin' there. Sweet kid. Prick tease, but really sweet. . . . I don't want that in the papers, understand."

"Understood."

His hair was dry. He shut off the drier, set it down, and selected a green vial of hair tonic and began drizzling it on. "So you busted Fat Ass' beak, I hear."

"You should know—he works for you, doesn't he?"

Cohen gave me a quick glare. "Says who?"

"That's the word on the street."

"What is?"

"That Sergeant Finis Brown is your bag man—I figure Lansom's running hookers outa the Gardens, and you're getting a taste. Why not?"

This glare wasn't quick—he held it on me and I would swear I could feel the heat. "Why *not*?" he growled. "Because Mickey Cohen don't traffic in no female flesh. I don't do that—that's fuckin' low, low as fuckin' dope. You tryin' to piss me off, Heller?"

"No. I just—"

Still frowning, Cohen returned his attention to his reflection. He put the hair tonic down and began massaging his scalp. "You just get them sleazy fuckin' thoughts outa your sleazy Chicago conk. I'm a businessman, not no fuckin' pimp."

"No offense meant, Mick. So who *does* Brown work for?"

"Himself! He's one of the biggest bookies in town."

"A cop is one of the biggest bookies in town?"

Cohen hacked another laugh. "Fat Ass is the fuckin' LAPD's in-house bookie, Heller . . . and Lansom, he covers all of Fat Ass' big bets."

I frowned, trying to make this work. "Mark Lansom is Fat Ass Brown's layoff man?"

Another quick glare, as Cohen began to brush his hair. "Do I fuckin' stutter? Yeah, that's what Fat Ass was doin' at Lansom's house, when you rearranged his nostrils—business with his backer. . . . Get me my hat, would you?"

"Where is it?"

"Should be on the dresser."

It was—a pearl-gray Borsalino that would have made Harry the Hat envious. When I reached for the lid, the bull terrier—whose corner I had neared—began to growl.

"Tuffy!" Cohen called. "Shut up, you little bastard!"

The dog stopped growling.

I handed Cohen the hat from the bathroom doorway.

Cohen put the Borsalino on—he would have looked absurd

enough in the oversize sombrero, but wearing nothing but a towel. . . .

"Listen, Heller, you mind me losin' the towel? It ain't no queer thing. It don't make me no faggot 'cause I like to stay clean—it's just, I'm just late for a meet and I gotta get myself ready."

"Do what you gotta do, Mick."

He removed the towel, folded it up, and set it on the counter. For an ugly little shrimp, Mickey Cohen had always attracted a good class of fine-looking women and I now knew what they saw in him.

The hairy naked little (in stature) gangster now selected a can of talcum powder from the battalion before him. He began shaking the talc all over himself, pausing now and then to put the can down and rub in the powder.

"Listen, I know all about these smalltime McCadden heisters," he said, standing in the little snowstorm (the hat, apparently, was to protect his hair from the talc blizzard), "and Fred told me about some of your thinkin', where this dead bimbo is concerned."

"I can tell you one thing, Mick—it's no sex crime. She was smiling the informer's smile."

"Tell me about it." The talcum can was empty; Cohen—who looked as if he'd been dipped in flour, awaiting a frying pan—selected a new can and started the process again. "But Brown is gonna keep steering the investigation in that sex maniac direction, 'cause if his partner the Hat starts diggin' into the Florentine Gardens, well, the Hat's gonna find out his fat-assed partner is the LAPD's house bookie."

"Don't you think Hansen must already know that?"

"Maybe, maybe not," Cohen said, shaking more talc on himself. "Sure bet the Hat knows his partner is a fuckin' crook—but not necessarily the department's win-place-and-show window."

"Or maybe the Hat does know," I said, thinking aloud, "and might relish exposing Fat Ass."

"Either way," Cohen shrugged, "Brown wants to keep that investigation outa the Florentine Gardens."

"And your old pal Jim Richardson likes the sex angle better than a dime-a-dozen mob rubout, anyway—sells more papers."

Nodding, powdering himself, Cohen said, "That's why no paper in town has noticed that cut-up bimbo got dumped in Jack Dragna's backyard."

I was leaning against the doorframe. "Then you agree with me, Mick—that Dragna had this murder done, to send a warning to Savarino, to shut him the fuck up?"

The naked gangster in the Borsalino shook his head, chin wrinkling. "I do not agree, in any way, shape, or form."

I almost fell over. "Jesus, Mickey—Jack Dragna tried to hire those McCadden boys to bump you off!"

He put down the empty can of talc, reaching for a third. "Yeah, probably. That's just business." He began salting himself again. "Gotta remember, Jack was the big boss in town before your buddy Benny Siegel and me got sent out here. We butted in on Dragna's territory, no question—two Jews, yet. But Dragna couldn't do nothin', not out in the open, 'cause he had ties to Lucky and Meyer."

Luciano and Lansky.

"So every now and then," Cohen continued, "Jack tries to stop my clock, but tries and make it look like it was somebody else's idea. But much as it would do me a favor having you go whack his wop ass, I can tell you without no doubt, Jack Dragna did not have that broad killed."

My head was reeling. "Why do you say that, Mickey? How can you be so goddamn sure?"

Patting himself with powder, he smirked at me. "Heller, how well do you know Benny Siegel?"

"Well."

"He's got this crazy reputation, right? Screw-loose killer? Do you believe it?"

I shrugged. "Not entirely."

"Do you think Benny or me, you think we would kill somebody just for the sheer fuckin' hell of it? Would I stick icepicks in some person, just to torture them?"

"I don't think so."

"Well, thank you. Thank you very fuckin' much." He was rubbing the powder in. His eyes were clenched tight in the shadow of the Borsalino brim. "I can tell you I never killed a man, or had a man killed, who didn't the fuck deserve killing by the standards of our way of life. The same is true of Benny, and the same is true of Jack Dragna."

I could hardly believe my ears—Mickey Cohen defending Jack Dragna.

"Dragna was going to have you killed, Mick!"

"From his vantage, I deserve it!" Cohen selected a blue bottle of cologne from the toiletry troops and dabbed some behind either ear. "I took business away from him! I stole his prestige! Tell me, Heller, when did you ever see any mobster bump a civilian? What did this good-looking piece of ass, God rest her soul, do to deserve that lousy fuckin' fate? Not a damn thing!"

"Then who did do it, Mick? Who marked Elizabeth Short as an informer, when she wasn't one? Just to warn an informer off?"

Carefully, Cohen returned the cologne bottle to its position. "Hell, I don't know. You're the detective. Who else would benefit from shutting Savarino up? Anyway, Dragna's old school—he wouldn't have the stomach for a kill like that."

"Are you sure? The sex-crime aspect of it sent the cops down the wrong path."

He gave me a brief Bronx cheer. "The only way that coulda happened was if Dragna ordered this girl killed, and some goombah went off his noodle, and got carried away havin' a little too much sick fun . . . In which case, Dragna woulda knocked this boy in the head. There'da been some Dragna gangster turn up dead in a ditch, and there ain't been any."

The bathroom floor, around his feet, was carpeted with talcum powder. He used a towel to rub some of the powder off, then looked at his naked reflection and held out his arms, as if in welcome.

"Now I can get dressed," Cohen said.

The powder crunched under his feet as he walked bare-ass-but-for-his-Borsalino into the bedroom, where—after pausing to bend and pet and exchange sloppy kisses with Tuffy (none of which was pretty to see)—he took the hat off, set it on the top of the dresser, and from a drawer selected a pair of monogrammed silk shorts.

"The rumor," Cohen said, climbing into them, "is Mark Lansom was trying to get the Short kid in the sack and havin' no luck whatsoever. So he loses his temper and kills her gorgeous ass. Now, at the same time, Fat Ass Brown is supposedly into Lansom for five grand—and agrees to help cover up the crime, if Lansom wipes the money slate clean."

"Is that what you think happened, Mick?"

Cohen shook his head. "Sounds like horseshit to me. First, Lansom don't got the balls. Second, the bastard is swimmin' in quality tail, so why's he chasin' some little cock tease? But, anyway, that's what I'm hearin', so maybe you should know."

Soon he was in gray silk socks and a white silk shirt with a red silk tie. He curled a finger for me to follow him into a walk-in closet smaller than New Jersey where he selected a blue-gray modified zoot suit with wide, long lapels and tapered trousers, from hundreds of similar suits of various shades hanging there.

"I never wear a suit after it's been dry-cleaned," he said, with a little shudder, leading me out of the closet, me carrying his suit on a hanger for him. "Makes me itch. . . . After a while, I give 'em to poor people."

"Mick, I still want to hear Dragna's version of this."

Cohen smiled tightly, put a hand on my shoulder. "You go see Dragna, if you like, talk to him about this, but Heller, I guarantee you one thing: *you'll* be dead in a vacant lot. No fancy cut job, just a bullet behind the ear, which will do the fuckin' trick, don't you think?"

"I can handle myself with gangsters, Mick."

He hacked one more laugh, as he stepped into his trousers, then looped in a black leather belt. "This ain't Chicago, Heller. These people got no history with you, no respect for you or dead Frank Nitti."

From a drawer he removed a snub-nose Colt .38 in a small holster, which he snapped onto the back of his belt, so that the gun rode his spine. Then he tapped my chest with two fingers; for some strange reason, he smelled strongly of talcum powder.

"You start sniffin' around Jack Dragna, tryin' to connect him with the worst, most fiendish murder since Jack the Ripper slashed them limey sluts, and *you're* gonna be Jim Richardson's next juicy headline. . . . Help me on with my coat."

I did.

"Speakin' of juice, wait'll you taste my fresh-squeezed. Gotta apologize, though, we yammered so much, I don't have time for breakfast. I'll have Johnny show you to the kitchen—just tell the chef you want my special lox-and-onion omelet."

"I think maybe I lost my appetite, Mickey."

The natty little ape glanced over his shoulder at me, snugging the Borsalino back on. "Don't offend me, Heller. I don't like that."

It was delicious.

# 21

For a change Jim Richardson wasn't pacing, that manic engine of his apparently having finally run down. He sat slumped at the head of the conference room table at the *Examiner*—he and I were alone in the narrow chamber—a cigarette drooping from slack lips. The city room editor was staring woefully at me with both eyes, even the slow one.

"This fuckin' story is runnin' out of steam," he said.

I had just reported what I'd learned from my conversations with Granny and Mark Lansom at the Florentine Gardens, including Lansom's missing address book. I also passed along what Harry the Hat had told Eliot and me about the sorry state of the LAPD's investigation, all of which Richardson already seemed to know. Anything of value I'd learned, yesterday, I of course withheld—the McCadden Cafe group's connection to Elizabeth Short, in particular; and certainly nothing about Welles, or Jack Dragna, who I had decided—on Mickey Cohen's sage advice—not to bother seeing. Dragna seemed not only a dead end, but a potentially deadly one.

"There's a lot going on," I said, shrugging. "Should be plenty of legs left in this thing."

Richardson shook his head mournfully. "Too many goddamn leads—too many boy friends, too many bars she frequented, too many lovesick letters she wrote to too many nobodies."

"None of your newshounds have turned up anything interesting?"

"Best thing we got lately is the Dahlia was seen at numerous joints in the company of a big 'bossy' blonde." He crushed out his cigarette in a glass tray, started up another one, then added archly, "If you can believe the cab drivers and bartenders and lushes who shared this hot information."

The bossy blonde was probably Helen Hassau.

"When was this," I asked, "that she was seen with a blonde?"

"Just two days before the body turned up. I hear the cops are starting to think Miss Short was a lesbian, and are hitting the dyke bars. The Hat tell you as much?"

"That he didn't mention." Didn't surprise me that Hansen was holding out on me like I was holding out on him.

"Fowley's still chasing soldiers up at Camp Cooke," Richardson said, shaking his head. "So many leads, and none of 'em cough up a clue."

"It's still early, Jim."

"Our readers are getting bogged down in this unproductive crap. I didn't want the cops to solve this overnight, but I didn't expect 'em to mount their horses and gallop off in all directions."

"She was a good-looking girl who got around town—sorting out her life and loves could take a year."

"Meanwhile, my readers get their asses bored off."

I rose from the hard chair. "Well, I'm takin' the rest of the day off. You can let me know Monday morning if you still want me in on this thing."

The editor nodded. "Thinkin' about headin' back to Chicago with that good-lookin' bride of yours?"

"Yeah. Maybe you could sit down with Fowley or somebody and do that puff piece, first—give my agency that boost you promised."

"Sure thing. Of course, it would be a better story under a headline about how you found the Black Dahlia's killer."

I was at the door, now. "I'll see what I can do, over the weekend."

"You do that. And I'll see if maybe I can figure out a way to goose this thing in the ass."

"That's the best place to apply a goose."

Richardson snorted a laugh.

Just as I went out, I glanced back and he was an oddly pitiful figure, sitting there alone in the big room, staring into nothing, one eye going this way, the other that, his bald head wreathed in cigarette smoke.

Back in the Beverly Hills hotel bungalow, I found a note from Peggy. She was going out shopping with Cathy Ross, for the afternoon—"while I still can." I knew this to be a reference to her time of the month—tomorrow, or later today, if the flow got really heavy, she'd be bed-bound. She had really hard periods, sometimes accompanied by blazing headaches.

Couldn't blame her for wanting to get in a little relaxation before the menstrual onslaught, but I felt helpless and as alone as Richardson had looked. For a case with so many leads, I was fresh out, particularly since Cohen had scratched Dragna off my list.

I walked the hotel's manicured, flower-flung grounds and slipped inside the lobby, and grabbed lunch at the Fountain Coffee Shop. When I was strolling past the front desk, an assistant manager called out to me, and handed me a note from my mailbox.

Lou Sapperstein had been trying to call, all morning—six little slips of paper represented as many attempts.

That put some spring in my step, and back in the bungalow I called Lou at his home number, and got him on the first ring.

"You found something," I said.

"I found something," Lou said.

"Well, it better be good, 'cause as we speak, Sergeant Finis Brown of the LAPD is in town—that is, the town you're in, partner, Chicago? And Sergeant Brown and I are not good friends."

"How unfriendly are you?"

"Well, if he finds his way to our offices, Lou, you'll notice a bandage on his nose."

Lou sighed. "You broke his nose. You broke the nose of one of the investigating cops."

"Why, doesn't that sound like me, Lou?"

"It sounds exactly like you, Nate," he said wearily. "Now I

want to ask you something, before I share my tidbit of information, which by the way only cost the A-1 three hundred bucks—"

"Three hundred!"

"Yeah—this comes from a doctor in Hammond, Indiana, a rabbit-puller who does not want the attention of the cops or the press, which being the Black Dahlia's doctor would certainly bring."

I frowned. "Black Dahlia? You know the nickname, so the case has hit the Chicago papers."

"Yeah, no pics of her yet. Just small, juicy articles; but with a moniker like that—"

"Right. So spill, Lou—what did this Hammond Dr. Kildare give you?"

"Let me ask you my question, first. Have you run across any men who say they slept with her? Who actually screwed this girl?"

"No. She went down on her share, though."

"And didn't you tell me you didn't remember screwing her, yourself? That you were drunk on your ass that night?"

"Yeah," I said. "My love life is a regular Cole Porter tune, isn't it?"

"Nate, there's a reason for this girl, this slutty girl, never fucking anybody. *She couldn't.*"

I sat up. "What the hell do you mean? She was pregnant, wasn't she?"

"No. She was not."

I was shaking my head, as if not sure my ears were hearing right. "Then what was she going to an abortionist for?"

Another sigh. "Like a lot of those guys, this quack in Hammond is also a gynecologist. The problem the Short girl had was *not* that she had your, or anybody's bun, in her oven. She requested a colposcopy."

"Talk English, Lou."

"A vaginal exam. But she couldn't have one. You see, Elizabeth Short had a physical abnormality that made even a routine vaginal exam impossible. The doc called it . . . let me check my notes . . . 'vaginal atresia.' "

"What the hell does that mean?"

There was a shrug in Lou's voice: "She had something the doctor said happens maybe once in a million births: an undeveloped vaginal canal."

"Undeveloped. You mean, like a . . . kid's?"

"Like a child, a female child—Nate, your beautiful Black Dahlia did not have fully developed adult genitals."

I just sat there, phone against my ear, staring at a vase of cut flowers on a stand across the room—lovely pink flowers, feminine, delicate. Dead.

"Nate? You still there?"

I nodded, then realized Lou couldn't see that, and said, "Still here. It's just . . . so many things make sense now. Of course she satisfied her boy friends orally—it's all she had."

"Sorry for the crudity," Lou said, "but she probably couldn't let them in her back door, either, without showing herself—without them seeing that she was . . . like a child, down there."

*So Harry the Hat's third piece of information, gathered in the autopsy, was* not *that the Dahlia was pregnant—but that she was physically incapable of having normal intercourse with a man!*

Something clicked. "Lou—the money she was raising . . . It wasn't for an abortion. It was for an operation—she wanted to be a normal woman!"

"I hadn't thought of that," Lou said. "I guess that's why you're the president of this outfit."

Her physical abnormality was why she had gone to Dr. Dailey—her old family friend—whose partner, Dr. Winter, was a gynecologist. The money she was saving up—that five hundred dollars she was scrambling after, blackmailing me and others for—was so she could become a complete woman.

Bobby Savarino had been talking marriage, and Elizabeth Short—like so many women, like so many men, in these sad, hopeful postwar days—wanted the cottage and the picket fence and the whole married American megillah. I'd been right, when I told Fowley that I figured Beth Short wanted to be a wife more than a movie star.

And so, after years of thinking about it, and dreaming about it, and after discovering that a doctor from back home was practicing in Los Angeles—a doctor specializing in "woman troubles"—she finally had taken the step, to arrange for an operation. An expensive one.

"What are you going to do with this information, Nate?"

"The cops already have it," I said, "or anyway the key cop does." And I explained how the Hat was keeping this and two other only-the-killer-knows items under wraps. "But it means I have to rethink every piece of information I've gathered, every individual I've spoken to."

Lou laughed humorlessly. "Whole new ball game."

"Different game entirely—though this one also starts with a butchered girl in a vacant lot."

We discussed Brown's presence in Chicago, and I told Lou to play it straight down the middle, should Fat Ass show up at the office with questions about me. Soon, perhaps today, I would tell the Hat about having known Short briefly in Chicago, and explain my reticence to come forward, due to the coincidence of having been along with Fowley for the discovery of the body.

"Now that we know Beth Short wasn't pregnant," I said, "I'm much less a viable suspect."

"That doesn't change the fact that she told you she was pregnant," Lou reminded me, "and tried to blackmail you."

"If she'd been pregnant by me," I said, "there was a good chance she could've told some girl friend or other, or a doctor, or even another boy friend. But since she was lying to me, scamming me, chances are strong nobody knew about her calling me from the Biltmore . . . but me."

"And me," Lou said. "But I ain't tellin' a soul. We'll talk about my raise, later."

"Fuck you very much. Don't you see, Lou? If she'd really been pregnant, a whole battery of men might have been suspects. They now have been turned into a meaningless bunch of former boy friends, whose tales of never having sex with the girl suddenly make sense."

"So the suspect field is narrowed," Lou said.

"Considerably."

I did not tell Lou about Watterson, because Eliot had requested I keep the lid on that; but, like a new Rosemary Clooney tune, the Mad Butcher of Kingsbury Run had just jumped back to the top of my personal Hit Parade.

"On the other hand," Lou said, "maybe one of those boy friends killed her—you know, flew into a murderous rage when he discovered she could not be fucked."

"Jesus, yeah—that does make a terrible kind of sense."

Another humorless laugh. "Poor kid was the only prick tease on earth who didn't want to be."

After hanging up, I just sat there on the couch in that bungalow, afternoon sun filtering in lazily through sheer curtains, my interview notepad in hand, and I paged through it as I mentally sorted through every fact, every facet, every suspect, every supposition, every rumor, every seeming coincidence, viewed through the new prism of Beth Short's disability.

Perhaps half an hour later, a frantic knocking at the bungalow door jarred me, as if I'd been sleeping and got jolted awake, and I went quickly to the door and opened it. Perhaps I had been in a trancelike state, but seeing Eliot Ness's uncharacteristically excited expression made me instantly alert.

"I have some incredible information," he blurted.

"You may want to hear mine, first," I said.

I sat on the couch and he pulled up an armchair, tossing his fedora on the coffee table, and listened to my retelling of Lou Sapperstein's bizarre news. Midway he got up and helped himself to some Scotch from the wet bar.

Visibly shaken, Eliot said, "It's all beginning to make sick, tragic sense."

"Parts of it are coming clear, but I have to admit, most of it is still pretty goddamn murky from where I sit."

"Wait—just wait." He gulped at the Scotch, then unbuttoned his suitcoat, set the drink on the glass top of the coffee table, and for several long moments sat with his elbows on his knees and his face in his hands; that unruly comma of brown, graying hair hung almost to his eyebrows.

"Are you all right, Eliot?"

"Where shall I start?" He sat suddenly straight. "All right, the beginning . . . I spent two hours with Detective Hansen, wasting time retreading the Butcher inquiry, making the case for this probably not being the same perpetrator. He seemed to buy it well enough. Then I asked Hansen if anyone was exploring abortionists in the city—and he told me, yes, but that he personally thought that was a blind alley."

"Considering his knowledge of Beth Short's deformity, that's not surprising."

Eliot nodded, and pressed on. "But I pushed him, saying that in Cleveland we believed the Kingsbury Run Butcher was a doctor or perhaps ex-doctor, due to the medical precision of the dismemberments. The Black Dahlia's corpse showed similar medical knowledge and the same sort of surgical skill."

"And," I said, "you naturally told Hansen that if he's really trying to see whether the Kingsbury Run Butcher committed this crime, then this is a logical path to go down."

"Yes. He put me with a young vice squad sergeant, Charles Stoker, and left us alone. I asked Sergeant Stoker for a list of known and suspected abortionists. Stoker gave me one, but Dailey's name wasn't on it. . . ."

"Of course. Dailey's protected."

Eliot nodded. "So I told the young detective that I'd heard about a doctor named Dailey, who was originally from Massachusetts, same as Elizabeth Short."

I winced. "Dangerous sharing that . . ."

He raised a palm, as if getting sworn in on the stand. "But necessary to get the information—and, anyway, I can play it down, if it gets back to Hansen. Stoker started looking around the bullpen furtively, then finally, uneasily, admitted that certain local doctors suspected of abortion were not 'bothered' by the LAPD. He said it rubbed him the wrong way, but the policy in the department was that abortion was a fact of life and a few of the more responsible practitioners were given a blind eye."

"And he admitted Dr. Dailey was one of these."

"Yes, a very respectable retired Chief of Staff of Los Angeles County Hospital, after all, retired USC professor. But Stoker had some other interesting information about Dr. Dailey—he was very much aware of Dailey's failing mental condition."

"Really?"

"Really." Eliot smiled tightly, nastily. "Seems Dailey's estranged wife has been trying to arrange a commitment for her errant hubby—it's been something of a minor scandal. Apparently Mrs. Dailey thinks this woman, Dr. Winter, is 'exerting undue influence' over her husband, using her 'feminine wiles.'

"As in, stealing the doc away from her."

Nodding again, Eliot said, "Yes, and changing his will to favor Dr. Winter."

"It's not a new story."

"But in the context of the death of Elizabeth Short, it makes a very interesting story."

I shook my head, confused. "How in hell could the Short girl's murder have anything—"

Eliot held up a traffic-cop palm. "Wait. Just wait. After Sergeant Stoker and I were finished, I came back here to the hotel and made a few phone calls . . . first to the main branch of the L.A. public library, to see if they had Harvard yearbooks on hand."

"Why?"

"Because I wanted to see if Lloyd Watterson's father and Dr. Dailey really were classmates. A librarian on the research desk said she would be happy to look into it for me, and she called me back, not half an hour ago. Both men did attend Harvard, just not at the same time—Lloyd's father graduated the year before Dailey enrolled."

"What does that mean to you, Eliot?"

The Untouchable leaned forward, his hands clasped as if in prayer. "It means Lloyd was lying to us about at least one thing. Getting the job with Dailey had nothing to do with him being a friend and classmate of dear dead dad."

"And why would he lie about that?"

A tiny shrug. "Possibly to make himself look better to us—make it look as if he really was trying to make a clean start, with his family's help . . . rather than going to work for an abortionist, through the efforts of some lowlife criminal acquaintance."

"This is all very interesting, but—"

"Nate." Eliot twitched a smile, sat back, hands on his knees. "Do you have a phone book?"

Huh?

"Well, sure," I said. "It's right there, in that drawer." I pointed to the nearby endtable where the phone sat. "Why?"

"Because I did one of my most effective if accidental pieces of detective work today just by looking up a number, and checking the address that went with it. Get the phone book, Nate—*get it.*"

I got it.

"From what Stoker told me," Eliot said, "I thought it might be interesting to have a talk with Mrs. Dailey. Possibly not worth a trip to her house, but a phone call surely wouldn't hurt. Look up her number, Nate. It's under her husband's name—until two and a half months ago, when he moved out, that was where the doctor lived."

Humoring Eliot, wondering what the hell had got into him, I looked up Dr. Wallace A. Daily in the phone book. The phone number was meaningless, but the street address was not.

Dr. Dailey—or at any rate, his estranged wife—lived at 3959 South Norton.

"Jesus Christ," I said. "That's . . ."

"One block from a certain vacant lot."

I tossed the phone book on the carpet with a thud.

"What the hell does it mean?" I asked, trembling.

"I'm not sure," Eliot said. "Presumably Doc Dailey and the Winter woman do their abortions at the clinic, not his private residence. But it is one hell of a . . . coincidence."

*Detectives do not believe in coincidence.*

"Now I have one more item to share with you," Eliot said, with a self-satisfied sigh, "and it makes all of the rest of these revelations . . . perhaps even that of Elizabeth Short's unfortunate physical condition . . . pale to insignificance."

I leaned back on the couch, wondering how much more I could take; I felt as if I'd been pummeled.

"Remember I said the name 'Arnold Wilson' rang a bell? And you said it was an ordinary name—unlikely that it would make any more connection in my mind than 'John Smith.' But we were in the presence of Lloyd Watterson at the time, weren't we? The new improved mentally balanced Mad Butcher of Kingsbury Run? And you may remember, prior to leaving for Los Angeles, I had just spent several hours with the thousands of pages of the Torso file."

"I remember."

"It occurred to me that perhaps the name 'Arnold Wilson' had turned up in that file. So I called Merlo at home, long distance, just a few minutes ago."

Detective Martin Merlo—who had lived and breathed the Butcher case since he was first assigned in the mid-'30s . . . .

"I knew," Eliot was saying, "that Merlo would know that file inside out, virtually have the damn thing memorized. I asked him if the name Arnold Wilson meant anything to him."

"And it did?"

"Remember I mentioned that in the original Butcher investigation we had explored the theory that Watterson had had an accomplice of sorts? That some of the murders, the dismemberments, would seem to have required a second pair of hands?"

"You had a suspect . . . some fag butcher. . . ."

"A young homosexual, yes, who worked on St. Clair Avenue. Like Watterson, he liked to prowl the skid row sections of town, preying on society's dregs. And his name, as you've guessed, was Arnold Wilson."

*But could he be the same Arnold Wilson—the McCadden Cafe short order cook who had been so helpful to me? That skeletal, gimpy war veteran Wilson? And was he one of those cooks who butchered his own meat? I wondered.*

"It's still a common name," I said, not knowing whether I wanted this to be true or not.

"Yes, but the description of the St. Clair Avenue butcher-shop boy was not common: he was a very pockmarked kid, very thin, very tall, Merlo said . . . perhaps as much as six four."

Just last night, Arnold Wilson had been sitting on this same couch next to Peggy—had been alone with her.

"This description perfectly fits, incidentally," Eliot said, "that of the eyewitness accounts of the one Mocambo robber who went unapprehended."

"Which," I said, "is no coincidence."

"I think it's time we had another talk with Lloyd Watterson," Eliot said, sitting very straight. "Nate, I think we had the Dahlia's killer in our hands—perhaps not the person who had her killed, and who provided this particular victim to Lloyd, for his perverse pleasures—but definitely the fiend who did the butchering itself."

The phone rang and we both jumped.

"Hello," I said numbly.

"Nate, thank God."

It was Fred.

"What is it, Fred?"

"I'm at the Bradbury."

"What? Working?"

"Yes—for you. I'm taking a turn at watching Watterson. He and Dailey and the Winter dame arrived here about half an hour ago—they're in Dailey's office. Listen, I don't know what this means, but you may want to get over here right away."

"Why, what . . . ?"

"I just saw your wife go in there."

# 22

On Saturdays, the Bradbury Building was locked up by one p.m.—about half the offices staying open until noon, the others dispensing with weekend hours—so Eliot and I again parked in the alley and I used my tenant's key in the rear door, near the service entrance.

I had an idea I knew what was going on, and I had explained my theory to Eliot, chattering like a demented tour guide running stoplights and stop signs and wildly passing other cars in the fifteen or so frantic minutes from Beverly Hills to downtown L.A. He said little, just taking it in—but if a detective as astute as Eliot Ness did not contradict me, I knew I had to be on to something.

We flew up the five flights of stairs, golden sun streaming down through the skylight, filtering through the ornate ironwork, casting delicate filigree shadows; our footsteps echoed off the iron steps like small-arms fire in the vast hollow cavern of the Victorian building. No sign of janitorial staff or other tenants. On the fifth floor, Eliot—as I'd instructed—ducked into the A-1 office, to fetch handcuffs and a gun from Fred Rubinski's small arsenal . . .

. . . while I barreled down the hall to the doctor's office, nine-millimeter Browning automatic in hand.

Fred Rubinski was already inside—and I could hear his voice, jovial through the frosted glass. I had directed Fred to bluff his way in and keep anything from happening till I got there. Since Fred was a referral service for this high-class abortion mill, he would be humored by Dr. Winter and her senile mentor.

I burst into the waiting room, where only one chair was taken—by Barney's wife, Cathy, sitting reading a *Ladies' Home Journal*.

"Nate!" Cathy said. Casually beautiful in white blouse and black slacks, her dark hair up, the former showgirl looked at me with the wide, horrified eyes of someone who'd seen a ghost.

"Hello, Cathy," I said. "You just sit there, all right?"

Everything in the coldly modern reception area looked aboveboard, nothing suspicious, nothing remotely sinister. Fred Rubinski, typically natty in a brown suit and green-and-yellow-striped tie, stood chatting with Dr. Dailey, in front of the receptionist's empty window.

Gray-haired, salt-and-pepper-mustached Dr. Dailey—not in his white jacket today, rather a rumpled blue-gray tweed suit—at first smiled, and began to say, "I'm sorry, sir," possibly to inform me the clinic was closed; then the plumpish, grandfatherly gentleman's expression froze. Senile or not, he'd noticed the weapon in my fist.

Seeing me, Fred's cheerful demeanor disappeared and the Edward G. Robinson face turned cop-hard.

Dr. Dailey said, "What's going on here? I don't understand . . . ?"

"You rarely do, you old jackass," Fred snapped, and he took the doctor by the arm and sat him roughly down in one of the waiting room chairs. "Sit there and shut up."

And now Fred had a gun in his fist, too, a .38. Cathy was covering her mouth with a red-nailed hand, and looked as though she might cry. Behind his wireframes, the doctor's rheumy green eyes were open wide, as was his mouth, as if he'd been struck in the belly.

Pointing down the hallway, to the right of the receptionist window, Fred said, "Third door on the left."

Cathy rushed over, catching me just as I was starting down. She clutched my arm. "Nate, you don't understand. . . . She just wasn't ready. . . . Please don't hurt her."

I lifted her hand off my arm. "She's in there with a murderer, Cathy—go sit the hell down."

Swallowing, a hand splayed to the side of her face, backing up, Cathy stumbled into a chair and collapsed into it, just as Eliot blew into the office. Seeing him—he too had a gun in hand, a big nasty-looking .45—she looked like she might pass out.

"Back me up," I said to Eliot.

He nodded, and followed me down the hallway.

Sick inside, trembling with fear, coldly enraged, I opened the third door on the left and the tableau within was one I would never forget.

Stretched out before me like an Aztec sacrifice, in a white hospital gown that had been lifted up and gathered about her waist, lay my wife—her private parts exposed, the unfolded flower of her in the centerstage spotlight of a ceiling-mounted flood—on crinkling white butcher paper on a shiny steel table with her feet in metal stirrups. Just beyond where she lay on the table was the sink, the faucet of which had been fitted with a hollow metal-and-rubber cylinder connecting to a coil of rubber hose attached to a hollow metal tube with a small slit on the end.

She looked so small, like a child, my petite bride; and quite astoundingly pretty despite the conditions and the locale—no makeup, her dark hair pinned up, her creamy pale skin lovely even under the harsh light, her big violet eyes startled, horrified, at the sight of me—and her mouth open but no sound coming out, as she stared at the intruder who was her husband, an intruder with a gun.

The smell of strong disinfectant made my nostrils twitch. The small operating room was as blindingly white and antiseptic looking as a House of the Future kitchen—cabinets and counters and sink and ceiling, chrome and Formica and tile and plastic—and I had not been in a room so blizzard-white since I awoke tied into a chair in Lloyd Watterson's basement.

They both wore white smocks and surgical masks and rubber gloves. Dr. Maria Winter—the almost-beautiful amazon with the luminous brown eyes, her dark hair piled in a bun—stood at the end of the table, between my wife's legs, a rubber pad beneath

Peggy's hips, the doctor washing her with a soapy sponge from a stainless steel basin, water running down over her pubic region, moistening the pad, and streaming down into a catch bucket.

At the counter, tall blond Lloyd Watterson—ice-blue eyes frozen over the surgical mask—half-turned from transferring hot instruments from a sterilizer into a flat metal basin of steaming water. The instruments were mostly a delicate assortment of scalpels and curettes, and Lloyd held in his rubber-gloved hand a long, slender instrument with a rounded end, which I didn't much like the looks of.

"Put down your spoon, Lloyd," I said. "And put up your hands."

Lloyd nodded and dropped the instrument into the water with a little splash.

Pushing herself up on her elbows, feet still in the stirrups, Peggy was looking at me, eyes huge, mouth moving, but nothing coming out. I yanked the hospital gown down over her. Dr. Winter stood there, soapy sponge in one hand, basin in the other, like a statue in the Abortion Museum.

A towering woman, Dr. Winter was, but when I shoved the snout of the nine-millimeter in her throat, just under the surgical mask, she seemed to grow even taller, as her chin lifted and long lashes fluttered over those patronizing dark eyes of hers.

Calmly, I asked the doctor, "Have you done anything yet?"

"What?" Her eyes and nostrils flared like a frightened horse. "No! We were just about to begin the procedure."

"I see. . . . Lloyd! Keep those hands up, and away from those instruments! Try to imagine how much I'm looking for an excuse to splash your fucking brains across those cabinets!"

That gave Lloyd a spasmodic start, and he thrust his hands higher.

I returned my attention to Dr. Winter, yanking the mask down, exposing the entire olive oval of her face. I lowered the nine-millimeter from her neck, and smacked the barrel of the gun against the brim of the metal basin in her hands, knocking it out of them, sending it clattering, splashing to the floor.

The amazon abortionist jumped back, unnerved.

"Well, we certainly do thank you for your time, Doctor—but the little lady and me have had second thoughts. We've decided to have this baby."

Peggy finally managed to say, "Nathan . . . please!"

I smiled over my shoulder at her. "Let's not air our trivial little personal disagreements in front of the good doctor, here, and her estimable aide. . . . *Eliot*!"

My friend stepped in, the .45 in hand.

"Eliot, this is Dr. Maria Winter—Dr. Winter, Eliot Ness. Oh, and of course, you know Lloyd, already."

"Dr. Winter," Eliot said, nodding politely. "Hello, Lloyd."

Lloyd said nothing, hands high, eyes twitching over the surgical mask.

"Would you mind watching these two for me?" I asked Eliot. "I have business with both of them, and wouldn't want them to go running off."

"Glad to," Eliot said, the big automatic trained on Lloyd.

I slipped my nine-millimeter into its holster under my sport-jacket, and moved alongside Peggy, whose body was in a cramped V, as she sat propped up on her elbows, her feet still in those damn stirrups, as she stared at me with an expression that managed to mingle indignation and alarm.

Then I scooped her up in my arms and carried her out of there like a bride over the threshold. Romantic and dashing as all hell, except perhaps for the way my wife looked up at me as if I were a lunatic.

Where could she have got that idea?

Once we were in the hallway, I eased her to her feet and asked her where her clothes were. Peggy had never seemed more tiny, more dainty, than when she stood there in her bare feet, pointing down the hall toward a door.

"Let's get your clothes," I said, as if to a child.

She nodded, and padded down the hall, and I followed her into a small dressing room, a cubicle with a couple chairs and barely enough room for both of us. I leaned against the wall, arms folded, as she took her clothes from the wall hooks and got into her bra and panties and a yellow blouse and tan slacks and brown sandals.

"How's the period going?" I asked. "Any cramps?"

"I know I lied to you," she said, dressing, voice trembling with emotion, some defensiveness mixed in, "but you had no right to make this decision for me. I wasn't ready to have a child. You—"

"You're just lucky an abortion was what I did interrupt."

She was dancing on one foot, getting a sandal on. "What?"

I beamed at her; I had never loved her more, or hated anyone so much. "Do you know who was about to jam a surgical instrument into you, my darling? His name is Lloyd Watterson. Lloyd's the guy I've been looking for lately—you know. . . . The maniac who killed the Black Dahlia."

"What?" She was fully dressed, and stood with hands on hips, facing me, looking at me through narrowed eyes, challenging me. "You're insane."

"Possibly, but I'm well balanced compared to that 'doctor' of yours—oh, not the woman, she's probably competent enough. Again I refer to Lloyd Watterson—that tennis-anyone blond fella? He is in fact, no kidding, the maniac who butchered Elizabeth Short."

Hands still on her hips, Superman-style, she coughed a laugh. "You can't be serious. . . ."

I pawed the air like a bored lion. "You're right. I'm just kidding around. But you know, dear, just like before getting any medical treatment, maybe you really should seek a second opinion."

"What are you talking about?"

"Ask Eliot about Lloyd. You do recall why Eliot came to town?"

She knew very well that Eliot was here to consult on the Dahlia investigation.

Her eyes tightened. "You're not saying . . ."

"That aging boy ingenue in there is the very psychopath who butchered all those whores and bums back in Cleveland, not so very long ago. A certified, certifiable fiend who, incidentally, I tracked down, the first time around—and helped lock up in the loony bin. So he may bear me a little grudge, though, hell, why would he take that out on you?"

She waved both hands, shook her head. "You're just trying to scare me. . . . You're trying to put me in my place. . . ."

I grabbed her by the arms—as if I were going to shake her. But I didn't, not physically, anyway.

I looked right into her sweet freckled face and said, "All right, lover. You still want this abortion? Fine. Maybe at this point, I don't want your goddamn fucking kid, any more than you want mine. I'll round up Fred and Eliot and we'll take a powder, and leave you to Lloyd. It might be interesting to see what he'd prescribe for you if you got back up on that table and spread your legs."

I let go of her, shoving her, just a little.

Staggering back, then planting herself on shaky legs, she swallowed, or tried to; her eyes began to tear up, her lips quivering with fear. "Then . . . then it's true?" She pointed toward the front of the clinic. "That . . . that *was* the . . . I was going to be . . . he could have been . . ."

I sighed. Nodded.

With a yelping little animal squeal, she threw herself into my arms and held me tight; she began to sob, and I patted her back, saying, "It's okay, baby, it's okay," loving her, hating her, feeling so damn sorry for her, and so goddamn pleased she'd got what she deserved.

"I'm sorry, Nathan, I'm so sorry," she said, sniffling, tears and snot streaming down her pretty face. "Can you ever forgive me?"

I took her face in my hands and I held her face and looked into the violet eyes and I asked, "Are we having this baby?"

She nodded emphatically. "We're having it. We're having it, and we're going to love it and it's going to be the best baby that two people ever had."

"It's not an 'it,' I told her sternly, face still in my hands. "It's a boy or a girl, understand? Our baby—our child. And no butcher is taking that away from us."

She hugged me and she kissed me, a sloppy snotty weepy kiss that was the sweetest I ever had.

We were halfway down the hall when Cathy came up to us, looking sheepish.

"I'm sorry, Nate," Cathy said.

I said, "It's okay. . . . You were just trying to help out a friend."

Cathy nodded, chagrined.

"Please take Peg to the hotel," I said, "and stay with her. I still have things to do, here."

I handed Peggy into her friend's care, and walked them out through the waiting room, where Fred was still holding the confused, slumping Dr. Dailey hostage in the doctor's own waiting room. Seeing me with my arm around Peggy, Fred said, "She's all right?"

"She's all right," I said.

"I'm fine," she said.

I gave Peggy a quick kiss, stroked her cheek, and she and Cathy slipped out into the hall.

Frustrated, Dr. Dailey asked, "I demand to know what is going on here!"

"Shut up!" Fred and I said simultaneously, and the doctor jumped in his hard chair, and shut up.

I walked back to the operating room and curled a finger at Eliot, who joined me at the doorway. I told him to take Dr. Winter into Dailey's office and wait for me. I had to talk to Lloyd—alone.

"All right," Eliot said, taking my orders unquestioningly, "but do me a favor."

"Don't kill him?"

He nodded.

I shook my head. "No promises."

After an "oh well" shrug, Eliot herded the amazon across the hall into the jade-adorned office of Dr. Dailey, and I returned to the blindingly white room with the delicate instruments and the butcher-papered table with stirrups.

Surgical mask dangling around his throat like a loose bandage, Lloyd was leaning with his back against the counter. I shut the door—the loud click was like the cocking of a gun. Speaking of which, my nine-millimeter was tucked away, under my left arm . . . but my sportjacket was unbuttoned.

"I didn't know she was your wife," Lloyd said, raising both hands, palms out. The ice-blue eyes were dancing with fright. "I wasn't going to hurt her, I swear to God. The name she gave was 'Smith'!"

"I believe you, Lloyd."

"You . . . you do?"

I stood across from him, leaning back against the operating table. "This was a last-minute referral, wasn't it, Lloyd? A favor you did for a friend."

Lloyd blinked. "She was just another patient."

"No—tell me about your friend."

"What friend?"

"Your very good friend—your best friend . . . except that he's not as good a friend as you think. Y'see, he stage-managed this so that I would come in on you, in the act, and most likely blow you to hell and gone."

Indignation flamed in Lloyd's face. "What? You're crazy! He would never do that to me."

" 'He'? Your friend, you mean?"

"No, I . . . I mean, no friend would do something like that."

I raised an eyebrow. "Not even your old friend from Cleveland . . . your St. Clair Avenue 'apprentice'—Arnold Wilson?"

He swallowed thickly. "I don't know anybody with that name."

"Sure you do, Lloyd." My left hand, leaning against the operating table, reflexively clutched butcher paper and crinkled and tore and wadded it; but my voice remained calm. "After all, it would take a real pal to convince you to leave the head on a torso, like that, right? But your buddy Arnold needed the head left on—needed that smile cut into Beth Short's face, 'cause he had a message to send. You compensated with other fun—torture, for example. And with your quaint sexual tastes, the fact that her female organs were unformed didn't bother you, did it? You tied her up and fucked her in the ass and made her suck your dick, didn't you, Lloyd? Oh, you wonder how I know that? She died with shit in her stomach, you sick fuck!"

Lloyd whirled and grabbed the tray of instruments from the counter and flung it all toward me, an armada of sharp flying objects riding a warm splash of water. I covered my face with my arms, and my hand took a tiny gash and my sleeves were cut, but that was all—the metal instruments bouncing off, clattering to the floor.

Still, it was enough to distract me as, lightning fast, Lloyd moved to a drawer and yanked it open and plucked out a shiny silver instrument, no delicate curette this, but an amputation cleaver, with a wide, wicked blade—just like the one he'd come at me with in that other blindingly white room, the murder lab in his Kingsbury Run basement—and he raised it high, where it caught and distorted my reflection like a Crazy House mirror, ready to swing that blade down and around, to take my head off in his trademark manner.

But I fired the nine-millimeter first, and the bullet at close range caught him alongside the edge of his cleaver-wielding right hand, just above the knuckle of his little finger, blasting through that little finger and into the next and the next and the next, shearing through the digits, which went flying, scattering, tumbling, as if he were so clumsy he had somehow managed to drop his fingers.

The cleaver clanked to the tile floor and Lloyd was screaming, holding on to his wrist, the four stumps where his fingers used to be spurting and spouting blood, a quartet of scarlet streams that—as he gripped his wrist and shook his mangled hand—traced Jackson Pollock patterns on the white counter.

Eliot came charging in, .45 in one hand, his other gripping the arm of Dr. Winter, dragging her in after him. Out in the hallway, an alarmed Fred Rubinski was peeking in.

"Jesus," Eliot said.

"Christ," Fred said.

"Oh dear," Dr. Winter said.

Howling in agony, Lloyd had slid down to the floor and, kneeling like a praying man, was gripping his wrist, blood still squirting, but less so now, nothing arterial. His fingers were littered on the floor like particularly unappetizing sausages spilled from an hors d'oeuvres plate; one of them had ended up on the cleaver, which I thought was kind of poetic.

My voice was high pitched and defensive, a kid denying blame, as I said, "I didn't kill him," holding up my hands, one of which still grasped the nine-millimeter. "I didn't kill him."

Dr. Winter went to Lloyd and covered the damaged hand with a towel, glancing back at us pointedly. "I have to attend to this."

Lloyd was crying, moaning, saying, "It hurts, oh God, it hurts!"

"Is your senile partner up to handling this?" I asked her.

She looked up at me, kneeling beside her wounded associate. "I think so. In fact, he's more qualified than I."

"Fred, haul the doc in, would you?"

Soon Fred was supervising as Dr. Dailey began attending to his patient with surprising speed and precision. I positioned Eliot in the outer office, to make sure we weren't interrupted by police or any other surprise visitors. Dr. Winter found me a small bandage for my gash, and I was a little wet from the water Lloyd splashed me with; but otherwise, I was fine.

And there were still things that needed clearing up.

In Dailey's office, I sat Dr. Winter down in one of the cushioned wooden chairs across from the older doctor's massive mahogany desk. Perched on the edge of the desk, I loomed over her the way she had me, on my last visit here. In the back of the office, the lighted display case of jade figurines served as a glowing reminder of Dr. Dailey's financial worth.

"I could use a cigarette," she said.

"Go ahead."

"They're in that box on Wallace's desk."

I got her a cigarette from a Chinese-carved walnut box, and fired her up with a faux-jade dragon-shaped lighter. Absent-mindedly, I lighted one up myself.

We blew smoke at each other for a while; then she asked, "Are the police going to be involved?"

"For crime-solving purposes," I asked, "or cover-up?"

She shrugged. "In whatever manner."

"I'm not sure yet. You do realize the man who killed the Black Dahlia works in your office."

Averting my gaze, she sent dragon smoke out her nostrils, her red-touched lips thin and tight around the cigarette. "I admit no such thing."

I grinned at her, my smoke mingling with hers. "I didn't say you admitted it—just that you realized it. Funny, isn't it?"

The big brown eyes in the oval face regarded me coldly. "What is?"

I shrugged. "How a person can be right and wrong at the same time. I think I can make this whole sorry affair go away, if you just answer a few questions."

Now the eyes narrowed. "Who are you, Mr. Heller?"

"The best thing that's happened to you in a long time."

She thought about that. Then she exhaled smoke, lowering her gaze, and said, "Ask your questions."

"How long has 'Floyd' worked for you?"

Still not looking at me, she said, "Not long. Late November, I believe."

"How did you come to hire him?"

"He had good references, at least in terms of our extralegal trade."

"He'd worked in other abortion mills, you mean."

A tiny sneer formed on the thin lips. "That's an ugly term."

"For a lovely business. Where had he worked?"

"San Diego. San Francisco. Here in L.A. He's very knowledgeable, medically speaking; he has skilled hands."

"As of now, better make that 'hand.' " That got a sharp look out of her, and when her eyes met mine, I said, "Tell me about Elizabeth Short."

The smooth brow tried not to wrinkle, and did not succeed. "What about her?"

"She came here to your clinic—why?"

A sigh of smoke. "Dr. Dailey was from the same part of New England where the Short woman grew up. She needed an operation."

"She had vaginal atresia."

That got her attention. "How did you know that?"

"The way this works," I said, giving her as nasty a smile as I could muster, "is I ask the questions. Was it the kind of operation Dr. Dailey could still handle?"

"I . . . I thought he could."

"What was Dailey doing here today, Dr. Winter? He wasn't assisting you."

She was smoking more nervously, now. "I . . . I keep my eye on him, now."

"You mean, since he killed Elizabeth Short."

The words hit her like a physical blow, but she did her best not to show it. "That's ridiculous."

"Really it is—you just don't know it. Ever hear of a guy named Arnold Wilson?"

"Common name . . . but I don't think so."

"He's six-four, badly pockmarked, pronounced limp."

Now the thin lips worked up a patronizing smirk. "What—no eyepatch? No parrot?"

"I'll do the jokes, lady. Do you know him?"

"No."

Actually, that figured. I had an idea Arnold Wilson had kept his relationship to, and with, Lloyd Watterson strictly between the boys.

"Tell me about Dr. Dailey. Tell me about how badly he's been slipping, lately."

She plucked tobacco off the tip of her tongue. "He's . . . I told you before. He suffers from cerebral arteriosclerosis . . . resulting in senile dementia."

"So when his patient, Elizabeth Short, turned up dead in that vacant lot, a block from where the doctor lives . . . or used to live, before heeding your siren call . . . you figured he'd tried to do that operation by himself, and botched it, and halved that girl for easy transport, and then absentmindedly dumped her close to home. Something like that?"

She folded her arms over the shelf of her breasts—the genie was pissed off again. "You must be insane."

"I must be—everybody seems to think so, today. Or maybe you figured the doc was trying, in his demented way, to get back at his wife."

Something close to tenderness crept into her hard-edged voice. "Dr. Dailey is a gentle soul . . . He'd never do such a thing. . . ."

"In his right mind, you mean?"

She said nothing.

"Listen, Maria—he wouldn't do it in his wrong mind, either. You've been scammed."

Now she looked at me—startled. "What?"

"Lloyd . . . I mean, 'Floyd' . . . convinced you that he came in here, one night, and discovered what Dr. Dailey had done, right?"

"How . . . what . . . ?"

"Work with me on this. I'm here to help. Tell me, Doctor. Maria—tell me."

She shook her head, heaved a big sigh of smoke. "He . . . Floyd said he came in on the . . . grisly aftermath. He said he helped Wallace cart the body out . . . even admitted helping to cut her in half. Said he'd tried to make it look like a . . . sex crime . . . to help throw off the police. But Floyd was too new in the office to know that where Wallace suggested the body be disposed of was near his own home."

I laughed, and she flinched.

I said, "I figured you'd been led to believe some line of horse hockey like that. It's not true, Dr. Winter. Floyd is Lloyd, by the way, Lloyd Watterson . . . *Lloyd* butchered that girl . . . Your gifted assistant abortionist is a former mental patient known to have committed at least thirteen torso murders back in Ohio."

"You must be joking. . . ."

"Yeah, I'm joking. This has been a lighthearted afternoon all the way 'round."

She was weaving in the chair. "My God . . . can it . . . is it . . . true?"

"It can, it is—true." I gestured toward the door with cigarette in hand. "My friend out there is a former Ohio police official who is helping Lloyd's well-connected family see that he's returned to a mental institution, and committed for life."

Hope leapt into the dark eyes. "And if that happened . . ."

"That's right, Maria—then the LAPD would not be involved, nor would the papers. You and Dr. Dailey would be untouched by this scandal."

Now her eyes no longer avoided mine—rather, searched them. "What do you need from me?"

"I need you to get that fingerless son of a bitch ready to travel by train."

"When?"

"The sooner the better."

Her eyes tightened. She stabbed her cigarette out in a jade-green tray. "Done," she said, rising.

In the hallway, I found Eliot standing outside the operating room, just as Dr. Winter was heading in. I caught a glimpse of Lloyd seated on the abortion table, looking pale, in shock or sedated or both, his right hand bundled in gauze and adhesive, with four side-by-side spots of blood leaching through where his fingers used to be.

"Looks like Lloyd'll never play the piano again," I said to Eliot.

"They've got him pretty well patched up," he said. "Since when do you smoke?"

"Only when I get nostalgic for Jap bayonets. Look, Dr. Winter's going to cooperate with us—Lloyd'll be ready to travel."

"When?"

"Soon. Very soon."

"Today?"

"Now. I'll help you haul him to the train station, but I have loose ends to attend, so you'll have to make the trip alone. Shouldn't be a problem—Lloyd'll be pumped so full of morphine, he should be nice and cooperative. . . . I'll see you in a few weeks—at the wedding."

Eliot smiled, shook his head, as if he were amazed, for some reason. "Thank you, Nate."

"For what? Not killing that bastard?"

"Yes. And if they ever let Lloyd out of that asylum?"

"Yeah?"

"When we take him out into the desert," Eliot said, a hand on my shoulder, "I will bring the shovel."

I didn't have the heart to tell my friend Eliot Ness that the real reason I hadn't killed Watterson was that Lloyd's friend Arnold Wilson had wanted me to.

# 23

The bright lights of Hollywood Boulevard took on a shimmering radiance, neon burning in the coolness of dusk, the hard, unpleasant edges of an ugly one-industry town blurred into blemish-free beauty. Like an aging screen queen with a great makeup artist, a gauze-draped key light, and a Vaseline-smeared camera lens, Hollywood didn't look half bad.

The little neighborhood around the corner from Grauman's Chinese also benefited from twilight's gentle touch, seeming even more idyllic, with its pastel stucco bungalows, nicely trimmed lawns, and scattering of palms and pepper trees, with flower gardens whose blossoms glowed vividly in the gathering darkness, lights struggling not to go out.

I parked in the driveway, purposely blocking it, and trotted up the winding walk to the two-story red-tile-roof pink stucco two-flat. I pressed the button and, on the third try, its little electric-chair buzz summoned an answer.

Framed there in the doorway, Patsy Savarino—her red hair tumbling to her shoulders, her mouth lushly lipsticked, the huge green almond eyes emphasized with matching eyeshadow—was proof positive that a woman eight months gone could still look alluring. The former stripper—though small in stature, she'd been voluptuous even before her pregnancy—wore a yellow-and-green abstract-pattern print maternity top and pedal-pusher denims. She was in her bare feet.

"If you're looking for my husband," she said, guardedly, "he's not here."

"Any of his pals over here? Your upstairs neighbors, maybe?"

"The Hassaus moved out."

"That was quick."

"This morning." She began to shut the door. "I'm alone here and you're not coming in."

"Sure I am," I said, pushing my way in, stepping past her, into the vestibule, at the foot of the stairs to the second-floor flat. It took more than an expectant mother to stop this detective.

Her eyes were wide with indignation—and perhaps a little fear. "Mr. Heller, you'll have to leave!"

I shut the door and took out the nine-millimeter, to encourage her cooperation, and her fright. But the lush red lips only sneered at me. "Do you often threaten pregnant women?"

"I think this may be a first." I nodded toward the living room with its array of new, mismatched furniture. "How about your friend Arnold Wilson?"

Her arms were folded over her bosom and her chin was high—for some reason, she reminded me of a barroom bouncer. "Who says he's my friend?"

"Is he here?"

"Of course not."

I gestured with the nine-millimeter. "We're going to have a look around."

"Are we?"

I took her by the arm and dragged her along—"Hey! Lemme go, you bastard!" —checking every room of the eclectically furnished flat, finding no Bobby Savarino or Arnold Wilson or anyone else. The master bedroom closet was bare, nothing but hangers and a couple empty shoeboxes; the dresser was half-emptied. No male clothing at all.

She stood sullenly in the doorway, leaning back against the jamb, folded arms resting on breasts that had been formidable even before they began revving up for the coming child.

I turned to her. "You have an upstairs key?"

"What if I don't?"

"I'll kick the fucking door in."

She sighed. "Yes, I have a key."

"Can you handle those stairs all right?"

"Do I have a choice?"

I shrugged. "I can leave you down here tied."

She grunted a humorless laugh. "Would that be another first, Mr. Heller?"

"No, I just did it the other day— Oh, with a pregnant woman? I believe so."

Soon, she was dragging her ass up the stairs—albeit a nicely shaped one in the denim slacks, and her legs didn't look heavy, either; the former No-Pasties-for-Patsy still had pride in her appearance, and hadn't allowed herself to gain any excess weight, beyond the kid she was carrying.

She unlocked the door and showed me in, and around, the Hassaus' apartment. The lights weren't on but they weren't needed—what was left of the afternoon sun was finding its way through windows whose drapes had been removed. The entire place was fairly emptied out, only a few larger pieces of furniture remaining, chiefly a Colonial-style maple china cabinet in the dining room and a big walnut-trimmed wine-velour overstuffed sofa in the living room.

Otherwise, tumbleweed was blowing through the goddamn place.

"Christ," I said, and—convinced I was now alone with the knocked-up former stripper—I slipped the nine-millimeter back into the shoulder holster.

Again, she positioned herself in the doorway, arms folded on her chest, like a harem eunuch on guard, if an improbably pregnant one. "They loaded up a trailer this morning."

I went right up to her, leaned a hand against the wall. She smelled like Chypre De Coty perfume. "Your husband go with them?"

Her expression was blank. "My husband's out on bail. You know he can't be leaving town."

"Henry Hassau's out on bail, too. They both skipped, didn't they?"

She shrugged—then nodded.

"Afraid of Dragna?"

"Afraid of doing time."

I could see that: they were facing twenty years, as her husband had pointed out to me.

I said, "The Ringgolds are going to be out some major scratch."

A tiny smile tweaked the full red lips. "Yes, but Bobby and Henry won't be testifying against them, will they?"

"That's why you needed my money, right? Raising a little traveling cash for Bobby?"

The green eyes were half-lidded now. "Gee. Ain't you the genius?"

I leaned in, doing my best to intimidate her, though with a tough little cookie like this, that wasn't easy. "And, now what? Bobby's going to get settled somewhere? Mexico maybe, and after you have the baby, you'll join him?"

She frowned—then she moved forward, so close her nose was almost touching mine. Her tone was near vicious when she demanded, "You want to talk? Let's go downstairs where I can take a load off. You think it's easy being pregnant?"

"Let's save a trip—why don't you go sit on that couch?"

Holding the small of her back with both hands, wincing in discomfort, she trundled across the empty room and sat. I plopped down next to her, giving her a little space.

"Did Arnold Wilson happen to go along with the boys on this bail-jump trip?"

She nodded. "Helen went, too." Her arms were at her side, now, and she was staring straight ahead at a wall whose wallpaper showed the shadows of absent framed pictures.

I sat sort of sideways on the couch, nestling in the corner, so I could look right at her, as she avoided my gaze. "Wouldn't happen to have been Arnold's idea, would it? Leaving town?"

She shrugged.

"Arnold's an interesting guy. To look at him, he seems like some small-potatoes lowlife—a nobody, a six-foot-four, pockmark-pussed nebbish. Not a leader, certainly, like your husband. But sometimes you have to watch out for these guys out on the sidelines, hugging the fringes. . . . You're in show business, Patsy—ever hear of a play called *Othello*?"

"No."

"It's by Shakespeare."

She shrugged. "*Romeo and Juliet.*"

I folded my arms, crossed my legs—comfy here in the big mostly empty room. "Right. Friend of mine is thinking of making a movie out of it—*Othello,* that is. I'm not much of a reader, and most of the time, when I go to the theater, it's to a house like your old stamping grounds, the Rialto."

Now she looked at me, smiling faintly, crinkles of amusement at the corners of the almond-shaped eyes. "Ever see me?"

"I saw all of you. Any man who had would certainly understand how you could get in your current condition."

"Is that your idea of a compliment?"

"Maybe you'd prefer me to commend your tassel work. Anyway, in that play, there's this character off to one side, whispering in the hero's ear, giving him bad advice. I forget the character's name, but Arnold Wilson, he reminds me of that guy."

"Does he?" Her gaze had returned to the wall of absent pictures. "That's so very interesting."

"For example, right before he brought me around here—to hear you and your husband expound on the subject of how Jack Dragna had the Short girl killed—Wilson stopped by the Beverly Hills Hotel. My wife and me, we're staying in a bungalow there. Kind of a honeymoon."

"What a lucky girl."

"Arnold's the kind of guy who knows how to seize an opportunity. That's what separates the merely selfish, greedy, immoral sons of bitches, like most of us, from the really evil ones. You believe in evil, Patsy?"

"I guess."

"You believe in God? In hell?"

Now she looked at me—apprehension creeping through her blank mask. "I suppose."

I shrugged. "Me, I don't know what I believe, other than I know that most of us are sinners, but that now and then you run into somebody who's . . . wrong to the bone. Evil the way the Bible would define it. The psychologists call these people 'sociopaths.' "

"Do they." Her eyes tightened. "What does this have to do with me?"

"Let me finish, Patsy—if you don't mind. I mean, you don't have supper to fix, now that your man flew the coop."

She granted me a sarcastic smirk. "Since I can't seem to stop you—and you have a gun—please continue."

"Thanks. So, anyway, Arnold waltzes into my bungalow at the hotel when I'm not around, convinces my wife he's an old buddy of mine, that we were in the war together. Now, my wife has been around and she knows a criminal type when she sees one—and she knows I number criminal types among my acquaintances and even friends. In the course of conversation—he must have been waiting there for me, a good hour—she asks him a question. 'Suppose I had a friend who was in trouble, and needed help?' 'What kind of trouble?' Arnold asks. Well, to make a long story short, Wilson helped out my wife's 'friend' . . . which is to say, my wife . . . and arranged for her to get an abortion."

That got her attention. "I thought you were on your honeymoon. . . ."

"I know, it disappoints me, a little, too, that my wife wanted to start out our married life by killing our kid. But we've worked that out—we've decided to have him, or her. The thing is, your husband's friend Wilson—manipulative weasel that he is—sent my wife to a specific abortionist because a special friend of his worked there—a very sick individual named Lloyd."

And, finally, I hit home. She couldn't hide the reaction: wincing, gritting her teeth as if a red-hot poker had been placed against her flesh, she turned away from me.

I remained casual, chatty in tone. "None of that is important—it is, after all, a kind of . . . coda to the real story, here. The real story begins with a pair of sick psychopaths, who have known each other for many years, and have visited all kinds of hellish torture and perversion and murder upon women and men, usually striking the nameless, forgotten souls who litter the skid row of any major city. Arnold and this friend of his named Lloyd share a secret bond, as well as any number of unspeakable interests. Were you even aware that Arnold Wilson is a homosexual?"

The green eyes widened. "What?"

"That's not really accurate—Wilson's a bisexual. Gate swings, as they say, both ways . . . and that doesn't offend me. I mean, whatever wets your wick, I always say. It's just that both of the ways that Arnold's gate swings are, well, a bit crooked. Arnold would quite naturally hide the homosexual aspect of his appetites from the all-male likes of your husband and the McCadden Group. He had to be one of the boys, right down to his war wound."

Her red hair flounced as she shook her head. "You've gone wacky—Arnold is no queer. . . ."

"Let me ask you this, where does Wilson live?"

That froze her. "I . . . I don't know."

"I'll wager you have the phone number and address of every other friend your husband did business with, certainly the entire McCadden crew."

She said nothing, but that was a confirmation of sorts.

"Late last summer and for part of the fall, Elizabeth Short was hanging around the McCadden Cafe. She and your husband became involved . . . Don't bother denying it, don't try to look surprised. Beth Short even became friendly with Hassau's wife Helen—the girl became sort of a mascot to the McCadden Group, a little more than that to your husband."

Staring at the wall again, her face hardened back into that blank mask.

I continued, saying, "Wilson was working for Al Green at the cafe as a cook, as well as being a member of the heist crew. So of course Wilson got to know Elizabeth Short, was friendly with her. But he also considered her a kind of . . . loose cannon. Wilson knew the Short girl was trying to raise money, for some kind of operation she was planning to get—he figured it was possibly an abortion, since she was consulting with a doctor who Wilson knew ran one of L.A.'s highest-class, most protected abortion mills."

She gave me a glance, and a flinch of a frown. "Why are you telling me this? What the hell does this have to do with me?"

Outside the windows, magic hour was over—the darkness of night carried with it muffled traffic noise from nearby Hollywood Boulevard. I got up, switched on the overhead light, which bounced off the varnished wood floor. She winced, preferring the darkness. I sat beside her again.

"Wilson knew the Mocambo heist was going to be a big score. He also heard about the Short girl's surprise when Beth discovered her new friends at the McCadden Cafe were a bunch of armed robbers. Wilson feared she might go to the cops, or otherwise sell them out, raising money for that supposed abortion. So he convinced his buddy Lloyd—who had been using his medical training to work for various abortionists on the West Coast—to apply for a job at that same abortion clinic where Elizabeth was enrolled as a patient. Fortuitously for Wilson, this was the perfect time for Lloyd to get work at the Dailey clinic: the chief doctor was failing mentally, slipping into senile dementia, and his female partner, a woman named Winter, could really use a good physician's assistant about now, particularly one trained in the abortionist's art."

Patsy had turned away again. "You must like the sound of your own voice. I'm not even listening."

"With Lloyd in place at the abortion clinic, the Short girl could be taken out, in a manner that—as a sick bonus—would allow these old pals in perversion to have a good old-fashioned debauched time. But Beth Short got spooked, with the Mocambo heist coming up, not wanting any part of a crime of that magnitude, and she fled to San Diego, where—typically—she freeloaded off a new friend she made. Several weeks later, before the heist, your husband and Helen and Hassau went down there to try to encourage Beth Short to come back to L.A."

Her sharp glance indicated the latter was news to her.

"And, a month or so later, after the heist had been successfully pulled, Bobby and the McCadden Group apparently getting away clean, Beth decides to come home to the City of Angels, where she gets back in touch with Bobby and Helen. She decides to keep a low profile, since she now knows her 'fiancé' already has a wife, a very pregnant one at that."

Patsy closed her eyes; she might have been asleep.

"Now, all through this time, Beth Short is still actively trying to raise that money—perhaps with visions of running off with your Bobby—and Arnold Wilson may have seen her as a blackmail threat. But Wilson wasn't the one, of course, who initiated the murder plan. That is where you come in, Mrs. Savarino."

Her head swiveled on a dime, green eyes flashing. "Me? You're a fucking lunatic!"

"Hey, it got me out of the Marines. We're up to where Bobby and his pal Henry are arrested, and Bobby starts shooting his mouth off about Dragna trying to hire a McCadden Group hit on Cohen. Your husband wanted to make a deal with the cops, but all he succeeded in doing was spurring Dragna's rage—that's when the onslaught of death threats began. You and the rest of the McCadden Group and their families were targets for mob retaliation, if your idiot husband did not shut up, and soon. That's when you went to Arnold Wilson with your plan."

"My plan to do what? I did no such thing."

"You suggested to Wilson that if Elizabeth Short were to turn up dead, in an apparent mob-style execution, Bobby would read it as a warning . . . and, at the same time, your competition for your husband's affections would be eliminated."

"That . . . that 'Black Dahlia' wasn't a gangland killing; she was murdered by a sex fiend!"

"It was both those things, Patsy. You see, when you expressed an interest in having Beth Short removed, Arnold Wilson already had his friend Lloyd in place—settled in as a good little physician's aide at the abortion mill, the very clinic where Beth Short was a patient. As I said, Wilson is a conniving sociopath of the first order: everything he did had sinister layers. He and Lloyd gleefully committed a sick sex crime that would send the police down the wrong road, even as the informer's 'smile' they gashed in the girl's face sent your husband a message. Then Wilson had the body dumped in a place where both Dragna and the abortion doctor could be implicated."

She frowned, truly puzzled. "Why would he do that?"

"Since Arnold Wilson's relationship with Lloyd was a secret one—a pact between human malignancies, a relationship acted out in the depths of human society, skid row bars and flophouses and the like—should Beth Short's murder ever be traced back to Lloyd, it would be Lloyd—a known psychopathic murderer—who would take full blame."

"Why wouldn't this . . . 'Lloyd' . . . tell the police about his friend, Arnold Wilson?"

"Because Lloyd likes to take full credit for his depravity. He has an ego as big as it is bizarre, which for example compels him to send taunting postcards to the detective tracking him. Wilson was suspected as Lloyd's apprentice in those torso murders in Cleveland, ten years ago—but Lloyd steadfastly refused to implicate his friend . . . either out of loyalty, or a desire to hog all the 'glory.' "

That was why Wilson—who obviously had recognized me and remembered my role in the original Butcher case—had maneuvered my wife into that abortion clinic today. Wilson had no doubt heard from Watterson that Eliot and I had cornered him—and released him, supposedly believing Lloyd's story—but Wilson would easily have guessed that we'd be keeping Lloyd under surveillance, and that I would be informed immediately when Peggy went into that clinic.

The diabolical bastard knew, too, that I was likely to kill Watterson, if I burst in on him either aborting my child or butchering Peggy (didn't matter to Wilson which), thereby closing off any investigatory avenue that might have implicated Arnold Wilson in the murder of the Black Dahlia.

"But, Patsy," I said to the lovely pregnant redhead, "you didn't just suggest this murder—you hired it done. Lucky devil, that Arnold Wilson: a murder he had been thinking about doing anyway, and somebody pays him to do it!"

She had a glazed expression, now. "What . . . what makes you think I paid Wilson to kill her?"

"Well, hell, that's where your money went, your husband's share of all that Mocambo heist loot. It was the Ringgold brothers who paid Bobby's bail, after all. And yet you and Bobby were willing to tell a stranger anything he wanted to know, for a lousy hundred bucks."

She mustered up a sneer. "And that makes me somebody who hired a murder? Is that what you call detective work?"

"Actually, it was Mickey Cohen who got me thinking like a detective again. . . .What did Elizabeth Short do to deserve her fate? Not a damn thing, he said—if a gangster like Dragna wanted to send your husband a message, he'd have hit another member of the McCadden Group, some deserving crook, not a civilian dame who happened to be somebody's mistress. So—why Beth Short? Who would benefit from her death? How about Bobby's wife—Bobby's pregnant wife."

I'd said my piece.

We sat there for perhaps two minutes, maybe three—a long time to sit in silence. A horn honked. A dog barked. Some kids squealed in play. Two minutes, maybe three, of no conversation—a prisoner to your thoughts, in the presence of another, who has appointed himself your accuser.

Still, I was surprised, even startled, when she blurted, "All I wanted to do was shut my husband's stupid mouth, before he got us all killed!"

I grunted a humorless laugh, then said, "You might have come up with another way."

"Not one that would get that bitch Beth Short out of our lives!"

That was when she broke into tears. I got a hanky out for her and she wept into it, and blew her nose a couple times, then offered the hanky back to me, which I declined.

Patsy Savarino had probably lived a tough life—I had no idea what her background was . . . Strippers came from everywhere, everywhere that was hard or abusive, that is. Good-looking girls with nice bodies like Patsy—who found themselves on burlesque stages with their talent hanging out, who ended up with guys who ran con games or gambled or did crimes—came from hardscrabble farms in West Virginia and Chicago slums and Podunk orphanages and even wealthy suburban homes where daddy liked to keep incest in the family.

But somewhere, at some point, Patsy had no doubt been a little girl with a doll, or anyway a little girl who wanted a doll, and maybe she had a dog or a fucking kitty, and played with blocks and jumped rope and, like all of us, started out as an innocent kid.

And while I knew that Patsy Savarino had initiated the murder of Elizabeth Short, I also knew that the horrendous depravity committed upon that girl by Arnold Wilson and Lloyd Watterson far exceeded Patsy's worst wishes for the black-haired angel-faced woman in black-seamed stockings who'd been trying to steal away her husband.

"I never . . . I never meant. . . . So savage, so cruel, so sick, so twisted . . . how could they . . . and make me part. . . ?"

Then she was crying again. I went to the bathroom and got her a big wad of toilet paper and she used that for her tears and to blow her nose in. I put an arm around her. This went on for quite a while.

"I . . . I have terrible . . . nightmares. . . . I see that girl. . . . I see terrible things being done to her. . . . Sometimes I'm standing there . . . in the dreams . . . watching myself do them. Cutting her . . . butchering her. . . ."

"You can't make a bargain with the devil," I said, "and not get your ass burned."

"What . . . what are you . . . ?"

"Patsy, sweetheart, when you decided to have that girl murdered, all bets were off—all nicety, all morality, all decency, went out the window. You can't commit a little murder just like you can't be a little pregnant. When you let Arnold Wilson into your life—maybe the most evil son of a bitch I've ever met, and I've met a few—when you invited him in, his sickness became your sickness."

"What . . . are you saying? That I'll . . . feel like this . . . fucking sick-in-my-gut-and-my-heart guilty like this . . . with these awful terrible nightmares . . . as long as I live?"

I patted her shoulder. "It'll let up, some. I only dream about combat once or twice a week, now. But to some degree, yeah—you're going to carry this with you. That guilt. 'Cause it's yours."

The lipstick had been rubbed off by the hanky and toilet paper, but the lips remained full, and sensual, trembling now. "How can I . . . how can I go on living?"

I put my hand on her swollen belly—gently. "Because you have to. You have to put this behind you, much as you can, and raise this kid better than you were raised."

She studied me for a moment, searching my face, then asked, "What are you going to do to me?"

I shrugged. "Nothing."

"Nothing?"

"A wife who kills to keep her husband, there's worse crimes."

Those almond-shaped green eyes were wide with astonishment, and relief. "You're not going to . . . no police?"

"No police. Not in this town." I sighed deeply, shook my head. "I'm goddamn sorry Elizabeth Short is dead—she really was a nice girl, somewhat screwed-up, like most of us . . . but she didn't deserve what she got, not that anybody would, except maybe Arnold and Lloyd. But sending you to jail, Patsy, to have your kid inside . . . what good would that do? Anyway, I have a friend who needs this kept quiet . . . He's the one who's taking Lloyd back to the Crazy House . . . and me, I don't much care to be in the middle of this, anymore."

"What about Wilson?"

I pointed a thumb at myself. "That's the deal you're going to strike with this devil—when you talk to your husband, if he knows where Wilson is, find out and let me know."

The green eyes narrowed. "You're going after Wilson?"

"If it takes me the rest of my life."

"What . . . what are you going to do to him?"

"Don't know yet. I'll think of something . . . appropriate. And it sure as hell won't involve any cops."

She was shaking her head, the red mane shimmering. "Mr. Heller . . . how can I thank you?"

I grinned at her. "If your marriage breaks up, and my marriage breaks up, maybe I can think of something. Otherwise, let's skip it."

"That another compliment?"

"I never saw anybody with better reverse-tassel action than you, Patsy."

Her smile surprised me; her laugh was a shock to both of us.

Downstairs, as I was about to go out, she touched my arm and looked up at me. That pretty face—stripper hard but still alluring—softened, suddenly, and I could see the child she'd been. I hoped her child turned out better than she had—like I hoped mine turned out better than me.

The gorgeous pregnant redhead seemed almost embarrassed as she gazed up and said, "I was just . . . just trying to hold my marriage together."

"Hey," I said, tipping my hat, "I know the feeling."

# 24

◆

The following Monday I called Richardson and told him I was heading back to Chicago, midweek, and wouldn't be available to work on the Dahlia story any longer. I did hope to get that puff-piece interview about the A-1, "Hollywood's detective agency to the stars," wrapped up before I left.

"Stop by tomorrow morning," Richardson said on the phone, a twinkle in the eye of his voice. "Something may turn up to change your mind about goin' home."

There was nothing ominous about the way he said it, but considering I alone knew that the Dahlia case had been privately solved, and would remain (if I had any say in it) publicly unsolved, the city editor's words made me uneasy.

I spent much of Sunday and Monday leading the L.A. A-1 staff of operatives (including Fred) in looking for Arnold Wilson, checking out the twilight world of the various skid rows of their city, of which there was no shortage.

The primary skid row was Main Street, with its low-end burlesque houses and stripper bars, and a platoon of B-girls who made Elizabeth Short seem innocent, in joints like the Follies Village, the Waldorf Cellar, and the Gay Way. Fred checked out the taxi-dance halls, Roseland (owned by Mark Lansom, incidentally) and Dreamland; and Teddy Hertel scoured the neighborhood around East 31st, where Lloyd had been living, and of course fine-tooth-combed Lloyd's shabby flat.

Me, I worked Fifth Street from San Pedro to Main, where winos sold their blood to buy booze and slept it off in all-night movies, and where you could see more soldiers and sailors than on your average military base or aircraft carrier. Finally, late Monday morning, the guy behind the counter at the cigar store at 5th and Gladys—a corner where you could buy anything from a policy slip to a reefer to a chippie—recognized Wilson's distinctive description (we didn't have a photo). By Monday afternoon I found the flophouse on Main where Arnold Wilson had been living.

He had cleared out Saturday, around noon—leaving no forwarding address.

On Tuesday morning, I told Fred what I wanted done. We would contact agencies with whom we had reciprocal arrangements and have Wilson looked for in both San Diego and San Francisco, two prior known haunts of his (according to Patsy Savarino). Concentrate on skid rows, I said, and bars catering to sexual deviants. Fred thought that was a good plan—but what did I want done if somebody finds him?

"Sit on the son-of-a-bitch," I said, "and call me. I'll fly in from Chicago, immediately."

Fred had a sick expression. "We're kinda asking for them to . . . you know, abduct the bastard."

"There's a five-grand bonus for the man that finds him."

"Five grand?"

"Not out of the business funds, Fred—my personal money."

". . . Okay. But a slimeball like this—knowing somebody's after him, as he's gonna gather when he learns about Lloyd—is gonna make every effort to disappear."

I knew Fred was right. A guy who moved in criminal circles, whose private life was down among the human dregs of big cities, could surely find some sewer to vanish into.

"You heading over to the *Examiner*?" Fred asked.

"Yeah—gonna see if I can finally shake that p.r. article out of 'em."

"D'you see the morning paper?"

"No."

"Better take a look."

The *Examiner*'s front page told quite a story. Seemed Jim Richardson had been working late, Sunday night, when he received a phone call at his desk.

"Is this the city editor?" said a voice that Richardson described as "silky."

"This is Richardson."

"Well, Mr. Richardson, congratulations on the excellent coverage the *Examiner* has given the Black Dahlia case."

"Thanks."

"But things seem to be getting a little . . . bogged down."

"Beginning to look that way."

"Maybe I can be of assistance. . . . Tell you what I'll do. Watch the mail for some of the things the Dahlia had with her when she . . . disappeared."

"What kind of things?"

"Things she had in her handbag."

And the phone had clicked dead.

So Richardson said.

In the conference room at the *Examiner*, Bill Fowley and several other reporters were standing around an array of material spread out like a banquet before them. At the head of the long table, Richardson—in shirtsleeves and suspenders, his cigarette angling upward—cast his fish-eye on me as I entered. Oddly, a scent of gasoline was in the air, mingling with cigarette smoke.

"Heller! Nate!" Richardson gestured grandly from the head of the table. "Come right in, come right in, and see what the Postal Service brought us."

Fowley, grinning, gestured at the table. "It's goddamn Christmas!"

Yes, it was, and the presents (all of them reeking with gasoline) included:

Elizabeth Short's birth certificate.

Her social security card.

A Greyhound Bus Station claim check for two suitcases and a hatbox.

A newspaper clipping about the marriage of an Army Air Force major named Matt Gordon with the name of the bride scratched out and "Elizabeth Short" written in, in ink.

Several photos of the beautiful black-haired girl with flowers in her hair and this serviceman or that one, on her arm.

A small leather item with the name "Mark Lansom" embossed on the cover—the fabled stolen address book.

Plus the oversize envelope these goodies had arrived in, a three-by-eight white number pasted with odd-sized letters cut from newspapers and magazines to form the following address and message:

To Los Angeles Examiner
Here is Dahlia's belongings
Letter to follow.

"Do the cops know about this?" I asked Richardson.

My less than gleeful tone seemed to make the gaggle of reporters nervous—a few even had embarrassed expressions. But not Fowley, and certainly not the boss.

"Of course they do," Richardson said. "Donahoe himself is on the way over, and so is Harry the Hat. . . . This opens up whole new avenues. There's seventy-five names in that address book."

"You been handling this stuff?"

"Carefully, with a handkerchief . . . but there's no prints."

"How do you know?"

"The, uh, fiend who sent this apparently was well versed in contemporary police science, and knew soaking that stuff in gasoline would wipe out all traces of fingerprints."

I nodded, and turned to head toward the door.

"Where are you going?" Fowley asked.

"I'm off this case. I'm tired of pretending I'm a newshound, and I don't have any desire to get in the thick of it with the cops, either."

Richardson hustled around the big conference table and cornered me at the door. His right eye stared at me while his left eye dogpaddled into position. "What about that interview?"

"Talk to Fred. You can call me at my office in Chicago. Glad to give you anything you need."

"This story is heating back up."

Very softly, I said, "You heated it back up, Jim."

"I don't know what you're talking about."

I nodded toward the table. "That stuff is evidence you withheld from those suitcases at the bus station that you beat the cops to. Or did you find that Express office trunk?"

"Fuck you! That came in the mail—"

"You sent it to yourself, Jim, just like you imagined that phone call you got Sunday night—or did you have Fowley or somebody call you from a booth?"

The left eye had caught up in time for him to glare at me. "What's got you so high and mighty all of a sudden?"

"I don't know. Something about this town—it's a turd dragged through glitter, all nice and shiny, but Jim, it's still shit. I'm ready to go back to Chicago—it's shit, too, but it doesn't pretend to be anything else."

The *Examiner* got several more front-page weeks out of the story, including a few fake letters, some of which Richardson may have sent to himself; but the cops didn't make any headway with the new evidence, even the address book. Between dead ends and LAPD cover-ups, the investigation fizzled out.

On the gray morning of January 25, 1947, a graveside service was held for a murdered young woman, on a hillside in Oakland's Mountain View Cemetery. Half a dozen family members were present, but her father, Cleo, did not attend. The stone was pink—Beth's favorite color, her mother said, not black—and bore this inscription: DAUGHTER, ELIZABETH SHORT, JULY 29, 1924–JANUARY 15, 1947.

In 1949 a Grand Jury investigation into a notorious call-girl scandal—the top madam in L.A. had been working hand-in-hand, so to speak, with LAPD vice—invoked the botched Dahlia investigation when its report spoke of "deplorable conditions indicating corrupt practices and misconduct by some members of the law enforcement agencies in the county."

Thus ended the eight-year regime of Chief Horrall, and began a shake-up and reorganization in the department that would soon lead to the sixteen-year reign of Chief William Parker, who would bring a new attitude to the LAPD—Parker was, after all, the man who had invented that dreaded self-policing unit known as Internal Affairs.

The Dahlia case did result in one notable contribution to society: the California state legislature passed a Sex Case Registry. The murder of Elizabeth Short had led to the creation of the nation's first required registration of convicted sex offenders.

I stopped in to see Harry the Hat before I left town, and told him about my having known Elizabeth Short, and apologized for having withheld the information.

"It was a coincidence," I said, "and detectives don't believe in coincidence."

"Actually," the Hat said, seated at his desk in his pearl-gray fedora and a loud green-and-red silk tie, "I do . . . If it wasn't for coincidence, most murders wouldn't get solved."

"You mean, a guy runs a red light, gets pulled over, and suddenly Jack the Ripper's been arrested."

"That's how it usually happens," the LAPD's top homicide expert said. "But don't quote me."

Harry the Hat continued to work the Dahlia case, off and on, until he retired to Palm Desert, California, in 1968. He became known as the detective obsessed with the Dahlia, and was frequently quoted in newspaper "nostalgia" pieces; he consulted on a TV movie about the case. He died at age eighty, a stroke mercifully ending a battle with lung cancer. His three cabinet files of Dahlia evidence shifted from detective to detective at the LAPD over the years, including the legendary "Jigsaw John"—John St. John.

Harry and Finis Brown had a falling out, during the call-girl fiasco; but Brown—with the blessing of his beloved brother, Thad, the Chief of Detectives upon whom Raymond Burr based the Ironsides character—continued working the case on his own, and was said to be at least as obsessed with it as the Hat. He chased leads out of state—Florida, New York, and the Great Lakes region—before eventually retiring to Texas.

Brown did discover my connection to Elizabeth Short, and was heartbroken (I was told by an amused Hansen) when the Hat told Fat Ass that he already knew it, and had dismissed it. Brown, bookie or not, did have skills as a detective and on his Chicago trip tracked down the same Hammond, Indiana, abortion doctor that Lou Sapperstein had questioned for me.

In the months that became years following the discovery of Elizabeth Short's body in that vacant lot, both Hansen and Brown and every other LAPD detective working the case was stymied by a succession of copycat kills, muddying the waters, naked dead women with "BD" carved in their thighs, killers hoping to pass the blame or perhaps claim it.

Robert "Red" Manley's marriage did not last. Nor did his sanity—about a month after he was questioned, Manley suffered a nervous breakdown and received shock treatments at a private sanitarium. In 1954 his wife Harriet committed him to a state hospital, where he was diagnosed paranoid schizophrenic. They were divorced shortly after, and once, in the early '70s—between stays at various psychiatric hospitals—Manley, living in a trailer, used an ax to chase away a researcher inquiring about the Black Dahlia. Manley eventually committed suicide.

Two years after the murder of Elizabeth Short, Mark Lansom was shot, nearly fatally, by one of his dance-hall girls. Photographs of Beth Short were found in Lansom's possession by the police, though the exact nature of those photos remains undisclosed. Actress Jean Spangler, a former Florentine Gardens dancer who resembled Beth Short, disappeared in the fall of 1949; Lansom was a suspect in what appeared to be a murder, but was not prosecuted. He died of natural causes in 1964.

Which was more than could be said for Nils T. Granlund. Granny, who finally exited the Florentine Gardens in 1948, took his showgirl-saturated showmanship to Las Vegas, where in 1957 he was hit by a taxicab in the Riviera parking lot, dying hours later of a fractured skull and internal injuries.

Dr. Wallace Dailey died of a heart attack in November of 1947. Dr. Maria Winter and Mrs. Wallace Dailey fought bitterly over the dispersal of the doctor's estate, half of which (including his medical practice and equipment) had been left by Dailey to his female partner. The spurned wife claimed that his "feminine office partner" had been blackmailing the good doc, having learned certain damaging knowledge concerning Dr. Dailey's "professional secrets," keeping him a virtual prisoner during the last months of his life. The struggle was played out in the L.A. papers, and many assumed that the "professional secrets" referred to Dailey's abortion mill; but I wondered if that cunning olive-skinned amazon had convinced the senile doctor he had indeed killed the Black Dahlia. In any event, the court rejected both their claims, appointing a trust to handle the estate.

Later in 1947, my friend Eliot Ness lost his bid for mayor in Cleveland. He was also voted down as chairman of the Diebold board, and efforts to gain another position in law enforcement never panned out. Quietly suffering with a worsening drinking problem, he remained in the private sector, where his business endeavors were less than stellar. His third marriage, however, was a happy one. In 1957, in the small town of Coudersport, Pennsylvania—where he was trying to make a go of a check-watermarking business—he died in his kitchen, having just returned from the liquor store, shortly after receiving in the mail the galley proofs of *The Untouchables*, the autobiography that would make him a posthumous household name, as the "man who got" Al Capone.

Capone, incidentally, died in January 1947, finally succumbing to syphilis-related ailments, sharing the front page with Black Dahlia coverage, about a week after I put Eliot Ness and Lloyd Watterson on the Union Pacific bound for a Dayton, Ohio, loony bin.

Which was where Lloyd Watterson died, far too peacefully for my tastes, in 1965. After Eliot's death, I began receiving Lloyd's taunting postcards—and it became my job to make sure the Mad Butcher of Kingsbury Run was still confined in that veterans hospital in Dayton.

Most of the Crazy House sequence was cut from Orson Welles's

*Lady from Shanghai*, a film Harry Cohn dumped into the second-tier slot of a double-feature release, further damaging the director's already crippled Hollywood career. In May of '47 Welles mounted his low-budget production of *Macbeth*, and in November he and Rita Hayworth were divorced. The next three years of his life were largely spent in Europe, filming *Othello* in fits and starts and bits and pieces, funded by acting jobs in other directors' movies, Welles frequently playing a villain. This was to be the pattern for a larger-than-life life that ended quietly in October of 1985. The shadow of Elizabeth Short's death casts itself over many of his later films, in particular *Touch of Evil*, in which director/cowriter Welles plays a villainous cop who strangles a victim in a seedy hotel room.

Richardson retired and eventually died; Fowley retired, wrote novels, and is still alive, at this writing. Hearst promoted Aggie Underwood to managing editor, to shut her up about the Bauerdorf killing. In 1949, Jack Dragna finally got somebody to hit Mickey Cohen, or try anyway, at Sherry's restaurant, with Fred Rubinski and me nearby—but that's another story. Barney and Cathy remarried, of course, very happily, Barney never needing the needle again. Barney lost a bout, to cancer, in 1967.

Most of the rest of them, cops and crooks, I lost track of over the years. A bail-bondsman named Milton Schaeffer sent his people after Savarino and Hassau and brought them back, from San Francisco, and they got sentenced to thirty years, not twenty. What happened to them after that, I have no idea. I always kind of hoped Savarino made it out on Good Behavior in, say, ten and picked back up with Patsy and their kid and went straight. But that is, of course, ridiculous Polly-fucking-anna thinking.

Peggy and me? We had our beautiful son—Nathan Samuel Heller, Jr.—on September 27, 1947. We had by that time moved to a brick bungalow in the Chicago suburb Lincolnwood, and she had already asked me for a divorce. We'd struck a truce, in those last few days at the Beverly Hills Hotel, and there had been no recriminations or accusations from either of us—we had even screwed each other silly, proclaiming our undying love and looking forward to the first of many babies. We didn't quite make two years.

Our relationship, postmarriage, remained stormy. We almost got back together a couple times, and for patches we were friendly, and there were stretches where we weren't. For a long time my son—who lived with his mom—believed all the terrible things she told him about me. When he got older, we started to get along better, but maybe if he reads this book, he'll know his mother wasn't perfect . . . and that without his dad, he might've ended up a few teaspoons of slippery, slimy cells floating in water in a metal basin.

The search for Arnold Wilson ended later in '47, in San Francisco. One of criminal lawyer Jake Ehrlich's investigators spotted our man in a second-floor saloon called Finocchio's that catered to the gay set. The investigator tracked him to a Grant Avenue flophouse in Chinatown, called me, and I flew out that night.

The next morning, in Chinatown, I found the hotel had burned down and sixteen people had died, mostly transients. A tall charred corpse was found in Wilson's room. God or kismet or somebody had seen to it that the Butcher's apprentice had met a fitting hellish fate.

But as I stood looking at the smoldering building, firefighters doing their job, I felt cheated somehow; then after an hour, I turned my back on it, and flew home, doing my best to leave my smoldering hatred for that son-of-a-bitch behind.

In February 1982 I made a trip to California. I had retired long ago, and my second wife and I lived in Florida, in Boca Raton. A healthy, spry old S.O.B., I was still chairman of the board of the A-1 Detective Agency, but my son was the president of the firm now, and had been for quite a while. He was working out of the Los Angeles office and I had traveled alone, to visit him, since he and my wife didn't get along.

Also, I'd been contacted by a writer named Gil Johnson about the Black Dahlia case. He was working on a nonfiction book about the murder, and my name had turned up in his research. He wanted to talk. At first I'd been reluctant, but then he caught my interest.

"I've solved the case," he said. His voice over the phone was a mellow, actorly baritone.

I was sitting on the patio of our house on the causeway, watching boats go by, sipping lemonade. "Really?"

"I've come across this old guy who knew the killer."

"Is that right?"

"He says the killer was named Al Morrison."

Now I was less interested. "Is that so?"

"Yes . . . but to tell you the truth, I have a feeling this old geezer . . . he's an alcoholic, skid-row type . . . may have been a sort of accomplice in the crime."

And now I was very interested. "What's his name, this geezer?"

"Smith. Arnold Smith."

"What's he look like?"

"Emaciated as hell. Bad acne scars. Maybe six four . . . walks with a limp. Says he got it in the war."

"Well, I might be able to talk to you about the case."

"Oh! That's great! I'd been warned you didn't give interviews . . . I heard you were writing your own book. . . ."

"I'm working on my memoirs, but I'm years away from the Dahlia. I don't mind giving another writer a helping hand. I've been wanting to get out to the Coast to see my son, anyway. How can I get in touch with you?"

Three days later we were sitting with draft beers in front of us in a booth in Musso and Frank's on Hollywood Boulevard, that no-nonsense dark-wood-paneled meeting place where actors, agents, and surly waiters converge.

Johnson was in his mid-forties, smooth, intelligent, leading-man handsome with a full head of silvering brown hair, wearing a brown sportjacket and a yellow sportshirt and looking, well, Hollywood. He had already explained that he was a former actor, occasional screenwriter and that he'd written a true crime book about the Manson family that had led to more work in that vein.

"I stumbled onto this character quite by accident," Johnson said. "A girlfriend and I were visiting this couple in Silver Lake, where I was living at the time. It was a little party, maybe half a dozen people, some of them fairly rough characters—I know my girl told me later she'd felt uneasy."

The host of the party had taken all his guests out to the garage, to see if he had "anything they wanted."

"It was full of stuff—stereo equipment, TVs, golf clubs, you name it—guy was a thief, obviously, or a fence. Anyway, as the night wore on, we were listening to old records from the '40s and '50s, and this tall, thin, sick-lookin' character starts reminiscing about Los Angeles in the '40s, after the war. I mentioned I was working on a book about that period. He asked me what the subject was, and I said the Black Dahlia murder. . . . And he said he knew her."

"Did you take this seriously? It was a party, you were all drinking. . . ."

"I took *him* seriously—there was something . . . intense and, frankly, creepy about his manner. He said he used to know Elizabeth Short when she hung out at a cafe on McCadden. He said he knew one of the members of a heist crew who hung out there, too, a Bobby Savarino."

"Really."

"Anyway, he asked me if I was willing to pay him for information, and I said yes, if it proved of value. Imagine my surprise when, over time, this developed into him saying he knew the killer, and that the killer had confessed to him."

"Have you checked up on this guy?"

"Shit, yes. He's got a five-page rap sheet and a dozen AKAs—burglary, theft, vagrancy, intoxication, lewd conduct. He's gay, or anyway, bi. Served a couple short stretches."

"What do you want from me?"

Johnson leaned forward, his passion for the subject palpable. "You worked on the Black Dahlia case—hell, you found the body."

I shrugged. "I was there when the body was found. I did background investigation for the *Examiner*."

"Here's where I'd like to start. I'd like to go over with you what Smith told me, and see if it gibes with what you know."

"Be glad to." I checked my watch. "But, uh . . . let's make it another time. I need to catch up with my boy."

Johnson smiled; handsome guy, should have made it big as an actor. "Mr. Heller, your son's got quite a reputation. What's it feel like, having your kid take over the family business?"

I shrugged again. "He's good at it."

"Are you two . . . close? Or is there competition?"

"We get along." I finished my beer. "I just wish he weren't such a cynical, skirt-chasing wiseass."

That seemed to amuse him, for some reason. Then he said, "Well, uh—let's set up a meet."

"Sure. How about tomorrow afternoon, same place—say, two o'clock? Maybe I should talk to this Smith. Where's he live, anyway?"

"Dump called the Holland Hotel. But let's have our meeting, first. Get you grounded in the basics. Then I'll put you two together."

I nodded. "Probably a good idea."

The Holland Hotel was at 7th and Columbia, near downtown L.A. I had called ahead to get the room number—Arnold Smith was in 202—and, just after dark, I went in through a rear, service door, carrying a bottle of bourbon in a paper bag. The place was just a step up from a flophouse, and when I knocked on the door marked 202, brown flakes of paint fell off, like dark dandruff.

"Who the fuck is it?" a raspy, reedy voice called.

"Gil Johnson asked me to drop by," I said, raising my voice. "Got a bottle for you!"

"It's open!"

I went in. The room was a glorified cubicle that reeked of urine, which was about the color of the decaying, water-damaged plaster walls. There wasn't much room for anything but a scarred old oak dresser, a well-worn armchair, a metal single bed, and a battered oak nightstand with a gooseneck lamp, a pink-and-black plastic clock radio from which emanated staticky country-western music, a couple paperbacks, a bathroom glass, a box of kitchen matches, and a half-empty pack of Chesterfield cigarettes.

A TV stand near the bed stood empty—if a TV had been there, it had long since been hocked. The corner room had two windows, both undraped, with ancient cracked manila shades, drawn. The light green carpet was indoor-outdoor and badly worn. The room was fairly dark but for a pool of light thrown by the gooseneck lamp, hitting the drunk on the unmade bed like a spotlight.

He was in his T-shirt and stained, threadbare brown trousers, a toe with an in-grown nail sticking through one of the frayed socks he wore. His bony frame was covered with loose flesh the color of a fish's belly, mottled with sores and scars. His left leg was scarred and shriveled and shorter than the other.

His features hadn't changed that much: same Indian-ish high cheekbones, brown eyes peering out of slits, pointed nose, balled dimpled chin. The Ichabod Crane face was grooved with years, with hard living, but not—I would wager—lines etched by a conscience.

"Jesus Christ," Arnold Wilson said thickly. "Is that who I think it is?"

He seemed a little surprised, a lot drunk, but not at all frightened or even concerned.

"Hello, Arnold," I said.

I pulled the armchair up next to the bed where he sat propped up by a flat pillow, using the wall as his headboard. He had an empty bottle of Muscatel limp in his lap.

His grin was yellow and green and black. "Wondered if you'd ever find me."

"Pretty tough tracing a guy who's willing to burn fifteen, sixteen people to a crisp, to cover his tracks."

"Shit—fuckin' lowlifes. Put 'em outa their misery. . . . So you talked to Gil Johnson, huh?"

I nodded. "He's researching the Dahlia. Of course he called me."

"And then he mentioned 'Arnold Smith,' and you put two and two together."

"I'm a detective. I hear about a six-four skid row alcoholic, and I'm able to deduce it might just be my old friend, Arnold Wilson."

He laughed, once—or was it a cough? "You look good. Christ, how old are you?"

"I'll be seventy-seven."

"Christ, I'm just sixty-six and I look like Methuselah!" Shaking his head, he said, "Shit, guy lived as hard as you—you don't look a day over fuckin' sixty!"

"I don't drink, I don't smoke, and I got good genes. That's all it takes, Arnold."

"Funny . . . seein' you makes me feel good."

"It does?"

"Remembering those days. Great days. I was in my prime!"

I grinned. "Playing all of us like a cheap kazoo. Sending me in Jack Dragna's direction, knowing it would get me killed. If it wasn't for Mickey Cohen, I mighta been."

He laughed, and coughed, and laughed. "And now I'm set to get out of this dump—finish out my life living a little better, for a change. God, four years of this! Worse than fuckin' stir."

"Don't kid me, Arnold. You and Lloyd always liked skid row—easy pickings, plenty of ass to hustle, male and female."

Wilson made a farting sound with his lips. "Too old for such foolishness. I wanna retire. Johnson's gonna pay me to hear all about the murder."

"And you're going to tell him about Lloyd?"

His grimace was grotesque; it was as if his face was trying to turn itself inside out. "Of course not! I made up some guy named Morrison. But I'm gonna give Johnson all the good, gory details. Would you like to hear it, Heller? Just how we did it?"

"Sure. Why not? . . . . You mind if I bum a cigarette?"

He nodded toward the nightstand. "No, help yourself. . . . I thought you didn't smoke."

"Not regularly. I smoked overseas."

"Guadalcanal—I remember. . . . Gimme one."

I held out the pack of Chesties and he plucked one out; then I lit him up with one of the kitchen matches, asking, "Were you really in the Army, Arnold?"

"Sure." He sucked on the cigarette, then exhaled slowly. "Got my leg bayonetted overseas; that was no bullshit."

"I quit the cigs when I got back in the States . . . only, now and then, I get the urge. You know all about giving in to urges, don't you, Arnold?"

"I guess I do."

I helped myself to a Chesterfield and lighted it up.

"Uh . . . that bottle . . . is that for me?"

"Let's hear the story first."

Wilson began to talk, an elderly man sharing precious memories. He told how the girl (he never referred to her by name) had needed a place to stay, since shacking at Hassau's was awkward with Bobby's wife downstairs. That had allowed him to lure her to Lloyd's apartment on East 31st Street, where the fun began.

"But you're going to be disappointed," Wilson said.

"Oh?"

"If you want gruesome shit. Hell, most of what we did to her was after she died. All we did before she died was fuck her in the ass and just kind of . . . you know, party. I think she drowned on her own blood—I mean we didn't strangle her, but she was alive when we cut the smile in her face, and that's the blood, you know, she choked on."

I unsealed the cap on the bourbon bottle and screwed it open. I reached for the bathroom glass on the nightstand and poured the dark liquid into it, right to the top.

Arnold was salivating. He held out his hand.

But I didn't give it to him. Instead I asked, "You and Lloyd didn't happen to do that other girl, did you? That socialite?"

"Bauer-what's-it? Yeah, we did her, had her in the tub to cut her up, but we got interrupted and had to duck out the back way. Hell, we did lots of 'em you don't know about. You bring me a bottle like that every night, and I'll tell you a new story every night."

I splashed the bourbon in his face; some of it splashed on the pillow and sheets.

"Hey! You fucker!" He sat up, the liquid streaming down the nooks and crannies of his pockmarked face.

"I'm sorry," I said. "I lost my temper . . . I'll pour you another. . . ."

And I emptied the bourbon bottle all over him, down his T-shirt, and his trousers, dumping it everywhere. He was too drunk and weak to do anything—he just lay there, looking at me astounded.

"What are you wasting that shit for?"

I reached for the kitchen matches.

Then he understood . . . and yet he just grinned at me—with those teeth that were yellow, green-caked decayed things, plus a few gaps. "You wouldn't, you fuckin' candyass. You don't have the balls."

I lit the match.

And now, finally his eyes showed fear—some small fraction of the fear his victims had felt. Soaked with the booze, he began to tremble, as if a chill had overtaken him.

I was holding up the match, flame dancing like a little orange-and-blue demon. "What are you afraid of? You already died in a hotel fire once, Arnold."

"What do you want, Heller? You want me to come forward? Want me to confess? Well, fuck you!"

He threw the wine bottle and I easily ducked it; it shattered on the wall behind me. I straightened—the match was still burning bright, had burned about halfway down.

"Do you believe in heaven, Arnold? Do you believe in hell?"

"No!"

"I'm not sure about that, either—but I do know you deserve hell."

The flame was fat now, burning within a quarter inch of my fingers, leaping orange, jumping blue.

"What the fuck are you doing, Heller? We're just a couple of old men!"

"You're old enough," I said.

And tossed the match.

The next morning I received a call from Gil Johnson. I was staying at my son's house in Malibu; I was out on the deck, watching young women (they apparently weren't called "girls" anymore) bob around in bikinis down on the beach.

"Mr. Heller," Gilmore said, his tone grave, "I have something terrible to report."

"Oh?"

"Seems Arnold Smith was burned to death last night, in his hotel room."

"Really?"

"No one else was injured—fire was confined to the tiny room that Smith lived in for the last four years. Horrible, horrible. . . . Somebody went up and down the halls banging on doors, yelling fire—over the sound of Smith screaming, apparently . . . Everybody was evacuated."

"Everybody but Smith?"

"Everybody but Smith. I guess a fire station was just a block and a half away. Only the one room was involved in the blaze, but the whole interior of Smith's was a charred mess. . . . Must have been a regular inferno."

"Jeez."

"The manager of the hotel says Smith was a heavy smoker and of course I knew he was a heavy drinker. But I guess there'd been three or four minor fires already in his room . . . from him falling asleep with a cigarette in his hand. They think maybe he spilled some booze and . . . Still, there definitely will be an arson investigation."

"Really?"

"Yes. See, I've been talking to the cops about this—you've heard of that famous detective, John St. John?"

A blonde and brunette came bounding out of the water and flopped onto towels, on their tummies. "Yeah, Jigsaw John, the Dahlia's his case now," I said. "You've told St. John about Smith, you mean?"

"Yes. I was going to try to get Smith to tell St. John about what this guy Morrison did. But St. John, based on what I've told him, thinks Smith may be . . . or I guess now it's 'may have been' . . . the Short woman's killer. Or, as I suspected, an accomplice. Which makes Smith a suspect in an unsolved murder."

"Ah. Which means there has to be consideration of the death possibly being something other than accidental."

"You don't miss much, do you, Mr. Heller? Plus, the cops are wondering who went through the hotel warning everybody."

"Was he seen?"

"No, but none of the residents take credit—they all just booked outa there."

I grunted, studying the brunette, who had turned over onto her back, and whose breasts seemed unlikely. "It's a puzzle."

"Sure is. Anyway, I still need to go ahead with this." He sighed, cleared his throat. "I guess I'm up to us getting together later today, like we planned."

I sipped my glass of iced tea. "Well, that's the thing, Gil. I've been giving this some thought. I'm thinking maybe I might want to do a Dahlia book myself, someday."

"I hope that doesn't mean—"

"I'm afraid it does. I've got to save what I know for my own book."

"Oh. Well. I guess I can understand that. . . ."

"Good." Now that little blonde down there, turning over; those looked real.

". . . I have to say, Mr. Heller, it is a strange coincidence."

"What is?"

"Smith dying in a hotel fire, with you in town, before I could get the two of you together."

"I suppose. But if you like, there is one thing I can tell you about the Dahlia case—you know, just as one author to another."

Hopeful expectation colored the writer's voice. "Any insight you can share, Mr. Heller, any scrap of information, would be appreciated."

Those girls down on the beach—they were about the same age Elizabeth Short had been, when she died; and they were out here in La La Land, no doubt with similar hopes and dreams. I hoped they'd fare better than the girl from Medford, Mass. But the way the world was going, I had no faith they would.

"Mr. Johnson," I said, "this goddamn case is just filled with coincidences."

# I Owe Them One

Despite its extensive basis in history, this is a work of fiction, and liberties have been taken with the facts, though as few as possible—and any blame for historical inaccuracies is my own, reflecting, I hope, the limitations of conflicting source material.

The basic theory of this novel—that Elizabeth Short's murder was not purely a sex crime, but a mob-style execution designed to serve as a warning to a potential "squealer"—is a new one, never proposed in the many articles and several book-length studies on this famous unsolved murder. Short's connection to the armed robbers known as the McCadden Group—alluded to in John Gilmore's *Severed: The True Story of the Black Dahlia Murder* (1994; revised edition, 1999) and Mary Pacios' *Childhood Shadows: The Hidden Story of the Black Dahlia* (1999)—has never been linked directly with the motive for her death. No one, until now, has pointed out that the Black Dahlia's body turned up in that vacant lot the day after Robert Savarino—arrested on the Mocambo robbery—blabbed about Jack Dragna's people approaching him and other McCadden Group hoods about killing Mickey Cohen.

I believe this theory is the key to the true solution to the murder, including the direct involvement of the self-admitted Mocambo robbery accomplice known variously as Arnold Wilson,

Jack Anderson Wilson, and Arnold Smith (among other aliases). Although my pairing of Wilson and the Mad Butcher of Kingsbury Run may seem fanciful, one of Wilson's aliases is in fact the name of a suspected accomplice of the Kingsbury Run Butcher. Wilson did indeed die in a suspicious hotel fire in February 1982.

This new theory was developed with my friend and research associate, George Hagenauer, who made the connection between the Mocambo robbery and Elizabeth Short's death by the lucky happenstance of a key newspaper article appearing next to a Barney Ross feature we'd been looking for. Newspaper research continues to be the cornerstone of our approach, and both of us pored over the Los Angeles newspapers of the day, including the *Examiner*, *Herald-Express*, and *Times*. George's contribution to the shaping of this theory and to the novel itself has been invaluable.

I have also interwoven elements of other key Black Dahlia theories, in an effort to make this novel an all-encompassing view of a compelling but convoluted case. Nonetheless, numerous fascinating aspects have been played down and even eliminated, in an effort to keep this narrative down to a (somewhat) manageable length.

Three book-length works were of tremendous value to me in the writing of this novel.

The aforementioned *Severed* took the first serious book-length look at the murder of Elizabeth Short, boasting landmark research, including Gilmore's discovery of the identity of a major player in the murder of the Dahlia, the man I refer to as Arnold Wilson (just one of his aliases). For anyone interested in this case, *Severed* is essential reading. Gilmore—his autobiography, *Laid Bare* (1997), contains more Dahlia material—is so key to the case that it became necessary for me to represent his role via a fictional character, Gil Johnson.

The previously mentioned *Childhood Shadows* by Mary Pacios is a compassionate, in-depth look at Short's short, tragic life, from the point of view of a childhood friend. Pacios did extensive research and explores all of the previous major theories and then proposes her own. Pacios is the source for the theory that Orson Welles is a Black Dahlia suspect—a notion I frankly find absurd, though Pacios makes a good enough case for me to justify the inclusion of the great filmmaker as a character, here.

Also helpful was *Daddy Was the Black Dahlia Killer* (1995) by Janice Knowlton with true crime expert Michael Newton. The theory proposed in this work does not seem terribly compelling to me, based as it is on latter-day "remembering" of suppressed traumatic memories; however, the material on Elizabeth Short—separated from the story of Janice Knowlton's homicidal father, her Black Dahlia suspect—is well researched and skillfully presented.

I am a big admirer of Jack Webb and his classic 1950s television series, *Dragnet.* Webb wrote an excellent (if typically laudatory) nonfiction work on the LAPD, *The Badge* (1958), with a section devoted to the Black Dahlia case. Reading Webb's version of the Dahlia case as a young teen sparked my interest in Elizabeth Short.

*Angel in Black* is a sequel of sorts to a 1984 Nathan Heller short story, "The Strawberry Teardrop," which dealt with the Mad Butcher of Kingsbury Run, and introduced the character Lloyd Watterson. That story was expanded into the Eliot Ness novel, *Butcher's Dozen* (1988), which represented in-depth research that George Hagenauer and I did into the Torso murders on site in Cleveland; at Case Western Reserve Library, among the long-forgotten Ness papers, we discovered the taunting postcards sent to the Untouchable by the Butcher from a mental institution. Prior to our research, the closest thing to an in-depth examination of Eliot Ness' role in the Butcher case was a single chapter of Oscar Fraley's *Four Against the Mob. Butcher's Dozen* was the first book-length work on Ness and the Cleveland Torso killings, and every nonfiction (and fictional) work since—as well as television treatments of the case—has used our research, uncredited, as a foundation.

Lloyd Watterson is a fictional character, but he has a real-life counterpart, identified as Dr. Frank Sweeney in Marilyn Bardsley's excellent article, "The Kingsbury Run Murders," available on the Internet at Dark Horse Multimedia's Crime Library (Bardsley, incidentally, does list *Butcher's Dozen* as a source). Also,

Bardsley's Internet article, "The Black Dahlia," is an excellent Gilmore-slanted overview of the Short murder.

Other Internet articles of interest include "The Undying Mystery of the Black Dahlia" by Lionel Van Deerlin (San Diego Online); and "An Original Black Dahlia Article" by Russell Miller, which is a part of the excellent Black Dahlia Web site (www.bethshort.com) maintained by Pamela Hazelton. Hazelton's Web site is a thoughtful, fact-filled tribute to the murder victim.

With few exceptions, the characters in this novel appear with their real names, despite receiving varying degrees of fictionalization.

Bill Fowley is a fictional character, a composite of Will Fowler, Sid Hughes, Bevo Means, and numerous other reporters active on the case, and is not meant to represent any one of them, though superficially the character's background resembles that of Fowler, whose excellent memoir *"Reporters"* (1991) was a helpful reference for this novel. Jim Richardson, however, was a real city editor, and my portrait of him is based on material in Fowler's book and Richardson's autobiography, *For the Life of Me* (1954).

While Bobby Savarino is a real person (portrayed in a fictionalized manner), his "wife" in this novel is a wholly fictional character. I do not know whether Savarino was married in real life but, if he was, it certainly wasn't to the fictional ex-stripper, Patsy, who I invented.

The unflattering portrait of Finis Brown in this novel is drawn from material in several sources, primarily Pacios (where Brown's supposed status as a bookie/corrupt cop is stated by several witnesses); but in fairness it must be stated that in various other sources, including Jack Webb's *The Badge*, Brown is depicted as an honest and effective detective. For the purposes of this narrative, the positive opinions were ignored and the negative opinions coalesced into my fictionalized portrayal of Brown, which in no way should be viewed as a portrait of the real man.

"Mark Lansom" is based upon Mark Hansen, whose name was changed to avoid confusion with Detective Harry Hansen. Fred Rubinski is a fictionalized Barney Ruditsky, the real life P.I. whose restaurant, Sherry's, was a Mickey Cohen hangout.

Dr. Wallace Dailey and Dr. Maria Winter are fictional characters with real-life counterparts, and this aspect of my novel reflects a fascinating theory developed by Larry Harnisch, whose in-progress Dahlia book, *Stairway to Heaven*, I eagerly await. Harnisch has an ongoing Web site at Geocities, where he shares his groundbreaking research.

The theory that the Mad Butcher of Kingsbury Run might have been responsible for the Black Dahlia slaying—a concept posited in my novel *Butcher's Dozen*—has been further developed by Lawrence P. Scherb, who has published several articles and, several years ago, corresponded with me, generously sharing his thoughts and theories.

My "backup" research assistant, Lynn Myers, provided photocopied articles and book excerpts as well as several movies and videos. A 1975 TV-movie, *Who Killed the Black Dahlia?* starring Efrem Zimbalist as Harry Hansen and Lucie Arnaz as Elizabeth Short, was too fictionalized to aid my work. More valuable was *Medford Girl*, a 1993 documentary by Kyle J. Wood, who has donated profits to erecting a monument in Elizabeth Short's name in Medford, Massachusetts. Also viewed were "The Black Dahlia Murder," an episode of E! Channel's *Hollywood's Mysteries and Scandals*, and *Case Reopened: The Black Dahlia*, a Learning Channel documentary.

I have written extensively about Eliot Ness and sources used in developing my ongoing portrait of the real-life Untouchable can be found at the back of the various Ness novels, including *Butcher's Dozen* (recently published in a hardcover edition by Five Star Mystery). To refresh my memory about the Kingsbury Run case, however, I turned to *Great Unsolved Mysteries* (1978) by James Purvis and the following Ness-related nonfiction works: *Eliot Ness: The Real Story* (1997), Paul W. Heimel; *Four Against the Mob* (1961), Oscar Fraley; and *Torso* (1989), Steven Nickel.

One of the great pleasures of researching this novel was revisiting many of Orson Welles' films, including *Lady from Shanghai*, *Touch of Evil*, and *Macbeth*. I also read a number of Welles biographies: *Rosebud: The Story of Orson Welles* (1996), David Thomson; *This Is Orson Welles* (1992), Orson Welles and Peter

Bogdanovich; *Citizen Welles* (1989), Frank Brady; *Orso*
*The Rise and Fall of an American Genius* (1985),
Higham; and *Orson Welles: A Biography* (1985), Barbar
ing, whose *If This Was Happiness: a Biography of Rita Hayworth* (1989) was also helpful.

Several biographies and autobiographies aided in my research, including *The Abortionist: A Woman Against the Law* (1994), Rickie Solinger; *Blondes, Brunettes and Bullets* (1957), Nils T. Granlund with Sid Feder and Ralph Hancock; *Headline Happy* (1950), Florabel Muir; *No Man Stands Alone* (1957), Barney Ross and Martin Abramson; and *Thicker'n Thieves* (1951), Charles Stoker. The portrait of Mickey Cohen drew upon *Hoodlums: Los Angeles* (1959), Ted Prager and Larry Craft; *Mickey Cohen: In My Own Words* (1975), Mickey Cohen and John Peer Nugent; *Mickey Cohen: Mobster* (1973), Ed Reid; and *Why I Quit Syndicated Crime* (1951), Jim Vaus and D. C. Haskin.

Numerous true crime books include a chapter on the Dahlia. Among such works consulted were *The California Crime Book* (1971), Robert Colby; *Fallen Angels* (1986), Marvin J. Wolf and Katherine Mader; *Hollywood's Unsolved Mysteries* (1970), John Austin; *The Mammoth Book of Unsolved Crimes* (1999), Roger Wilkes (editor); *Open Files* (1983), Jay Robert Nash; *They Had a Way with Women* (1967), Leonard Gribble; and *True Crime: Unsolved Crimes* (1993), editors of Time-Life Books. *To Protect and Serve* (1994) by Joe Domanick provided excellent historical background on the LAPD. *The Super Sleuths* (1976) by Bruce Henderson and Sam Summerlin provided material on Harry Hansen.

A number of books on L.A. and Hollywood were also useful, including *City of Nets* (1986), Otto Friedrich; *Cruel City* (1991), Marianne Ruuth; *Death in Paradise* (1998), Tony Blanche and Brad Schreiber; *Great American Hotels* (1991), James Tackach; *Hollywood Babylon II* (1984), Kenneth Anger; *Hollywood Goes on Location* (1988), Leon Smith; *Landmarks of Los Angeles* (1994), Patrick McGrew and Robert Julian; *My L.A.* (1947), Matt Weinstock; *Out with the Stars* (1985), Jim Heimann; *Raymond Chandler's Los Angeles* (1987), Elizabeth

Ward and Alain Silver; and *Sins of the City: the Real Los Angeles Noir* (1999), Jim Heimann. The WPA Guides for California and Illinois were extremely helpful, as were *Chicago Confidential* (1950) and *U.S.A. Confidential* (1952), both by Jack Lait and Lee Mortimer.

I would again like to thank my editor, Joseph Pittman, for his belief in Nate Heller and his creator, and his patience when a death in the family made me miss a deadline; and of course Dominick Abel, my friend and agent, who also was gracious and supportive at a rough time.

*Angel in Black* is a novel about relationships, in particular, marriage. I am grateful for the love and support of my wife, Barbara Collins—Nate Heller never had it so good.

MAX ALLAN COLLINS has earned an unprecedented nine Private Eye Writers of America Shamus nominations for his Nathan Heller historical thrillers, winning twice (*True Detective*, 1983, and *Stolen Away*, 1991).

A Mystery Writers of America Edgar nominee in both fiction and nonfiction categories, Collins has been hailed as "the Renaissance man of mystery fiction." His credits include four suspense-novel series, film criticism, short fiction, songwriting, trading-card sets, and movie/TV tie-in novels, including such international bestsellers as *In the Line of Fire*, *Air Force One*, and *Saving Private Ryan.*

He scripted the internationally syndicated comic strip *Dick Tracy* from 1977 to 1993, is cocreator of the comic-book features *Ms. Tree, Wild Dog*, and *Mike Danger*, and has written the *Batman* comic book and newspaper strip, the mini-series *Johnny Dynamite*, and a graphic novel, *Road to Perdition.*

Working as an independent filmmaker in his native Iowa, he wrote and directed the suspense film *Mommy*, starring Patty McCormack, premiering on Lifetime in 1996; he performed the same duties for a 1997 sequel, *Mommy's Day*. The recipient of a record five Iowa Motion Picture Awards for screenwriting, he also wrote *The Expert*, a 1995 HBO World Premiere film. Subsequently he wrote and directed an award-winning documentary, *Mike Hammer's Mickey Spillane*, and in 2000 wrote and directed his third independent feature, *Real Time: Siege at Lucas Street Market.*

Collins lives in Muscatine, Iowa, with his wife, writer Barbara Collins, and their teenage son, Nathan.